A PAIR OF BLUE EYES

THE YEARS BETWEEN

JJ MARSH

PREWETT
BIELMANN

Copyright © 2025 by Prewett Bielmann Ltd.

The moral rights of the author have been asserted.
All rights reserved. No part of this publication may be reproduced, distributed, or transmitted in any form or by any means, including photocopying, recording, or other electronic or mechanical methods, without the prior written permission of the publisher, except in the case of brief quotations embodied in critical reviews and certain other non-commercial uses permitted by copyright law. No other party may reproduce and/or otherwise use the Work in any manner for purposes of training artificial intelligence technologies to generate text, including without limitation, technologies that are capable of generating works in the same style or genre as the Work, or sublicense others to do so without specific and express permission from the publisher.
Cover design: JD Smith
Published by Prewett Bielmann Ltd.
All enquiries to admin@jjmarshauthor.com
First printing, 2025
eBook Edition:
ISBN 978-3-906256-30-6
Paperback:
ISBN 978-3-906256-31-3

PROLOGUE

December 1929, Basel

Her first thought upon waking in the little wooden room was to reach Switzerland by nightfall. Five hundred kilometres, crossing a border, filling the fuel tank, finding her way on unfamiliar routes, and the wild card of weather were all challenges. *You are a modern woman. You can do anything.* In Gasthaus Adler's parlour, a maid was lighting a fire. Eloise wished her a good day and was on the road by six o'clock. The fuel gauge showed a full tank and the rain had given way to a clear dawn. She drove south as the sun rose, bumping along in the driver's seat, her whole body aching, cold and complaining of hunger. The Laubfrosch was not much happier, sputtering and threatening to stall every time she changed gear. Eventually, they came to an arrangement as she attuned to the sound of the engine, and they motored in relative peace into a bright morning.

The sun made intermittent appearances and the little car reached dizzying speeds of 50kph on the open road. Of all the dangers Eloise had considered when deciding to drive from

Germany to Switzerland – causing an accident, falling foul of thugs, sleeping at the wheel, losing her way, being apprehended by the authorities or running out of fuel – the one factor she had not considered was having time to think. Her mind must have spent the last few days in shock, but had now recovered and was asking insistent questions. She shut out every *how could you?* and *what were you thinking?* and the most plangent of all, *who are you?* to concentrate on her woefully inadequate motoring skills.

In her naïveté, she assumed she could refuel at a garage in Karlsruhe like any other driver. Undisguised curiosity from the attendant and amused stares from fellow motorists shook her confidence. She paid the attendant with a small tip and asked permission to park her car on the forecourt while she sought sustenance in a nearby café. He took her coins and agreed, still smirking.

The scent of fresh coffee lured her across the road and through the door before she had even registered the clientele. Ladies whispered behind gloved hands and one waitress actually stifled a laugh at her practical motoring clothes. Her temper flared. They ought to recognise and admire a trail-blazing modern woman, instead of measuring her against their own provincial yardstick. But this place was a long way from Berlin. Rather than wilt under their judgemental gaze, she ordered a Bratwurst with mustard and onions to raise eyebrows still further. Once finished, she paid the bill, wished everyone a good day and returned to her car. By midday, she would be in Switzerland. Home at last.

Three hours driving under the grey monotony of low skies, and the landscape became a blur. Her concentration strayed. Twice she had to right herself after drifting to the centre of the road. All she had to do was keep going, watch the fuel gauge and stay awake. One mistake would prove fatal. *You are a modern woman. You can do anything. Keep going.*

. . .

At the Swiss border, she hardly imagined a welcoming fanfare. However, the smooth re-entry to her homeland she expected was anything but. This time, it was not her innocence that betrayed her, but her confidence. The *Grenzen* guards regarded the Laubfrosch with its Berlin plates as suspicious and treated her with aggression and hostility. First they studied her papers and asked her to come inside while they examined the vehicle. She spoke Swiss German and answered politely. Then she answered the same questions again and invoked her family name.

The younger man raised his shoulders to his ears. "What were you doing in Germany?"

"As I said, I was a journalist for *Vogue*. It's a women's fashion magazine."

"You must have been very well paid to afford one of those." He nodded through the window towards the Laubfrosch, where two German Shepherds were sniffing the chassis.

The older man sporting a dense moustache chuckled, an unfriendly sound.

"Once again, Frau de Fournier, your address in Berlin?"

Her brain froze and she looked down at her hands, still clad in leather. She pulled at each finger, easing off her gloves and giving herself time to think.

"The last place I lived in Berlin was Charlottenstrasse 125. A boarding house which is currently up for sale."

The two men had a muttered conversation and the older one left the room. The younger soldier folded his arms and watched as his colleagues removed her holdall from the car.

She shifted in her seat. "What do the guards want with my luggage?"

He ignored her.

"Sir? I would like to know when I can continue my journey. I am a Swiss citizen, returning home to my family."

"You can continue just as soon as you tell us who's paying you."

"I'm sorry?"

The door opened and the older man returned with a senior officer who did not introduce himself. With a jerk of his chin, he dismissed the younger soldier and took the seat opposite Eloise.

"Who are you and who are you working for?"

"As I said, my name is Eloise de Fournier from Fribourg. I'm a mother of two children and until recently, I was a journalist for *Vogue* magazine in Berlin."

He shook his head with a patronising sneer. "I'm sure you thought it would be easy to slip past some country soldiers with no experience of foreign agents. Wrong. We are professional Swiss border guards, trained to identify and apprehend malignant forces which threaten our nation."

Eloise was so blindsided that she actually laughed. "Don't be ridiculous!"

The atmosphere cooled.

"Let's try that again, shall we?" The officer curled one hand into a fist and covered it with the other. "I am a military man, well disciplined, fair minded and not prone to fits of temper. The interrogation squad are rather less predictable. That said, no one can deny they certainly get results. Your choice is simple, madam. You can talk to me or I hand you over to them."

Eloise stared at him, unable to think of a thing to say.

"I have a few questions about some anomalies in your story. If you answer them to my satisfaction, you may go on your way. If not, the interrogation squad will get the information we need using their own methods. Do you understand me?"

"I ... yes, of course. I have nothing to hide. I am a Swiss citizen, returning home to her family. There is no need to treat me like a criminal."

"Good. In that case, please allow the sergeant to inspect your handbag."

Instinctively, Eloise clutched it tighter. The moustached man held out a hand and she relinquished it with as much dignity as she could manage. Her throat swelled at the injustice, but she would not allow herself to cry. Tears should be reserved for people who mattered.

"To business: I want to know why you are driving an expensive vehicle whilst unemployed. Please tell me why you are travelling home with nothing but a holdall, which contains a large amount of jewellery. For what reason would you be carrying a valuable artwork wrapped in Russian newspapers? Who are you working for and what information do you seek?"

"And why are you carrying a large amount of Reichsmarks?" added the sergeant, showing the contents of her purse.

Eloise closed her eyes and placed a hand over her mouth. She had a sudden recollection of a visit to her brother when he was studying in Zürich. An elderly couple on the train had regarded her with some censure and she chose to make sport of their obvious disapproval.

Oh, Bastian! With all manner of allusions and hints as to my top-secret mission, I more or less convinced them I was Mata Hari. Ha, ha! They'll be talking about me the entire weekend.

She inhaled deeply and wished she hadn't. The air was stale, the soldiers smelt of sweat and mouldy uniforms, and she herself was none too fragrant after driving all morning.

"Are you seriously accusing me of being a spy?"

"Unless you can prove otherwise, madam, a charge of espionage looks likely. Treason carries a heavy penalty."

Unbidden, her brother's response floated into her mind. *As a matter of fact, Mata Hari was executed by firing squad during the war.*

1

Winter 1925-26, Fribourg

Losing a husband was an onerous task, or so Eloise had been led to believe. Death certificates to procure, funerals to arrange, wills to be read, paperwork to manage and all that official business with dour men in dark suits. What a dreadful bore. Yet in those rootless days since Sylvain died, family fussed, friends pressed her hands and staff moved around the house like ghosts, fading into the shadows if her head happened to turn their way. Other than receiving an incessant stream of visitors bearing condolences, she had precious little to do.

"You need not worry about a thing," said Bastian, his hands resting on her shoulders. The stiff black crêpe dress rustled at his touch. "Papa and I are taking care of all the formalities. No one shall intrude upon your grief, my dear."

She curved her mouth into a smile, and this time it was unforced. The sight of her beloved brother genuinely lifted her heart. If only the occasion had been less gloomy, they might have taken their favourite walk down to the banks of the Sarine.

Perhaps they would try and fail to describe the colour of the river, criss-cross some bridges and indulge in some scurrilous gossip. Bastian invariably made her laugh.

"Thank you. Without my family by my side, I would drift at the mercy of strange currents. In truth, I hardly know what to do with myself. The fact he is gone is impossible to comprehend."

"All of us feel the same way. Losing such a fine man was a cruel blow for so many, but above all, you. I cannot imagine how my niece and nephew must suffer. Have no fear, Eloise, you and your family are not alone. Yet if our attentions become oppressive, you must speak. My concern is that you would prefer solitude."

"No!" Her voice was louder than intended. "No, not at all. I am grateful for the company. The house feels oddly hollow without him. Even the children are hushed at play."

He released her shoulders and as if he had been the only thing holding her upright, she sagged into the window-seat. Her gaze took in the lawn. Today, the expanse of green was a stage and the window frame a proscenium arch. Bare branches conducted by the wind danced an elegant ballet to music she could not hear. She sighed, wishing with all her heart she could shake off this miserable weight, discard the restrictive dress, run out into the wind and whirl like a dervish.

She straightened her spine and reprimanded herself. No joy danced in her heart at Sylvain's demise. He had been a good man, a kind husband and admirable father. Of the two of them, he was without doubt the better parent, demonstrating patience and forbearance, exemplary behaviour and on rare occasions, paternal pride. His children respected and replicated his demeanour. One word or stern look from him could bring them to heel. Never in his presence did they behave like little demons, whereas she found them unpredictable and exhausting. She sighed once again and Bastian drew a chair from the dining table to sit by her side.

"Can I do anything to ease your sorrow?" he asked, his tone solicitous.

She caught his hand and placed it to her cheek. "You are a man of science. Do you know of a way we can turn back the clock?"

He shook his head, his eyes drooping and his forehead creased in sympathy.

"No, I thought not," she said, and rested her temple against his, the power of touch a salve on an old wound. It was not enough. Nothing would ever be enough to rid her of this paralysis.

"How about a hot drink and a pastry? You look so pale. Perhaps it's that dress."

She reclined against the heavy drapes. "Widow's weeds are rarely flattering. Ring for refreshments if you want some. I cannot summon the energy to eat or drink. Is it normal to feel in a dense fog, somehow etherised and at one remove from reality?"

Bastian rang the bell and the maid appeared before he had retaken his seat. He ordered two hot cups of Ovomaltine with a slice of apple-almond cake. It was so typically Bastian that a smile spread across Eloise's face. A malt drink supposed to promote strength, and their favourite afternoon treat. On rainy days, brother and sister used to sit beside the fire, drawing with coloured pencils, sharing the one slice of cake they were permitted. Ever the gentleman, he always gave her the bigger portion. If anything could tempt her to eat, it would be *their* cake.

"Grief has no rules, Eloise. What is normal to someone recently bereaved may differ entirely to another. Keep going and do what you can. The children maintain a stoical air."

"Laurent is too young to understand. What four-year-old

grasps the concept of gone forever? His sister is taking it harder but Sylvia is a closed book. Had I not personally birthed the child I would swear she was my niece, not my daughter."

"Your niece?" Bastian's eyebrows rose in astonishment. "Whatever do you mean?"

"Do you not see the resemblance to Charlotte? Studious, self-contained, withdrawn and lacking in spontaneity, both seem to resent having a family at all."

The maid knocked, entered and set down a tray. Eloise looked away but Bastian thanked the young woman for such kind attentions to his sister. Only after the girl had closed the drawing-room door did he speak.

"Sylvia is six. She is trying to make sense of her world, especially now. Charlotte does indeed lack the genial touch, but she has passion. No one can deny her enthusiasm for ..."

"... dusty old books and hours closeted in the university library. Could we describe that as passion?"

Bastian broke the cake into two pieces, one noticeably larger than the other. He placed the bigger piece on a plate and pushed it across the table to Eloise. "Do not underestimate our sister's lust for learning. She is fascinating on the topics of language, geography and biology. Last time I visited, she took us around the garden, talking at length on the topic of butterflies, pointing out caterpillars and a chrysalis. Your children were enthralled. Charlotte differs from us in terms of sociability. That does not mean her engagement with the world is worth any the less. I admire her fine mind."

Eloise dabbed her finger onto some cake crumbs and put them in her mouth. The sweetness and fragrance awakened her appetite. "A fine mind is not enough to snare oneself a husband." She took a bite of cake, and only when reaching for her Ovomaltine caught her brother's expression. "What's the matter now?"

His face cleared. "Nothing is the matter. I must say this apple cake is quite delicious. May I ask Cook for the recipe?"

A spark flared in Eloise's brain, the first since her husband's passing. She replaced the cake, sat upright and pointed an accusatory finger at her younger brother. "What is it? Tell me now or I shall winkle it out of you the usual way."

He affected a patronising air. "I, a respected doctor with the ear of the Swiss government, and you, a recently widowed mother of two, both have reputations to uphold. It would be undignified to be seen wrestling on the rug like a pair of toddlers."

"Stop that and tell me what ruffled your feathers, Bastian. I can read your face as easily as Charlotte reads Ancient Greek."

He took his time, refusing to meet her eyes, dusting pastry flakes from his fingers and patting his moustache with a napkin. "Of all the ladies in my acquaintance, I consider you one of the most modern. You believe in female suffrage. You applauded Seraphine for gaining a nursing qualification. You championed Rosa Bloch and her revolutionary demands for women's rights. To hear you dismiss Charlotte, our brightest sibling, with 'a fine mind is not enough to snare oneself a husband' strikes me as backward looking and frankly disappointing. Is that the best your daughter can hope for? A good marriage?"

His words stung, all the more so because they were true. "You are supposed to console me, not lecture me on my principles. In any case, it's all very well for you."

"That I will not deny. Which is precisely why I use my advantaged position to balance inequalities. Women should be able to follow any path they choose. Surgeons, lawyers, business owners, architects, and professors, why shouldn't such roles be female?"

"Perhaps because we still have not earned the right to vote?"

He inclined his head in acknowledgement of her point.

"That will come very soon if Germany is any kind of benchmark. Probably in your lifetime and undoubtedly in Sylvia's."

Eloise finished her cake, considering his remark. "Women can vote in Germany?"

"Yes, of course. You are aware of the revolution across the border and that the country is now a republic? Do you ever read a newspaper, Eloise? The world is changing."

The cake and malted drink gave Eloise a sudden burst of energy. She jumped to her feet, cradled her brother's face in her hands and kissed his cheeks three times. "So many revolutions these days, one can hardly keep up. Let's walk around the garden so long as the rain holds off, shall we? I want to ask your advice about what to do with this house. But first, tell me all about Julius."

Her aim was true and she hit her target.

Bastian's stern expression melted into fondness. "Yes, fresh air would do us both good."

They donned coats and outdoor boots and he offered her his arm. "Julius is growing so fast I am afraid to blink. You will meet him shortly when they travel here for the funeral. He has Seraphine's eyes, lucky boy, and my verbosity. Yet to form a recognisable word, he nonetheless chatters like a starling. He reminds me of you. That is why I want you to be his godmother."

Twice in one day Eloise experienced a surge of emotion other than hopeless grief. "Me? Are you sure? Does Seraphine approve? Oh, Bastian, nothing would make me happier. A godmother! Surely that makes me somewhat respectable?"

Respectability, she reflected after her brother had left to meet the undertakers, could hardly be considered a life's ambition. She paced the library, casting resentful glances at the shelves housing tome after tome of adventure, drama and passion, all of which eluded her. After all, what was she to do with her life now?

Mother. Aunt. Widow. How did such passive duties fill a person's day? As Madame Eloise de Fournier, she had no choice but to make daily decisions. Approving Cook's menus, planning activities with the nanny, rearranging the furniture, meeting friends at a coffee shop, discussing a curriculum with the tutor, supervising the children's playtime and dealing with correspondence before Sylvain returned for dinner could occupy an entire day.

As a young woman, she had desired nothing more than an advantageous marriage. Her parents compiled a list of acceptable bachelors and pretended to consider each one on his merits before plumping for the obvious. Sylvain de Fournier, a childless widower from a neighbouring estate, was prosperous, well educated and a family friend, meeting everyone's requirements. Eloise would have no need to change anything other than social status and move into her new home along the street. *Les jeux sont faits.*

The Favre family operated as a pack, seducing the man with youthful charm (Eloise), fulsome flattery (Maman) and hints of power consolidation (Papa). Against such a unified front, de Fournier never stood a chance. The poor man capitulated with a sigh of relief and asked her parents' permission to court their daughter. Affecting surprise and delight, they agreed.

Her role was to play the ingénue, fall in love and accept the 'entirely unforeseen' proposal with a modest blush. A kind man, Sylvain indulged her as if she were his niece and treated her like a piece of fine china. Their intimacy was discreet, always conducted under the cover of darkness and never discussed. Somehow, those awkward, blessedly brief fumbles resulted in two children. He was delighted. She was appalled. The damage wrought on her body could never be undone. Once she had borne him an heir, Eloise considered her side of the contract fulfilled.

Then in late November, seven years after she had walked down the aisle, Sylvain complained of a headache. She suggested calling the doctor, but he demurred, retired to his bed and failed to wake up the following morning. At the age of thirty years old, Eloise went from a glamorous society wife to a pitiable widow with no future.

2

Summer 1926, Fribourg

Widowhood was even more tedious than being married. Since the funeral, no one asked her opinion on anything. Eloise and the children moved back to the parental home, she in her old bedroom, the children upstairs in the nursery and she had, quite literally, nothing to do.

Every day she was woken by the same maid who assisted with her toilette. Her clothes were always the same – a black crêpe dress, as befitting a grieving woman. She descended for breakfast, made polite conversation with her children and parents, and Charlotte on occasion, then when everyone departed for their busy days, she took her book into the winter garden. An existence, not a life.

Even writing letters, which used to be one of her chief pleasures, became a chore. She had nothing to say. Yes, she was well. Condolences were much appreciated. The children had recovered from that nasty winter cold. The funeral had indeed been a tribute to a great man. No, she was unlikely to travel before the autumn. Temperatures had risen but ... she bored herself and put down her pen.

A movement outside caught her eye. The delivery boy, whistling something tuneless, dropped the newspaper on the doorstep.

Do you ever read a newspaper, Eloise? The world is changing.

She opened the door to the hall. The maid, Greta, bobbed a curtsey and asked if she needed anything.

"When my father has finished with his newspaper, would you mind bringing it to me?"

The girl attempted to conceal her surprise. "Certainly, madam. Is it only today's news that interests you or would you like to read yesterday's sheet? We generally save them for the fire, you see. There's a good half dozen below stairs."

"I would very much like to read them all, please. Thank you so much."

Day after day, Eloise pored over columns of newsprint, her fingers often smudged and grey when she folded the pages for the maid to remove. Her head pulsated with new information and she yearned to discuss it with a like mind. She wrote to Bastian several times, but only received one reply. He apologised and excused the delay by saying he had so little time for correspondence in his new advisory role to the government. Indeed, he agreed wholeheartedly with her points about women playing a role in politics. She should act upon her convictions, in his view. Since the press had made such an impression, why not apply for a job as a journalist? She could argue her points to willing ears and gather a groundswell of support for full female participation in society.

Her parents looked askance when she raised the topic at dinner. Was not motherhood enough of a role for any woman? Whenever would she find the time? Would Sylvain have approved? On what sort of topics was she qualified to opine?

"I should like to address the shameful lack of female representation in public life, for one thing. A series of articles on pioneering women in medicine, in business, in entertainment and, why not, in politics?"

Her mother expressed the view that journalism already had an imbalance of loud opinions. Her father segued neatly into the question of Lausanne's radio station and whether it was worthwhile buying a licence. That led to her mother's dismissal of Swiss radio and Charlotte's enthusiasm for a new medium for public information, a debate her father refereed. Eloise's tentative attempt to create a role outside the family was lost.

As usual after dinner, she peeked in on the children, both already asleep, and bade the nanny goodnight. On returning downstairs to her own bedchamber, she was startled to see Charlotte waiting outside, a package in her hand.

"Should you wish to learn more on the topic, I would recommend starting at the beginning with these two volumes. A journalist should always have an authoritative quote at her fingertips. Please use a bookmark, as I would like both returned in pristine condition. Goodnight."

"Goodnight, Charlotte, and thank you." She took the parcel inside and unwrapped two books. One was *Déclaration des droits de la femme et de la citoyenne* by Olympe de Gouges. The other was in English by a writer called Mary Wollstonecraft. Eloise quailed. English was her weakest language. Even so, she understood the title: *A Vindication of the Rights of Woman*. She sat at her desk and began to read.

. . .

Each day, she took a walk to the old town and stopped at Frau Theurer's news kiosk. When it was not too busy, she and the proprietor would spend a pleasant few minutes discussing headlines of the latest newspapers or magazines. She always bought something, perhaps *L'Illustré, La Revue de Genève,* or *Schweizer Illustriete*. Some days, Frau Theurer had a new issue of *Berliner Tageblatt* or *Le Figaro*. On the occasions French editions of *Vogue* arrived, the kind-hearted lady hid one beneath the counter, especially for Eloise. They were shockingly expensive but provided hours of entertainment and thrilling ideas for the day when she could finally wear something other than widow's weeds.

In the afternoons, she frequented the library. She sought out publications in English, poring for hours over the writings of Millicent Garrett Fawcett with a dictionary at her side. Staff grew familiar with her frequent enquiries about ordering this volume or that from another library. By and large, they tried to satisfy her requests or direct her to similar works. She only ever borrowed one book at a time, tucking it into the bottom of her handbag.

When the children came home from school, Eloise was always waiting in the winter garden. *Le goûter,* their afternoon snack, was the one meal she prepared herself. Mainly because it involved nothing more than bread, butter, jam, cake and hot chocolate. In response to her questions, they chattered semi-comprehensibly between bites while she observed the light in their young faces. Even Sylvia, who had worshipped her Papa, was now bursting with enthusiasm for her music lessons. Laurent ran about, demonstrating a game he had won, and Eloise applauded. All too soon the doorbell rang announcing the arrival of their tutor. Both trooped upstairs to the nursery to be schooled in German accusative cases, as the maid cleared the table.

In her bedroom, Eloise kept her reading material in a knitting bag, concealed beneath a never-to-be-finished blanket. The only times she attempted to emulate the professionals' style of journalism were when she was alone. All her drafts, good, bad or mediocre, went onto the fire.

One unpromising October morning, she dressed in a navy dress with a white trim. Since the year and a day of mourning had elapsed, Eloise craved colour and light, but her mother's disapproval forced her to stay with sober tones. She tied a bright scarf around her neck and picked up an umbrella, ready to leave the house. Just at that moment, Charlotte came through the front door, looking damp and somewhat dishevelled.

"Eloise! Just the person. This saves me coming through to the winter garden."

"Good gracious, my dear, you look wet through! I'll call for Greta to light the fire in the breakfast room. Be careful not to catch a chill."

"I'm fine, there's no need to fuss. I have something for you. A colleague at the university mentioned a magazine you might enjoy, so I ordered a copy to be delivered to her house. Papa would not like such a thing to come here. She sent a message boy to tell me it arrived this morning and I've just been round there to collect it." She opened her carpet bag and drew out a rain-stained brown-paper parcel.

"How very kind of you!" Eloise put down her umbrella and used the letter-opener on the sideboard to cut the strings. Inside was a perfectly dry copy of a magazine she had never seen before: *Die Dame*. It appeared stylish yet practical, containing articles on fashion, dress patterns and household tips, and all of it in German. There were also features on women at work, doing jobs such as machine operating in factories or driving school buses. She struggled to find words for her gratitude. "Charlotte, this is quite marvellous. I'm most touched by your thoughtfulness."

Charlotte looked over her shoulder at the pictures of hats. "Looks shallow and frivolous to me. Nonetheless, the publishing company is advertising for women journalists. Why not send them some of your work?"

"My work? I have nothing to send! I have never submitted a single piece."

"That's because you keep burning them rather than sending them to an editor. Think of it, Eloise. Writing for a magazine, earning your own money, enjoying your freedom and living in Berlin. This is your opportunity to be a New Woman."

"Don't be silly, that's absurd," Eloise laughed. "How could I move to Berlin and support two children on a journalist's wage?"

Charlotte unpinned her hat and shook off the raindrops. "I have never been silly in my life. You couldn't support the children. Obviously Sylvia and Laurent stay here with their grandparents and their doting aunt. They have the same nanny, go to the same school and take extra lessons with their tutor. Very little in their everyday life changes, apart from regular thrilling letters from their mother, who is right in the thick of things. Once you are established as a journalist, who knows? I must go and change my stockings, my feet are soaked. See you at lunch."

Eloise put the magazine into her handbag as furtively as if it were contraband. Then she changed her plans. Rather than a visit to Frau Theurer, she walked in the other direction until she reached the library, found a quiet table and withdrew her treasure.

. . .

It took over two weeks before Eloise had three pieces she judged good enough to send: The Benefits of Nature Walks on Children's Health; The Tragic Story behind Löwendenkal, The Lion of Lucerne; and A Lady Skier – What to Wear on the Slopes. Her letter of application took days of rewriting and agonising over every word. Her father's professional views would have been valuable but she dared not broach the subject, neither to him nor her mother. When she had finally finished her articles, she asked Charlotte's opinion. She did not emphasise the need for honesty. With Charlotte, you expected the whole truth with no varnish.

"The first word that comes to mind is vapid. Perhaps less so with the background to the lion sculpture but that will not matter. Although the essay demonstrates your ability for research, an editor will dismiss it without reading the first paragraph. Think of your readership, Eloise. Since the Treaty of Versailles, how many Germans want to read about Swiss Guards defending the French royal family against revolution?"

Once the words were out of her sister's mouth, Eloise's insensitivity struck her like a lightning bolt. "Of course! You're absolutely right. How foolish of me!"

"At the same time, you do show a certain flair for descriptive language. Why not write a companion piece to your fashion item about the charms of a ski resort such as St Moritz, Grindelwald or Zermatt, for example? Somewhere your readers can practise what you preach. Your application letter I found mediocre and have annotated it with some suggestions. Do not dally. The final date for accepting applications is the end of this month."

"No! It is simply impossible for me to write another article in that time."

Charlotte raised her eyebrows. "A journalist works to a deadline, if she is a professional. Good luck." She marched out of the winter garden with her usual purpose, stopping only to scoop up a biscuit Laurent had left on the arm of a chair.

Fewer than forty minutes remained before she must change for dinner. Eloise drew out a sheet of paper and began to write.

3

Winter 1926-27, Fribourg

BLUE SKIES ABOVE THE ENGADINE
By Eloise de Fournier

The charm of St Moritz begins to work its magic even as the train travels through dense pine forests with jagged snow-covered peaks reflected in the lake below.

For centuries, tourists have flocked to bathe in the health-giving mineral waters of this Engadine town. Nowadays, it holds a different kind of allure for visitors: the thrill of winter sports. Skiing, sledding and hiking opportunities draw energetic men and women from all over the world, who also appreciate the relaxing evening atmosphere in top-class hotels after a day of healthy fresh-air exertions.

It was not always so. People used to travel to the region only in summer months, fearing the winter too cold and gloomy. An enterprising hotelier named Johannes Badrutt made a legendary wager with a group of English guests. If they returned for the winter and did *not enjoy the sunny climate, he would foot the bill. They took the bet and told their friends. The rest is history.*

Each year, more and more pleasure-seekers visit St Moritz for exceptional landscapes, unparalleled activities, sophisticated après-ski and an opportunity to mingle with the bright and beautiful. If that is not enough, one can sit on the terrace with a cup of hot chocolate and absorb the most breathtaking scenery in the world.

Hastily written and overflowing with adjectives as it was, that was the piece which got her the job. The editor wanted to run it in the very next issue, alongside her fashion item about ski wear, accompanied by illustrations. When could she start as a full-time employee at *Die Dame*?

Every morning since she posted her three articles and application to Berlin, Eloise had been the first to descend for breakfast. The morning staff laid the post on a table beside the front door, ready for her father to inspect. Whenever there was an invitation for her mother, a note for Charlotte or far less frequently, a letter for Eloise, he would set each missive at their respective places. A German postmark would excite curiosity and provoke questions which Eloise was ill-prepared to answer, so she beat everyone to the dining room. Greta, evidently puzzled by this change in household habits, offered to light the fire earlier if Madame de Fournier wished. She refused, saying she was perfectly content to wait for the rest of the family. One grey December morning, a knock came at the door before she had even got out of bed. Greta entered, carrying a tray with a coffee pot, a jug of milk and an envelope.

"Good morning, Madame de Fournier. A letter from Germany arrived this morning, addressed to you. I thought you might like to read it in your room with a cup of coffee."

"Greta, you are a treasure! Thank you."

She read the letter three times, took a sip of coffee and read it again. The management of *Die Dame* were willing to pay her for the articles she had written and publish them in the very next edition. Should she wish to join them on a permanent basis, a position as staff writer would be available from next January. The terms and conditions swirled into a blur and the coffee cup clattered as she replaced it in the saucer due to her shaking hands. She had landed the job of her dreams. By next year, she could be a professional journalist. With a calming intake of breath, she set the letter down and began rehearsing her speech to her parents. A sudden panic gripped her and she tore open the door, rushed down the corridor in her nightgown and knocked on Charlotte's door. Her sister was completely unpredictable, sometimes leaving the house before it was light, other times dawdling over breakfast until ten. Eloise simply could not tackle her parents without Charlotte's support.

"What is it?" Her tone was snappish, reminding Eloise of the reason why she never knocked on this particular sibling's door.

"It's Eloise. May I come in?"

"No, you may not. Go to your room and I will join you when I am ready."

The elation bestowed by the letter was like a bubble of joy, enclosing and insulating her from insult and offence. Charlotte's curt dismissal made no impact, although Eloise followed her instruction and returned to her room. She picked up the letter and read it again. ... *accompanied by illustrations*. Whose illustrations? How could they be sure the images were precisely what the writer of the article imagined? She gave herself a sharp reprimand. Making demands before she had even accepted the job?

Three short raps announced the arrival of Charlotte.

She came inside and closed the door. "You've heard from the magazine, I suppose."

"I have. Here, read this."

Charlotte took the letter, poured more coffee, sat in the armchair, drank a good half a cup and read. When she looked up, a rare smile graced her face. "Congratulations! I am extremely impressed. Write back to say the salary is acceptable and you give them your permission to publish both pieces. When your work is to be accompanied by illustrations, you expect to have final say over which images are best suited. Tell them you will be at your desk by the first of February and wish them an excellent Christmas."

"The first of February is far too soon. The arrangements ..."

"Arrangements can be arranged. Let us break the news to Papa and Maman this very morning. Talk to the children this afternoon during *le goûter* and remember to make it sound like a gain rather than a loss. They will follow your lead. Do you know, Eloise, I am extremely proud of you. With your aptitude, you were always destined to be more than a pair of blue eyes. Now I'm going downstairs for some coffee that is not lukewarm."

She swept out of the room, leaving the letter on the table. Eloise considered her unvarnished words: *with your aptitude, you were always destined to be more than a pair of blue eyes.* She recalled her own: *a fine mind is not enough to snare oneself a husband.* She snatched a scrap of paper from her writing desk and wrote both down. If nothing else, she had the beginnings of an article.

Her dreams crumbled to ash before the coffee pot was empty.

"Absolutely not! How could you even think of such a thing? Your role is as a mother to your children. Why would you want to work, and in a cesspit like Berlin of all places, when you have everything you need under this roof? To even propose such an idea shows disgraceful ingratitude and if I may say so, self-indulgence. One of my daughters going out to work! It's unthinkable!"

"But, Papa, Charlotte goes out to work!"

"At the university! A respectable Swiss seat of learning, not a filthy den of iniquity in a country which just lost a war, suffered a revolution and will need more than a decade to pay off its debts. I blame myself. A young woman sheltered from reality has a rose-tinted view of the world."

"A very good argument for why Eloise should accept this offer," Charlotte interrupted. "Papa, she is not proposing to tramp the streets of Berlin begging for employment. She has a firm offer of full-time work at a highly regarded publication, secured by her own skill at writing. I think it praiseworthy that she wishes to contribute to society by using her intelligence."

Monsieur Favre flared his nostrils. "I would be prepared to countenance Eloise playing some role in journalistic endeavours for the benefit of Switzerland on the condition it was part time and left her free to continue her maternal duties."

"Think of your children, Eloise," said her mother. "Nothing is more important for a woman than raising a family."

"Exactly! Your mother sacrificed everything for you, your brother and sister."

"Times have changed." Charlotte shrugged. "Maman, may I have the coffee pot, please? *Merci*. We are all grateful for our upbringing and should probably say so more often. But this is 1926. Women took control of the farms, the factories *and* the families while men went to defend Swiss borders. We have proven ourselves capable of so much more than bearing children. A New Woman no longer expects to sacrifice everything and actively wishes to participate in all echelons of society. Why shouldn't she?"

In the silence that ensued, no one lifted their eyes from their plates.

Greta opened the door with a fresh pot of water but Monsieur Favre dismissed her with a flick of his fingers. He stood, his hands braced against the table and expression stony.

"As the head of this household, my decisions are final. Should you wish to return to your own home, pay your bills, arrange staff to care for your children and maintain your property, you are perfectly free to run off to whatever hellhole you choose. While you live under this roof, such a proposition is out of the question. The topic is now closed. I wish you all a good morning."

At the sound of the front door closing and her father's footsteps crunching down the drive, Eloise burst into heartbroken sobs. Her mother rushed to her side, patting her hair and advising against upsetting herself.

"Why would I not be upset?" she wailed. "My life is over!"

"That's not true, my darling! You cannot think that way. Consider your wonderful children who fill us all with pride. Is that not enough?"

Eloise brushed away her tears and shook her head. "No, it is not enough. Not for me."

"Finally!" Charlotte applauded. "If you start with honesty, the rest will follow. Now, dry your eyes, for goodness sake, because I have no time for waterworks. Let us discuss the situation from a practical perspective. Eloise has done her duty to you and Papa, as the obedient daughter she always was. She married Sylvain and produced two children. It's not her fault he died so soon, but after the decent period of mourning, why shouldn't she have a second opportunity?"

Madame Favre fussed with the bow at her neck. "Do you mean she ought to remarry?"

"That is one option of many. However, rather than rushing into another marriage of convenience, she might wish to choose for herself. After the loss of Sylvain, a beloved husband and superlative father, she may have broader horizons."

"Poor Sylvain. We miss him, both as a son-in-law and a dear, dear friend."

Charlotte handed her a napkin. "Why is everyone in this family so weepy?"

The two daughters waited until Madame Favre had composed herself. "I will speak to your father. Ring for Greta, this coffee is cold."

It took four days and complex manoeuvres from all three women but Herr Favre eventually granted his daughters an audience. He chose an evening when his wife was attending a recital at the *Musikhalle* and received them in his study.

As agreed during their rehearsals, Eloise went first, emphasising her good behaviour, cooperative nature, bright mind and adventurous soul. Like her father, she devoured newspapers, keen to form her own opinions from a variety of sources. Journalism was a highly respected profession with a significant role to play in the fabric of society. She had done everything asked of her and now gained the chance to pursue a career as a New Woman, earned on her own merit.

He nodded once or twice, but mostly examined his fingernails.

Charlotte's voice was modulated and calm, but her words lit a fire in Eloise. "Please understand, Papa, this is all your fault. You look surprised. My sister is not an ungrateful child kicking against the traces. If anything, she holds true to the values you instilled. Our parents raised their children to be enquiring, curious, interested in our environment and eager to engage with the world. You wanted Bastian to study medicine and he became a credit to the medical profession. You encouraged me to go as far as possible with my education and as a result, I gained a respected status at the university. Your plans for Eloise were a good marriage. Did she disappoint?"

His eyes softened. "Never."

"Therefore, give her wings. Let her do a trial period at the magazine, writing articles alongside other brilliant journalists to learn her trade. If the role is not for her, she can return home and apply her knowledge to the Swiss media. If she swims in a competitive market, we celebrate another Favre success. A credit to her family, your daughter looks to the future and champions progress."

He stood, his hands behind his back and looked out at the gardens. "There is the question of the children. Sylvia and Laurent already lost one parent."

Eloise had no answer for that. However, her sister was never lost for words.

"Your realism, Papa, is a trait I have long admired. To perceive the truth of the matter without sentimentality allows you to reach the best compromise. Using the same clarity of thought, Eloise spends an hour with the children each day. The rest of their care is supervised by the nanny, Greta, their tutor and school. In order to see my sister fulfilled and happy, I volunteer to prepare *le goûter* and listen to the stories of their day while she throws herself into the life of a political journalist. As a family, we can raise two bright, happy children who take pride in their lineage."

They waited in the shadow of their father's back, hardly daring to look at one another.

What Eloise said next was not rehearsed, but whispered from desperation. "Over generations, the Favre family has always led by example. Fellow citizens look to us when making decisions, more often than not seeking your advice. Everyone talks about progress, in communications, in politics, in international relations and domestic stability. One evening at dinner, I heard you and Sylvain exchange views on that very topic. So many of those ideals can be achieved by educating female minds and harnessing their power. Papa, allow me to forge my own path. There is no greater honour than holding the Favre flame as a beacon."

No one spoke for a full minute until their father cleared his throat. "Leave me now. I must have time to consider. At dinner, you will limit your conversation to the mundane unless I speak of the subject. Thank you both."

The two women left the study and closed the door behind them.

"Thank you, Charlotte. I am overcome with gratitude."

"As you should be. I was perfectly right to suggest journalism as your profession. As the mistress of manipulative purple prose, you'll go far."

No announcement, no official acceptance, yet in the smallest of gestures, Eloise's parents gradually acknowledged the positive sides of her move. Her father advised her to contact the magazine with a view to a probation period in February. Then he began making enquiries with his bank colleagues as to a suitable *quartier* of Berlin and a recommended ladies' rooming-house. Once his approval was clear, Madame Favre fell into line, assuming control of the packing when she was not absorbed in preparations for Christmas. The children accepted the news so easily Eloise wondered if they understood what it meant. Nonetheless, she was relieved to have precious little drama around the topic. The only person who balked at the idea was the one who suggested it – Bastian.

When her brother, Seraphine and Julius travelled to Fribourg for New Year, they brought good news. Seraphine was expecting a second child. After the delighted congratulations subsided, Eloise, nudged by Charlotte, proffered her own modest achievement. Seraphine was the first to express her joy, sincere in her praise, followed by Bastian standing to shake her hand. Nonetheless, she caught the reproachful look he exchanged with their father. During the Silvester celebrations, there was barely a moment for a private conversation, what with the children's excitement, a formal dinner and party games until Midnight Mass at Cathédrale Saint Nicolas.

The next morning, the first day of 1927, everyone dressed warmly for the traditional family stroll around town. Seraphine, it seemed, was suffering from morning sickness and could not participate. Eloise pulled a sympathetic face to hide her glee at having her brother's full attention and insisted on sending up mint tea to quell the poor woman's nausea.

The outing served several purposes. First, the aim was to walk off the excesses of the previous evening. Second, the Favre and de Fournier families took the opportunity to mingle, stopping for a brief conversation with significant friends or calling out good wishes to lesser acquaintances. New Year's Day was an occasion to be seen. Eloise normally loved parading around in her finery beside her husband and showing off her children. Today, the whole event struck her as provincial and dull. Neither did it escape her attention that no one boasted of her imminent change in circumstances. However, she had the opportunity of walking beside Bastian. With his wife indisposed and her husband deceased, nothing was more natural than for the siblings to fall into step.

For a while, they made no other conversation than exhorting one another to look at the children playing in the snow or exchanging opinions on the cathedral's new stained glass windows. As they reached the tree-lined Place des Ormeaux and the statue of Père Girard, Bastian adopted a casual tone and said,

"You cannot seriously consider moving to Berlin." It was not a question.

Eloise bristled. "I most certainly can. Good heavens, the wheels are already in motion. The boarding house is expecting me, my train ticket is reserved and by the time I arrive, two of my articles will be in print. I am going to be a journalist, on *your* recommendation, if you recall."

"Always pushing things to the limit, my dear. Yes, I do recall encouraging you to put your intelligence and enthusiasm to work, largely in the service of others. What I had in mind was a way of occupying your time, contributing to the community and exhorting other countrywomen to join the cause, all the while fulfilling your other role – that of a mother. Writing for a Swiss publication would allow you the freedom to do both. Taking a job in Berlin is the opposite. You will neither play a role in the emancipation of your Helvetian sisters nor in the upbringing of your children."

Anger choked her throat, rendering her unable to speak. She strode ahead of him, trying to catch up with her parents. Behind her, footsteps crunched in the snow.

"Eloise, stop! Can we not debate the issue like adults? Or must you flounce off like a petulant child? My concern is for my niece and nephew, in the main. But I admit to serious reservations about your welfare. Berlin under the Weimar Republic is unstable, dissolute and not the place for a vulnerable woman. I am simply asking you to explain your decision in order to understand what provoked such a reckless move."

She whirled on her heel and faced him, her teeth clenched. "I owe you no explanation! You cannot sit on the fence, *mon frère*. On one hand, you say women should have greater power over their lives. Yet you stand here demanding I beg your approval for my course of action. I will do no such thing. You have no right! I require nothing from you. I am happy you and

Seraphine have found a balance of equals. Yet how I navigate my life is none of your business." She stalked away, calling to the children. "Laurent, you made a snowman! *Formidable*! Where are your gloves, Julius? Your poor hands are frozen. Should we find you a scarf? Sylvia, go ask Grandpère for his."

For the rest of the visit, she and Bastian remained civil but avoided being alone together. Her temper, once roused, took more than a day or two to subside. She spent time in the winter garden with Seraphine, talking about the doctor's practice in Brienz, drinking tisanes for their health and discussing baby names.

"I always wanted to call my daughter Chantal," Eloise sighed. "That was impossible when our first child was a girl. Tradition states the child must be named after the father and Sylvain was a stickler for tradition. So she is Sylvia Chantal de Fournier. Why did you call your first born Julius?"

"After Bastian's friend Julius from university. He was a brilliant young doctor who died in the influenza outbreak. I never met him, although I feel as though I did from my husband's glowing words. He calls him the brother he never had." Seraphine winced. "I'm sorry. That was thoughtless of me. His love for both his sisters is evident, but I know you are the closest to his heart. This is why he worries so."

Eloise was playing with a myriorama, creating an ever-changing landscape from eighteen illustrated cards. Sustaining her anger and indignation to Seraphine's angelic face was impossible. She abandoned the cards with a sigh and joined her sister-in-law on the chaise longue.

"I know, and he is the closest to mine. Even though he is the baby of the family, Bastian believes he knows what's best for his sisters. Why? Because he is a man. Seraphine, I have no desire to be miserable for the rest of my years. A widow at thirty years of age, am I to retire from life and take up needlepoint? No, I am determined to experience life in all its beauty and ugliness. Where better than as a *Neue Frau* in Berlin?" She shrugged. "I'm practising my speeches on you. Pay no attention. Is it not always our nearest and dearest who drive us to distraction? Surely you and your siblings must quarrel?"

Seraphine rested a hand on her belly. "I cannot say we ever did. As a child, I lost two brothers. Henri died before his tenth birthday and Anton was still an infant when he succumbed to the white death."

"I'm so sorry." Eloise hesitated to sympathise. No one had ever raised the topic when her father was alive. "Did Bastian tell you we lost our older sister to the same terrible disease?"

"Yes. I know about Françoise. That must have been very painful."

"Truthfully, our parents protected us from the worst. At the time, Bastian was in the army and I was at a finishing school in Lausanne. Neither of us knew until after the funeral. Papa forbade us to speak of it for fear of upsetting Maman."

Seraphine placed a hand on Eloise's arm. "It is understandable to avoid the subject at first. But I hope you have happy memories of your sister. I have precious few of my little brothers but I treasure every last one."

"Françoise was twenty-two years of age and the kindest, most beautiful woman in the world. She was the peacemaker of the family." Eloise clenched her fists, refusing to scratch old scars. "No one is perfect, but in my mind, she remains a saint."

"Yes, departed souls will always be pure. That is why we decided to name our children after our siblings in heaven. My instinct tells me this is a girl. She shall be called Henrietta Françoise Favre and this time we will ask Charlotte to be godmother. Should God bless us with another baby, he or she will be Anton or Antonia. You are fortunate, Eloise, to have a happy family. Treasure the time you have together because one day will be your last." Her lovely blue eyes clouded and she reached for a handkerchief.

They clasped hands in silence, both lost in thought while the January rain pattered on the glass roof. After a few moments, Eloise bent to kiss Seraphine's hand. "I promise to take my godmotherly duties to Julius with the utmost seriousness. Thank you for the honour. Now I shall find Bastian and offer an olive branch. Seraphine, my brother is lucky to have you. And so am I."

She hurried away before her emotions got the better of her. From the study, laughter alerted her to a noisy game of draughts. When she opened the door, she saw Bastian was playing Laurent, with his sister as his advisor.

"Maman! Come help us! Uncle Bastian is cheating!"

"He is, Maman, he is just making up the rules. You must be the referee."

Eloise widened her eyes at her children. "Your uncle is a professional doctor with the ear of the Swiss government, not to mention a respectable husband and father. Are you calling him a cheat?"

"Yes!" they chorused.

"Well, I wouldn't be at all surprised. He was a rotten player when we were little and nothing has changed. I shall be the judge of this."

She settled herself on a chair with an aloof expression towards the children and a sly smile directed at her brother. The game began.

. . .

The children won, since the referee was unashamedly biased and the cheat had long since given up trying to hoodwink his niece and nephew. The maid knocked to say Julius had awoken from his nap and *le goûter* was served in the winter garden. The children scampered out of the study while Eloise and Bastian stayed behind.

"You never told me Seraphine lost two brothers," she said, scooping all the counters into their cloth bag.

"It is her place to talk about her past, not mine. Those two little boys and many others like them were an avoidable tragedy. That is why I championed iodised salt. I knew it would change the lives of people like Seraphine's family." He folded the board into the box that bore all the scuffs and scratches of their shared childhood. "Since the iodine intervention, Seraphine's mother has borne another child. Peter is healthy and full of vigour, with none of her family's previous afflictions."

"Just like Julius."

"Just like Julius," he agreed. "Eloise, will you allow me to apologise? Your decision to apply for a job and gain it on your own strengths is to be applauded. I say again, congratulations."

"I accept your apology and your congratulations. I sense there is a 'but'?" She remained on the chair, like an umpire.

"There is no 'but'. Truthfully, I admire your drive and talent, and wish you luck. Berlin must be tremendously exciting at a time like this. My only concerns are for your safety and the children's wellbeing. As your brother and their uncle, you would expect nothing less. That said, if you are sure this is the right thing, I give my wholehearted support. In a way, I envy you."

Her defensive carapace softened. "Don't envy me. You have a wonderful wife, child and career. I am stepping into the unknown. If you want the truth, I'm frightened."

"Good." He stood up. "If you are frightened but proceed regardless because it is the right thing to do, that is the definition of bravery. Shall we join the others for some Ovomaltine and apple cake?" He offered his arm and she took it.

4

February 1927, Berlin

The right thing to do. All the signs confirmed it. Her articles were published as promised in the January edition of *Die Dame*. At the news kiosk, Frau Theurer was so proud of her regular customer's new identity, she placed a regular order for the magazine. Papa found a Berlin boarding house, run by a respectable woman who only admitted decent young ladies. It augured well that the establishment was on Charlottenstrasse, and even her sister allowed herself a smile. Two of Mama's acquaintances in Basel were travelling as far as Frankfurt to visit their brother and would be only too pleased to accompany a young woman on the second leg of her journey. Everything was prepared and Eloise was ready.

She faltered only when saying goodbye to Sylvia and Laurent. Losing both parents in two years was too dreadful for them and she lay awake night after night, questioning her choice. On this subject, she consulted no one. In the final analysis, the only people whose opinions counted were the children.

The day before she was due to depart, they came home from school to find her waiting in the winter garden as usual. On the table was the usual hot chocolate, plum cake, slices of dark bread and a slab of cheese. On the floor sat two huge presents, wrapped with ribbons and labelled 'For Sylvia' and 'For Laurent'.

They entered, neither able to ignore the presence of two large, gift-wrapped objects, and kissed her cheeks. She asked if they had washed their hands (they had), if they were hungry (they were) and invited them to sit because she had something to say. They ate and drank, watching her with concerned eyes. Her throat swelled and she blinked several times, trying to clear her vision.

"Is the cake tasty? Last year's plums were quite exceptional."

"It really is very good, Maman. Won't you try a piece?" Sylvia used her knife to cut a delicate sliver, slid it onto a plate and handed it to her mother.

The act of eating and swallowing helped Eloise find her voice. "My goodness, this is delicious. I doubt very much if I shall enjoy such cooking at my lodgings in Berlin. On that topic, I want you to know that I will miss you both terribly and write to you as often as I can. Leaving you is a wrench, I cannot deny, but you are better off at home with the family, seeing your school friends every day while Nanny looks after all your needs. I have a present for each of you, just to remind you of me. Sylvia, this one is yours. Laurent, wipe your fingers and open this."

They undid the bows, peeled away the paper and exclaimed in unison, although Eloise saw Laurent had no idea what his gift might mean.

"*Une maison de poupées!*" breathed Sylvia. "You bought me a dolls' house! I always wanted one of my own. Thank you so much, Maman, I love it!"

Eloise kissed her daughter and waited for Laurent to

discover his own world of invention. "There are lots of little bricks," he said, lifting the first tray out of the box.

"Exactly, my darling. Lots of little bricks for a little architect. You can build houses, castles, churches, farms and a whole village. The only other thing you need is your imagination."

Absorbed in unpacking the box, he had to be reminded by his sister to express his gratitude. "Thank you very much, Maman."

The three of them sat by the fire, exploring the elements of each diversion, until Charlotte entered the room.

Sylvia started and clapped her hand over her mouth. "Our German tutor! We forgot!"

"Your tutor has a free afternoon seeing as this is your mother's last day at home. What do you think of your presents?" Charlotte bent to examine Laurent's rudimentary construction. "I'd say this is much better than one of those silly stuffed bears. Good choice, Eloise. Can I have a slice of that cake?"

The car was ready by six in the morning, when the children were still asleep. Her parents and Charlotte accompanied Eloise to the station, ready to wave her off. She tried to oppose the scheme but was overruled. She did not protest. On one hand, she wanted to embark upon her journey alone. On the other, she was grateful for their support and less likely to break down into embarrassing tears on the train platform than at their own front door. Her face was still puffy from when she had kissed the children goodnight eight hours ago.

The fuss of putting her luggage onto the train and getting assurances the porter would be able to assist in Basel made the final goodbyes less emotional. With a flurry of kisses and warm embraces, Eloise stepped onto the carriage. The whistle blew, she took her seat and with one last wave at her family, she left

Fribourg for the unknown. She held her head high, clenched her jaw and twisted her wedding ring around her finger. *Sylvain, have I made a terrible mistake?*

Twelve hours later, she was convinced she had. The delay between Basel and Frankfurt meant she missed her connection to Berlin. The kindly friends of her mother's offered her a place to stay until the following day, but Eloise was determined to press on. If she could not reach Berlin tonight, she would get as close as she possibly could manage. The stopping service to Leipzig was equipped with neither first-class carriages nor porters, so she had no choice but to sit in a freight car on top of her trunks. The journey was interminable.

When she enquired about onward trains to Berlin, the conductor shook his head, his moustache as droopy as his eyes. Her best hope, he advised, was to take rooms in Leipzig overnight. He could vouch for the hotel beside the train station, as cheap and relatively clean.

"Best hotel in town. Just be sure to lock your door."

His advice alarmed her, but she had little choice. She paid a porter with a trolley to transport her luggage to the 'best hotel in town', which appeared run down and shabby. As she approached the entrance, shapes emerged from doorways, some bandaged, others limping and all converging on her and begging for a few Pfennigs. The porter threatened them with a stick, enabling her to get inside safely while he manhandled her luggage.

Shaken, she checked in and paid extra for a larger room so that she could keep her luggage in sight. Once the formalities were complete, she asked about the possibility of a meal. The kitchen was closed. All the manager could offer was a plate of cold cuts and a glass of wine. He insisted on payment up front, examining her Reichsmarks with narrowed eyes. On receiving her keys, she immediately sought out the communal bathroom. Latrines on railway stations were vile.

A bored young woman with a thick accent brought her food and Eloise locked her door for the night. She ate some meat, cheese and pickles with stale bread, forced down some sour wine, performed a basic toilette and out of sheer exhaustion, fell asleep too tired to even cry.

R ain lashed the windows at seven in the morning, which did nothing to improve her mood. She hurried to use the bathroom before any of the other guests, her stomach churning with nerves. It was always possible to turn around and go back to Switzerland. Ignominious, obviously, but why should she endure such discomfort and danger when there was an alternative? Someone banged on the door, startling her to the extent she smudged her eyeshadow. She tidied her make-up and opened the door to see a man wearing nothing more than undergarments and a frown.

She apologised, ducked past him and was hurrying to her room when she smelt coffee. The girl who had brought the food was taking empty plates to the kitchen. Aware of her improper attire, Eloise attempted a bright smile.

"For a small fee, could you bring some coffee and pastries to my room? Perhaps an egg? I find it awkward to eat alone in the dining room, you see."

The girl held out her hand.

"Oh, I don't have money on me. I just came from the bathroom. Payment on delivery?"

The girl shrugged and walked away. Eloise had no idea how to interpret that. She packed her bag and dressed for the journey. Another long day of travelling was in store, whether she continued to Berlin or returned to Fribourg. She sat on the bed, dithering and counting by how much she had already exceeded her budget. Someone knocked.

"Do you still want this?"

Eloise unlocked the door to see the girl holding a wooden platter with an assortment of breads, a boiled egg, yogurt, preserved fruits and a pot of coffee. Her gratitude nearly overwhelmed her as she laid it on the table. "Thank you so much! This is exactly what I need. What does it cost?"

"A hat."

"I'm sorry?"

"You wear nice hats. The modern style. You give me a hat, there's no charge."

Without hesitation, Eloise took the straw cloche she had been planning to wear that day and placed it on the girl's head. "Does that fit?" She turned her towards the looking glass. "If you don't like this one, I have others."

The girl turned to all angles, assumed various expressions and adjusted the hat a little lower over her brow. "I like it very much indeed. Thank you and enjoy your breakfast. When you are ready to leave, the porter is right outside."

Whether it was the coffee, the fruit or the negotiation, something shifted in Eloise. Yes, Germany was very different to what she had expected, but where was the excitement when everything stayed the same? Onwards, to Berlin!

This last leg of her journey was exactly how she had imagined. A first-class seat in a quiet carriage, her luggage stowed by the porter, and once the rain cleared she enjoyed some marvellous views of Saxony. She read the newspaper she had purchased at the station with half an ear on other people's conversations, attuning herself to the sound of the sharp Germanic tongue. All thoughts of running home to Fribourg and the safety of Switzerland were forgotten. As the train heaved into Berlin in the late afternoon, daylight was fading. Eloise hardly noticed for the dazzle of streetlights, warm glows from windows and bright signs advertising everything from cigarettes to motor vehicles.

It was exhilarating and nerve-wracking all at once. The amount of people on the platform overwhelmed her even though a porter helped get her luggage into a taxicab. She gave the driver her new address and stared out at the chaotic traffic, bustling pavements filled with fashionable folk and a plethora of entertainment palaces. Never in her life had she felt more of a country innocent. How on earth could she compete with all these sophisticates?

She paid the driver a little extra for heaving her trunks to the door and wished him a good evening. A chill wind crept under her collar so she rang the doorbell, eager to get inside.

The door opened to reveal a handsome woman in a bottle-green dress holding a wine glass and a cigarette. "The new lodger. You should have arrived yesterday."

"Yes, I know and I apologise but the train was delayed and I was forced to stay overnight in Leipzig. My name is Eloise de Fournier."

"Leipzig?" The woman's lip curled into a sneer. "You are to be pitied, not judged. My name is Ruth Gartner. You brought all this luggage? Levi! On this occasion, you may come in through the front entrance. In future, you must enter through the back door on Charlottenweg. My lodgers live at the rear of the building. The front is my private domain and I am fond of entertaining. Levi! Oh, here he is."

A stooped man wearing braces and an open-necked shirt came out of the shadows. He looked up through round spectacles and gave a curt nod in Eloise's direction.

"Levi is our caretaker and we treasure him. This house

simply could not function without his knowledge. Levi, this is Eloise and she's in Room No. 1. Good thing it's the ground floor, no? Look how many bags she has! Will you take her things to her room while we complete the formalities? Thank you so much. In here, Eloise, I expect you need a drink." She led the way into a small salon, lit with Art Deco lamps and a cosy fire.

"Thank you, Frau Gartner. A cup of tea would be most welcome."

"Tea you can make yourself in the guest kitchen. And I dislike the formality of family names. My name is Ruth." She poured two glasses of sherry. "All I need from you is a signature and a brief glance at your *Ausweis*. Please be aware that the house is non-smoking and anyone who flouts that rule will be given notice. The fire escape is exempt for obvious reasons."

Eloise produced her identity card before she took the glass. "I don't smoke. Never have."

"I'm pleased to hear that. Our agreement is for three months' probation and thereafter an extension for one year, yes?"

"That is correct. If my employers wish to retain me, and I hope they will, I intend to stay for a year at least."

"Good. Sign here and here. Ah, you wear a wedding ring."

"I am a widow."

"Likewise. The war took so many of our men." She picked up the contract and examined the signature. "Perfect. One copy for you and one for me. *Prost*! Welcome to Berlin, the city where everyone gets a second chance!" They raised their glasses and drank. "Come, let me show you your new home."

The bedroom was almost as large as the one she had left in Fribourg. Huge heavy wardrobes lined the wall, a jug and basin sat on a side table, one window overlooked the back alley and another had a view of the side street. She had a table at which to work, an armchair, a large bed and across the hall, a bathroom. Officially, it was shared with the other lodgers, but since there was another bathroom on the first floor, she was likely to keep it to herself. Next to that was a small kitchen, with all the necessary amenities. She noted each lodger had their own shelf. LILI. HILDEGARD. VERONIKA. It seemed Lili and Hildegard cooked a lot, judging by the vegetables, herbs, canned beans and bouillon, while Veronika's was empty other than some mouldering cloves of garlic. One could tell a lot about a person by looking at their provisions.

Eloise expressed her thanks with all sincerity. Ruth gave a kindly smile, bid her new lodger a good night and returned to her own quarters. The moment Eloise closed the door to the bedroom, the discomfort and uncertainty which had plagued her throughout the journey melted away. Something told her this was a safe place. The decor was neutral, but not in a careless way. Pale pink walls, dove-grey woodwork and a patchwork eiderdown in pinks and purples coordinated well with the charcoal rugs. There were a few bland prints on the wall, easily replaced by something more personal. Her trunks and holdall sat beside the bed. She could not yet face unpacking, so dug her tea caddy from her travelling bag, made a pot in the kitchen and settled into her armchair, gazing out at the street. *Welcome to Berlin, the city where everyone gets a second chance*!

5

February 1927, Berlin

The whole idea of travelling on the Friday was to give her the weekend to recover, unpack and explore her surroundings. Due to the Leipzig interruption, she had one day in which to do everything. Eloise woke before eight and went to the bathroom, wondering where she would be able to purchase bread, milk and butter on a Sunday. As she returned to her bedroom, she saw a little basket on the floor outside the door. It contained a jug of milk, half a loaf of bread, a pot with curls of butter, another with a spoonful of jam and a little posy of wild-flowers tied with a ribbon.

"Oh! How lovely!"

"Good morning!" Two smiling faces looked out of the kitchen doorway. "Those are just a few little things to welcome you to the house. I'm Hildegard and this is Lili. You must be Eloise, all the way from Switzerland."

"Thank you so much! Yes, I'm Eloise and it is a pleasure to meet you."

Lili beckoned. "Bring your basket in here. We've just made coffee so let's have breakfast together, shall we? Do you have plans for the day, because we can show you around, if you like?"

"Let the woman sit down, Lili. We don't want to steamroller her the minute she arrives. How was your journey, Eloise? When Ruth brought the post, she mentioned an unfortunate delay."

"Please take a seat." Lili poured the coffee and cut a slice from the other half of Eloise's loaf. "We came downstairs yesterday evening to invite you for a drink, but seeing as your lights were off we didn't knock."

"That's very thoughtful of you. I missed my connection in Leipzig and had to spend the night there. The journey was very tiring so I went to bed without even unpacking. Unfortunately that's how I must spend my Sunday in order to be prepared for Monday morning. Are you both in employment?" She added milk to her coffee and took a grateful sip.

"We are indeed. New Women, both of us. Lili is a saleswoman in a clothing store."

Lili beamed with pride. She was a classic Teutonic beauty, with creamy skin, lively blue eyes and a ready smile. She wore her hay-coloured hair in high waves away from her face. The rest was tucked into a flat bun at the nape of her neck.

"Whereas I manage an office for a law firm." Like Lili, Hildegard wore her hair in a bun, although hers was darker and a good deal more severe. "You came to Berlin for work, I imagine?"

"That's correct. Tomorrow I take up my role as a staff writer for *Die Dame*. I must confess I am terribly nervous. This is my first job and I have no idea what to expect."

Lili stopped eating and stared.

"*Die Dame*? That is wonderful to hear! I read that magazine and so do all my clients. You can give me the inside track on trends and style, and I will be the best informed girl in store!"

Eloise laughed at her enthusiasm. "You are probably better

informed than I when it comes to fashion. We can advise one another." She began buttering her bread, oddly unselfconscious even though she was not yet properly dressed. "Can you tell me a little about this area? Is it easy to circumnavigate? I'd hate to arrive late at the publishing office."

"We'll help you." Hildegard's manner was practical and no-nonsense. Lili was probably a decade Eloise's junior, while Hildegard seemed closer to her own age. Even so, she dressed in the contemporary style, in a simple shift dress with pearls at her neck. "Tell us where it is and we'll show you how to get there. I've lived in Berlin all my life and Lili's from Potsdam, so not a complete outsider. We know our way around the city. You are the exotic stranger from Switzerland. How does Berlin compare?"

"I may be able to give a better informed answer to that question in a month or so. One thing I can say is that Berlin is bigger, brighter and far more thrilling than my home town. But since meeting you two professional women, I already feel very comfortable in this ladies' boarding house. What about Veronika? What line of work is she in?"

The atmosphere changed in an instant and neither woman met her eyes. Hildegard poured more coffee and in an offhand manner, said, "The entertainment business, you could say. She keeps very different hours to the rest of us. I doubt you'll meet her often, as she's quite nocturnal. Unless you smoke, of course."

"No, I don't smoke." Eloise changed the subject. "February in Berlin. I can already see I shall need my winter coat and warmest hat. Somehow I expected here to be less chilly than home."

The conversation moved on to the best attire for winter weather, and her new housemates regained their friendly animation.

. . .

Monday morning dawned cold, rainy and grey. Eloise fussed and fretted over her clothes, convinced everything made her look like something out of the last century. Eventually she chose a long lilac skirt and jacket, black ankle boots and a white blouse. Lili showed her where to get the correct tram and wished her luck. Her wish was in vain. The streets were infernal, with buses, motor vehicles, trams, horses and pedestrians all crossing one another's paths with no discernible organisation. Aboard the tram, people pressed and crammed and brushed wet umbrellas against her skirt. She got off a stop too soon and had to walk the rest of the way in the rain, accosted twice by men begging for money. One used a crutch to compensate for his missing leg and asked politely, but Eloise was too nervous to stop and rummage in her handbag. The second man made a grab at her skirts, demanding she give him some coins. When she arrived at the offices on Kochstrasse, she was hot, wet, flustered and daunted.

Once again that voice in her head told her she was making a terrible mistake. She took a moment outside the Ullstein building to compose herself, tucking a few stray hairs under her hat. Then with her head high, she pushed open the door and announced herself to the receptionist. The girl checked her name was on the list and pointed towards the doors.

"Take the stairs to the second floor and turn left."

She trudged up two flights, wishing she could take off her coat. She was hesitating on the landing when the door flew open and a stylish woman in a calf-length wool dress faced her.

"Eloise de Fournier? The receptionist told me you were on your way up. I'm Vicki Thal and I am very happy you are joining us. Come in and let me take your coat. The weather is dreadful, don't you think? One has no idea what to wear."

The room was bright and filled with desks where around a dozen people were working, talking, smoking or carrying papers to and fro. A few faces looked up and Eloise returned their smiles as she hung up her damp coat, wishing she'd worn something less old-fashioned.

"I'll give you a quick tour and assign you a desk because we have no time to lose. Our deadline is the fifteenth of the month and I want you to do a piece on bathing suits."

"Bathing suits? In winter?"

"No, no, this is for the June edition. We always work three months ahead. It just so happened we had space in the January issue for your item. Why don't I put you next to Martha, who is very experienced and can show you the ropes. Martha, this is Eloise, our new staff writer."

Martha, like Vicki, appeared chic and confident. She stood up and held out an elegant hand. "Hello, Eloise. Welcome to our magazine. I hope you like it here."

"Thank you, I feel sure I will."

In the next fifteen minutes, Vicki introduced her to everyone in the room, stopping for a quick conversation at each desk. The ratio of women to men was 2:1, which came as a surprise, and everyone was more fashionably dressed than her. People seemed warm and friendly, but there were far too many names to remember. Finally, Vicki showed her how to use the coffee maker, then dumped a pile of catalogues and magazines on her desk.

"Devise an approach and an approximate sketch of how you see the finished piece. We'll talk about it at the editorial meeting tomorrow morning. Remember, it's all about the individual's sense of taste. How does *she* want to be seen? Is that fine for you?"

"Yes, certainly," answered Eloise, who had no idea where to begin. She began looking through the catalogues' section on bathing suits, making notes on the variety of materials, cut, patterns and types. Some manufacturers were now calling the garment a 'swim suit', which sounded much neater to Eloise's ears. Some of the swim suits now leaned towards practicality rather than modesty, since an Australian lady athlete by the name of Annette Kellermann had made competitive swimming acceptable. Her figure in an all-in-one suit cut well above the knee was most admirable. Indeed, many women were persuaded that swimming could be good for the body. An idea occurred to Eloise and she began to scribble some notes.

By the end of the working day, after looking up facts in the manufacturers' catalogues, fabrics, cross-checking references and earmarking examples for the illustrator, she had the makings of an article.

NEW LOOKS FOR THE BEACH
What kind of swimmer are you?

For the bathing belle to look pretty yet respectable, the latest version of the dress-over-bloomers ensemble remains an attractive classic. If exercise is your aim, inspired by the Olympic Games, one of the bright one-pieces will not impede your movements. Or perhaps somewhere between the two, such as a close-fitting dress over shorts would be your ideal compromise. Swim suits are now part of the modern woman's wardrobe. Even Coco Chanel has designed bathing costumes for Les Ballets Russes in Paris, marrying fashion and high culture.

Depending on your budget, why not opt for a knitted maillot or a sleek jersey silk, both light and excellent at holding their shape. Say goodbye to the heavy, saggy flannel of yesteryear. When it comes to colours, the nautical theme will not go away any time soon. Blue and white stripes are a perennial favourite, as is the light belt against a darker colour to accentuate the waistline. Beware pale shades as they tend to transparency when wet. In addition, beige, white or peach can make pale skin appear grey and wan.

As we all know, accessories can make an outfit. Matching shoes and bathing hat signify a woman who pays attention to detail. Why not add a coordinating parasol to keep the sun at bay and turn heads?

Come on in, the water's lovely!

She fiddled with it again once she arrived home, tempted to show it her housemates, but could not bear to seem so lacking in confidence. Instead, she contributed an apple to the evening meal, which Hildegard and Lili prepared together. Sausages with potato mash, gravy and red cabbage with apple. They ate at the kitchen table, each relating anecdotes from their days at work. At one point, footsteps came down the stairs, but whoever it was went straight out into the street, leaving behind a trace of strong perfume and cigarette smoke.

When the back door closed, Eloise glanced at the other two. "Was that Veronika?"

"Hmm." Hildegard looked up at the clock. "She's late tonight. Normally out before we get home and in bed before we get up. Do you want to wash, Eloise, and I'll dry? Thank you for the sausages, Lili. My turn tomorrow."

"Yes, thank you, Lili. It was kind of you to invite me to join your meal. I would like to return the favour. Can I cook for you both on Wednesday?"

Lili boiled water for tea. "That would be lovely! Hildegard and I take turns making dinner every other day, except weekends. If you want to fit into the rota, you could take Wednesdays."

"I would love to participate. I'm not the best cook in the world, as my children will testify, but I'm sure I can rustle up something edible."

The two women stared at her.

"You have children?" Lili's eyes were huge.

"Yes. Sylvia is seven and Laurent is five."

"Where are they?" Hildegard glanced into the corridor as if the children might be hidden in a trunk under Eloise's bed.

"At home in Switzerland with my parents and older sister. Happily, a proper cook is in charge of that kitchen."

"Good gracious!" Lili's brow creased. "Don't they miss you dreadfully? And you them?"

Eloise considered those questions as she rinsed the cutlery. "I'm sure they're absolutely fine. As for me, that remains to be seen. Let's finish up here and I can write my letters home."

In the event, the only letter she wrote that evening was to her children. She penned a lively account of Berlin's streets, emphasising the number of people, amount of traffic and ubiquitous advertising, including a few observations to make them laugh. She knew her parents and Charlotte would read what she had written, so decided their own letters could wait until the weekend, when she had a little more substance to relate about her life. She performed her toilette, chose her clothes for the following day and sat in front of the mirror, bunching her hair behind her head. Perhaps a shorter cut might suit her face.

6

Spring 1927, Berlin

Her swim suit piece was accepted eagerly, with only minor tweaks from Vicki. Next, she was charged with two collaborative pieces. One with travel illustrator Ulrich on the best bathing spots in and around Berlin. He was the man who had added the image to her description of St Moritz, and showed excellent taste. Her second assignment was on the best materials for a dancing dress, with her desk mate Martha.

Her colleague instantly began planning a trip to every fashion house in and around Hausvogteiplatz, dashing off messages to all her connections. Eloise agreed with great enthusiasm. She had never visited a major dress designer and thrilled with excitement at the thought. However, their original idea of taking a week to visit all the designers was quickly quashed by Vicki, who permitted them one day out of the office and no more.

Her bathing spots piece, she assumed, would also involve

seeing a little more of Berlin than her street and the tram ride to the office. Ulrich had other ideas.

"Not necessary, my dear. This article can be completed with a short tour around the office. Take your pad and pencil, ask half a dozen of this lot which is their favourite and why. If two of them say the same thing, choose someone else. See if you can't get a riverside spot, a lake and at least two upmarket *Baden*. You write it up in pretty language, I do some generic waterside illustrations and we're finished."

She must have looked surprised because he laughed, not unkindly. "Always take the easy road, my dear, because the best results often come from the least effort. Do you have a preference when it comes to bathing?"

"Not in Berlin, no. I've only been here two days. But at home in Fribourg, I loved to swim in the river Sarine. It's the most extraordinary greeny blue. You can float along with the current and gaze up at the trees lining the river bank."

"Ah, well, I imagine a Swiss river is a good deal cleaner than the Spree. You wouldn't catch me in there. I have heard talk they are planning to forbid bathing due to the state of the water. Who knows? You might find one hardy soul who chances it. Come back to me tomorrow when you have six different locations and we'll get to work."

Ulrich was absolutely right. She asked seven of her colleagues for a recommendation and each waxed lyrical about the absolute 'best' place to take a dip. The disappointment at not going out on the streets was outweighed by the fact it was the worst possible weather to visit lakes and rivers. In addition, by interviewing a few others in her workplace, she learned their names and got to know a little about them. By the end of the day she was feeling quite proud of herself.

One girl, Julia, asked some questions of her own in return. She had spent time in both Geneva and Zürich, and enquired as to Eloise's opinion of those cities. While they conversed, some of the journalists began leaving for lunch. Julia asked Eloise to join her at a nearby café and they continued chatting over soup and a *Butterbrot*. After they finished eating, she drew out a packet of Eckhart cigarettes and offered one to her companion.

"Oh, thank you, no. I don't smoke."

Julia lit hers with a smile. "You will. Everyone does. Especially if you work in fashion."

It was fascinating to watch her ritual. She placed the cigarette in its holder, clipped two fingers around the stem and placed it between scarlet lips. With one flick of her lighter, she inhaled and released a cloud of smoke to wreathe around her face in mysterious swirls.

That evening, Hildegard cooked stew with some offcuts of mutton and vegetables. Eloise outlined her new assignment regarding dancing dresses and her plan to visit fashion houses. It was, apparently, Lili's favourite topic.

"Taffeta is very good because it bears the beadwork well. The most important thing is that it swishes around the legs as you dance. Silk is divine, of course, although terribly dear and awfully delicate. Gabardine and cotton are strong but look rather dull. The evening wear we have in stock at the moment is all about drapes. The material must fall elegantly, even when there's much less of it."

The conversation clearly bored Hildegard as she made two attempts to change the subject. When she saw Lili was not to be deflected, she made a pot of tea and retired for the night. Eloise promised to share all her findings with the younger woman and was about to say her goodnights when a knock came at the connecting door. One could never predict when or how that morning's post would arrive. Mail sometimes appeared on the kitchen table in the morning or Ruth came round with a bottle of sherry if she felt like company. Tonight the caretaker entered the hallway like a cat unsure of its welcome.

"Hello, Levi. How are you?"

"Very well, thank you, Eloise. Ah, here's Lili, I have a package for you." He bowed his head, his thick black curls glinting in the overhead light. "There are also two notes for Veronika and for you, Eloise, a letter from Switzerland!"

He handed over the bundle and waited.

"Thank you, Levi. It's kind of you to bring our mail. Well, goodnight, then."

"You're welcome. You know, I was in Switzerland once." His moustache expanded as he smiled.

"What did you think?" asked Eloise politely, itching to open her letter.

He pushed his glasses up his nose. "Everything was distant. Scenery, people and language, all very beautiful but rather removed. Goodnight, ladies."

With that, he left.

D*ear Eloise*
I trust this finds you well and that you had a good journey. We have been waiting for news since Saturday. Your mother insists she told you to call us from a public telephone on arrival and I clearly recall asking for a telegram at the very least.

We are growing increasingly concerned. Yet as I have heard nothing from your landlady or your employer enquiring as to your whereabouts, I must assume your journey went as planned. I hope you will respond to this letter at your earliest convenience.

The second reason for writing is an unexpected development regarding the de Fournier house. A gentleman of my acquaintance is looking for a property in either Bern or Fribourg to house his numerous offspring. He is a wealthy industrialist who travels regularly to oversee civil engineering ventures. I have assured him that Fribourg is the perfect city in which to raise a family. We took a tour of the city together and as an example of the kind of residences available, I showed him around Sylvain's house and gardens. He was most taken with the amenities and location and asked me to name a price.

Before I continue with any kind of assessment of its value, I wanted to consult with you on the subject. Obviously the property is in your name. All proceeds will go to you and the children, which would set you up for life. You then have no need to work and can buy a smaller house for you, Sylvia and Laurent, thereby maintaining complete independence.

Please communicate your opinion soonest since I am ready and willing to undertake any negotiations on your behalf. I do hope you see this opportunity in a favourable light, especially as such fortunate circumstances do not occur very often.

With fondest regards

Papa

Fribourg, 3 February 1927

The letter put her out of sorts, mainly because her father's rebuke was deserved. Why hadn't she sent a telegram or made a telephone call? She countered her better nature by saying she had been far too busy. Enough time to go window shopping, visit a food market, join Julia for lunch, sit at the kitchen table with her new housemates and even write to the children, but not to pay the most basic of courtesies to her parents?

She crossed the hall to wash her face and clean her teeth. The letter to the children should arrive the day after tomorrow. Even so, she should send a telegram. She resolved to do it the very next day, before she arrived at work. Something simple and to the point.

SAFE ARRIVAL FINALLY STOP LETTER TO FOLLOW STOP LOVE TO ALL

That should keep him quiet for a week or so.

Even as she typed up her article on Berlin bathing spots, revised once again after editorial advice, she pondered the vexing question of the de Fournier house. She had lived there for less than a decade yet felt protective of her marital home. It signified safety and echoed with happy memories, until more recently. It was where the children had grown up. It was where she herself had grown up, since she was little more than a spoilt girl when she became Madame de Fournier. The house belonged to her and the children. Selling it was too painful so soon after Sylvain's passing. A decision was required at some point, she knew, but for as long as possible she would defer it.

Another pressing decision was what to do with her hair. On Friday, she and Martha had appointments with four of the biggest fashion houses and Eloise was the complete opposite of chic. Her clothes were outmoded and dowdy, her hair took far too long to pin into a bun and it was high time she acquired some proper make-up. Trying to achieve all three before Friday was ridiculous and she needed some advice. She completed her text, checked it for errors and delivered it to Ulrich.

While he was reading, she glanced across at the woman on the opposite side of the desk. She too was an illustrator and at that moment, was inking in some designs for summer hair. She stopped work and looked up at Eloise in enquiry.

"Oh, I'm sorry, I didn't mean to poke my nose in. It's just your designs are so pretty and I am trying to decide what to do with mine."

The woman sat back and assessed her. "You have good bone structure. What about something like this?" She indicated her own sleek head, ears and the nape of her neck exposed.

"Oh my goodness, I'm not that brave. But it looks lovely on you. I want mine shorter, certainly, because it is such a bore to keep smart. Maybe something like that?" She pointed to the drawing of a curly bob which framed the model's chin.

Ulrich rose from his seat and came to add his opinion. "It's a good starting point. No doubt short hair will suit you and if you feel braver next time, you can experiment. I'll give you the name of a barber."

"A barber?" Eloise was aghast. "Surely there must be a ladies' hairdresser who does ..."

"Ulrich is right. Only a barber can manage these shorter cuts. If you like, I'll go with you as it's your first time. My name is Hannelore." She stood up to shake hands and Eloise saw she was wearing trousers.

She blinked, trying to act as if she hadn't noticed. "I'm Eloise and I'm new here."

Hannelore tilted her head with an amused smile. "I'd never have guessed. The barber's is only a two-minute walk. Let's meet at midday, downstairs by the front door. I'll give him the instructions and leave you to it while I buy us something to eat. Nice to meet you, Eloise."

Her protestations shrivelled before they reached her mouth. "How very kind of you. Midday it is. Ulrich, what do you think?"

"Of the hair or the article? I'm teasing. Your piece is fine. I'll do a few sketches and if I think a word or two needs changing, I'll consult you first. Good work. Didn't I say you could get all the material you need from within these four walls?"

· · ·

When she returned from the barber's, still shocked by her audacity, Hannelore went ahead, clapping her hands for attention.

"She's been with us less than a week, but look who's becoming a *Neue Frau!*"

The attention terrified Eloise and she hissed at Hannelore to hush, but it was too late. Applause rang around the office and several colleagues wandered over to admire her glossy bob.

"You look so different!"

"How pretty you are – I think it's perfect!"

"I cannot take my eyes off your hair!"

She accepted the compliments as graciously as she could manage and reached out a hand to Hannelore. "This is all thanks to you. Next week, I'm taking us out to lunch."

"I'll look forward to that. You look beautiful." Hannelore caught her chin and lifted her face, then pressed a finger to Eloise's lips. "You *are* beautiful. See you later."

The reaction when she returned to the boarding house with all the ingredients for *Älplermagronen* was less enthusiastic. Hildegard was the first to enter the kitchen, clasping a hand to her throat on catching sight of her housemate.

"Good heavens, Eloise! Your long, thick hair, what happened?" She sat down in the nearest chair as if in shock.

"I'm a New Woman, Hildegard. No more getting up two hours before work to arrange my locks. Tomorrow, I will get out of bed, give my bob a brush and walk out the door. I'm making *Älplermagronen* for dinner. Macaroni in a cheese and bacon sauce."

"That sounds very nice. Why did you, I mean, it looks perfectly modern, but how long will it take to grow back?"

Mischief entered Eloise's voice. "Grow back? I shall never

wear it long again. If anything, I'm thinking of cutting it shorter. Aha, it sounds like Lili's home."

"*Guten Abend, zusammen.* I brought some roasted chestnuts from that funny little man on the corner ... oh! Eloise! You are so brave! Let me look at you." She studied the haircut from every angle, a smile creasing her face. "You look so chic! And how much easier to manage than all this." She pushed up her bun with one hand. "I wish I had your courage. Hildegard, don't you think this suits her?"

"It does look practical, if less than ladylike. I know you two think I am an old tartar, but isn't long hair one of the most attractive features of a woman?"

Eloise stirred the cheese sauce and considered the topic. "Long hair *was* thought of as feminine and therefore attractive. Nowadays, women prefer to personify elegance, independence and capability. I believe there is more to me than my looks." She checked herself, aware she was writing an article in the air, rather than talking to her friends. "Although there is a long way to go before I gain the same respect you have earned. Let's look at this as a first step of many."

"Did you weep?" asked Lili. "Whenever I have to cut my hair, I cry to see those locks swept up by the hairdresser."

"I did not weep. Partly because I went to a barber, not a hairdresser. There's something about men with clippers that stems one's tears."

"A barber?"

Their astonishment echoed her own so accurately that she burst into giggles, no longer able to feign nonchalance. "Sit down, I'll serve the food and tell you everything."

7

Spring 1927, Berlin

Her first two weeks in Berlin passed so fast it seemed like two days. She had delivered six articles, only one of which needed a serious rewrite. She had made friends: Julia, Martha, Ulrich and Hannelore at work, Hildegard and Lili at home. Trams no longer intimidated her yet she kept alert, since she had once drifted off in a daydream and found herself in a poor neighbourhood of ragged children and hard-faced women. The driver advised her to remain seated until he began the return journey. "Elsewise, they'll have the shirt off your back." On the streets, she grew adept at dodging the ubiquitous beggars, having learned to spot them from a distance and avert her eyes from their horrifying deformities. She kept her purse inside her coat to deter thieves and only donned jewellery once inside the office.

The high point so far was the visit to the fashion houses, where she had soaked in all the beauty, learned vast amounts about the skills involved in dress design, gained confidence in speaking to impossibly sophisticated auteurs and come away with a handful of samples in return for a positive slant in their article. This was her dream come true.

The low point was her father's pressure to sell her house in Fribourg. One breezy letter detailing all her adventures and a throwaway line about sentimental attachment did not satisfy him. He wrote straight back, detailing the advantages of selling now, reminding her how much the house cost in maintenance, exhorting her to be reasonable and asking her to telephone on receipt of his letter. She ignored his request and sent another note, reiterating her decision. They could, she assured him, discuss it when she came home for the Easter holiday. To her horror, his next move was to telephone her at work, meaning Vicki's office.

Eloise kept the conversation brief, as Vicki went outside in order to give her some privacy. Naturally, she assumed a personal call to the office must signify a family emergency. Her father was overbearing and made several mentions of her responsibilities. Eventually, she snapped, and told him to respect her wishes and never to call the office again. The incident distracted her to the extent she forgot it was her turn to cook that night and did not stop at the market on the way home. Her housemates were understanding and ate herb and onion pancakes without complaint. She resolved to use some of her savings fund to buy a decent cut of meat for Thursday night.

Her second weekend in Berlin took her by surprise. She had nothing to occupy her time. The previous Saturday she had spent doing her laundry and visiting the *Frauenbad* to get a decent bath. On Sunday she went for a walk in the neighbourhood and did a little sightseeing. The house was quieter than normal. Her housemates both spent weekends visiting their families, absent from Saturday morning until Sunday evening. Lili went home to Potsdam, Hildegard travelled south to the suburb of Lichterfelde, where according to her, nothing much happened.

Nothing much happened for Eloise either, until early Sunday morning. She repeated the Saturday routine of laundry, bathing at the ladies' public facilities, choosing her wardrobe for the following week and writing letters home. She addressed her parents as one and did not mention the altercation with her father. To the children's dutiful missive, she replied with lots of questions and a description of the Brandenburg Gate. It was harder to write to Charlotte, knowing that any mention of fashion houses would make her yawn. Instead, she related facts about her job, her housemates, the streets of Berlin and the number of injured ex-soldiers on the streets. To Bastian and Seraphine, she allowed herself a little more frivolity, whilst emphasising how much she missed her children. She sealed the envelopes, marvelling at the many faces of Eloise de Fournier. At four o'clock, she made the most of the remaining light and walked a few blocks, just to get a little exercise, until rain drove her indoors.

Dinner was a lonely affair, consisting of the same kinds of things she would prepare for her children's *goûter*: bread, cheese, jam and an apple instead of cake. She indulged in a hot chocolate and thought of the meal her parents would be enjoying. Three courses, not including the consommé, with fine wines to enhance each dish. Then she thought of the accompanying conversation and decided she was better off where she was. By nine o'clock, she was in bed with her book.

The noise sounded like a heavy coat slipping off a hook and crumpling onto the floor. She could have explained it as such and gone back to sleep but her coat was on a hanger in the wardrobe. Moreover, coats did not make small coughs, sneezes or sobs. She switched on the lamp and checked the clock. Ten minutes to five. The sounds from the corridor stopped for a moment and then a feeble scratching came at her door, as if a cat required admittance.

Eloise got up, dressed in her robe and opened the door to her bedroom. The rectangle of light from behind her illuminated a figure on hands and knees, drooling from the mouth.

"Oh my goodness!" She stepped into the corridor and switched on the light. The smell hit her before she saw the pool of vomit inside the open door. The figure was a woman with cropped blonde hair and fringed dress, clutching a bunch of keys and a still lit cigarette.

"What on earth is wrong? Are you unwell?"

At the sound of her voice, the woman's elbows buckled and she collapsed onto the hall floor face first. Eloise dropped to a crouch to remove the cigarette and keys from under her forehead. Had the wretched creature not been soaked to the skin, she could have suffered a burn. Eloise's rudimentary knowledge of first aid taught her that someone who had fainted should be placed on their side. With some difficulty due to the slippery skin of the patient and the fact she was a dead weight, Eloise manoeuvred her sideways, with one knee drawn up for balance. She bent closer to the woman's mouth to listen for breathing and recoiled at the stench, watching instead for the rise and fall of her chest. Reassured by signs of life, she fetched a cushion from her room, wrapped it in a towel and slid it under the damp blonde head.

Wind and rain blustered through the back door, still open to all manner of intruder. She stepped over the foul-smelling puddle but just before she shut out the weather, spotted a glint of silver on the step. A small handbag covered in reflective discs with a chain to be worn around the wrist lay in the rain, its contents spilled across the wet path. Eloise scooped everything up in both hands and carried it all inside, kicking the door closed behind her.

She ran the cold water tap and soaked a dishcloth to wash the woman's face. Smudged eyeshadow, red lipstick, dribble and mucus washed away easily, leaving a fragile, ashen face beneath the mess. She covered the woman with a blanket then she set to cleaning up the mess. It took three buckets of hot water and plenty of soap before she was satisfied. Then she boiled the kettle one more time to make some tea. While she waited for her unexpected guest to regain consciousness, she stuffed newspaper into the soggy handbag and tidied up its contents, drying each item with a tea towel. A cigarette case, a cigarette holder, an Art Deco lighter, a perfume atomiser, a powder compact, a beaded bag stuffed with notes, some loose change, assorted business cards, mostly water damaged, and a tiny silver box which looked as if it might contain earrings but instead held some fine white powder.

She was nodding off on the kitchen chair when a soft moan jerked her awake. In the corridor, the patient had pushed herself up onto one elbow and was blinking at her surroundings like a child waking from a nap.

"Hello. How are you feeling? Would you like some tea?"

The woman squinted at her. "Water?" she croaked.

Eloise filled a tumbler. "Here you are." She waited until the woman had taken three long draughts and set the glass on the floor before continuing. "I think you must be Veronika. My name is Eloise and I am the new occupant of the ground floor."

The woman covered her eyes with her hand. "For the love of everything holy, turn that light off!"

Eloise obeyed, switching off the hall light and observing the woman by the illumination from the kitchen.

"Where's my handbag?"

"You dropped it outside. I picked everything up and brought it into the kitchen. At least I think I got it all. Do you want to come and check? If I missed something, I can have another look when it's light."

Veronika drank another gulp of water. "Yes. No. I think I'm going to be sick."

"In here!" Eloise opened the bathroom door and switched on the light. Veronika scuttled in like a heaving beetle and just got her head over the toilet before she vomited. It didn't seem decent to stand and watch, so Eloise returned to her room and got dressed. It was just after seven o'clock. Soon the sun would rise. When she came into the corridor, she could hear the sound of splashing water.

Ten minutes later, Veronika, dressed in Eloise's bathrobe but still wearing her dancing shoes, shuffled into the kitchen and slumped into a chair. She rested her head in her hands and muttered, "Sweet Lord in Heaven, last night nearly killed me." Finally she looked up, her eyes bloodshot and sooty. "Can we start again? You mentioned tea?"

"I did. This is a fresh brew." Eloise poured two cups.

"Thank you very much. For the tea, for the water, for the bathrobe, for rescuing me and my handbag and ..." she gestured vaguely "... everything. I'm Veronika. I live here." She held out an unsteady hand which Eloise shook.

"Eloise. You're welcome. I guessed you might be a resident, rather than a random stranger who broke into the house and vomited in the hallway."

"Oh, hellfire and damnation." Veronika clasped her hands over her eyes and groaned. "Not the best way to introduce myself, I suppose." For the first time, she held Eloise's gaze. "I am deeply ashamed of myself and mortified to have intruded on your Sunday morning. Please accept my sincere apologies and my assurance it will never happen again." Her dipped chin and mournful brow was too rehearsed to be genuine.

"It's not the first time you've used that line, is it?"

With a tired laugh, Veronika dropped the pretence. "No. And all the other times I've used it, I never meant a word. You have a weird accent." She reached for a cigarette. Her lighter didn't work after three tries so Eloise lit a kitchen match and opened the window.

"I'm Swiss."

"That explains everything. I won't offer you a cigarette for two reasons. One, your complexion tells me you have no vices. Two, I've only got seven left and cannot face going out until I've slept off this hangover."

She smoked, holding the cigarette between her first two fingers, while wiping sleep from the corner of her eye with her thumb. Her eyelids drooped and she propped up her head with her left palm. Eloise moved her saucer closer to catch the perilously fragile tube of ash. Her age was impossible to determine. Under the harsh bare bulb of the kitchen light, she seemed at once haggard and grey yet with the underlying tautness of youth.

Her gaze fell on something and she sat upright, spilling ash onto the table and reaching for the curling business cards. "*Scheisse*! I can hardly read these. What do you think, is that a one or a seven? I need to call this guy or I will have no work next weekend!"

"It's a seven. Just let them dry out and they'll be functional. Like your handbag."

"If only that worked for me." Veronika heaved herself up with the aid of the table, tipped everything but the faulty lighter and damaged cards into the pockets of the bathrobe and swallowed her tea. "Thank you, Saint Eloise of Switzerland, and I'll repay your kindness one of these days. Goodnight and sleep well."

With a faint smile, she edged out of the kitchen and padded up the stairs. Eloise opened all the windows, cleared up the kitchen and went to empty the stubbed-out cigarette and ash into the toilet. On the bathroom floor was Veronika's filthy wet dress and undergarments. Eloise dumped them in the sink, ran the water, fetched the soap flakes and boiled the kettle. Again.

Hildegard returned to 125 Charlottenweg just as the light faded into dusk. She brought three slices of *Apfelstrudel* from her sister, a slab of cheese from her brother-in-law and some peacock feathers her mother wanted to give away.

"I thought you and Lili could make use of them for your hats," she said, laying the iridescent feathers on the table. "My mother's latest superstitious whim is her conviction that peacock feathers bring bad luck. She will no longer have them in the house. Bad luck? Never did the peacocks any harm, did it? How did you spend your weekend?"

"Quietly, on the whole. I must say, I have never heard of peacock feathers as a harbinger of doom. As a matter of fact, I vastly prefer feathers to fur. A feather has a dash of elegance without overdoing it. Do you not want to use them as an embellishment yourself, Hildegard?"

"In my line of work, feathers and frippery detract from the seriousness of the profession and I am hardly the type to parade around the Tiergarten in my finery on Sundays."

"Oh, the Tiergarten! That's where I meant to go today."

Hildegard frowned. "You forgot to go to the Tiergarten? That's a little more absentminded than forgetting to cook dinner."

"Ha ha, you're right. I intended to spend my day in the park, but had a thought about an article, so spent much of my day writing and researching. Having an idea makes next week smooth sailing, you see. And the Tiergarten will still be there next weekend. I think I hear Lili coming up the path. Shall I boil the kettle for tea?"

8

Spring 1927, Berlin

After that startling encounter one Sunday morning in February, Eloise did not see Veronika again for another month. Had she not initiated contact, it could have been longer. She washed, dried and pressed the fringed dress, wrapped the clean undergarments in brown paper and left both items outside Veronika's room one evening. Two days later, she found a flamboyant bouquet of roses bound with silver paper propped against her door. In a childlike scribble, the note said, "For my guardian angel, Eloise. With grateful thanks, V.' The grand gesture was somewhat undermined when Eloise removed the paper before putting the flowers in a vase. An embossed card fell out which read, 'None of these could ever smell as sweet as you, my beautiful rose. Yours as ever, Reinhart xxx.' Second-hand or not, the yellow and red blooms made a luxurious addition to her bedroom, filling the air with a heady scent.

At the end of February, Eloise received her first pay packet. Her own money, earned from her own hard work, could not have been more precious. All month she had made the most of her lunch hour, visiting the more upmarket clothing stores at least once a week. She often asked advice and usually bought something small, until she was on first-name terms with several of the salesgirls. Now she waited until Saturday and went shopping for a whole new wardrobe. A new calf-length skirt, a neat cloche hat and two blouses, along with beads, ribbons and a length of navy-blue crepe material with which to make herself a dress. All employees of Ullstein Publications were entitled to a discount on their dressmaking patterns.

As a result, she spent the rest of her weekend cutting out panels of fabric and pinning them together. Hildegard had promised to borrow her mother's Gritzner sewing machine and carry it across the city in return for some of the more sober clothes Eloise no longer wanted. It seemed a fair trade. She spread her material and paper patterns out in the kitchen to make use of the table, secretly hoping Veronika might stop by on her way in or out. She was disappointed. She heard and saw nothing whatsoever of the other occupant and by Sunday afternoon, had grown tired of her own company. When Hildegard arrived complete with sewing machine, Eloise could not hide her delight.

At work, she was invited to join an 'ideas' meeting, looking at which direction future issues should take. The invitation came as a surprise, even when Vicki explained the reasons why. A 'new girl' had no preconceptions and was less likely to base her ideas on what had gone before. Not only that, but Eloise and her ilk were the magazine's target readers: modern, earning an independent income, well educated and with a strong sense of identity. She found the roomful of people somewhat intimidating but listened intently. She nodded at some points, but said very little until directly asked to contribute.

"What do women want, in your opinion, Eloise?" asked Hermann Ullstein.

Without hesitation, she answered in one word. "Mobility. We want to be able to change, whether that's our looks or our habits or even our location. The past was all about rigidity of roles and fulfilling other people's expectations. The way I see it, the future is about shaping our own roles and challenging what is expected of us. Women nowadays want to be spontaneous, unexpected, in control and alive to the possibilities. A magazine aimed at women must be more than clothes and cosmetics. We are interested in what's going on in the world and want to be part of it. Sorry, I didn't mean to say quite so much."

"We asked for your opinion," said Max Adalbert, one of the bosses from the publishing house. She had never seen him before. He was strikingly good looking, not the type of man one forgets. His personality filled the room and several women, including Martha, seemed too shy to meet his eyes. "When you say 'what's going on in the world', can you give us an example?"

"Oh, everything that's new. Frightening films by Herr Lang or Herr Murnau, influential German artists and architects, modern European music, the latest motor vehicles, great German cities and why one should visit, what's happening close to home, such as Berlin's nightlife and theatre scene, and how it compares to the rest of the world."

Adalbert gave Ullstein and Vicki a meaningful look. "Some very good suggestions there, no? I particularly like the concept of the cabaret and club perspective. Send someone to investigate and take a photographer. Martha, you're very quiet. Can we hear what you think should be in our magazine?"

Martha was playing with her pencil and did not look up but her voice was clear. "We are a fashion magazine. I think we should focus on Paris. That is where all the key couturiers are. For example, I'm thinking along the lines the evening-dress feature I did with Eloise. We could go to Paris, pick up the most modern developments both from fashion houses and the boulevards, then run several pages on contemporary French fashion."

Eloise nodded eagerly. A trip to Paris would be marvellous!

"Or you could read the French magazines and save yourself a trip," remarked Vicki drily. "I like the idea of street fashion, though. All right. Martha, you can have a day out next week to spot trends. Work with Philippa on the design side. Eloise, you can have two half-days off as compensation for a couple of late nights on the cabaret scene. As usual, outline the article and if I like it, you can go back with a photographer. Anything else, Max, Hermann? Or shall we break for lunch?"

Much as the idea of investigating infamous nightclubs appealed to her professional pride, Eloise's personal side was rather more intimidated. She couldn't possibly go to a cabaret on her own, but she didn't know anyone well enough to ask them to accompany her. She was leaving the building for the nearest café when she saw Max Adalbert waiting on the street.

"Who will accompany you into the dangerous underbelly of the city, Eloise? Obviously it would be unthinkable to send you alone."

She stammered and hesitated, too flustered to find a reply.

"If you don't have someone in mind, may I volunteer? Friday would be a good night for it. Send a note to my office with your address and I'll collect you by car at eight o'clock. Enjoy your lunch." He strode away across the street, leaving Eloise speechless.

. . .

Not one of the nightclubs seemed an appropriate place to attend with one's boss. At Eldorado, couples of the same sex danced together and transvestites performed torch songs. At the Toppkeller, chorus lines high-kicked through routines, ironically often wearing nothing up top. The Palais Heinroth was much more glamorous but more of a dinner and dance location, with American jazz bands and inflated prices. Eloise was distraught and even considered asking Veronika's opinion. The only thing that stopped her was the fact her housemate appeared to frequent a less salubrious type of establishment.

The problem gnawed away at her for two days until she finally asked the worldliest woman of her acquaintance – Hannelore. On the pretext of thanking the woman for holding her hand through the haircut, Eloise asked her to lunch. Her speech was carefully prepared because she had a feeling Max Adalbert would not want the office gossiping about his after-hours activities. So she spoke of a 'gentleman' who had kindly offered to help her research her nightlife article. The problem was, she didn't know him at all well and was afraid of giving the wrong impression.

"Where does one take a respectable man to see what's available without giving him a terrible shock?"

"There are almost a thousand clubs in Berlin. Something for everyone, even your mysterious friend. Tell me what you're looking for."

"More than one place, because I need to get an overall impression. Maybe start downmarket and then go a bit more elegant?"

Hannelore gave her throaty laugh. "I recommend the reverse. Test him. Open with dinner and dancing at the Resi or better still, the Barberina which has an English jazz band in residence. Then move a few doors down to Mitzy's. Have a few drinks, enjoy the cabaret and take his temperature. If he is not concerned by the risqué nature of the acts, why not extend the boundaries at Amuse Bouche? You can prepare him on the walk there. Whatever your heart desires is there on a plate. If that's too rich for his blood, send him home and come over to The Dorian Grey. Join me and the girls for a nightcap."

Eloise scribbled furiously in her notebook then looked up and dropped her voice. "I thought The Dorian Grey was a lesbian club."

"It is." Hannelore widened her eyes in mock drama. "A very exclusive club which only admits the best lesbians. And their guests, of course."

Eloise was nothing if not an opportunist. "In that case, could I accompany you one evening, just to get a sense of how the other half lives? I mean, I'm not that way inclined, but in terms of a balanced article, it seems only right to include all elements of Berlin's nightlife."

"Everyone's a little bit 'that way inclined'. You'll never know until you've tried it. All right, how about next Saturday? Meet me at The Bluebird at eight and we'll go from there. Good luck on Friday. I can't wait to hear all about it."

They walked back to the office together without making conversation. Of the two evenings out on the town, a night in homosexual venues superseded dining and dancing with her boss, in Eloise's opinion. Then she remembered her manners just as they reached their building.

"You're very kind to show me another side of Berlin. Thank you, I would love to come along next Saturday night. What sort of thing should I wear?"

Hannelore lit a cigarette. "Whatever you want. Just nothing too 'office'. Plenty of men and women have a thing for 'half silks', by which I mean an office girl by day and a prostitute by night. Dress like a classy woman out to enjoy herself on her terms. I'm going to the kiosk for more smokes. See you upstairs."

Eloise watched her go, open-mouthed.

Max arrived a few minutes before eight, but like a true gentleman, sat in his car smoking until the clock struck the hour. Eloise knew all that because she, Lili and Hildegard were waiting in the darkness of her bedroom, peering out at the street. They spoke in strangled whispers, although there was no chance he could hear them.

"From what I can see at this distance, he has a very handsome profile," breathed Lili.

Hildegard snorted. "One can barely make out his face under the streetlamp, but I will say that is a very sophisticated motor car. You are very fortunate to ride in such a conveyance."

"My stomach is full of butterflies. I wish I smoked."

"Don't be ridiculous, Eloise. Take some deep breaths and tell yourself you are a professional at work. Your role is to observe the details and record them all faithfully. Lili, stop twitching the curtains. He'll see us."

"Sorry. Yes, you are so lucky, Eloise. Just imagine riding in that motor car, going to one of the glamorous hotels, dining with a handsome man and then going dancing! Oh, I have butterflies on your behalf. Will you tell us everything in the morning? Ooh, look out, he's coming!"

The bells rang out from Charlottenburg's church and the knocker sounded three sharp raps. Eloise shooed the others into the kitchen and answered the door.

"Good evening, Herr Adalbert. You're precisely on time, sir."

"No need to call me sir. We're not at work now. May I say how lovely you look? The peacock feathers in your hat match your dress to perfection. Shall we?"

"Thank you. I made the ..." She stopped short, aware that a homemade dress and creative millinery might not be as impressive as she thought. "I made the effort to investigate a few establishments we might explore. Unless of course, you have other ideas?"

Max offered his arm and walked her to the car. "I am contented to be guided by you when it comes to cabaret, revue and dance floors. As for dinner, however, I do have a preference. I reserved a table for two at the Palais Heinroth. After all, who can dance on an empty stomach?" He opened the passenger door and helped her in.

Perhaps the most thrilling evening of her life until that night was when Sylvain asked her to be his wife. As they stood on a beautiful balcony overlooking the river, she had been giddy, overcome with emotion and unable to suppress a certain smug vindication at seeing her plan come to fruition. This was different. For one thing, she was out of her depth. Max was a familiar figure at the Palais Heinroth, evidently, as waiters hurried to escort them to the table, addressing him by name. En route, he stopped to greet a party of associates, taking pains to introduce Eloise as one of the bright new writers on the staff of *Die Dame*.

The Palais was indeed palatial, with huge murals, imposing columns, dazzling chandeliers and an ornate ceiling. Awe-inspiring enough to make one stop and stare before even taking in the glamorous clientele. She and Max were seated at a corner table with a heavy white tablecloth and an unimpeded view of the dance floor.

"Your first time here?" asked Max, amused by her owlish gazing around the huge space.

"My first time almost everywhere," she said. "It is not yet a full month since I arrived in the city. I find it exciting and intimidating in equal measure."

"I'll tell you a secret. So do I. That's why I'm hoping our adventures tonight will throw some light on an aspect of Berlin I scarcely know. What would you like to drink?"

Normally opinionated and informed on food and wine when she dined out in Fribourg or Berne, on this occasion she opted to leave the decisions to Max. Not to flatter his ego, but to take at least one pressure off herself. They ate Cordon Bleu with spring vegetables and duchesse potatoes, accompanied by a light red wine. Unused to large portions, she could not finish her meal and refused a dessert. Max was an excellent conversationalist, demonstrating a comprehensive knowledge of Swiss resorts and showing interest in her perspectives. She observed his refined manners, the light from the chandeliers reflecting in his brown eyes, how other diners watched their interaction, and she began to relax in his company. An American jazz band struck up while they drank coffee, and in minutes several other couples were already on the dance floor.

Eloise itched to join them. Dancing was one of the pleasures she indulged whenever she had the opportunity. She had specifically designed and made this dress to shimmer and sway with movement. Her toes tapped, her shoulders twitched and she looked at Max with an appeal in her eyes. He laughed and got to his feet.

Instantly she knew they were perfectly matched. They danced the foxtrot, his right arm pressing her body against his and his left hand holding hers at shoulder height. They revolved around the rectangle, twisting and weaving between other dancers, moving as one. The music filled the room, drawing people to find partners, generally men and women, while several female to female pairs shimmied among them. The atmosphere was celebratory and energetic, and Eloise didn't want to stop.

But the band changed tempo and she seized the moment to

visit the ladies' room. She was quite sure all the exertions had wrecked her carefully painted face. When she returned, powdered, lipsticked and ready for another round, Max was standing at their table.

"Shall we move on? I am eager to see what you have planned because I feel quite sure you mean to shock me. Let's get our coats and I'll have the boy bring the car."

"We don't need the car. Mitzy's is just a few doors down the street. But yes, the night air will be chilly so coats are essential."

It seemed perfectly natural to hook her hand into his elbow as they strolled past cafés filled with theatregoers and dodged loud parties on their way to the next venue.

"I must warn you, all the establishments on my list are recommendations. I have no personal experience of any for which I beg forgiveness in advance. It is perfectly possible I will be shocked."

"What a pair of innocents we are! Is this the place?"

A metal black cat, back arched and eyes lit red, protruded from a doorway where flashing lights announced 'Mitzy's'. A few people were queuing to enter, all of whom looked as though they had stepped from the pages of *Die Dame* themselves. Once inside, she and Max deposited their coats with the coat check girl and entered the main room through some velvet curtains. The stage dominated the space, even though it took up less than a quarter of the area. A spotlight illuminated a man in a suit who was introducing the next act. Directly in front were cabaret tables, each lit with its own small lamp, with chairs in a semi-circle facing the stage. On the upper level were rows of seats on a gradient so everyone could watch the action. To the left there was a bar with stools at regular intervals.

"If we sit there, we can make a fast exit should it be necessary," said Max, his expression faux serious.

"Very wise. Perhaps we should have an emergency signal."

"Good idea. Take out one of your peacock feathers and waft it under my nose. I will understand immediately and whisk you to safety. What do you say to a cocktail?"

"Nothing too strong. I'm supposed to be working."

"In that case, I'll order champagne."

Maybe it was the bubbles or the novelty of being in the thick of things, but Eloise found the cabaret hilarious. The female impersonator sang a risqué ballad ripe with innuendo, which had her in fits of giggles. A trio of dancing girls came next, showing off supple limbs in French knickers and camisoles. Their movements were so synchronised, they might have been mechanical but for their bright smiles and fluttering eyelashes. They received a huge round of applause, which made Eloise feel somewhat sorry for the man who had to follow that performance. He was a small chap in round glasses, wearing a crumpled suit and carrying an accordion.

He sang a traditional ballad but with the words changed. At first, the audience frowned and muttered, but then he rhymed the word '*Kaiser*' with '*Scheisse*', eliciting laughter and a smattering of applause. She glanced at Max, who was nodding approvingly. The song continued, using political references Eloise didn't understand, but there was no mistaking their effect. Women gasped and clapped hands over their mouths while grown men thumped their thighs and wiped away tears of mirth. The man finished his performance with a flourish and bowed several times to his public, many of whom were on their feet, cheering.

Max was one of them. "Bravo, *mein Herr*! Bravo!" He placed a hand on Eloise's shoulder. "This was an excellent choice. Where next?"

"It's a little stroll from here, but that will help clear my head. We're going to Amuse Bouche. My acquaintance tells me there's something for everyone."

. . .

The atmosphere was different the moment they stepped inside the door. Assorted extravagant characters assessed them in the lobby, some grinning lasciviously. As Max paid their entrance fee, the doorwoman, dressed a backless waistcoat and glittery shorts, whispered something in his ear. He gave her a puzzled look and she indicated an array of little pill boxes on the shelf behind her.

"*Nein, danke*. Looks like you were right, Eloise. There really is something for everyone. Come, let's see what all the fuss is about."

More velvet curtains screened the interior. Once inside, the surreal scene reminded Eloise of London, swathed in a dense fog, with only vague shapes to indicate inhabitants. She had only been to the British capital once, at Sylvain's side on a diplomatic mission, but had never forgotten the miserable grey miasma draped over it like a shroud. Here, smoke rose in layers, offering glimpses of sequins, bare arms, cocktail glasses and sleek heads locked in an embrace. Instinctively, she drew closer to Max, who placed a protective arm around her waist. He guided her closer to the podium which passed for a stage and managed to snag a table when another couple departed.

A woman with dark skin sang a heartrending song in Italian, which as far as Eloise could comprehend concerned a lover lost at sea. Before she could protest, Max had ordered another bottle of champagne. Her head was already hot and spinning, and she wished they were once more outside in the fresh night air. The chanteuse left the stage and the master of ceremonies told the audience to expect an unforgettable performance from the dancer everyone wished to see. Amid the cheering and the waitress bringing their champagne, Eloise only caught the first name – Anita.

A hush descended and the lights dimmed. All eyes were on the empty spot-lit circle until an arm holding a red ribbon appeared. Amid whistles and whoops, the arm twirled, whipped and drew patterns with the fabric, before dropping it to the floor. The room seemed to hold its breath. All at once, a woman leapt from the wings like a bat, her upper body concealed by a black cape. She began to caper and prance, twirling the garment like a conjuror, revealing her insubstantial underwear at every turn. The music built to a crescendo and the dancer flung off the cape to reveal bare breasts and nothing more than flimsy red French knickers. The audience bayed like wolves.

She danced, arching and curling, splaying and balancing, interpreting the music like a muse unleashed. Her body was only part of her repertoire: she used her painted eyes and red mouth to add drama to the performance, finally snatching up the cape and collapsing on the floor like a wounded matador.

The lights switched from the stage to the uproarious audience, stamping, cheering and calling for an encore. When the spot found the stage once more, she was gone, leaving only her cape behind. It was the most extraordinary event Eloise had ever witnessed.

"How will you render *that* in your little notebook?" asked Max, pouring her another glass of champagne. She had barely registered drinking the first one.

Eloise searched for a witty reply but her attention was drawn to the couples drifting onto the dance floor. It must have been the interval, because now everyone wanted to move their bodies. Two men clasped one another's waists, each matching the other's footwork. A woman lifted her arms and leant so far backwards she looked like a dying swan. Female partners laughed or nuzzled as they shuffled along to the beat.

"One more dance?" Max extended his arm and drew her close. She nestled her cheek against his lapel, inhaling the scent of oriental spices. They bumped and brushed against other couples until she grew dizzy and could bear no more.

"Max? Please will you take me home?"

"Of course! This way."

Within minutes, they were on the street, breathing cold air and gazing at the stars. He helped her into her coat and placed his arm around her shoulder. She was grateful that he did not speak, simply supporting her until the boy brought the car.

He drove her home, kissed her hand and told her he'd rarely enjoyed himself as much. She mumbled something similar and tottered up the steps to the side door, barely managing a wave before she fumbled her way inside. First stop was the bathroom, where the urge to vomit immediately disappeared. She washed her face and cleaned her teeth, poured a glass of water and went to bed. Once again, her body lied. She was convinced she would pass out the second she hit the pillow. Instead, she lay wide awake, replaying the scenes she had witnessed while her head spun.

Finally, she got up and opened the window. Cold air poured in, bringing a welcome chill to her agitated body. She sat on the window ledge in her nightgown, looking up at the stars, tiny glows in the night sky. After a moment, she noticed another glow, two floors above on the opposite side of the street.

A man was smoking on the fire escape opposite. She watched the rhythm of the glow, exhaled cloud, silence and glow again. They were the only two people on the street; her dangling her legs over the sill, him on the metal landing with his tobacco. She sat there for a long time, appreciating her silent companion. Finally, her feet grew numb and she swung her legs inside. Before closing the window, she looked up and said, "*Gute Nacht.*"

In the silence that followed, she shrugged and reached for the window latch. Then she heard a quiet, rasping voice.

"*Gute Nacht, Fraulein.*"

9

Spring 1927, Berlin

The nightlife feature met with unconditional approval. Vicki seized on the concept as highly topical and made it the lead story for the May issue. One of the senior female designers was immediately tasked with creating a cover. But one article was not enough. She must produce another, different in tone but as a companion piece, and both would be accompanied by a photographic spread. Eloise was stunned and delighted. Since sketches were much cheaper and easier to control, only a rare occasion merited photographic images. Vicki paired her with Friedrich, a sculpture student and freelance photographer who sometimes worked for Ullstein Publications. He would come in that very afternoon to discuss possibilities.

On learning her partner was a student and not a professional, she was a little disgruntled, believing a spread such as hers deserved better than a part-time amateur. All indignation deflated when she returned to her desk and saw a multi-coloured bouquet of flowers on her desk. The card read, 'For

Eloise. My sincere thanks for an entertaining and eye-opening evening. With friendly greetings, M.'

When all the interest and teasing from her colleagues had subsided, she sat at her desk and composed herself. Martha had not paid any attention to the ostentatious gift, simply continuing to frown at her typewriter. Eloise was grateful, and cupped her hands over her eyes to focus. Another night spent visiting homosexual clubs might well provide a different angle but was it sufficiently distinct from her first? She feared not. She jotted down four or five ways to approach the story from a new perspective, but couldn't settle on a single clear concept. In frustration, she went out into the streets at lunchtime, where she posted a note for Max Adalbert, thanking him for the flowers and apologising for being a wilting lily at the end of their evening.

When she returned, Friedrich Seidenstücker was waiting in the boardroom. To her surprise, he was close to her own age and extremely pleasant. His hair was neatly parted, and behind round glasses his dark eyes radiated intelligence. He read her outline and pronounced it as atmospheric, evocative and powerful. He was eager to take the right kind of images to visualise her words. They agreed to revisit the same haunts the following Friday and sat for an hour discussing potential compositions. Then he asked the dreaded question.

"I understand there is to be a second piece?"

"Yes, there is to be a second piece, when I think of the right approach. Can I beg your patience while I try out a few ideas?"

His eyes slid to the left and he went very still.

"Friedrich? Is everything fine?"

"I spend a lot of time at the zoo. Let me show you." He withdrew a folder of pictures: people gasping at elephants, children laughing at penguins, men crouching to get a good view of a walrus, the view of a crowd from behind the head of a brown bear. "Do you see how the spectators are equally as fascinating as the spectacle? What do you think about looking from the opposite side of the stage? You interview performers, I photograph the crowds and we show the collusion between artist and audience. It is in the interests of both to trust the magic of smoke and mirrors. After all, cabaret is a distraction, a momentary escape from reality. That way, your article is less about participation and more about observation. Sophisticates love to believe they can maintain an intellectual distance."

His softly spoken voice and accurate piercing of social delusion rendered her speechless. All she could do was nod and scan the pictures he had spread on the table.

"I apologise, Eloise. You are the journalist. My role is to illustrate your points as best I can."

"No, no, absolutely not. Your idea is quite inspired. I can almost see the two articles bookending your photographs. You read the first piece and interpret the images one way. Then you read the second and see them in a whole new light. Friedrich, you are a genius!"

He ducked his head as if to dodge the compliment. "Ideas are one thing, execution is another. Do you think we will be able to work together?"

"I am quite sure of it. What say I contact some clubs and ask permission to conduct interviews and take photographs next Friday? This is very exciting!"

"Perhaps two nights would be prudent. In that way we can visit a wider variety of locales. Unless of course you have plans for Saturday?"

"As a matter of fact, my plans for Saturday dovetail rather well with our mission. Two nights on the town and we'll have this in the bag. I am so glad Vicki suggested you."

. . .

Two late nights entitled her to two more days off. She decided to save up all the extra time and add it to her Easter break. A week in Switzerland was pitifully short when two of those days were spent cooped up on a train. Instead, she took a full seven days of her holiday entitlement, added three extra and planned a whole fortnight with her family.

Her next problem was a wardrobe issue. She had only one modern dancing dress, the one she had made herself. There was simply no time to make another, even if she did raid her savings to buy more material. Lili and Hildegard had nothing she could borrow, and to go out two consecutive nights in the same frock was unthinkable. One evening, she made *Rösti*, put the baking tin into the oven, washed her hands and ran up two flights of stairs with a perfume sample she had brought home from work. The lights were on beneath Veronika's door. She tapped with one fingernail.

A moment later, Veronika opened the door in full make-up and a faded peignoir. "Yes?"

"Hello, Veronika. Do you remember me, Eloise from downstairs?"

"Hello, Eloise-from-downstairs. What can I do for you? I'm preparing to go out, you see."

"I understand. Could you possibly do me a favour? I have to go dancing twice this week and I only have one dress. We're close enough in size and I wondered if you had anything you could loan me. Naturally, I will wash and dry it before returning the item. Also, I brought you a perfume sample I thought you might like." She was babbling and bribing and making a complete hash of her request.

Veronika took a step back and assessed her. "Yes, some of my dresses will probably fit you. I have a couple I don't wear anymore. Strange, I remember you as much fatter. Come in, you can try them out and if you like, make me an offer."

The room, to Eloise's astonishment, was three times the size of her own. Or it would have been had half of it not been cluttered with clothes rails, hat stands and a triple-mirrored vanity table. The central feature was a huge double bed. A chaise longue beneath under the eaves had prospects through double windows to the south and west.

Veronika rummaged in a wardrobe the size of a caravan and finally pulled out a calf-length puce dress with a drop waist and embellished hem. "That one makes me look like a *Blutwurst*. Or how about this one? Boring black, but with the right accessories, it works. Try them on."

After a moment's hesitation, Eloise slipped off her work dress so that she was wearing nothing more than her camisole. The purple dress was not an attractive colour, but a stylish cut. The black fitted her as if tailored, with an opaque bodice but transparent skirt and sleeves. Veronika watched from the chaise longue, sipping at a cocktail and smoking a powerful cigarette. With a flourish, Eloise threw out her arms for approval. Only then did she see the other observer. The smoker on the fire escape was directly opposite and staring through the window.

Veronika caught Eloise's alarm and with a *tsk* of exasperation, drew the curtain. "*Scheisse*, I forgot about Jan. Poor bastard lost an eye in the war. Insomniac, shell-shock, addiction, he has the full house. We have an agreement. I leave the curtains open, he watches me. Nothing else. Sometimes, when I get in late, we sit and smoke. Him on his side of the street, me on mine. He's not a big talker. Look, I need to go. Take the dresses and we'll work out a deal. Have a nice evening, Eloise-from-downstairs, and thanks for the perfume."

Eloise expressed her gratitude and hurried down to the ground floor. Hildegard was peering into the oven, her brow creased.

"Good evening. I think this dish is about to burn. It's not the best idea to leave the stove unattended. Were you upstairs?"

Eloise dumped the dresses, switched off the oven and used a tea towel to withdraw the cooked potato. Hildegard was right, certain parts were dark brown. She'd rescued it just in time.

"Gracious me, that was close. Thank you so much for checking. Yes, I went upstairs to see if Veronika could loan me some dancing dresses. I have two jobs this weekend, and wearing the same old thing again simply will not do. Let me put these frocks in my room and I'll start on the eggs. Did you have a good day at work?"

"Am I to understand you are dining out on Friday? In which case I will need to alter my preparations. In future, I would appreciate being notified."

Chastened, Eloise gave an apologetic smile. "My working hours might be a little irregular for the next month, but I will be sure to give you and Lili fair warning. Excuse me one moment."

"Very well. Just understand that Lili and I keep regular hours and respectable habits. Are you meeting the man who sent you flowers again?"

"Oh, no. This is a joint job with a photographer. I'll tell you all about it over dinner."

The man who sent her flowers certainly did want to meet again. Max responded to her card the very next day, inviting her to dinner on Friday. She explained her situation and expressed regret at the prior engagement, with the hope they could enjoy one another's company some other time. She thought that was that and threw herself into arranging reservations at various clubs, a press card for Friedrich, interviews with performers and access to backstage. In the evenings, she dedicated herself to altering and embellishing Veronika's dresses, adding silver ribbons to the purple frock and red trim to the black. Each night she spent an hour penning letters home, but noticed she could barely fill two sheets of notepaper. Instead, she added little sketches of a comical hat or a funny little dog she thought would amuse her children. Then she closed the curtains, with a nod to the wounded soldier smoking in the cold, and fell into an exhausted sleep.

To her surprise, Max wrote back immediately, advising her to go to the Barberina on one of her exploratory nights out. He had left a message with the manager to admit them on his recommendation. He also suggested an outing to the Tiergarten followed by Sunday afternoon tea. She accepted eagerly, as her previous excursions to the park had always made her feel the odd one out. Strolling the paths in the company of a handsome man would be vastly preferable to wandering around alone. She sent her reply by return. A whole weekend filled with activity and pleasure! How things had changed in a matter of weeks!

On Friday night, she ate a bowl of what Lili called 'Leftovers Soup' and bid her housemates a good weekend, before catching the tram to meet Friedrich at The Wintergarten. Their instructions were to make themselves known at the stage door. Eloise was in a state of high excitement as her first interview was with The Codonas, an acrobatic troupe everyone was talking about. Indeed, there were already queues of people outside the main entrance. A stage manager escorted them to a dressing room, where three members of the Codona family were preparing for their performance. They were friendly and excitable, often talking over each other and offering to pose for Friedrich. He tried to explain he wanted unforced, candid shots, but every time he lifted his lens, Alfredo or Lalo would stop talking, inflate their chests and plaster on a showman's grin. Eventually he conceded defeat and asked them to pose as a trio. The beautiful muscular Clara placed her hand on each man's shoulder and threw a sultry look at the camera.

Eloise and Friedrich thanked them sincerely for their time and followed an usher towards the stage. Two chairs had been placed in the wings where they were to sit until the Codonas were on their platform, high above the heads of the audience below. Only when the stage was in darkness and the spotlights on the trapeze artists were they permitted to come out and watch the show. A pair of ballroom dancers finished their routine, took their curtain call and trotted past Eloise and Friedrich, their faces sweaty. Eloise could understand, it was very warm under all the lights. The MC was encouraging further applause and building up anticipation for the imminent arrival of the Codona troupe.

His pitch rose as he introduced them and an enthusiastic round of applause greeted them as they stepped on stage. Unlike the white athletic gear they had sported in the dressing room, now all three were cloaked in long black satin capes. They bowed in synchronisation, threw off the capes to reveal their body suits and made their way down the steps and into the auditorium. Three spotlights followed, each trained on a different acrobat. Eloise and Friedrich crept from their chairs to stand in the centre of the darkened stage and watch. The artists walked up the aisle almost to the back wall and scrambled up rope ladders. In a trice, Alfredo was on his swing, rocking back and forth, and gaining height with each swing. He rolled down, dangling his torso from the swing and holding on with his legs.

Eloise clapped her hand to her mouth, only too aware of the danger. Many acrobats performed with nets to break their fall if the worst happened. Not the Codonas. Soon Clara was whirling through the air, her body hanging below her swing, to meet her husband. Once, twice, three times and then she let go, sailing through the air and into Alfredo's grasp. The crowd gasped as one and then again as he flung her upwards to catch her own trapeze.

They changed positions, flipping and flying, each time appearing to catch one another at the very last second. Finally, Lalo took the role of catcher and Alfredo performed his legendary triple somersault in the air. Applause thundered through the auditorium as the trio descended the ladders and ran to the stage to take a bow. Eloise and Friedrich scuttled back to their seats just before the lights came up.

"I've never seen anything like that in my life," she breathed.

"Neither have they," Friedrich grinned. "We'll have some marvellous shots of open-mouthed wonderment, if the light is not too dark. So, where to next?"

The pair spent an hour at Mitzy's, talking to dancing girls and photographing the patrons' laughter at a comedian. Eloise found it so convivial she was reluctant to leave. But they had another engagement. The last stop of the night was Eldorado, mainly because it was an easy walk for Eloise to get home. It was renowned as a homosexual haunt, for its beautiful female impersonators and relaxed attitudes. Cross-dressing was common and same sex dancing was not only permitted, but actively encouraged. Her interviewees would include Daisy the barkeeper and Ooh Là Là, who referred to himself as a chanteuse.

It was a wonderful venue, loud with chatter and live music, yet welcoming to everyone. The doorman pointed out Daisy, who apologised but had no time to chat. Instead she asked Amelia, a striking woman sitting at the bar in a tuxedo, if she would talk to a journalist about the club. Amelia raised her pencil-thin eyebrows, which Eloise took as acquiescence and sat on the next stool.

"You'll have to buy me a drink," said Amelia, her face stony.

"Oh, yes, of course. Daisy, could I ..."

Before she could finish her request, Daisy uncorked a bottle of champagne and thrust four glasses over the bar. "On the house. Just make us sound fabulous!"

Amelia poured the bubbly and Eloise wondered if the fourth glass was for Daisy herself until an incredibly tall and astoundingly beautiful apparition reached from behind Friedrich to scoop up a drink.

"Good evening, lady and gentleman of *Die Dame*. I think this is for me. My name is Thomas, but you can call me Ooh Là Là. Mister Photographer Man, please note my left side is my best. Shall we toast the incomparable bliss of Eldorado?"

"To Eldorado!" Friedrich surprised them all by raising his glass first. "I am so looking forward to seeing you perform. Are you willing to be photographed, Amelia? I try to catch casual shots, in the hope of finding something unusual."

Ooh Là Là answered for Amelia. "Her? Unusual? Hardly. *Garçonnes* are like sand in the sea round here. Whereas I am anything but run-of-the-mill. Do you plan to write about Berlin's depraved underworld? If so, count me in. What do you want to know?"

Eloise asked about the club's clientele, how long it took him to get dressed for a performance and if there was any rivalry between artistes. He talked non-stop, embellishing his answers with anecdotes and wild cackles at his own jokes. Eloise was enthralled and just about to embark on the topic of intoxicating substances when he shrieked, emptied his glass and hurried away, shouting, "I'm on next!"

She turned to Amelia, who was smoking with one hand and rotating a finger around the rim of her champagne glass with the other. Friedrich had disappeared, possibly to follow Ooh Là Là onstage.

"What did he mean by calling you a *Garçonne*?" she asked.

Amelia opened her arms, inviting Eloise to study her. "The kind of woman who scares men. We wear our hair like a boy's, which is why they call it a *Bubikopf*. We dress sharply in trousers, jackets and even a tie. We're sexually predatory and see no reason to apologise."

"The very definition of a New Woman."

A frown crossed Amelia's face. "There is more than one definition. I imagine you think of yourself as a New Woman but we have little in common."

"Would you say that in the same way that Thomas, or Ooh Là Là, celebrates his feminine side, you are comfortable with the masculine aspects of your personality?"

"Not at all. Ooh Là Là is a caricature of a woman, a costume that Thomas puts on and takes off. He plays a role and plays it very well, as you shall see. But it is not a reflection of who he is. This is who I am. My attitude and style are statements, signifying how I wish to be seen. All of us wear masks."

"A friend of mine dresses in a similar way. She is a lesbian and she says everyone is a little bit that way inclined. Is that why you come to a homosexual club?"

The question appeared to amuse Amelia. "I come to Eldorado because it is open to everyone. People here do not judge or make assumptions. In other clubs, if I am drinking alone at the bar, men take it as an invitation. If I want male company, I ask for it. If I want female company, I find it. If I want to be alone, I come here."

"Until a nosy journalist interrupts your evening by asking lots of impertinent questions," Eloise smiled. "Thank you for talking to me. I will leave you in peace to watch the performance."

Amelia topped up both their glasses and nodded a farewell. The club was even busier than when they had arrived and people were positioning themselves for the next act. Eloise found a spot beside a marble column and leant against it, sipping her champagne. Her eye was drawn to two young men, arms wrapped around one another, swaying to the music. The band reached a crescendo and most dancers turned to clap. Bowing and waving, the musicians left the stage for a break and the curtain descended. In front of it stood an upright piano and a microphone. A man dressed in tails crossed the stage and sat at the piano. Into his own microphone, he announced, "Ladies and gentlemen, please welcome our radiant Parisian chanteuse, Mademoiselle Ooh Là Là!"

The curtain parted and the spotlight found the striking figure, posing with arms stretched wide as if to embrace them all. Under the lights, all the make-up, wig and sequinned gown did not appear as overdone and jarring as it had done close up. In an instant, Eloise forgot all about garrulous Thomas and applauded Ooh Là Là.

She began with a rendition of 'Was machst du mit dem Knie, lieber Hans', complete with facial expressions and a theatrical delivery. For all the overacting, it was clear to everyone that the singer had a clear, beautiful voice. The next song was titled 'Oh How That German Could Love' and sung in English. Ooh Là Là managed to wring all the humour from the lyrics by singing them with a cod French accent. The audience laughed and squealed with glee, some wiping their eyes. For her final offering, the pianist was replaced by a cellist. Together, they created a heart-breaking ballad about a woman whose husband never came back from the war. Her range of her voice and the passion it contained transfixed Eloise, along with many other members of the audience. No shifting, no whispering, not even any drinking. The room was in the palm of that graceful hand.

On the last chord, the place erupted into cheers, stamps and rapturous applause. For a second time, more than one person patted a handkerchief to his or her eyes. Eloise herself had a lump in her throat which took half a glass of champagne to shift. The chanteuse bowed modestly, blew kisses and exited into the wings. No amount of stamping or calls for an encore could tempt her back.

Friedrich appeared at her elbow, his face glowing. "What an extraordinary night! I have more material than I know what to do with. Shall I walk you home? Just think, we can do it all again tomorrow!"

His enthusiasm was endearing and she happily listened to his impressions as they walked the short distance to Eloise's lodgings. She shook his hand, wished him a good morning, since it was already half past two, and went indoors to sleep off the excitement. The house was silent, and for a change Jan was not smoking on the fire escape. She switched off the light and presumed even insomniacs needed a change.

Before she fell asleep, Amelia's words rang in her ears. *I imagine you think of yourself as a New Woman but we have little in common. All of us wear masks.*

It was true. Eloise was every bit as much a pretender as Ooh Là Là. She could only hope that if she kept up the act for long enough, it would come naturally. For now, she maintained the mask.

10

Spring 1927, Berlin

Both Saturday and Sunday, she slept till eleven without a shred of guilt. Her hours had been long and she deserved a long lie-in. She spent Saturday afternoon doing household chores and laundry, ate a light dinner and wrote out her notes in a more comprehensible format. Then it was time to get ready, get on the tram and start all over again. On Sunday, she went to the public baths and organised yesterday's material. She had enough for at least three different articles. It would be very difficult to choose which interviews to discard. After lunch, she prepared herself for Max, surprised to find herself more than a little nervous. At exactly three o'clock, he rang the bell. He cut quite a dash in his spring coat with his left hand behind his back.

"Max, you're right on time." She held out a hand for him to shake, but he took it and kissed it instead.

"Hello, Eloise. You look far too fresh and lively for someone who's spent two nights trawling the clubs of Berlin. These are for you." He withdrew his left hand and presented her with a posy of spring flowers.

"How pretty! That's most kind of you, especially after the beautiful bouquet you sent last week. Have you enjoyed a pleasant weekend?"

"It was pleasant, if dull, and I doubt it can compare to yours. Going to the park must seem quite pedestrian after all that glamorous nightlife. Shall we?"

"Yes, let's. As a matter of fact, I am very much looking forward to our excursion. For one thing, I have excellent company, and another, since I am not working, I'm able to relax."

He gave her a brilliant smile and helped her into the car. The afternoon seemed simultaneously intense and relaxed. Max wanted all the details of her investigation into the entertainment world and he was the perfect audience. He laughed at her descriptions of Ooh Là Là, widened his eyes at the songs she had heard at the Cabaret of Comedians, shook his head in disbelief at the acrobatic feats of the Codonas and nodded in recognition as she described the dancers at The Barberina.

"And did you take to the floor? Half of me hopes you did, as you are an excellent dancer. The other half wishes to keep you to myself. Was Herr Seidenstücker a masterful partner?"

"I was working," she protested, turning away to hide her blush. "As was Friedrich. In fact, the only time we really spent together was walking between venues. Otherwise we were fully engaged with our mission. It was truly an eye-opener and I have no doubt next weekend will be even more so."

"Next weekend? One has to commend your dedication. If you plan to spend your weekends visiting all the clubs in Berlin at a rate of three per night, you will be finished before Christmas."

Eloise laughed. "Goodness, one would need a far stronger

constitution than mine. Not to say I didn't enjoy the entertainment, but it's more a monthly treat, I would say. The reason I am out again on Saturday is thanks to a friend. She has offered to show me some ladies' venues."

He stopped and inclined his head. "Ladies' venues? Pray elaborate."

To her annoyance, Eloise was blushing again. "Places where ladies can let their hair down. Or perhaps better put, cut their hair off. I'm joining Hannelore for an introduction to some homosexual bars. I couldn't include those this weekend because of Friedrich."

They began walking again and Max was strangely silent for a while. Finally he said, "You cannot take Friedrich to such establishments because he is a man? Are men prohibited?"

"To tell the truth, I don't really know. I suppose I shall find out on Saturday. It's all very new to me. Do you know, I think Hannelore is the first lesbian I have ever met? Although now I think about it, my sister has never shown the slightest interest in men."

"While you are quite different?"

"Oh, yes. I always enjoyed male company. My interest in such places is partly curiosity and partly balance. It's hardly fair to include Eldorado without The Dorian Grey, don't you agree?"

He laughed loudly, throwing his head back so that his hat almost fell off. "What an intriguing person you are, Eloise de Fournier. Now tell me, when might you find an evening in your hectic schedule to dine with someone who requires no other entertainment than yourself?"

"Well, I have no plans for Friday." She gave him a sideways glance.

"Good. That's settled. We shall dine and dance at The Russian Tea Room, somewhere you have yet to see. Oh dear, are you cold? The wind is getting up and I fear it will rain. I vote we cut short our stroll and scurry back to the car. The café is just a few minutes' drive and their pastries are unforgettable."

Coffee and cakes stretched into an early evening glass of Sekt and by the time Max drove up outside her house on Charlottenstrasse, it was dusk. This time, he took her chin in his hands and kissed her lightly on the lips.

"I cannot wait to see you again. Friday seems so far away."

"It will be here before you know it," she said, quoting one of the lines she so often used with her children. "Thank you for a blissful afternoon. Goodbye."

"The pleasure was all mine. Goodbye, Eloise."

The effect of his warm lips on hers had a strangely dizzying effect and she walked up the wet steps with caution. At the door, she turned with a wave and he raised a hand before driving away. Was it possible, she asked herself while unlocking the door, she could be falling in love with her boss? What an appalling cliché!

By the end of March, she was in his bed. Max wooed her with charm, romance, flowers, thoughtful gifts, entertaining conversation and rapt attention. For three weeks, they spent every Friday evening dining, dancing and seeking entertainment. He always knew the best bands and the newest acts, and never had a problem gaining access to an exclusive restaurant. Saturdays and Sundays, he regretted, were always spent with his elderly parents. As their only son, it was his duty. She took that as a sign of his noble nature.

When he announced he had a rare weekend free and invited her to spend it at a lodge in Königswald, she prepared herself for the inevitable. Her finest undergarments, French perfume, a silk peignoir and the most essential of accessories, a Dutch cap. Eloise had read plenty about the precautions a woman could take to avoid an unplanned pregnancy. A visit to the pharmacy was all it took. She bought a little rubber device which took a little practice to insert, but could be reused. According to the pharmacist, it was apparently undetectable by her 'husband'.

It was a good job it was reusable since Max was a greedy lover. He wanted her morning, noon and night. Sexual activity with Sylvain had waned into non-existence after the birth of Laurent, but she found ways to satisfy Max without exhausting herself. All that reading of French erotic fiction had equipped her well. He was also generous, taking time over her pleasure. After two days of love-making, she returned home like the cat that got the cream.

As for conversation, it was only natural they should talk about the magazine, as it was a large part of both their lives. Max was always looking for something different, fresh ideas, exciting angles. He mentioned the fact he was searching for a new creative director, a visionary who could lead *Die Dame* to greater heights. He entertained Eloise's ideas, even helping her develop some concepts, and encouraged her to pitch them to Vicki. His one stipulation was that she did not mention him. Eloise could take all the credit and their relationship remained a secret.

The Friday after their weekend at the lodge, he took her for dinner at the Eden Hotel and mentioned he had booked a room for the night. The entire dinner was an erotic dance of intense anticipation and lustful gazes. They dispensed with dessert and tried to make a dignified exit from the restaurant. The moment Max closed the hotel room door he clasped her to his chest, whispering in her ear.

"I have thought of nothing but this all week. Oh, Eloise, you make my head spin. How is it possible to fall in love at the speed of an express train? Kiss me, you spellbinding creature. You are a glass of cold water to a man dying of thirst."

She kissed him, her own head spinning at his declaration of love. His hands slid up her legs until her reached her stocking tops and suspenders. She pulled away. "Give me a moment, Max, I must use the bathroom. Oh, and to answer your question, I find it certainly is possible."

He took her face in his hands. "Aren't we the luckiest devils to have found one other?"

"We are, we truly are. I'll be right back."

When she returned, he was already under the sheets, his chest naked. He growled at the sight of her revealing underwear and reached out to pull her onto the bed. With a giggle, she fell into his arms. He unwrapped her like a gift, stopping to kiss each area he had exposed until his desire overtook him. The first time was over in seconds, but Eloise knew that was not the end of the matter. When he had recovered, he opened a bottle of champagne, standing naked and unembarrassed in the lamplight.

They toasted each other and lay side by side, not talking, just drinking one another in. He began caressing her thigh with his fingertips, his eyes watching her face. Her lips parted and her breath caught at his touch. That was the signal he was waiting for. The second bout of love-making was slow, gentle and almost teasing until she exploded with a little cry at the shuddering high point. They lay on their backs, recovering their breath, and Eloise couldn't help replaying his words. *How is it possible to fall in love at the speed of an express train?* She hadn't been fantasising. This was the kind of love affair she had always dreamed of, where two people were not drawn to each other's status, or prospects, or sound reasons for business consolidation. This was pure, intoxicating desire. She waited until his breathing grew slower and heavier signalling sleep, then she sat up in bed. She reached for her champagne glass and toasted her scandalous self in the mirror. Like an acrobat trusting she will be caught, she had thrown herself into his arms without a safety net. *To second chances!*

She rose before him in the morning and took the opportunity to bathe in the tub. It was a rare luxury to wallow in warm water she did not have to share with strangers. She emerged, fragrant and soft, to join him under the covers, wishing she had thought to bring a change of clothes. With little kisses on his back and neck, she woke him and embraced his immediate passion. He was even more handsome with ruffled hair and a shadowy chin.

"You are a peach and I could eat you up in two bites," he murmured as she laid her head on his chest. "I must use the bathroom and then I have a surprise for you." He bounded out of bed.

She dropped her eyes to below his waist. "Another one?"

He laughed, kissed her again and went into the bathroom. She sat up against the pillows, marvelling at the luxury of this huge room, the size of the entire ground floor of Charlottenweg 125. The swagged curtains, piles of pillows, white monogrammed towels, deep carpet and most impressive of all, a bathroom exclusively for their own use, were all overwhelming. Would this be her life with Max? Five-star hotels, expensive restaurants, pretty presents and a head-turning car? If so, she might adapt rather well. Her stomach grumbled and her thoughts turned to breakfast. Perhaps they could eat in the room, feeding each other slices of fruit and drinking quality coffee.

Max came out of the bathroom wearing a towel around his waist and releasing a billowing cloud of steam. He saw she was still in bed and gave her a wolfish grin. Then he rummaged in his jacket pocket, pulled out an object and sat beside her, hiding whatever it was in his fist.

She gulped, scarcely daring to believe he was about to propose.

"I called in a little favour. A colleague has a forest hunting lodge near Fürstenwalde, merely a couple of hours' drive from here. It's very wild and romantic, and ours for the whole Easter weekend. Four whole days together, just you and me. I can't imagine how we'll fill the time, can you?" He opened his palm to reveal a key.

Her face fell.

"What is it, my treasure? Are you not pleased?"

"Max, I won't be here for Easter. I'm going home to Switzerland. Vicki agreed to my having two weeks' holiday."

He reached out a hand to stroke her knee. "You can easily change your holiday dates. Spend Easter with me and go home the week after."

"No, I'm afraid that's impossible."

He tilted her chin to face him. "Nothing is impossible if you want it enough."

"You don't understand. Everything is arranged. I take the train next Saturday morning. My children are expecting their mother and I cannot disappoint them."

"But you can disappoint the man you claim to love? Very well." He stood up and walked to the other side of the room.

"I am a mother, Max. My children must come first."

"If you say so." He pulled on his clothes, his back to her.

Tears filled her eyes. "And in any case, what of your parents? How can you leave for so long when you spend every weekend at their sides?"

"That's none of your business. I am going downstairs to settle the bill. Please deposit the key at reception when you leave. Goodbye, Eloise."

"Max!"

The door closed silently behind him.

11

Spring 1927, Berlin

Saturday was unbearable. On returning home, she thanked her lucky stars neither Lili or Hildegard was present to see her puffy, tear-stained face. But after sobbing into her pillow for hours, she desperately wanted someone to talk to and willed them back. It was no use. She was alone with her pain until Sunday evening. Finally, she washed her face and went out to the shops before it got dark. Despite her having no appetite, it was foolish to have no food for the weekend. Fierce April wind, at first cooling her hot cheeks, soon became painfully harsh, and the tears it induced were nothing to do with her state of mind.

The humiliation was the hardest to bear. She considered herself a modern, sophisticated and independent woman. But after a few dinners and the occasional trinket, she had succumbed to a fantasy. It was unforgivably stupid. Her marriage to Sylvain might not have been a whirlwind of passion, but it was clear-eyed and practical. Not to mention based on mutual esteem. Her husband would never have spoken to her with the cold dismissiveness Max used that morning. Shame suffused her once again and she made a promise to herself. She deserved respect and unless a man treated her with such, he was not worth her time. With a determined snort, she turned her attention to the groceries.

With some eggs and bread which had increased in price by ten percent since last weekend, she pulled her scarf around her ears and returned to Charlottenweg. A car was driving away from the front door and her heart leapt, forgetting her resolve of ten minutes earlier. She quickened her pace, praying it had been Max with flowers and an apology. But there was nothing outside the door and when she got inside, the hallway was empty. She frowned when she saw the kitchen light. To leave it on whilst out shopping was very scatterbrained of her. Then she heard the sound of rustling paper and went to see if it was Levi with a message.

A fur-trimmed coat draped over a chair and the smell of cigarette smoke alerted her to Veronika's presence. On the table was a bottle of champagne, a grocery bag and a basket of fruit. Veronika leaned against the sink, smoking. Her make-up was sooty, her dress creased, and even her hair looked a little fluffy.

"Eloise! Thank goodness it's you. If it was either of those judgemental witches, I would have had hysterics. Come, sit with me a while. Let's have some breakfast."

"Hello, Veronika." She opened her mouth to observe that it was almost six o'clock in the evening and closer to dinner time than breakfast, but the phrase 'judgemental witches' gave her pause. "I saw a car outside. Was that someone bringing you home?"

"My dear friend Leonard is most solicitous of my comfort. He bought me some treats because we've been up all night and I am ravenous. A darling man, everyone adores him. Now, what do we have here?" She upended the grocery bag so that the contents scattered over the table. "Asparagus, smoked salmon, butter, bagels, soft cheese, radishes, caviar and ham. And in the basket, there are pears, grapes, peaches and gooseberries. Hmm, I could live without the asparagus and gooseberries, but never mind. You get some knives and plates, I'll find the glasses. Or should we take this upstairs? How long do we have before the harpies return?"

"You shouldn't call them that. They've been very kind to me."

"Lucky you."

"Lili and Hildegard always spend the weekends with their families. They won't return until Sunday evening. Didn't you know that?"

"No and I wish I'd known sooner. So we can relax and indulge ourselves for as long as I can stay awake. Hurry, woman, let's eat!"

The sight of such unusual and luxurious delicacies awakened Eloise's appetite, and her yearning for company made her rush to assemble the tableware. The pop of the champagne cork startled her into a nervous laugh. They toasted the generous Leonard, then Veronika sat in a chair and gave orders, while Eloise sliced the bagels and slipped them under the grill.

For someone usually taciturn, Veronika was exceptionally verbose. "No idea where he gets these things from. Two streets from here people are surviving on one bowl of cabbage soup per day, but last night I dined on trout pâté for first course with tiny little toasts. Chicken Chasseur with a mushroom ragout was the main, then a lemon sorbet to cleanse the palate before a dessert of meringue with raspberries. Raspberries, in April? All I know is that he has connections. Keep an eye on those bagels, we want them golden and not burnt."

"I'm watching, don't worry. Are you romantically involved? I mean, are you a couple?"

"We certainly do 'couple', but there's precious little romance involved. He hires me to flatter his ego, sleep with him and pretend that he's the only man in the world in front of his friends. Then I pocket a roll of cash and he drives me home. I'm a practical woman. Love them, leave them and take what you can on the way out. Food! Now! Or I shall expire in a heap on this floor without reapplying my lipstick."

With a jolt, Eloise understood what Veronika was saying. In this boarding house for respectable working ladies, one of them was an actual prostitute. She immediately chastised herself and turned off the grill. Who was she to judge? After a little flattery, Madame de Fournier had dropped all her dignity and her drawers for her boss. As a result, she'd found herself treated like a common tart. At least Veronika's clients paid for her time.

"Freshly toasted bagels! Let's eat."

"Hallelujah!"

They drank champagne and tried every combination of bagel; cream cheese and salmon, ham and radish, butter and caviar until Eloise could not manage another mouthful.

"But what about the gooseberries?" demanded Veronika and they collapsed into helpless giggles.

"Gooseberry fool!" spluttered Eloise.

"Gooseberry surprise!" Veronika gasped.

"Which is asparagus stuffed with gooseberries!"

They laughed so hard, both lost the power of speech for a moment, and Eloise realised she was extremely drunk.

"Oh, my dear Eloise," said Veronika. "You are a tonic. No, listen, I have a better idea. I'll give this fruit to Jan. God knows what that man eats because he refuses to beg and won't use the municipal kitchen. It's as if he wants to starve out of stubbornness."

"Yes, that's a very good plan. I think I need to lie down now."

"Me too. Either I drink a coffee and have another snort or go to sleep like a good girl. Let's open the window to get rid of the smoke and leave all this till the morning. Goodnight, Eloise, and thank you for breakfast."

They stumbled their way to their rooms and Eloise just about managed to clean her teeth and close the curtains before she collapsed onto her bed. She switched off the light and caught the sound of voices outside and high above. Veronika and Jan, she assumed with a smile. She curled under her blankets, closed her eyes and recalled Veronika's words. *Love them, leave them and take what you can on the way out.*

H eartbreak and a hangover were the worst combination. Eloise slept until ten o'clock, when her stomach rejected all that rich food and champagne. She just managed to reach the toilet before vomiting and shedding more miserable tears. Then she washed her face and vowed never to touch alcohol again. The kitchen resembled the aftermath of a Bacchanalian feast. She could not face clearing up, so drank two glasses of cold water and returned to her bed.

A half-dream, half-nightmare jerked her awake and she checked the clock. Quarter to two! Her housemates would be home in a few hours and she was completely unprepared for Monday morning. She threw off her blankets and froze at the sound of the doorbell. Who on earth would be calling on a Sunday afternoon? She peeked through the curtains but saw no vehicles other than a motorcycle in the street.

She opened the door to a delivery man, who took in her dishevelled appearance with a twitch of an eyebrow. "Must have been a good night. Delivery for Frau de Fournier?"

"That's me."

"Here you are, milady. Have a pleasant Sunday afternoon." He handed over an enormous bouquet of multi-coloured flowers, a box of chocolates the size of a manhole and a beribboned letter bearing the name Frau Eloise de Fournier. He was almost at the gate when she remembered her manners.

"Thank you and same to you."

He waved and she returned indoors to her room, where she immediately opened the letter.

Dearest Eloise

I cannot imagine what you must think of me and hang my head in shame. The last twenty-four hours have been utter torment. It is true, I was sorely disappointed when my planned surprise was ruined. Nonetheless, a gentleman must take such a blow on the chin and with good grace. I did neither. To behave like a spoilt child was quite unforgivable.

There is nothing I can say to excuse my behaviour other than to plead the madness of love. Your words on Friday evening led me to believe you feel the same way about me as I do about you. Dare I hope you might give me a second chance to prove I am not the brute you think I am?

Eloise, I love you with my whole heart. The thought of losing you is insufferable. You are so beautiful, intelligent, witty, erudite and dare I say, individual in a way so many women wish to be but rarely achieve. I have never met anyone like you and wager I never will.

Your family commitments surely take priority and I respect your honourable stance. If anything, it makes me admire you more. Please, my treasure, leave me a crumb of hope by dining with me one last time before you leave for Switzerland. Send word and I will collect you on Friday at eight. I hope these tokens of my appreciation demonstrate my sincere apologies.

Yours with the greatest affection
Max

. . .

She put the flowers in water, read the letter again, cleared up the kitchen and read the letter another time. Then she made herself an omelette while considering his words. Finally, she put all evidence of last night's excess into the waste bin and took it outside to the municipal container. On top of the festering heap, she threw Max's letter. The flowers and chocolates, she decided, should not be wasted. Upstairs, she left the huge bouquet outside Veronika's door and stepped onto the fire escape. Jan sat with his back to the wall, the cigarette between his lips as much a part of his personality as the eye-patch. Close up, she saw his remaining eye was a piercing blue, shot through with turquoise and green. It reminded her of glacier lakes like Blausee.

"Hello. My name is Eloise."

He pressed a finger to his lips and then to Veronika's window. "Ssh. She's still sleeping," he whispered. "You two had quite a party last night."

"I'm still recovering. Listen, someone sent me chocolates and I don't want them. Are they any use to you?"

"Go to hell!" His exhortation to keep quiet was abruptly abandoned. "Stuff your chocolates, you dirty whore! I don't want leftovers from your rich pimps. You think you're so modern, don't you? New Women? Don't make me laugh. New women pursuing the oldest profession in the world. Take your chocolates and your pity. Go to hell! I despise you."

Eloise gasped, as shocked as if she'd been slapped in the face. Her instinct told her to turn away and leave the horrible gargoyle to spit venom at someone else. Yet she stood her ground.

"You know nothing about me, not even my name, but you pass judgement on how I live my life. All I know is that your name is Jan and you're my neighbour. Why would I pity you?"

He dropped the limp end of his homemade cigarette

through the metal grille and began rolling another. He spoke, his voice low and scratchy, like an overused record. "You shouldn't pity me. I only have one eye but I see more than most. You're right, I don't know your name, but I know you come from Switzerland, so I christen you Heidi. I see you have a rich man who drives here in his big car and takes you to nice places. I see it wasn't long before he took you to his bed. I see he only socialises with you on Fridays, and I ask myself why he is not free at weekends. I see you are making a fool of yourself. Poor little Swiss miss."

Eloise sat on the top step, her head in turmoil, sifting through his observations with a sense of admiration for him and shame for herself. Finally, she got to her feet and faced him, her chin held high. "I'm not stupid, you know."

"That remains to be seen. Oh, and if your beau ever offers you cigarettes, cocaine or schnapps, you have my permission to pity me. Good luck, Heidi."

She gave him a nod and went downstairs, puzzling over the strangest conversation she could ever remember and put the chocolates into her suitcase. Sylvia and Laurent would not refuse a selection of sweet treats, she was sure.

12

April 1927, Berlin

On Monday, Friedrich came into the office to show her a contact sheet of photographs. Eloise was astonished. Even at such a diminutive size, the images struck her as quite extraordinary. They pored over each tiny square, pointing out particular features and exclaiming over the subjects' expressions. The only problem was choosing the half dozen that would make the feature.

"What if ..." said Eloise, as an idea surfaced. "What if it was more than two features? Between us we have enough material for a whole series and we can make full use of your wonderful work."

"Will your editor entertain that idea?" Friedrich looked dubious.

"There's only one way to find out." Eloise jumped to her feet and picked up the portfolio. "Let's go and ask her."

Friedrich grinned and followed her to Vicki's office. As they approached, she saw through the window that she was not alone. Sitting opposite her was none other than Max Adalbert.

Her hands began to sweat and her mouth dried. She stopped so suddenly, Friedrich almost cannoned into her.

"Oh, she's in a meeting. In that case, I'll come back later. May I keep the contact sheets to illustrate my argument? I promise to take great care of them."

"I trust you, Eloise. How about I come by tomorrow morning to hear how she reacts?" Friedrich picked up his hat and briefcase.

"Hold on. I'll walk downstairs with you. I need to pop out for ... something." She slipped the portfolio into her desk drawer and snatched up her handbag, desperate to get out of the office before Max emerged. She simply could not face him, not now and certainly not in front of all her colleagues. In her hurry, she forgot her coat. She chatted to Friedrich until his tram came, went to the Post Office to buy some stamps, queued at the bakery for a cheese roll and spent a chilly quarter of an hour walking around the block. When she had been away from her desk for fifty minutes, she crept up the stairs, prepared to run down again if she heard anyone coming in the other direction.

Back in the office, Martha was putting on her coat. "There you are! Julia and I are going to the café. Do you want to come with us?"

"Thanks, but I took my lunch hour to run errands. I'll eat this at my desk."

"Suit yourself. By the way, Max Adalbert was asking for you. He left a note. If he suggests a date, run for the hills. See you later."

She turned to ask Martha what she meant but she was already on the way out with Julia. Instead, Eloise looked over at her desk. Sure enough, there was an envelope bearing her name in Max's distinctive penmanship. It was tempting to throw it straight in the bin, but he was a senior member of the magazine's parent company and that would be most unprofessional. She postponed her decision, tucked it into her handbag, ate her roll and outlined the content for a series called 'After Dark – Berlin by Night'. At twelve-thirty, when almost all her colleagues had left the office for lunch, she took his letter out and read it.

Dearest Eloise

I cannot bear your silence. I am unable to eat, or sleep for thinking about you. Please, please, my beloved angel, have pity on me. Your forgiveness is the only thing that matters. Say yes to dinner on Friday. The thought of your leaving for Switzerland on these terms torments me. I must see you. Send word to my office this afternoon. I understand you wish to punish me but if you had the vaguest idea of how I suffer, you would relent. Please, my darling, reply soonest.

Yours as always

Max

She tucked it into the envelope, completely unmoved by his entreaties, and considered her response. Across the room, she saw Hannelore lifting a piece of her work up to the light. She wandered across to have a look. It was a magnificent rendering of Neuschwanstein Castle to accompany an article on the beauty of Bavaria. She complimented her on the delicate brushwork.

"Thank you very much. I put quite some hours into this piece, which is why my stomach is reminding me I'm late for lunch. Have you eaten or do you fancy joining me for something disgusting at the Bierkeller?"

"Since you make it sound so appealing ... no, thank you. Anyway, I took an early lunch. Can I ask you a question? What do you know about Max Adalbert?"

Hannelore shrugged. "Not much. We illustrators just do as we're told and don't have much to do with management. All I know is that he has a bit of a reputation as a ladies' man. You're not going to fall at his feet like all the other silly girls, are you?"

Eloise faked a bright laugh. "Certainly not! All I can say is more fool those silly girls."

"Good. I knew you were smarter than that." She stood up, her short bleached curls slicked close to her face as if she had just emerged from water. "You understand that you and all the other female writers have a responsibility here? Fashion journalism is changing, Eloise, and not before time. Soon Hermann, Max, Rolf etcetera will be dictating how we should look, what we ought to desire, and the way we should feel will be ancient history. Why? Because we, *die Damen*, the very women who design, make, model and observe what fashion means to us have taken up their pens, paints and cameras. We can speak for ourselves. Our mouthpiece is *Die Dame*."

Eloise was transfixed. "Why aren't you in charge?"

"Of what?"

"Everything! I would follow an orator like you to the ends of the earth. Oh, there's Vicki. I must catch her. Enjoy your lunch."

Vicki was not convinced that two nights on the town merited an entire series, but when she saw Friedrich's photographs, she became more persuadable.

"We can't do a whole series on Berlin. It may be the biggest city in Germany, but we get enough accusations of elitism and self-obsession as it is. We'll do a series, but only three on Berlin, using a dozen of these pictures. You contact someone in Hamburg, Munich and maybe Cologne to send us something similar and we'll spread it over six months. Tell them we'll pay for a journalist and a photographer. I think we'll use this one for the cover." She pointed to one of Friedrich's shots of the audience gazing up in wonderment at the Codonas' trapeze act. Eloise was pleased. Not only did she get three features out of it, but Friedrich's work on the cover was an unexpected bonus.

When she got back to her desk, Martha had returned.

"Good lunch?" she asked.

Martha waggled her hand. "So-so. Watery onion soup, even worse than last week and the bread was so thin you could see through it. What did Adalbert want?"

"Oh, he had some comments on the nightlife article. Vicki wants to run it over three issues and get similar pieces from other cities. I'd better get down to work. That reminds me, what did you mean when you said I should run for the hills if Max asked for ..." She was interrupted by Martha's phone ringing.

"Martha Falken?" She rolled her eyes. "*Guten Tag*, Frau Krüger, nice to hear from you again." She continued listening to the caller, but looked meaningfully at Eloise and pointed to the third finger of her left hand.

"Married?" mouthed Eloise, aghast.

Martha nodded. "I know exactly the one you mean, Frau Krüger. Just let me get a pen and I can take down a little more detail."

Eloise walked to the bathroom in a haze, Jan's words ringing in her ears. *I see he only socialises with you on Fridays, and I ask myself why he is not free at weekends. I see you are making a fool of yourself.* Of course. It was so obvious, she must have been wilfully blind to ignore all the signs. The elderly parents. The colleague's lodge. The knowing looks at The Palais Heinroth. For their romantic weekend together, his wife must have been out of town. She wondered where the poor woman was going over Easter. Maybe they had children. The thought made her feel sick.

She pulled out the letter and turned it over to the blank side. With her Montblanc Meisterstück fountain pen, one of the last presents Sylvain had given her, she began to write.

Herr Adalbert

This is to be our last communication. Your conduct has been despicable and dishonest from the outset. On learning of your marital status, I was appalled at your duplicity and my own foolishness. The only bright side is that you showed your true colours before I grew too attached. You should be ashamed of yourself. Please refrain from all future contact unless it is for professional reasons.

Eloise de Fournier

On the envelope, she crossed out her own name and replaced it with his, then took it downstairs to the receptionist. The final post round was at four so unless he left early, he would receive it today. Then she returned to her desk and started looking up journalistic colleagues in Hamburg.

Her holiday in Switzerland came at exactly the right time. She cleared her desk of all duties, filed both her Berlin nightlife articles, worked with Friedrich to select exactly the right images, refined 'After Dark' guidelines for fellow journalists in other cities, and packed her suitcase for the trip. On the Friday before she left, she gathered Easter gifts for her family and housemates. On a whim, she decided to include Jan. The magazine office always had plenty of samples sent from advertisers and companies hoping for a mention. Eloise asked permission to take some phials of perfume, a red velvet coin purse, lipsticks, decorative hairpins, a silk scarf, two packets of cigarettes, an eyeshadow, three pairs of earrings, a selection of sweets and trio of miniature Kirsch bottles.

She spent a contented hour in her room after dinner, filling hand-painted papier-mâché eggs with carefully selected treats. For Hildegard and Lili, perfume, earrings, hairpins and chocolates. For Veronika, cigarettes, eyeshadow, the scarf and a lipstick. For Jan, all three bottles, cigarettes and a few Gummibears. At six o'clock on Saturday morning, she crept upstairs and left the eggs outside the respective rooms. Then she opened the door to the fire escape, planning to throw Jan's egg across the street. But there he was, watching and smoking in the pre-dawn light.

"Good morning."

He did not reply but his eye fixed on her face.

"I'm leaving today. Because I won't be here for Easter, I wanted to give everyone an egg. You included. Rest assured, none of this came from a rich beau."

"Are you coming back?" His voice sounded feeble, as if his throat hurt.

"Yes. In two weeks. I have to go now because my train leaves at seven. Catch this, will you?" She swung the paper bag containing the egg once, twice, three times and let it fly over the railing. Jan stretched out both hands and grabbed it before it hit the ground.

"You know, Heidi, you're very strange," he said, looking into the bag.

"So are you. But I've seen stranger. Goodbye, Jan."

A taxi turned the corner and parked outside her building. She closed the door and hurried downstairs to answer the door before he rang. The driver helped her with her suitcase and she cast one last glance up at the fire escape. Jan gave her a salute.

She saluted back and got into the cab. "To the station, please."

Two weeks in Switzerland was not quite the triumphant return she had envisioned. Everyone had made plans for her and not all were to her liking. Of course she was happy to spend hours with Sylvia, admiring the tiny items of new furniture in the dolls' house and the dear little clothes she made for the inhabitants. Her patience was limitless when Laurent wanted to demonstrate his building skills or the paintings his teacher had awarded prizes. She spent most of Sunday in the nursery, lavishing attention on her children.

By the time she got up on Monday, only Charlotte was in the breakfast room.

"Where is everyone?" she asked, pouring some apple juice.

"Papa is in his study. Mama is instructing Cook on the menu for Easter and the children have gone to camp."

"Camp? Oh, good morning, Greta. Yes please, an egg and some ham with a cup of coffee. Thank you. Charlotte, what camp are you talking about?"

"We must have a serious conversation about their education. Both are doing poorly in German and getting low grades."

"At their age, Charlotte, so was I. Young people learn at different paces and they already have a German tutor three times a week. They'll catch up, as I have done."

Eloise's refusal to see it as a serious concern clearly irritated her sister. "No, I'm sorry, that will not do. They must do as well as their peers or join a lower class. This week, I booked them into an activity camp in Schwarzenburg. Lessons in the morning, fun and games in the afternoon while socialising with their German counterparts. They will return on Thursday for the Easter weekend. If it works as it should, I will book them another one during the summer holidays."

"Oh goodness gracious, I'm only here for two weeks and you send my children away for four days? Why didn't you consult me?"

"I did. I also know for a fact their teacher wrote to you on the topic. In the absence of a reply, we took a decision on what is best for the children. I will leave you now as Papa wants to see you in his study. While you're in there, you must ask him if he will foot the bill for the summer camp."

Eloise watched her go with the guilty realisation that she had only given Charlotte's letter a cursory glance and dismissed the teacher's altogether. She ate her egg and ham alone, wondering how to resist her father's demands. With a long-suffering air she knocked on the study door, already sighing at the thought of his frown.

As expected, he made some cursory enquiries about her journey and her job then turned to the topic at hand: the sale of her house. However, on this occasion, he put on the thumbscrews.

"I quite appreciate the fact you don't know what the future holds, yet provision must be made for your children. By selling the house now, for an extremely fair asking price, you will have a handsome nest egg for when you return from Berlin. I have personally identified several town houses you could easily afford, some within walking distance of their school."

"Well, that all sounds very good, but I would really rather not sell that house. It has a great deal of emotional significance to me."

"That I don't doubt. It also entails a great deal of financial investment simply to keep it from going to wrack and ruin. It is a crying shame to allow such a magnificent property to stand empty and if I may be honest, too much for you and two children. Why would a family of three require seven bedrooms and two reception rooms, a staff of eight and three acres of orchard? More importantly, how would you manage the expenses on your widow's stipend and journalist's pay?"

She had no answer to that.

"Furthermore, I must be blunt when it comes to Sylvia and Laurent. They are growing fast and require new clothes, materials for school, in addition to the usual maintenance. On top of that, Charlotte proposes a summer language camp after this Easter experiment. No doubt it will become an annual occurrence. All of this costs a considerable amount. In the absence of a breadwinner, of course I am happy to provide for my grandchildren. But knowing you are able to realise a small fortune if only you chose pragmatism over emotion makes me more than a little disappointed."

There was no way out. "May I have a little time to consider, Papa?"

"I'm afraid not. I have waited patiently since February and will tolerate no further delay. I have already lost one buyer along with a good deal of his respect thanks to your intransigence. This is no longer a request, Eloise. You must sell that house."

She capitulated. Then she asked permission to take the children and visit one last time.

"You may visit, but there is no need to take the children. Firstly, they are not returning here until Thursday. Secondly, it will upset them unnecessarily, particularly if you are affected. Thirdly, I want to you to complete your farewells today. Take the keys and go after lunch. Thank you, Eloise, and I will keep you informed as to progress."

Before she could retreat to the winter garden to consider the double shocks of absent children and lost house, her mother accosted her in the hallway, with a mournful expression.

"Oh, Eloise, your lovely hair. You used to be so proud of your lustrous, thick locks. Do you remember sitting with me at the looking-glass, combing it until it shone? I know it's very modern and you can choose your own style as a busy woman about town, but it does make me very sad."

"It's much more practical this way, Maman."

"If you say so. Have your spoken to your father yet? Good, then you must come with me to the café. Madame Berger invited us to her morning salon and I accepted. The salon itself is nothing special but she has two very eligible sons I want you to meet. Will you go and change into something a little more sober, please?"

You must ask, you must sell, you must come ... once again, Eloise had no free will, took no decisions, and simply followed orders. Not once had a member of her family showed any interest in her work. 'Do you like Berlin?' they asked, as if enquiring if she enjoyed tripe. 'And journalism suits you? Well, as long as you're happy'.

She changed her clothes, arranged her hair and accompanied her mother to the café for tedious small talk on banal topics. Whenever Eloise contributed by mentioning Berlin's house prices, fashions, parks or coffee shops, she was met with pursed lips and an awkward silence until someone changed the subject. It was a fruitless exercise in matchmaking since the eligible sons evidently found her as repellent as she found them. Maman was not pleased.

After the first few days at home, she yearned to return to her little room on Charlottenweg. Only the pleasure of spending Easter with the children and the anticipation of Bastian and Seraphine's visit prevented her from changing her train ticket. On Good Friday they were all together, including baby Henrietta, a mere month old. Everyone was enchanted with the beautiful little cherub, even Charlotte, who never showed much interest in children before they could talk. They had the baby's christening service on the Saturday, meaning that the family visited church on four consecutive days.

"Makes up for the last three months, I suppose," Eloise muttered to Bastian as the priest said his goodbyes after the Easter Monday service.

"Don't let Maman hear that. What do you usually do on Sunday mornings in Berlin?"

The vision of Max crawling up the bed like some kind of panther flashed across her mind, but she dismissed it with a blink. "Sleep late, do laundry, prepare myself for Monday. If it's nice weather, I take a tram to the Tiergarten."

"Alone?" Her brother had an instinct for when she was hiding something.

"Yes, because my housemates go back to their families at weekends. I do have friends from work, but I generally spend all week with them and enjoy a day of solitude."

"Solitude is all very well, but today is a special occasion. Shall we let the others go on home while we take a stroll along the Sarine?"

"Oh, yes please!"

He signalled their intentions to Seraphine, who lifted a hand in acknowledgement and blew him a kiss.

"Your wife is a perfect angel. I'm not sure you're good enough for her."

"I say the same thing every single day. It's so good to see her happy again. I have not yet said anything to the family, but Seraphine lost a baby two years ago. That's why we left it very late to announce it when she got pregnant with Etta."

"Oh poor Seraphine! And poor you." They walked down the steep cobbled streets to the river. "I'm so glad you have your baby girl. Does Seraphine mind when you call her Etta? It's just that she told me Henrietta was after her brother Henri, who died."

"That's Julius's fault. He can't say her whole name, so she's Etta at home. Now my wife is no longer under a cloud of grief, I can turn my attentions to my sister's happiness. How is it, being a working woman in a big city?"

"Mostly thrilling, sometimes a little lonely and no matter where I go or what I do, I'm always gauche and unsophisticated."

"With your new haircut? Surely not?"

"Don't mention my hair. Mama is in mourning over my shorn locks. If she could see some of my colleagues! Everyone is glamorous, devil-may-care, modern and worldly. There's a man in the opposite building with one eye. He lost it in the war."

"Yes, I hear the streets of Berlin are littered with the bodies of broken soldiers reduced to begging for survival. What kind of a reward is that after risking one's life for one's country?"

Eloise hunched her shoulders. "I try to be kind and give what I can, but what my wages can buy on Monday is often less than half by Friday."

"Your trial period was for three months. Either party can say it's not for them. Now you've decided to sell the house, you could live a very comfortable life in Fribourg and work as a journalist here. Not that I'm trying to influence you. This is entirely your decision."

They reached the riverbank and turned left at the bridge. Ducks tilted their tails in the air and a moorhen fluttered to a stop in the shallows.

"You're the first person not to tell me what I *must* do. The issue is this. One element of my new life is that I make lots of mistakes, some minor and others too embarrassing to recount. But I am learning, Bastian. I am developing as a person and I dare say, as a journalist. Giving up now seems wrong and for one thing, it would give Maman carte blanche to open husband-hunting season. As we discussed last year, I want more from life than a wedding ring."

He laughed and guided her past a muddy puddle with his hand on her elbow. "I see. My sister wants career success, independence and a chance to fulfil her potential. But, Eloise, what about love?"

A line from Max's letter came back to her. *Eloise, I love you with my whole heart. The thought of losing you is insufferable.*

"Love," she sniffed, "is overrated."

13

Summer 1927, Berlin

The new creative director was supposed to bring a breath of fresh air to *Die Dame* and change things for the better. Instead, he soured the atmosphere and made things worse. Ernst Dryden was a well-known artist and fashion designer from Vienna who now lived in Paris, with very dogmatic ideas. Firstly, he wanted to dispense with many of the fashion and travel articles, opting to turn the magazine into something more heavyweight, including the serialisation of a novel. He took over much of the illustration work, leaning away from the concept of individual style and into chorus-line imagery. Several staff illustrators and photographers were dismissed, including Hannelore.

Eloise, Martha and Julia treated her to lunch on her last day, intending to cheer her up. As it transpired, Hannelore was the one who felt sorry for them.

"I see which way the wind blows. Look at who lost their jobs. Most of them are illustrators and photographers and nearly all are women. He's going to use his own people to make the magazine a vehicle for his own work. Mark my words, you will be next. The staff will become predominantly male, he will systematically replace us with his colleagues and transform the contents into his vision of the future."

"Vicki won't allow that!" said Martha.

"Vicki will be side-lined, her input worth less and less. Not only is she a woman but she's also Jewish. There's a growing unfriendliness to Jews and not just in the media. Expect that to get a lot worse."

"Not here," said Julia. "People in Berlin are not afraid of a few Bavarian extremists. You mustn't get paranoid, Hannelore. I'm worried you're seeing a small group of nasty, noisy brownshirts as typical."

"Don't worry about me. I intend to find work in Austria or maybe Switzerland. I hear Swiss girls are pretty." She grinned at Eloise.

Six months ago, Eloise would have blushed. "The prettiest, but must you leave Germany? Why not try a different publication in Berlin, or settle in another city like Hamburg?"

"Because I don't like the way this country is going. Women made a lot of progress under democracy, maybe too much, too fast. Now there is going to be a counter reaction. My advice to you, ladies, is to look out for your careers. Start now. As modern women, what do you want?"

"To use our voices," said Julia. "To write about what matters to women."

Martha agreed. "Yes, freedom and independence at work. When it comes to the home, our own income and the choice of how to spend it."

"And you, Eloise?"

"I agree with Julia and Martha, but I would add choice. One does not need to be a mother or a worker or a revolutionary. The New Woman can be all three."

"In our utopian dreams, perhaps we can," said Hannelore. "In the Weimar Republic, we have to fight tooth and bloody nail for every step forward. Becoming a New Woman isn't an identity we can slip over our heads like a string of pearls. This is a war. Our fight for independence will last a thousand years. We have won some battles but our progress must be defended. The worst, I'm sad to say, is yet to come."

No one had an answer to that.

Ever since she was little, Eloise was a doubter. She always tested what she had been told, sometimes to her detriment. One such example was the warning not to touch the poker even when it no longer glowed red. The pad of her index finger still bore a smooth spot. She tested Hannelore's theory with Vicki, or at least part of it.

Since she had taken up smoking, Eloise preferred to do it in the fresh air. The irony was not lost on her, but smoking at her desk seemed like fouling her own nest. The truth was that she smoked more as an accessory than as an addiction. Another person who liked to smoke outside was Vicki. She would often float past Eloise's desk, waving her cigarette case and arching her eyebrows. That summer, pale skin was especially fashionable, so it was often just the two of them on the balcony, wearing sunglasses and overlooking the courtyard below.

Conversation revolved around work. The closest they ever got to personal was to offer a compliment on new shoes or admire a shade of lipstick. Still, being outside somehow levelled their status. Eloise never felt intimidated or hesitant to ask questions, and Vicki was amenable to off-topic subjects. Such as office politics.

"Do you ever think we're offering an unrealistic dream? All

our articles and advertising promote an impossible lifestyle, unless of course, you're very wealthy."

"That's the entire essence of *Die Dame*, Eloise. Have you only just realised and are now suffering a crisis of conscience? Too late, my little idealist. Anyway, some people are thriving: those who made a killing in the war, those who used hyperinflation for their own ends and those with family money. Why shouldn't they look at lovely pictures and feel a part of modern life?"

"I suppose you're right. To tell the truth, I prefer the culture of distraction. Beautiful clothes, glamorous people, and the ideal woman we all aspire to being. Although, I can't help feeling we're moving away from that in the current environment. The magazine is not the same as it was."

Vicki blew a long stream of smoke into the cold air. "Of course it's not. No new creative director is likely to come in and say, 'Everything's going very well here, you just carry on as you are'. Why bother paying him? Dryden has to put his stamp on the enterprise, adding his own peculiarities to our look. Should circulation rise, he will be deemed a success. On the other hand, were ladies to find his style uniform, bland, detached from real modern women and with a focus on male interests, they will stop buying it."

"Is that what you think will happen?"

"Time will tell. The one thing I will not tolerate is men lecturing me on what women want." Vicki looked above their heads towards the management offices and lowered her voice. "I'm already seeking work elsewhere. Never a good idea to put all your eggs in someone else's basket. You're good at what you do, Eloise. I'd advise you to look out for opportunities."

She went inside, leaving Eloise to conclude she had not yet disproved Hannelore's point, but rather underlined the sentiment.

. . .

The question of personal aspirations pursued her all week, especially as the government were championing female contributions to society with the slogan "*Kinder, Küche, Kirche*" (children, kitchen, church). None of those three came naturally to Eloise.

On Friday evening, she sat down to dinner with her two German housemates and asked them the question directly. "What do women want?"

Their answers were unexpected.

Lili answered without hesitation. "To do our duty and serve our country. We want to be decent citizens, hard workers, loyal wives and good mothers, in order to restore the German race."

"I see. That's a very honourable response. Still, I was hoping for something a little more specific to you. Imagine your ideal future, Lili. How does it look?"

Tonight's 'feast' was *arme Ritter* or poor knights, also known as stale bread soaked in egg and milk then fried in whatever fat was available. Towards the end of the month before payday, mealtimes grew increasingly lean. At least Lili and Hildegard could go home for a decent feed at the weekend. Eloise bit her lip, reminding herself of the large empty house in Fribourg and her parents' three-course dinners prepared by the cook.

Lili put down her forkful of food. "In my future, I am a housewife, married to a good man who works for the railways. We have a small house and garden in Potsdam, halfway between my family and his. Our children, two boys and a girl, help me grow vegetables and raise chickens. We live a simple, healthy life. Church on Sundays and we never fail to exercise our civic duties by using our vote."

Her eyes filled with light at this vision, and despite her cynicism, Eloise was touched for her friend. "I hope that comes true for you."

"An honourable response from an honourable person,"

agreed Hildegard. "I am quite sure you will find the pair of us disappointing in your quest for female advancement, Eloise, but you must understand that German women have moved mountains in the last ten years. The freedoms people like Veronika find so attractive hold no appeal for the average lady. Our desire is to play a role in society, stand up for our communities, put our shoulders to the wheel and show what we are capable of achieving."

"Another honourable answer," exclaimed Eloise, adding cinnamon to her poor knight.

"Honourable, yet unexciting. Lili and I read your articles about Berlin nightlife, the near-naked dancers, the lady couples, the female impersonators and the debauched decadence which passes for modernity in some circles. Some see that as progress. I'm afraid I disagree. What women want is respect. Taking off one's clothes degrades and cheapens the dignity of womanhood. The real answer to your question, I suggest, is that women want different things."

They ate in silence for a few minutes, digesting their food and Hildegard's words.

Then Lili spoke. "What about you, Eloise? How does your future look? What do you want out of life?"

For a moment, she didn't have an answer. Possibilities raced through her head like a meteor shower before she answered as honestly as she was able. "I want everything life has to offer. Or in other words, I want fulfilment."

"I don't know what you mean by that."

"That's all right, Lili. Neither do I."

Searching for another journalist position was awkward, in that many editors knew one another socially. Some were even married to each other. Still, she sent off one or two applications every week, to no avail. Most publications failed to respond, while others expressed an interest in seeing more of her work. One even offered to commission her piece on *femmes fatales*. She said no thank you and continued her search.

Halfway through July, nearly seven months after her arrival in Berlin, Eloise accepted the facts. Staff writing jobs were as common as white ravens. She either stayed where she was, which was becoming more uncomfortable daily, or sought out freelance work. Her financial situation was precarious enough as it was, and patching a living out of unreliable commissions would remove any semblance of security. Her reasonable side reminded her that she could give up and go home any time she wanted. Her unreasonable side wondered why on earth her father *still* hadn't sold her house. Then she would have a very comfortable cushion with which to fund her lifestyle. If only she had agreed to the first buyer. By having allowed her sentimental heart to rule, she had made a foolish mistake. Perhaps her whole ambition was a mistake and she should go home, be a decent mother and be grateful that she had that option. Jan and Veronika had nowhere else to go.

She was heading out for some lunch between some summer showers, when she spotted Friedrich Seidenstücker sitting outside a café on Alexanderplatz. She ran across the street, jumped over a puddle and landed on the pavement in front of his table.

"Eloise! What an unexpected surprise! I do wish I'd had my camera ready just then. You leapt across that puddle like a ballet dancer. Will you join me?"

"I'd love to. I've hardly seen you in months. Are you very busy?"

Friedrich hailed the waiter and Eloise ordered a coffee. The prices here were extortionate and she would get a bagel from the bakery on the way back to work.

"Busy is an understatement. I'm turning people away, can you believe? Those who don't pay on time, change the brief at the last minute or pair me with incompetent journalists can find another photographer. *Die Dame* is on my list of favourite clients, I assure you."

"Oh, I'm sure it is. They're bound to keep you. Not only are you good at your job, but also male and not Jewish. It's the rest of us who have to worry."

Friedrich's smile faded and his forehead creased with concern. "Please tell me they have not terminated your contract."

"No, no, at least not yet. But many of my colleagues have lost their positions and I am looking over my shoulder."

The waiter brought her coffee with a little beaker of water. In the saucer, a little chocolate sat on a triangle of paper. Eloise popped it into her mouth.

"They would have to be out of their minds to sack you. I've worked with all sorts of journalists and you are one of the best. No, don't give me that polite smile, I'm serious. You have passion, ideas, commitment and you are wonderful with people. Hasn't your new director noticed how much you contribute to the magazine?"

"Our new director hasn't noticed anything because he lives in Paris, directing operations from the fashionable *quartiers*. For him, *Die Dame* is an abstract concept, not a room full of creative minds. Put simply, he thinks he knows best."

Friedrich closed his eyes and shook his head. "Another of Adalbert's brilliant schemes to ruin something that's working perfectly."

"You know Max Adalbert?"

"By reputation and that's as close as I want to get. Monstrous ego, apparently. Are you implying you are looking for opportunities elsewhere? Only this morning someone asked me if I could recommend a wordsmith with an open mind."

Eloise's coffee cup halted en route to her mouth. "An open mind?"

"An acquaintance specialises in photographing nudes. Such images, accompanied by a little vignette, are published privately for a ravenous audience. He simply cannot produce enough to satisfy them. It's highly lucrative. Let me be clear, I am not suggesting pornography. These pictures are coy, suggestive, flirtatious and exciting. Erotica, if you will. A large portion of its consumers are ladies. An inventive writer capable of penning something subtle, arousing and sophisticated which appeals to both sexes could earn a good deal of money."

She sipped her coffee in silence.

"I've offended you and I am mortified. Eloise, I apologise. The only reason I brought it up was your all-embracing enthusiasm of the nightlife scene. You seemed unshockable, but now I see that was your professional demeanour. Please forget I ever spoke."

"Not at all. The idea intrigues me. My reticence is not due to affronted morality, but insecurity. You see, I've never written anything of the sort. To be truthful, I'm not at all sure I'd be any good at it. Shouldn't one have a great deal of worldly experience for such an undertaking?"

He dabbed his mouth with a linen napkin. "Either that or an unfettered imagination. Are you busy on Friday night? Good. Then meet me here at eight and I'll introduce you to my friend. In the meantime, take a copy of his latest, to appreciate the house style. I must run. Your coffee is on me."

14

Summer 1927, Berlin

For the third time, a prospective buyer pulled out of the house sale in Fribourg. This meant further frustration for her father and an asset which was rapidly becoming a liability. It also left Eloise in a grave situation. Since being demoted to merely a 'contributor' at *Die Dame*, she struggled to maintain an income and cover her expenses. Rent and food absorbed all her money, leaving nothing to fund the clothes she needed for her new lifestyle, leave alone travel. The train journey to Fribourg for 1 August and Swiss National Day was far too expensive and since the children were once again going to a holiday camp, she expected her family to accept the situation with only minor qualms.

However, when she communicated her decision to stay in Berlin for the whole summer, the reaction was furious outrage. Her mother, her father, Charlotte and even the children wrote to express their dismay. As always, Charlotte's words were the bluntest.

Have you altogether forgotten your responsibilities? Your children have not seen you since Easter. Sylvia confessed she could not recall the last time you wrote. You have absented yourself from their lives and from ours. We, who shouldered the burden of raising your children to give you a second chance at both being a mother and having a career, are now forgotten. Now it seems the latter eclipses the former and you abandon your own offspring to chase glory in print. You are shallow, selfish and undeserving of these wonderful young people. Each of us, but most of all Sylvia and Laurent, deserve a heartfelt apology. Your dear departed husband would be shocked by your behaviour. Look in the mirror, Eloise. You will not like what you see.

For a few days, she managed to stifle her sister's criticisms by frequenting bars and cafés, flirting with anyone who would buy her a drink, dancing, smoking and laughing as if she was happy. The weight of her situation pressed on her like a wet mattress.

Early one Saturday morning, Eloise woke with a champagne headache. The church bells were ringing and her bladder was full. She went to the bathroom, relieved herself and drank a glass of water. When she opened the door, Lili and Hildegard were coming downstairs, about to leave for the weekend. Their eyes widened when they saw the state of her. Politely, they wished her a good weekend and scurried out into the street. She returned to her bedroom and did as her sister bade her. She looked in the mirror.

It was a horrible sight, all the worse for being familiar. How many women had she passed on the streets, feeling pity and disgust at their grey skin, make-up-smudged eyes and red wine-stained lips? The stench of cigarettes and alcohol was nauseating, her head throbbed and her own breath offended her. She opened the window to allow something fresh into the stale fug.

How had she got home? The man she danced with outside Café Karloff paid for a taxi, didn't he? Or was it those girls from Mitzy's who linked arms with her to walk down Charlottenstrasse? Sometimes, when she got in late, she went upstairs and sat on the fire escape, mostly being insulted by Jan. But not last night.

She stumbled into the kitchen to drink some more water. Her stomach craved something heavy and full of fat. What she wouldn't give for a plate of *Rösti* and a fried egg. But her kitchen shelf was empty apart from some Knorr dried soup and her post propped up against the coffee pot. Soup was better than nothing. While she waited for the water to boil, she opened the first of three envelopes. It bore only her name, with no address. Eloise recognised the handwriting. Ruth's tone was friendly but pointed out that her rent was overdue by one week. If there was a problem, please let her know and they could talk about it. Eloise turned down the heat and stirred the powder into the water while wondering what to say.

The second was a letter from Dietmar, pleading for more of her erotic stories. The man didn't give up easily. After delivering half a dozen saucy tales, loosely plagiarised from her own youthful reading, she gave him notice there would be no more. She found the process of refashioning other people's lurid fantasies utterly mortifying. In any case, Dietmar paid a pittance, barely enough to keep her in cigarettes. Still, she had to pay the rent somehow. The soup was ready and she poured it into a bowl, putting off the third envelope for as long as possible. It was from her brother and she dreaded his judgemental tone. The trouble with Bastian was that he regarded parenthood as the greatest achievement in the world. No matter that as a doctor he had been a significant part of a major medical breakthrough to transform Switzerland. Nor that he was so highly regarded in the town of Brienz it was almost impossible to take a stroll along the lake without two dozen well-wishers tipping their hats and smiling. He was a father and husband, first and foremost, who could never understand Eloise's priorities.

Eventually she opened it to find a brief note, not the long and earnest lecture she had anticipated, and a return train ticket from Berlin to Fribourg.

Dearest Eloise

Please consider this an early birthday present to use at your convenience. However, you may recall it is our father's birthday on August 3 and this year he will be sixty years of age. We are planning a party to celebrate such a special occasion. I know nothing would give him greater joy than to have his entire family around him. Why not combine 1 August and the party in one trip?

With love always,

Bastian

PS: Fear not, I can and shall manage Charlotte

Her face twisted into a tearful grimace and she covered her face with her hands. Her dear beloved brother! She cried for a little while, washed and dried her face, then finished the cooling soup. She allowed herself a smile of acknowledgement at Bastian's cunning. He had not sent money for a train ticket, but the ticket itself. She could not use his gift for anything other than a trip home. He knew her too well.

Eloise sighed. Perhaps it was a sign. She was no longer a journalist at a glamorous magazine, visiting fashion houses and cutting a dash on Kurfürstendamm, but a scrabbling hack, reduced to writing smutty stories and visiting debauched bars in the hope of getting someone to buy her a drink. Why not return to Fribourg and live a comfortable, if stultifying existence? There were worse things. If she were brutally honest, the oldest profession in the world was merely a few missteps away. Surely that was not the reason she had left her children and come to Berlin?

All day long, as she washed her clothes and cleaned herself in the sink since she could no longer afford the bathhouse, she considered how different life would be at home with her parents. Servants to remove her dirty laundry, a cook to prepare nutritious meals, a car to take her wherever she desired and a library full of fascinating literature, assembled over the years by her erudite mother. Would it be so terrible to see Sylvia and Laurent on a daily basis, attend social occasions with an eye cocked for a suitable bachelor/widower? There was no shame in surviving, if not quite thriving in Berlin for half a year.

On Monday, she would write to Bastian and assure him she would be in Fribourg for the first week of August. Perhaps then she could have a realistic conversation with Papa and plan her return. No need to give up her dreams of journalism just yet, but perhaps a country still suffering under the yoke of wartime reparations was not the place to burst onto the scene.

Even so, she painted her face, put on her pearls and fringed frock, and went out into the night, praying to encounter a man with pockets deep enough to buy her dinner.

Her luck was in. But her benefactor on this occasion was female. She was threading her way through tables outside Café Coco when someone called her name.

"Eloise, isn't it? Hannelore's friend? I'm Romy and we met at The Dorian Grey a few times. How could I forget those beautiful blue eyes? If I'm not mistaken, you and I danced a most impressive Charleston."

"Hello, Romy, how nice to see you again!"

"Everyone, this is Eloise. Eloise, meet Edith, Genevieve, Irmgard and Louise. Won't you join us for a drink? We're celebrating Genevieve's divorce."

"Good evening, everyone. My friends are yet to arrive, so I'd love to join you, thanks."

Romy sloshed some champagne into a half-empty glass.

"That was Marlene's but she's run off after some slutty little dancer. Her loss, your gain. *Prost!*"

"*Prost*! And congratulations to Genevieve. Or should it be commiserations?"

Genevieve was a striking woman who wore her long hair piled high on her head. Kohl ringed her eyes, making the whites stand out as if she were startled. Perhaps she was. "Oh, congratulations, most certainly. Not only am I rid of the loathsome beast, but I take half his fortune with me!"

That provoked a round of toasts and Genevieve called to the waiter for another bottle of champagne. Eloise disliked her attitude, but was well aware she had come out of her own empty house with the express purpose of relieving some gentleman or other of his cash. One way or another, she had to sing for her supper. Unless she became part of the gang and adopted the same cynical tone, it was unlikely they would invite her to the next stop on their itinerary.

"That's another first I can tick off my list. Before I came to Berlin, I'd never a met a lesbian, an acrobat, a female impersonator or a divorcée."

Her assertion provoked gales of laughter and when the party recovered, conversation turned to other types of enthralling people they would like to meet. Eloise joined in where appropriate and gauged the mood well. By her third glass of champagne, Genevieve insisted she join them for dinner.

"We're going to order caviar, swill champagne, trough steaks, scoff desserts and dance between every course. The best part is that it all goes on my ex-husband's tab!"

The party howled and clapped with glee, Eloise amongst them. For a fleeting second, she wondered what Sylvain would think of her now.

· · ·

At quarter to two, an early night for her, she waved her new friends goodbye, found a business card for fellow journalist Irmgard, thanked Romy for a wonderful night and blew a kiss at Genevieve, who was sobbing in Edith's arms. The gay divorcée was drunk and filled with regrets. Tomorrow would be worse, Eloise knew from bitter experience.

The evening was still warm or perhaps it was the champagne coursing through her veins. She walked briskly along the streets, keeping near the kerb to avoid beggars, dodging drunks and attaching herself to groups whenever possible. When she turned into her own street, she looked up automatically and raised a hand when she saw the little orange glow.

Such a successful evening should not end prematurely, so she kicked off her shoes, and climbed the stairs with her cigarettes and all the little goodies she had pocketed. Jan's face was in shadow, lit only by the moon and the lamp at her back.

"Good night, was it, Heidi?" he asked, illuminated in the glow of her match.

"Highlight of the week. I had a slap-up meal, drank far too much champagne and made a useful contact. And the cherry on the cake? I didn't pay for any of it."

"Which poor bastard was footing the bill this time?"

"Even better than that. No subterfuge required. An acquaintance just got divorced and she took us all out on her husband's account. We had a wonderful evening."

"You are shameless, the lot of you. Do you ever have the slightest twinge of bad conscience, knowing what men sacrificed to keep you safe? No, of course you don't. You're too busy shaking off any vestige of morality and fleecing the opposite sex for everything you can get."

"Talking of what I could get, I filched some stuff to bring home. After-dinner chocolates, bread rolls, a packet of cigarillos, a lighter, some miniature bottles of whisky and a silk cravat. Which would you like?"

"All of it except the chocolates. Give those to Veronika." He shuffled forward to tug on the makeshift pulley system they had rigged up between the two fire escapes. The metal colander that served as a basket inched its way across the alley. Eloise filled it and sent it back. While he rummaged through the contents, she gazed up at the sky. Her neighbour was self-conscious about eating and would often save whatever she had given him, rather than consume it in front of her. She wondered if he had sustained other, less obvious injuries than his missing eye.

"There's another one," she gasped, as a shooting star whizzed into oblivion. "I saw two as I walked home."

"Perseids. Next month, you'll see one every few minutes if we get clear skies. Mid-August is the peak time for meteor showers."

"Oh. Are they visible from Switzerland, do you know?"

"Everywhere in the Northern Hemisphere. You going home for a visit?"

She blew a stream of smoke into the air, her focus ranging across the sky. "Yes, but it might be more than a visit. I'm about ready to admit defeat."

"Why?"

"Because I'm behind with my rent, my work is irregular and I spend my weekends flirting with people I don't like in order to eat."

"Oh, poor little Heidi." His tone was scathing.

"You asked, I told you the truth. *Die Dame* has very little work for me, none of my job applications even got a response and the only one who's offering me paid writing is that erotic publisher. I've already turned him down twice."

"Oh, I see. It's beneath such an elegant lady to earn a crust writing something more lowbrow than articles on ski-resorts and fur coats. You have no idea how the world works, do you?"

As always with Jan, she was just one comment away from stubbing out her cigarette and leaving him to fester in his own bitterness. "It's not that I think it's beneath me. I just can't do it. You may think of me as a scarlet woman, sexually adventurous and wildly experienced, but I'm not. I've only been with two men in my lifetime. The first time I read any erotica was before I got married and only then to learn what was expected of me. I didn't like it one tiny bit. The sad fact of the matter is that I don't have the background or imagination to write what they're looking for. For example, I struggle to find the appropriate terminology for people's ... parts."

Jan began to laugh, a painful, racking sound. Finally, he caught his breath. "How many words does he want?"

"More than 500 and under 1,000. Nothing too graphic but steamy enough to satisfy his clients, whoever they might be. I haven't the faintest idea how to write that kind of smutty stuff."

"If I do a couple for you, will I get half the fee?" He lit a cigarillo and held the match aloft, casting a warm glow on his remaining eye.

A dozen reasons why that would be a bad idea flashed through her mind, but she made a rapid decision. "Depends how much editing I have to do. If it takes me an hour to knock it into shape, we'll split it 60-40. But if it's just a matter of light corrections, you get half. How soon can you deliver?"

"Depends when my muse comes to me. But I should have something for you by tomorrow."

"Are you serious? That would be great! Then I can reply to him on Monday morning. If he decides to publish, we get paid by return post." She yawned. "Time for bed now, but I'll come up here tomorrow night."

"Sweet dreams, Heidi."

"You too, Jan."

15

Summer 1927, Berlin

Of all the many shapes Eloise fantasised her saviour might take, the one guise she had not foreseen was a one-eyed man with a filthy imagination. When she first transcribed Jan's erotic stories, she was shocked, incredulous and even though she would admit it to no one, somewhat aroused. Without changing anything other than grammar and punctuation, she sent all three to Dietmar, with a brief note to say she was trying something different.

Dietmar's reply arrived the very next morning, complete with full payment, enthusing about what 'she' had written. He could not be happier. Please send more like that, he urged, especially the last one. He would publish as many as she could produce.

Eloise kept her promise and split the money equally between herself and Jan. She also gave him a clean notebook, some pencils and a sharpener.

"He loved them and wants more," she said, drawing the

colander across the alley. "Here's your half of the money and his letter so you can read it for yourself."

His face impassive, he withdrew the letter and read it slowly. Then he counted out the notes and folded them into his pocket. Only then did he look at her, half his mouth curving upwards. "Not bad." He picked up the notepad, his expression reverting to its usual scowl. "But I don't need your charity."

"It's not charity, you impossible man. The reason I want you to use a decent notebook and proper pencils is to save my eyesight. It took me ages to decipher what you wrote and I don't have hours to waste on what is actually a side-line to my career."

He lifted one eyebrow. "Your career?"

"Yes, I sent off another three pitches this morning and one of them is bound to succeed. So what do you say? Can we give Dietmar what he wants?"

"I'll do my best."

What with a commission from *Deutsche Elite*, two pieces for *Die Mode* and a regular income from Dirty Dietmar, July turned out to be a relatively healthy month in financial terms. She filed her last article the day before she left for Fribourg and returned home to finish her packing. Hildegard and Lili were eating pumpernickel with cheese and pickles in the kitchen. Eloise's erratic hours meant they had long given up the routine of sharing the cooking, although sweet-natured Lili sometimes offered her a plate of whatever she had made.

"Hello, ladies! Have you had a good week?"

"Hello, Eloise! Yes, we have. Who wouldn't in this lovely weather? What about you? Are you all ready for your trip?"

Eloise flopped into the spare chair. "Nowhere near. I will sit down for two minutes, then I have to tackle my luggage."

Hildegard poured her a cup of tea. "If you need a hand

carrying things to the station, I am walking that way tomorrow morning."

"It's kind of you to offer, Hilde, but I have so much stuff, I'm getting a taxi. I'll give you a lift as far as the station, if you like."

Before Hildegard could respond, Lili burst out, "Levi delivered the post before you arrived. There are two letters for you and one is from *Vogue*!" She thrust two envelopes into Eloise's hand.

The usual from Dietmar but the other was in a hand she didn't recognise. As Lili said, the stationery was marked as from *Vogue* magazine.

"Aren't you going to open it?" Lili's blue eyes were huge.

"Perhaps Eloise would prefer to read her correspondence in privacy," said Hildegard, but could not conceal her own curiosity.

Eloise slid a knife under the flap of the envelope and withdrew a sheet of quality writing paper.

Dear Eloise

It was a pleasure to meet you a few weeks back at Genevieve's dinner. Considering how 'merry' we all were, I am amazed I managed to hold on to your business card. My good fortune that I did, because our conversation stuck in my mind. We talked about the dearth of German publications for women and saw an opportunity to address a particular demographic. Unfortunately at the time, I was unable to discuss my upcoming venture, but now I have permission to approach people. Hence my letter. Early next year, we are launching the German version of Vogue. *This will not be a translation of the American or French magazine, although some material will be shared. German* Vogue *will be targeted to the German market, with a central focus on Berlin.*

I am seeking a team of experienced writers and illustrators to produce the highest quality material on a regular basis. The planned publication schedule is for three issues per month. Please understand that were you still a staff writer at Die Dame, *I would not have approached you. It is unethical and immoral to poach other editors' staff. Yet you are freelance, as I understand it. If that is still the case and you are interested in being part of our permanent staff, I want to invite you for an interview. This would be with me and two of my colleagues in the first two weeks of September. Please let me know at your earliest convenience if this is a possibility.*

With friendly greetings

Irmgard Baum

The top of Eloise's head seemed to be floating somewhere near the ceiling. *Vogue*? A staff writing job at *Vogue*? She clapped her hand over her mouth to stifle wild laughter.

"What is it?" asked Lili, her face already wreathed in smiles.

"Ladies, you are looking at a future staff writer of German *Vogue*. Assuming I pass the interview, that is. Oh, heavens, I cannot believe my enormous good fortune! Who would have thought such an opportunity could arise from accidentally joining a divorce party? Oh, Lili, I am saved!" She jumped up, caught Lili's hand and waltzed her around the room.

"A divorce party?" asked Hildegard, with an indulgent smile.

"It's a long story involving lesbians and shooting stars. To think I was considering returning home to Fribourg, with my tail between my legs, ready to admit defeat! The job is not mine yet, I shouldn't get ahead of myself. But can you imagine?" She released Lili. "Never mind tea, this calls for a very small celebration!"

She ran to her room and pulled out her trunk, where she had squirreled away a half bottle of champagne. The man who had given it to her, she couldn't recall his name, had been 'hypnotised by her sapphire eyes'. In the kitchen, she popped the cork and poured a little into three tumblers, for a lack of flutes. Lili was already flushed pink with excitement and she hadn't yet touched a drop.

"I never before drank champagne in my life," she gasped.

"It's no different to Sekt, Lili. Congratulations, Eloise, good luck with the interview and remember us when you are rubbing shoulders with the glamorous set."

They toasted *Vogue*, Eloise, Berlin and each other, and laughed so hard even Hildegard wiped her eyes.

"What's going on in here?" Veronika stood in the doorway, perfumed and lipsticked and wearing a dancing dress.

"Eloise has an interview with *Vogue*!" breathed Lili. "And we're drinking champagne!"

"That's wonderful news, my friend!" She switched her unlit cigarette to her left hand to shake Eloise's right. "I wish you all the success in the world. Is there any champagne left?"

"Yes, just a drop," said Hildegard. "I'll get you a glass."

They toasted again, this time to Charlottenweg, and stood there smiling at each other for a moment until Veronika looked up at the clock.

"I'm late already. Have a fine weekend, one and all. *Schönen Abend*."

They wished her the same, Hildegard began washing up and Eloise excused herself to continue packing.

Lili reached out to touch her arm. "Don't forget the other letter."

"Thank you. If I don't see you in the morning, have a very good month and I'll see you in September."

The letter was from Dietmar and must contain the most recent payment. She ran up the stairs to see Jan's spot on the fire escape empty. She dropped the unopened letter into the colander and scribbled a note on the back. *All yours this time. See you in two weeks.*

Then she went downstairs to face her packing.

. . .

Her father's birthday party was a special occasion, not least because his whole extended family made the journey to Fribourg. She met long-forgotten cousins, ancient aunts and an entire gaggle of children she hadn't known existed. The mood was cheerful and summery, one whole weekend of celebrations. Under different circumstances, Eloise would have scoffed her way along the buffet, making up for all those nights going to bed hungry. But as a *Vogue* staff writer, she had to pay attention to her figure. Long, lean and svelte was the aspiration.

Occupied with the party preparations, social duties and post-event gossip, her parents did not subject her to a series of lectures. On the one occasion they raised the subject of her coming home, she played her trump card. Even they had heard of *Vogue*. She might have exaggerated a tiny bit, making it sound as if the job was already hers, but she would move heaven and hell to make it so. The children were sweet, if a little distant. They answered politely when she asked about the dolls' house, German language camp or Laurent's building blocks, but she could not shake the feeling they were humouring her. Neither showed any inclination to seek out her company, although they practically smothered Bastian the minute he crossed the threshold.

Mentioning her disappointment to Charlotte would only invite a lecture on maternal responsibilities, so she kept her bruised feelings to herself until Seraphine invited her to take the air. Little Etta sat in her perambulator, gurgling and squeaking to herself, while the two women strolled along the riverbank.

"She's a very calm child," said Eloise, watching reflections from the river dance across Etta's face.

"Yes. The complete opposite to Julius. If he's not talking at the top of his voice, he's dragging a stick along the railings or throwing stones into a bucket. Anything to make a noise. It's as if he needs to constantly remind us of his presence."

"Perhaps it's a girl thing. Sylvia is a quiet little creature, whereas Laurent thunders around the place like a baby elephant."

"Bastian tells me you two were quite the opposite. According to his account, he was a little angel whilst you were the troublemaker. I find that hard to believe."

"What a tell-tale!" Eloise laughed. "I'd love to deny it, but my parents and Charlotte would soon confirm the worst. Bastian was the sweetest boy, always smiling and quite happy to sit alone, playing with his toys. Whereas I yearned for adventure, thrills and spills, anything to ease the boredom. I dragged him into most of my hare-brained schemes and he usually came off worst. Every childhood scar my brother bears is either directly or indirectly attributable to me, I'm ashamed to say."

"How lucky you were to have each other. Currently, Julius shows more interest in the dog than his sister, but I hope that will change." Her face softened. "Mothers! We always want something more from our children."

"I'd settle for anything. Sylvia and Laurent behave as if I'm a visiting aunt, not their mother. Getting one syllable more than a yes or no out of them is like pulling teeth. I know, I know, since I have been absent for months, I can expect nothing less. But how am I to build a relationship with my offspring *and* pursue a career?"

A cloud crossed Seraphine's face. "I don't know. A rapport is not something you can force. Perhaps you need to let it develop naturally. Be yourself and if they like that person, they will be drawn to you. One thing I can say is that the relationship between my mother and me improved immeasurably once I moved out. Distance is not always a bad thing."

Eloise released a huge sigh. "I hope you're right. All I can do is work hard and hope to make them proud of me."

"You wait. This time next year you'll hear them boasting to

their friends in the playground. 'My mother works for a major fashion magazine in Berlin. Not just any magazine, but German *Vogue*. She's every bit a New Woman!' You'll be a badge of honour."

The thought filled Eloise with optimism. "You're a good person, Seraphine. I'm lucky to have a sister-in-law I can talk to about anything."

"Thank you. I am grateful to have married into a warm and welcoming family. What about your friends in Berlin? From your letters, you seem to have quite a social life."

Eloise thought of Lili and Hildegard, of Veronika and Jan, of Martha, Friedrich and the lesbians at The Dorian Grey. "My friends in Berlin are a wonderful, if wildly different bunch, and quite unlike anyone else I've ever met. To use that classic Swiss observation, they're special."

With promises to return at Christmas, Eloise took her leave of Fribourg. Her case was heavier than ever, filled with cans of food, packets of oats, rice and barley, bars of chocolate and a bag of fruit her mother had pressed upon her. But the real weight came from her brand new Merz typewriter. Her father could not have made a better choice of present and she was touched by his thoughtfulness.

"Well, a *Vogue* journalist can't just write on any old thing. I'm proud you stuck at something and made a success of yourself. My children are very different but all strong-willed. Just like their father," he'd said.

The minute she arrived in Charlottenweg on Saturday evening, she cleared a space for the Merz Simplex on her desk and spent twenty minutes admiring it from every angle. She regretted the fact her housemates were away because she was itching to show someone. Instead, she took all her canned food and some chocolate for her housemates into the kitchen and sat down to read the post.

The only letter she cared about was the one from *Vogue*. There, in black and white was the confirmation of the interview date. She had eight days to prepare. She skimmed the remaining mail, another commission from *Deutsche Elite,* two rejections from other magazines, a wheedling request from Dietmar and a postcard from Hannelore, who was happily living and working in Brussels. The attractive picture and necessity for brevity gave her an idea. Why not send postcards to her children? One each, chosen for her or his particular interests and a jolly update from their mother on the back. They could start their own collection. It was a fine notion and she got up to make a note in her diary. As she crossed the hallway, she heard voices on the step outside and a key turned in the lock.

The door opened and she was startled to see Hildegard and Lili enter the hall. Her presence obviously took them by surprise, to the extent that Lili released a little squeak of alarm.

"Eloise! Thank heavens!" said Hildegard.

"Hello, ladies. I wasn't expecting you on a Saturday evening, but I'm happy you're here." She noted their miserable expressions. "Is everything all right?"

Lili promptly burst into tears and Hildegard guided her into a kitchen chair. "Sit down, Lili and take some deep breaths. Put the kettle on, would you, Eloise? I must check all is well next door and then I will explain everything."

To the sound of Lili's exhausted sobs, Eloise made a pot of tea and then sat beside her, stroking her shoulder and offering her own handkerchief to replace the sodden rag the girl was using.

Hildegard returned, her face drawn and hollow. In response to Lili's upturned face, she gave a small smile and a nod. "No change, still sleeping. Thank you for the tea, Eloise. We were up all night. Lili and I spent this morning at the hospital and the rest of the day at the police station. It has been the most draining twenty-four hours of my life."

"Horrible," said Lili, reaching for a cup with shaky hands. "Too awful for words."

"Do we have any sugar?" asked Hildegard. "After nothing to eat since last night, I for one feel quite weak."

"I brought you some chocolate from Switzerland. Here, eat this. You too, Lili. It will give you strength."

She gave them a moment to savour the sweetness and boiled the kettle for another pot. Whatever the problem was, it would take some time.

"This is more welcome than you can imagine, Eloise, and I am so very relieved to see you. Let me start at the beginning. Lili, can you bear it, or would you rather go and lie down? You are worryingly pale."

"No, I want to hear what you have to say. Everything is such a muddle I can't be sure what happened myself."

"Very well. I shall start at the beginning for all our sakes." She took a sip of tea. "Last night, Lili and I were eating dinner when we heard a dreadful commotion from Ruth's half of the building. Screams and cries and the most terrifying sounds of running boots, then something hit our connecting door with such force I feared it might collapse."

Lili whimpered.

"Then a gunshot rang out. For a second, there was silence, followed by heavy footsteps running off into the distance. We sat here, frozen with fright until we heard a woman crying. I braved the door and found Ruth kneeling beside Levi. A group of thugs had chased him home, burst in after the poor man and attacked him in his own house. Ruth fired a shot over their heads and they fled. We tended Levi's wounds and Lili suspects he may have more than one broken rib. Despite all our entreaties, he refused to go to the hospital. Thanks to Lili's first-aid training, we were able to patch him up and make him as comfortable as possible. Ruth gave us a little sherry for our nerves and we returned to our stew."

"That poor man," interjected Lili. "They beat him with sticks!" Her eyes filled with tears once more.

"Don't upset yourself, my dear. We ate cold stew and were in the middle of washing up when we heard the sound of breaking glass from next door. We rushed to help and saw the windows of both reception rooms smashed in, Ruth white with shock, the revolver in her hand and bricks lying on the carpet."

"Bricks wrapped in flags!"

"The flag of the National Socialists, I'm sure you have seen it. Red, white and black."

Realisation dawned in Eloise's mind. "I know the one. Are you saying they attacked Levi because he's Jewish?"

"There is no doubt. On Ruth's front door, we found the Star of David daubed in yellow paint, marking the house as a Jewish residence."

Eloise gasped. "No! Surely not here!"

"You can see for yourself," said Hildegard. "Because try as we might, we could not erase the symbol in its entirety. Ruth called some colleagues and a group of men came with wooden panels to block the windows. Otherwise, she and Levi would have been exposed to whatever those violent thugs decided to do next." She stopped to drink some tea and rub her eyes.

"What a nightmare for you all!" Eloise reached out to squeeze her friends' arms.

"That was only the start," said Lili, resting her forehead in her palm.

"Indeed. It must have been almost one o'clock in the morning by the time we retired to our own beds, quite worn out by the shock. I fell into a deep sleep until Lili banged on my door around two hours later. Lili?"

The girl's expression when she realised it was her turn to assume control of the story was the epitome of stoicism.

"Unlike Hilde, I found it hard to let go of the evening's tension. I lay awake for a long while and even heard Veronika come in, bumping her way up the stairs to her own room. It was very soon after that when I heard a strange clanging from the fire escape. Obviously, I was terrified the thugs had returned to attack the rear of the property and were marching up to our bedrooms. But it wasn't the sound of boots, more like a bell. Then something hit my window. And again. Not bricks, but pebbles. Someone was trying to attract my attention. So I opened the curtains."

"You were very courageous," said Hildegard.

"Thank you. I opened the curtains and saw nothing below. Then a flash drew my eye to the upper floor of the building opposite. It was that man with the eye patch. He's always up there so one hardly notices him. But he was waving his arms about and pointing above my head, saying words I could not hear. I stuck my head out of the casement and listened. His voice was hoarse and indistinct but he said, 'Veronika is dying! Help her!'

"I unlocked my door and ran upstairs to find Veronika collapsed at the foot of her bed, having some kind of seizure. She was spasming and bleeding from her nostrils. Her eyes were rolled back in her head. I have never seen anything like it, nor did I know how to treat such a person. I woke Hilde and we made the decision to take the poor woman to hospital." She looked at Hildegard for confirmation. "Around three o'clock, I believe?"

"Yes, certainly after three. We dressed in whatever was at hand, then I carried Veronika downstairs while Lili ran into the street to find a taxi. At the hospital, they told us it was a drug overdose and asked us all kinds of questions about what she had taken. Naturally, we had no idea, but they regarded us with disgust. Twice they told us she would likely die and if not, suffer serious brain damage. Finally my patience snapped and I told them we were good neighbours trying to help someone we barely knew. After that, they left us alone. We waited until quarter past eleven this morning until a nurse said Veronika was alive and we should come back during visiting hours."

"Alive? Is that all?" The words 'brain damage' ricocheted around her mind.

Lili glanced up at the clock, biting her lip. "One can visit between five and seven in the evening. We only left the police station an hour ago and now it's too late."

Eloise had plenty of questions about the police station, but judged her housemates to be completely worn out. "You two have been heroic and I take my hat off to your mettle and sense of neighbourly duty. Now it's my turn. You go to bed and get a good night's rest. I will ensure our house is secure tonight. Tomorrow morning I will offer assistance to Levi and Ruth, then present myself at the hospital promptly at five o'clock to ask for news of Veronika. In the evening, I will cook dinner for us all. That way we can all recover our equilibrium for the week ahead."

Hildegard blinked hard. "Thank you, Eloise. I am truly glad you are home." She left the kitchen and trudged upstairs.

Once her footsteps had faded and her bedroom door closed, Lili looked at Eloise with bloodshot, swollen eyes. "Will you also tell the man on the fire escape? He saved Veronika's life."

"I will. Goodnight, Lili, sleep well and please don't worry. I'll watch over us all."

Eloise embraced her, noting how fragile she felt. After the girl had gone, she sat for a moment, thinking about Veronika,

Levi and Ruth. Then her maternal side took charge. These people needed her. She checked her own bedroom windows and bolted the front door. Back in the kitchen, she grated an apple, mixed it with water and oats, added some cinnamon and covered it with a plate. She gathered some cleaning equipment for tomorrow morning, tossed a few items into a net bag and crept up the stairs.

16

September 1927, Berlin

Jan was waiting.

"Do you know how she is?" he whispered.

She kept her voice equally low, conscious of her sleeping housemates. "Alive, apparently. That's all the nurse told them. I'm going to the hospital tomorrow to find out more." She lit a candle to be able to see the pulley. "Oh, what happened here?" The colander dangled from one side, the rope used to convey it back and forth now broken and limp.

"I pulled too hard, trying to get their attention, and snapped the cord. That's why I had to throw shards of glass at the blonde one's window."

"Thank God you did. The blonde one, whose name is Lili, woke Hildegard and between them they took Veronika to hospital. She'd overdosed on something. Without you, she most certainly would have died."

They perched on opposite sides of the alley, smoking and thinking. A night breeze fluttered the candle flame and wafted their exhalations up to the stars. From the streets below, stone and asphalt released residual heat, like a cooling oven, and the steps on which they sat emitted irregular clanks and pings as the metal contracted.

Eloise stood up. "Long day today and another tomorrow. I'll come up to tell you how she is when I get home."

"I'll be waiting. By the way, I have more stories for you."

"Pleased to hear it. Dietmar is champing at the bit. Look, I'm going to throw this bag over, will you catch it? It contains breakables."

He stood up with a good deal of effort.

"*Achtung, fertig, los!*" She swung the bag forwards, back again for momentum and across the empty space between them. He caught it with outstretched hands and clutched it to his chest.

"*Danke*, Eloise. *Gute Nacht.*"

She blew out the candle and closed the door, wondering what had happened to Heidi.

On Sunday, Eloise threw herself into domestic duties. She cleaned Veronika's room thoroughly until the stench of vomit and urine was barely detectable. Whilst on the top floor, she repaired the pulley between the fire escapes and righted the colander, securing it with double knots. She worked alone in Jan's absence. Downstairs, she served breakfast for her housemates, who both seemed restored by a long sleep. Thankfully, she had no need to do laundry or visit the public baths. She cleaned the kitchen and cooked a hearty risotto for lunch, enough for six people. The extra portions were for Ruth and Levi.

The caretaker's appearance came as an unpleasant surprise, despite Lili's description. His face was swollen and shockingly bruised, and it was clear the man was suffering a good deal of pain. Eloise promised to find something that would help. Ruth appeared nervy and ill at ease, smoking one cigarette after another, but ate the risotto washed down with several glasses of sherry. With some flattery and an appeal to her decency, Eloise persuaded her landlady to call one of her grocery suppliers. They delivered handsomely. A rich chicken and vegetable stew was bubbling on the hob by the time Eloise left for the hospital,

Veronika was conscious, but only just. The effort of opening her eyelids seemed to exhaust her and her jaw dropped, revealing stained teeth. Her body beneath the hospital shift was horribly thin, her collarbones and wrists protruding as if covered by wet tissue paper, not flesh. A doctor walked by, his head bent to read some notes, and Eloise adopted her most precise Hanoverian accent.

"Excuse me, doctor, I can see you're busy. My name is Frau de Fournier. My husband and I are most concerned about our tenant. We understand she was admitted yesterday as an emergency but are yet to comprehend what happened. Could you enlighten me?"

"She's your tenant?"

"Yes, Veronika lives in one of the Charlottenstrasse rooms we let to respectable ladies. She is unfailingly polite, pays her rent on time and has never caused us any concern."

"Frau de Fournier, this woman suffered a seizure as a result of ingesting an excess of cocaine, morphine and alcohol. She has a venereal disease and breathing issues due to her smoking habit. Her life expectancy if she continues in this way will be less than one year. My apologies, but the word 'respectable' is not one I would use. In your shoes, I would serve her notice."

Eloise bristled. "When will she be released?"

"As far as I'm concerned, you can take her home tomorrow evening. We need this bed for serious cases. Good day to you." He stalked away, pomposity personified.

She kissed Veronika's pale forehead and whispered in her ear. "I'm taking you home. Rest and recover. Soon you shall sleep in your own bed."

Her eyelids flickered but did not open.

Eloise caught the tram to Charlottenstrasse, tightly wound with tension, and filled with outrage at high-handed judgemental men. Compare him to Bastian, the essence of decency, tolerance and good manners. If only he were here to treat Veronika. An idea fluttered in the back of her mind, yet refused to take any recognisable shape.

At the house, she served bowls of stew for Hildegard and Lili. Before taking the pan next door, Eloise ran up two flights of stairs, closed the curtains against Jan's observation and rifled through Veronika's bedside drawers. As expected, she located a clutch of morphine capsules. She weighed them in her hand considering whose need was the greatest. It didn't take long. She tucked them all into her apron pocket, threw open the windows and trotted downstairs towards Levi.

Circumstances turned the house upside down. Living on the second storey was now impossible for Veronika. She needed to be on the ground floor, near a bathroom. Eloise had to move. She spent all of Monday packing her belongings and relocating upstairs. No one helped, since Hildegard and Lili were at work and Ruth was supervising the glazier. The amount of clothes and accessories Veronika owned would never fit into a normal-sized room, so Eloise packed two-thirds of the woman's things into trunks and pushed them right under the attic eaves. Three rugs still carried a foul whiff, the dusty curtains stank of smoke and the stained mattress had bedbugs. With Ruth's permission, she threw them all out.

By Monday evening, her vacant room awaited the patient.

She chose a comfortable outfit, clean underwear and the simplest pair of shoes she could find, then set off for the hospital to collect Veronika. The woman was meek and biddable, if not particularly coherent. The nurse gave Eloise medicines to help cure the infection and advised a healthier lifestyle with as much conviction as if she was whistling into the wind. The taxi driver ranted about communists, oblivious to his uninterested passengers, and dropped them outside the back door. Eloise opened her red velvet purse and paid the fare while Hildegard and Lili rushed to Veronika's aid. In response to all their solicitous enquiries, she merely smiled and said, "Thank you." Once she was in bed and apparently resting, Eloise left her and joined her housemates in the kitchen for sardines on toast and whispered discussions.

A chameleon adapts to its environment, changing colour to blend in. During those topsy-turvy days, Eloise wore several hats. In the mornings, she was a nurse, aiding Veronika's recovery. In the afternoons, she edited erotic stories and prepared an evening meal for Hildegard and Lili. After dinner, she read articles on contemporary fashion, prepared interview questions and occasionally slipped out to meet a friend for gossip. The attic room suited her perfectly. Her typewriter sat at her desk below the window overlooking Charlottenstrasse. The season was about to change, one could see the signs. A chilly breeze shook loose golden leaves which fell at people's feet. Horse-chestnuts, burst from their spiky jackets, lay on the ground gleaming like oiled leather. Low afternoon sun sharpened the colours, turning the grass a brilliant emerald, throwing long shadows from figures on the street below. All Berlin passed under her nose as she pondered modern hats, stylish footwear, beaded bags and how elegance was an attitude. The windows facing the alley were covered with gauzy nets to admit light but deter her neighbour's gaze. In the evenings, she would sit with Veronika for an hour, smoke some cigarettes on the fire escape with Jan, and type late into the night before falling asleep on the firm new mattress courtesy of Ruth.

"We could send you home and say wait for our decision, but I see no need. We love your ideas, admire your energy and your experience speaks for itself. Eloise, we want you to be a part of German *Vogue*."

For a moment, Eloise could not breathe, fearing the words she was hearing were an echo of her fantasies.

"Really? You mean it? This is a dream come true. Thank you so much, Irmgard, Karin, Georges, I take this as an honour."

"We're honoured to have you. Let me show you around and find you a desk. We're planning a launch issue for next April and two of your articles will fit the theme. Can you start office hours on the first of October?"

Eloise floated around the offices. The floor space was smaller than that of *Die Dame*, yet somehow more spacious, probably because there were only four people in the room. She spotted a table between two windows, similar to her home desk, which was flooded with morning sunshine.

"How many people are going to work here, Irmgard? I'd hate to take the place of an illustrator who needs the light."

"Don't worry about that. We're using the same artwork as Paris, likely the same covers too. Our unique angle is the Berlin interpretation. Where can we find haute couture in Berlin, how should adapt the latest style to the streets of this city, and the establishments in which to be seen. We use the French content with a German twist."

"I see." Eloise considered her words with care. "You mention French *Vogue* in terms of Paris. Does that mean German *Vogue*, in a similar vein, will focus on Berlin? I ask merely because my previous editor warned me against a bias towards the metropolis."

Irmgard placed a hand on Eloise's shoulder. "You have ethics, as well as style! I admire your integrity. Listen to me, my dear. You are a staff writer, given a topic, word count and suggested angle. Editorial decisions are far above both our heads. That said, why not bring ideas to the table? Everything is under consideration. Next, we need to organise business cards and pay attention to your wardrobe. From this day onwards, you are a representative of the most fashionable magazine in the world!"

Her joy lasted until she got off the tram on Charlottenstrasse and saw an ambulance standing outside Ruth's house. She ran across the street, heedless of her own safety, thinking only of the last words she had spoken to Veronika. *Here goes, wish me luck!*

The door to the front of the house was open. Disregarding protocol, Eloise flew up the steps and entered without so much as a knock. A burly man in medical uniform held up a hand to prevent her going any further.

"Stand aside please, lady."

She pressed herself into the study doorway and watched the man and his colleague take a covered stretcher out down the steps and into the waiting vehicle. Through the white noise in her head, she heard sobbing and turned to see Ruth crumpled over her desk, her face covered by a handkerchief. In less than a second, emotions raced through Eloise like a train in a tunnel: relief, shock, sympathy, grief, guilt and self-preservation.

"Ruth, I'm so sorry. Levi was a lovely man. He didn't deserve what happened. Can I do anything for you? Let me get you some tea."

The ambulance was driving away. She closed the front door, slipped into Levi's room and located the remaining morphine capsules, still in his glasses case where she had hidden them. Of the original half dozen, only three remained. She tucked them into her purse and stared at the empty bed, wondering if her actions had hastened his demise.

She returned to her landlady. "On second thoughts, I think you need a sherry. Here, have a glass to steady your nerves."

"He didn't deserve it, Eloise. Levi was a good person. One of the best, in fact. How can this be?" Ruth accepted the schooner and attempted to stem her sobs. "Pour yourself one. We'll drink a toast to a fine man." Her skin seemed ragged and dry, her expression wretched, and wisps of hair spiralled away from her head.

"To Levi!" proposed Eloise, clasping her hand around her glass to hide the fact it contained a mere drop of fortified wine.

"To Levi, may he rest in everlasting peace." In the ensuing silence, tears slipped from the corners of Ruth's eyes, even as she swallowed. "I don't suppose you recall," she hiccuped, "what I said when you arrived. *This house simply could not function without him.* It's the truth. This house cannot function without Levi and neither can I."

Eloise placed a hand on Ruth's arm. "It's natural you should feel this way at the moment. Tomorrow, it will get easier."

Her deep brown eyes fixed on Eloise's face. "It will never get easier. You cannot possibly understand how I feel but that's not your fault. Berlin is no place for people like Levi. No place for people like me. How did we end up this way?" She cried quietly, bent over her sherry.

There was no answer to that. Eloise sat with her until the light faded and switched on some lamps. She closed the door to Levi's room and promised to clear it in the morning. Ruth expressed her thanks in dull tones, and Eloise left to check the other patient.

Somehow, since the weekend dramas, the three women had assumed responsibilities best suited to their personalities. Eloise nursed Veronika, Lili tended Levi and Hildegard took charge of the kitchen, conjuring nourishing meals for six people out of whatever they could muster. That evening should have been a celebration of Eloise's new job, but instead it turned into a vigil. Everyone blamed themselves. Lili's first aid had been insufficient. Hildegard's determination to get Levi to a hospital lacked force. Ruth should have never allowed him onto the streets during a brownshirts' parade. All this self-flagellation was vocalised and countered by the others. Only Eloise kept her mouth shut and dug her nails into her palms. Did morphine kill Levi? Was her kindness actually cruelty? She closed her eyes and told herself that if he died as a result of her actions, it had at least been a peaceful death.

The thought gave her little comfort.

17

Winter 1927, Berlin

Vogue meant escapism in every sense. Released from the gloom of the house, Eloise hurried to the *Zeitungsviertel* and absorbed herself in flights of fancy, unreal perfection, luxurious samples and imaginary women. She inhabited the future, namely next spring, where everyone looked forward with optimism in their eyes. Grey skies, ugly newspaper headlines, unpleasant confrontations in the streets and the drumbeat of political rallies were banished from the office. Here all was beauty, sunshine and distraction.

Eloise's choice of journalistic style was the *feuilleton*, a neat vignette or observation of what was happening in the world. She wrote from a woman's perspective with a contemporary flair targeted at a female readership. Her aim was to reflect the fascinating variety of ladies in Berlin, who redefined womanhood in their own terms. Above her desk was a quote from Johanna Thal, one of her contemporaries at *Die Dame*. It read: 'sartorial beauty no longer depends only on the judgement of the observer, but also on the individuality of the wearer'. In Eloise's eyes, the fact that observer (*der Betrachter*) was a masculine noun and the wearer (*die Trägerin*) feminine seemed apposite.

She wrote about mannequins and models, such as the lovely young Hilde Zimmerman, recently crowned Queen of Fashion. Her portrait of the infamous dancer Anita Berber had only a tangential relationship to fashion, as the woman was better known for what she wasn't wearing. Actress Brigitte Helm, who had recently starred in Fritz Lang's *Metropolis*, was hugely in demand, but thanks to the *Vogue* name, Eloise managed to secure an interview. She constructed a profile of fashion designer Sonia Delaunay, using photographs of her film and theatre costumes. But most of all, her pen sketches were of everywoman. How women made fashion a statement of their own personalities, in the street, at the café, in the office or on the factory floor.

One of her duties, in addition to writing features and observational *flânerie*, was to attract and secure investors. These people provided the magazine's lifeblood: advertisements. In the months leading up to the spring launch, Eloise attended fashion shows, watched beauty contests, accepted invitations to try new cosmetics, visited design houses and charmed businessmen with impressive bank accounts. The social butterfly act was wearying, not to mention a strain on her wardrobe, but she painted her face, changed her accessories, altered a dress and smiled as if she were the face of a toothpaste brand. At least she was doing it for something more important than her next meal. Irmgard was impressed by her dedication and said so after Eloise agreed to represent the magazine at the opening of a new restaurant.

"Are you ever bored, my dear? Don't get me wrong, we're all grateful for the extra effort you put in, but it must become tedious."

"Never. I'd work all the hours God sends to make this magazine a success. If that means batting my eyelashes at wealthy sponsors to raise our social standing, I can bear another late night. Let's not forget, there's always free food."

"Good girl! Eat your fill and take any free samples going."

Eloise didn't need telling twice.

Winter was vile, cold, comfortless and devoid of hope. Lili gave notice in November and departed with a tearful farewell before Christmas. The poor girl had never recovered from the fatal attack on Levi. She jumped whenever the doorbell rang and scoured the newspapers for any stories of unrest on the streets of Berlin. Political clashes between communists and various brutal factions loyal to the National Socialists made the city unpredictable and its citizens insecure. News of the violence spread to other parts of the country, vastly exaggerated enough to cause alarm. It only took a gentle suggestion from her family and Lili returned to Potsdam, where she believed she'd be safer.

And more likely to snag a husband. Eloise chastised herself for even entertaining such a shallow notion.

Rather than find a new tenant, Ruth moved into the room Lili vacated, and locked up her side of the house, saying she could not bear to rattle around alone in her own quarters. While Eloise and Hildegard went out to work, Veronika slept and Ruth rattled around alone in *their* quarters. In the evenings, three of them ate together while Veronika sipped at her hip flask. Once the convalescent had left for work, Eloise smoked a cigarette with Jan until the cold drove her inside. Then she typed out his latest story. Sometimes, she woke in the small hours and heard the low murmurs of Veronika and Jan conversing in the icy moonlight. One night, half-asleep, she mistook the soft whispers in the darkness for a pair of lovers sharing intimacies. In a way, she supposed, that was true.

Eloise missed having a man in her life. Someone whose company would bestow security and respectability, whose conversation would fascinate and whose embrace would make her feel like the most beautiful woman on earth. In the circles she frequented, eligible, successful, good-looking and most importantly, unmarried men were ten a Pfennig. True, the same could be said of beautiful, chic, vivacious and most importantly, young women. With Max, she had enjoyed sex and loved the sensation of being desirable. With her newfound knowledge of erotic literature, she was confident of being a skilled and sophisticated lover. All she needed was a willing partner. She rolled over in bed, and through the chink in the curtains gazed at the night sky. Something flashed across the blackness but no explosion followed. It was not the season for shooting stars and more likely to be some kind of flare set off by a gang of thugs looking for trouble.

Nonetheless, Eloise chose optimism and made a wish. *Please let me meet a nice man. That's all. Thank you and goodnight.*

Maybe it really was a star or a comet or simply a sign from the heavens, because the very next day, she met Otto.

In contrast to other cities, Berlin no longer had a fashion season, but a year-long rolling calendar of events. Significant occasions tumbled into one another with such frequency no journalist could keep up, although some did their best. Early on Friday evening, Eloise hurried away from a show at the Gerson salon in order to watch a new *Konfektionskomödie*, or fashion farce at the cinema. She jumped off the tram, rummaging in her handbag to ensure she had her complimentary ticket, when she heard a shout behind her. Shouts on the street nearly always meant trouble, so she increased her pace, intent on reaching her destination without becoming involved in an altercation. Running footsteps overtook her and a man stepped into her path. He was breathing heavily and holding a red velvet purse.

"That's mine!" she said, pointing an accusatory finger.

"I know," he puffed, handing it over. "A pickpocket took it from your handbag as you left the tram. I saw him do it and raised the alarm. He dropped it and ran off, but so did you."

She checked the purse and found her money still there, along with her cinema ticket. "That was a very honourable thing to do. Thank you."

He removed his hat, took out a handkerchief and ran it over his brow. "You're welcome. Well," he smiled awkwardly, "I won't detain you as you're obviously in a hurry."

Without the shadow of his hat, she saw strong eyebrows, kind eyes, thick blond hair and a high forehead. In an instant, the idea of sitting alone in a dim cinema looking at more pretty clothes lost all its allure.

"I was in a hurry, to tell the truth," she lied, glancing at his ringless left hand. "Mainly to get away from the office. Could I buy you a drink by way of a thank-you? There's a very nice café on the corner. My name is Eloise de Fournier."

"Otto Graz. There's no need to thank me. I acted out of common decency. But it's Friday night and it's getting cold. Why not? I'd be glad to join you for a drink."

It turned out that Herr Otto Graz sold automobiles. Eloise had no interest whatsoever in cars unless as conveyance or fashion accessory, but passion was passion, even if it was for combustion engines. She asked intelligent questions, under the guise of understanding his attraction to the topic. It took a second glass of Riesling before she discovered her companion was unmarried, committed to building his business and at the cutting edge of social change. He invited her to dinner. She accepted, but insisted on paying the drinks bill before they left the café. While they waited at the tram stop, Otto pointed to her handbag.

"Better close that clasp. You've already had one lucky escape today."

She flashed one of her brilliant smiles and noted how he glanced away. She reminded herself she was not trying to charm an investor, even if the alliance would have been mutually beneficial. Tonight, she simply wanted to talk to another human being. In order to do that, she had to drop the act.

"Thank you. I'm afraid I'm a classic journalist, always distracted by a potential story." The tram was approaching. She pulled off her hat, aware her hair would be flattened and shapeless beneath. "The writer is taking a night off. Here is the woman instead. I warn you, it might come as a disappointment."

He took a pace back to allow her onto the tram first. "Let me be the judge of that."

Dinner at a small traditional restaurant no one had ever heard of with unremarkable wine and a complete absence of notable guests was a novelty. It was also unexpectedly refreshing. She savoured her food, relished the wine, forgot about her hair and relaxed into comfortable conversation. For a second, she had the strangest sensation that she was talking to Bastian.

He walked her home, laughing as she demonstrated a mannequin's walk along Charlottenstrasse.

"That cannot be true! You're exaggerating."

"Goodness knows it's accurate. I've seen enough of those poor show ponies. Ogled, poked, groped, criticised and robbed of personality. I wouldn't do that job for all the tea in China."

"Would you say the same of a chorus line?"

Eloise turned to face him, taking his question seriously. "Not at all. Chorus girls dance at a remove, performing a carefully choreographed routine. They deliver what the audience expects, that's all. They are answerable only to the director, not every embittered dowager who resents the fact that designer dresses suit svelte frames and slim ankles. Oh, here I go again. I apologise."

"No need. I asked a question, you answered. Is this where you live?" The street light illuminated boarded-up windows and faded daubs.

"I rent a room at the back. Thank you for walking me home, for dinner and rescuing my purse. I was supposed to watch a film for work but I had a great deal more fun with you. Perhaps I should thank the pickpocket."

"I enjoyed myself enormously. How long is the film playing?"

"A week or two, I imagine. I can see it another time."

"In that case, may I come along? You can introduce me to your world and I can show you mine. There is a great deal of beauty and style in a modern motor car I think you would appreciate. I could even teach you to drive, if you are willing."

"Me behind the wheel of an automobile? What an extraordinary idea! I accept your offer, Otto, which I suspect you might regret. Here's my card and if you are free tomorrow night, I'll be at Kabaret Kino from eight o'clock."

"See you there. Goodnight, Eloise." He bowed, gave a broad grin and walked away towards the main street. No attempt at a kiss or even a shake of her hand. Otto Graz was a most unusual man.

18

Winter 1927–28, Fribourg

At Christmas, Eloise returned to Fribourg for two weeks. This time, she was not the pauper relying on her brother's charity, but a well-paid professional earning decent wages. Coupled with her steady income from Morgengrauen, the pseudonym under which she published Jan's erotica, she was able to afford quality presents for her family and housemates.

Winter was much more enjoyable when one was protected against it. In Berlin, the months between November and March were to be survived. In Fribourg, the season was an excuse for light, warmth, colour and conviviality. Especially when there was a new baby in the family. Seraphine and Bastian had recently been blessed with a little girl. Antonia had her mother's wide eyes and placid demeanour. Every one of her relatives fell in love at first sight.

The house was filled with festivities and laughter, lifting Eloise's spirits and acting as a balm to her soul. She took walks with her brother, played games with the children, ate fine food prepared by other people and attended social events with her parents. Whenever possible, she curled up by the fire with a book. Her father and Bastian channelled all their persuasive abilities into luring her home. Bastian applauded her success and said she had proven herself. Her father pointed out the significance of her children's ages and encouraged her to take an active role in their education. It was time, he believed, she should return to Switzerland. Her mother and sister supported the notion. For the first time, Eloise gave it some serious thought.

With her credentials, it was more than possible she could earn a living wage as a Swiss journalist. Her expenses would dwindle to nothing, laundry and cooking would be someone else's problem, and she could spend her wages on the latest fashions instead of scrag ends of meat at the butcher's shop. Far more importantly, she could cultivate a closer relationship with her children.

Two words pierced the comfortable bubble of future domesticity. The first was *Vogue*. When would she ever get a similar opportunity to work for an international fashion magazine? The German version had not yet launched and its potential was huge. As one of the key staff on a publication, she was in a position to shake the foundations of German publishing. This was the chance she'd been waiting for and her time to shine. On top of all that, working as a journalist made her feel alive like nothing else.

The second word was Otto. One half of her said, 'But nothing has happened'. The other half shook its head with a knowing smile. No, nothing had 'happened' in that she had not fallen into his bed within a month of their first meeting, but everything had happened in the context of a new friendship.

He came with her to the cinema to see *Die Königin des Schrotthaufen*, laughing at the comedy plot and admiring her knowledge of the costumes on display. The next day, they walked through the Tiergarten and took turns mimicking the actors. He surprised her with his observant eye. The visit to his car showroom was rather more intimidating, but his enthusiasm swept her into the moment. Sitting in the driver's seat of a 5,000 Mark Opel Stadt-Coupé, albeit stationary and indoors, was an exhilarating experience. He promised that on her return from Switzerland when the weather improved, he would teach her to drive. Not once had he hinted at romantic inclinations, behaving at all times with complete propriety. She found herself looking forward to their meetings, saving up little stories to amuse him and wondering what it might feel like to kiss those lips.

She was still cogitating on the problem of her career, and no closer to a decision, at Silvester. As tradition dictated, the family ate a fondue and attended the celebrations in the main square to welcome in the New Year. Laurent's face as he stirred the cheese, her mother's laughter as she danced with Sylvia and Seraphine, their neighbours' welcomes and the music playing under the Christmas lights were almost enough to tip the balance.

"It's not so bad, this little place," said her father at her elbow.

She linked her arm in his. "*Klein aber fein*. It might be smaller than a big city but it has plenty of charm."

"That's what I said the day you were born. Two weeks early, impatient as always, you took us all by surprise. A tiny scrap of a thing bursting into the world, with a loud voice and a fierce frown. Then you found the breast and looked up at me with an extraordinarily wise pair of blue eyes. *Klein aber fein*, I said to your mother. Small but perfect."

On New Year's Day, the whole family were eating lunch when her father dropped his fork with a clatter and collapsed. Before the doctor could be summoned, Albert Favre passed away under the dining table.

Eloise's reaction took everyone, including herself, by surprise. She wept with her siblings, comforted her mother, spoke to the doctor and priest, consoled the staff and made arrangements for his wake. Upstairs, she explained to the children that their grandfather was too good for this world and had been taken by God. With a whisper in Sylvia's ear, she encouraged her to take care of Etta. As the youngest family member who understood what had happened, she was the most vulnerable. She asked the same of Laurent with a nod towards Julius, who was busy building a kite.

Bastian was waiting outside the nursery. "Are they ...?"

"Distressed? Naturally. But I offered soothing words and suggested they care for one another. How are you?"

He rubbed a hand over his forehead. "I hardly know. Everyone is in shock, unable to function. Apart from you."

Eloise drew him into an embrace. "That's because it's not my first time."

She stayed on for the funeral. It was an enormous ceremony and she was on duty from morning to night. She, Charlotte and Seraphine moved like nuns through the crowds, offering sustenance and accepting condolences. It was the longest day of her life. It also made up her mind. She would return to Berlin by the end of the week and initiate the departure process. It was time to leave Germany. The thought saddened her, even though she knew it was the only decent course of action.

She announced her decision at breakfast. Julius and Laurent cheered, joined by Etta, who followed her brother's lead regardless of whether she understood why. Sylvia said nothing, her expression doubtful. Bastian, his emotions already fragile, was unable to speak, but nodded with his eyes closed as he clutched

Seraphine's hand. Her mother pressed her palms together and raised her eyes to the ceiling.

"Thank you, Albert," she whispered.

Only Charlotte kept buttering her bread, unimpressed. "Initiate the process? Which could take another month? Two months? Can you assure us you will be home by Easter?"

"That depends. I can promise you I shall wind down my activities in Germany with the intention of returning to Fribourg. If my editor agrees, I will continue to work for *Vogue*. How that might work and how long it will take, I cannot be sure. In the meantime, I trust you and Bastian to assist Mama with the daily routine."

"As opposed to the usual run of things," said Charlotte, with a sharp exhale.

Seraphine's voice, soft and warmed by her smile, added a gentle note to the discussion. "I am very happy to hear you will return, Eloise. It will be a comfort to us all. We are so very proud of you but at the same time, we miss your presence, your energy, your brilliance. In circumstances such as these, you are like a ray of sunlight at dawn."

Dawn. *Morgengrauen*. The reference to her alter ego made her feel strangely soiled under Seraphine's pure gaze.

"Thank you. I shall do my best."

Two days later, she was packing the last few items into her suitcase when a knock came at the door.

"Come in," she called, expecting her mother, who had spent the last few days wandering from room to room, at a complete loss. She remembered that unanchored feeling only too well.

"I apologise for the interruption," said Bastian. "I know you have a lot to do before the train tomorrow morning and I have no wish to be a distraction."

"You are only ever a welcome distraction. Is everything in order?"

"May I?" He indicated one of the chairs beside her writing table.

"Please do. Bastian, is something wrong?"

He hitched up his trousers and sat down, his bearing upright and serious. "Seraphine and I have been talking. My doctor's practice in Brienz was perfect for a young couple and their first child. Now that we are a family of three, we need more space. Moreover, I would like to raise my children in a city, ideally the one where I grew up. Papa's death throws a huge amount of responsibility onto Mama's shoulders and I feel as the man of the family, I should be here to help. The third factor which affects my thinking is the empty de Fournier property for which Papa failed to find a buyer. I am aware that house and land represents both an inheritance and an emotional attachment for you. This is why I would like to propose ..."

She dropped the shawl she was folding and rushed to sit opposite, leaning forward to rest her hands on his knees. "Yes! What a wonderful idea! Oh, Bastian, I can think of nothing finer than you and your family living under that roof, within walking distance of Maman and Charlotte. Our children will live close to their cousins and you will become a city doctor. It's perfect."

His smile spread across his face and he placed his hands atop hers. "Do you really think so? To me, it seems ideal, but I am aware my perspective is not wholly altruistic. What I can promise is that I will pay you proper rent and maintain the property to the highest standards. When you feel ready to return, there is enough room for both of us and our children. Unless of course you would prefer sole occupancy?"

"Not at all. The idea is preposterous, as is the idea of rent. You would be doing me a favour by living there. This is so exciting, don't you think? Can you imagine us all together under one roof? What a joy! How clever of you to devise such a plan. When do you think you can move?"

He got to his feet and planted a kiss on her brow, then went to stand by the window. "I must be honest and tell you the seed of this idea was planted by Charlotte. I discussed it with Seraphine and neither of us could see a disadvantage, other than the idea might offend you. I confess I am greatly relieved to see you embrace the notion. As for timescale, I would first have to find a replacement to take over. That may be relatively simple as my junior doctor is eager to take on a practice of his own. If everything falls into place, we could be installed within a month." He turned. "Eloise?"

"Yes?"

"I realise that my permanent return to Fribourg removes much of the imperative for you to do the same. Nonetheless, I hope with all my heart you will return. We all miss you very much."

She moved into his embrace, welcoming the weight of his chin on her crown. "I miss you too. I will come home, I promise. It's just I have unfinished business."

"Unfinished business?" He squashed her ribs as if extracting secrets. "Professional or personal?"

She released a muffled gasp, laughing at their childhood technique to make one another confess. "Both have potential."

Brother and sister gazed out at falling snow as it blanketed all the familiar beloved shapes of their world in a pale shroud.

19

Winter – Spring 1928, Berlin

The taxi to Charlottenweg on a Saturday afternoon took twice as long as usual due to demonstrations along main thoroughfares. The taxi driver simply shrugged when she asked who was angry about what.

"Whatever their leaders tell them to be angry about. Commies, the government, loose women, brownshirts, the French, uptight women, blackshirts, artists, Jews or the price of beer. I sympathise with the last one."

On the approach to the house via a backstreet, she found she was holding her breath. Yet there was no ambulance or broken glass, just glowing lamps in the windows. The taxi driver helped her heave her suitcases up the steps and she tipped him generously.

"Have a beer on me."

"*Dankeschön, Fräulein.*"

With a glance up at the fire escape, which was empty, Eloise let herself in. The sound of a rancorous dispute reached her ears and she closed the door with a firm bang to announce her arrival.

Hildegard stuck her head out of the kitchen. "Eloise! Thank heavens we can get some common sense in this house at last. Come in here, please."

"Hello, Hildegard. Did you have a pleasant Christmas? Happy New Year to you too." She did not speak the words aloud, but put down her bags and gathered her courage.

At the kitchen table sat Veronika, smoking a cigarette. This was an alarming sign. Smoking was strictly forbidden in all shared areas of the house. It was Ruth's only house rule. Of Ruth herself, there was no sign. The tension in the room was similar to that on the streets, seething with the threat of harsh words or provocative actions.

"Is something wrong?"

Both women spoke at once, so that Eloise was unable to decipher one clear sentence.

"... the minute her back was turned ..."

"... will pay rent ..."

"This house ..."

"Will you shut up and let me ..."

"... respectable young ladies!"

"You have no right ..."

Eloise clamped her hands over her ears, but that did not remove the spectacle of furious gestures and faces ugly with anger. She closed her eyes. When she opened them again, the atmosphere had changed and both women were staring over her shoulder.

In the doorway stood Jan, his fists balled and eye glaring. It took a second to comprehend how something she regarded as an architectural feature of the house opposite was now in their kitchen. It was as if the tram stop had appeared in the corridor.

Eloise sensed an opportunity to defuse the situation by

claiming centre stage. "I'm sorry I'm late. On New Year's Day, my father had a heart attack at the dining table and before we could summon medical assistance, he passed away. My family substituted Christmas decorations for funeral mourning. Today, I spent seven hours on the railway and another alarming hour crossing Berlin to avoid political demonstrations. Now I would like a cup of tea and an explanation for all this shouting. Jan, please take a seat. Hildegard, would you be so good as to boil the kettle? Put that cigarette out, Veronika. You know the rules."

Veronika obeyed and placed a hand on her breastbone. "I'm sorry for your loss."

"Yes," said Jan, limping to the nearest chair. "Sorry."

"That's shocking news. Please accept my sincere condolences. Come sit down and I will make us all some tea." Hildegard busied herself with cups, the kettle and tea caddy.

In the moment's peace she had imposed, she thanked them for their kind words and bowed her head while planning her strategy. When she looked up, it was directly at Jan.

"Hello. It's rather strange meeting you without an alley between us. May I ask you to summarise the situation?"

Jan's eye strayed to Veronika's cigarettes, but instead of smoking, he folded his arms across his chest. The pulsing of muscles between wrists and elbow indicated he was still clenching his fists. "He threw me out. Not just me, all of us. They want the house."

"Who's he, us and they?"

"The landlord kicked me and all the other tenants out just after Christmas. I don't know who 'they' are, but I do know they won't take no for an answer."

"It's the ..." Veronika began.

Eloise held up a hand. "Just a moment. I do want your side of the story, just as soon as I've listened to Jan. Your landlord asked you to leave after Christmas. He didn't give you notice?"

Jan gave her a scornful glare. "No. His place, his rules. Most people won't rent to men who can't work and ..."

"If you can't work, then how do you pay rent?"

"Hildegard, please! So he threw you and all the other tenants out in the middle of winter? Where did he expect you to go?"

Jan's shoulders almost touched his ears. "We can die in the street for all he cares. Some of them probably will."

That sobering thought settled on the party. Hildegard poured the tea and everyone reached for the warmth.

"I told *her* I had to get out," Jan continued, pointing at Veronika. "She said there was a spare room here, just until I could find something permanent. But *she* reacted as if I had the plague!" He glared at Hildegard.

"That's because this house ..."

"... is open to anyone who pays rent!"

"*Nein!*"

"*Doch!*"

"Enough, ladies! This is not a Hamburg fish market. In any case, neither of your opinions matters. Ruth is the landlady and her decision is final. Rather than continuing this uncivilised shouting match, should someone ask what she thinks?"

No one met her eyes.

"What?"

Hildegard pushed her chair back and lifted a pile of post from Eloise's kitchen shelf. The topmost item was a sealed envelope marked PRIVATE AND CONFIDENTIAL.

Dear Eloise

Excuse the hurried nature of this communication. My friends will be here to collect me and my belongings within the hour. The house is under siege by those who feel I do not belong in Berlin. I considered leaving after Levi's death but convinced myself to stand firm.

Since then, I have been harassed, insulted, refused service in shops and cafés which previously welcomed my custom. Add to this broken windows and ugly slogans painted on my walls, poison pen letters and a complete dissolution of my social circle.

In short, I must leave the city, perhaps even the country until this evil wave of violent prejudice is over. Until that time, I shall close my house and remove one of their targets. However, I feel strongly that my tenants should not suffer. The rear of the building attracts no such aggressive attention, and thus I am happy for things to continue as they are.

May I ask you to act as my right-hand woman? Collect the rent, deposit it into my account (details below), ensure the place is kept clean and call on next door's Hauswart *for everyday repairs. All decisions regarding departures and arrivals I entrust to you. For this service, your rent is henceforth written off.*

Under normal circumstances, we could have discussed this but since your return is delayed without word, I can only hope this arrangement is acceptable to you.

Although I have no forwarding address as yet, I will communicate my whereabouts soonest.

With sincere regards and please accept my eternal gratitude.
Ruth Gartner

F ive eyes were watching her as she replaced the letter in its envelope.

"Well?" asked Hildegard. "We already know what the letter says because Ruth explained she was leaving you in charge. Which means this decision is down to you."

Eloise needed some time to consider Ruth's request, to ponder why she had not chosen either of the longer-term tenants and reflect on how this affected her own decision to leave Berlin. There was also the incomprehensible fact that the poor woman had been chased out of her home for no other reason than her Jewishness. Eloise wanted to drag her bags upstairs and lie on her bed in perfect silence. Instead, she was forced to act as arbitrator in this dispute.

"I see." She pressed her fingers to her temples. "Very well. Let's discuss this like civilised human beings. Hildegard, what is your objection to Jan joining us as a co-tenant?"

The woman appeared affronted. "You actually need me to state the obvious?"

"I'm afraid so."

Without looking at Jan, she enumerated her reasons, indicating each on her fingers. "Firstly, this is a house for respectable young ladies."

"I'm not respectable," said Veronika.

"Please, Veronika, allow Hildegard to speak without interruption. You will have your turn to answer her concerns."

"Thank you, Eloise. As I was saying, this house was advertised as having a female landlady and female-only tenants. I am most uncomfortable at the idea of sharing my bathroom with a man. Secondly, as he says himself, he cannot work. So how will he pay rent?"

Eloise forestalled Jan's response by holding up a hand. "So if I understand correctly, his sex and financial situation are the problem?"

"Plus the standards! He's been here under a week and look at the place! The kitchen is filled with smoke, dirty dishes and beer bottles. It's like living in a doss house!"

Eloise noted that neither Veronika nor Jan countered that particular point. Indeed, as she looked around, she saw the normally tidy surfaces were cluttered with unwashed plates and cutlery, empty bottles stood next to the waste bin and one saucer was overflowing with cigarette butts.

She addressed Veronika. "What do you say to Hildegard's points?"

"I'd say she should learn some compassion for a fellow

human being. All right, all right, don't start that again. Yes, the kitchen is a bit of a mess after Christmas and New Year, but we can clean that up. The idea was to give Jan somewhere to stay until he finds another room to rent. But if you'll accept him as a tenant here, I'm willing to switch rooms with Hildegard. That way she has a bathroom to herself on the ground floor, and I share the upstairs one with Jan."

"You mean *we* share the upstairs one with Jan," Eloise pointed out.

"Well, yes, all right then, but it works out well. You and Hildegard keep regular hours, right? Jan and I usually sleep in the day and get up at night. Our paths will hardly ever cross."

Jan nodded his agreement. Even Hildegard seemed to be considering the advantages of the downstairs room.

"What about the question of the rent? I take your point about compassion, but ..."

"I can afford the rent," said Jan. "You of all people know exactly how much I earn."

"Yes, that is true."

Hildegard and Veronika both looked at Eloise for an explanation. "Jan has been helping me with one of my writing jobs and we split the fee. It's a steady income, particularly because he has quite a knack for the material. Now that the *Vogue* job takes up so much of my time, Jan could take over that job entirely. If so, he can easily afford the same rent as the rest of us."

Hildegard's frown was suspicious, but she did not press the point. "Leaving aside the bathroom and the rent, what about the house rules?"

"Good point." Eloise swept a hand towards the kitchen worktops. "This is completely unacceptable. Our shared spaces must stay clean and smoke-free. We all take responsibility for keeping the kitchen, the bathrooms and the hallway clean and tidy. Is that something we can all agree on?"

They all nodded with great solemnity.

"In that case, Jan, you are subject to the same terms as us. Three months' probation and if any one of us feels things are not working, we must ask you to leave. I'm going to my room now. It's been a long day."

She trudged upstairs, already composing a letter to her family in her mind.

Thus the house on Charlottenweg began to change, not without a certain amount of chafing and friction, yet the mixture of personalities found a way to inhabit the same space. Two diurnal and two nocturnal inhabitants made for a relatively comfortable co-existence. Each morning Eloise and Hildegard left for work, returning after six in the evening. Sometimes they ate together, taking turns to cook. On occasion Veronika came in to say goodbye before leaving for the night's activities. Other than the evening she had arrived with a hamper from one of her men friends, Eloise had never seen the woman eat. She seemed to subsist on cigarettes, alcohol and opium.

As for the fourth lodger, he moved like a shadow around the building, spending most of his time on the fire escape, regardless of the weather. Eloise usually joined him for an after-dinner smoke and was pleased to hear the arrangement with Dietmar continued to keep them both happy. Once she came downstairs to make a cup of tea before bed and found him in the kitchen, standing at the counter with a bowl of soup. He behaved as if she'd caught him in the middle of some transgression and waited until she left to continue eating.

. . .

The bitter fist of winter finally released its hold on the city and gave way to spring. Tiny yellow and purple crocuses poked their way out of the earth to line the garden path, making Eloise smile as she left to catch her tram. Primulas sprouted on the neglected lawn at the front of the house and the first bundles of asparagus appeared in the market. On Alexanderplatz, dull black and grey coats were replaced by baby blue or rose-coloured jumpers, while women lifted pink-lipsticked faces to the sunshine.

At weekends, Hildegard went home as usual to see her family. Eloise joined friends from work on Friday night and spent most Saturday evenings and Sundays with Otto. His political activities occupied Saturdays and although he had invited her to join him, she found the endless earnest arguments from passionate Social Democrats soporific. She was no fan of the communists and even less so the Nazis, but politics depressed her to the point she would rather do her laundry while Otto canvassed support.

On the rare occasions neither Eloise nor Veronika had commitments on Saturday evening, they took bottles of wine onto the fire escape along with cushions, blankets and an extra glass for Jan. Somehow, no one ever suggested sitting in the kitchen. That metal staircase above the streets below might have been cold and cheerless, but it belonged to them.

"You should invite your boyfriend to join us one evening," said Veronika, blowing smoke circles into the air.

Eloise shook her head. "Not a good idea."

"Why? Are you ashamed of us?"

"Yes," said Eloise, causing Jan to break into one of his hacking laughs. Painful as it sounded, Veronika and Eloise could not help but join in.

"I'll have you know some people would pay good money to sit in a back alley with a drug-addicted whore and a one-eyed pornographer." Veronika was wearing no make-up or jewellery or hair pomade. Despite her coarse vernacular, she looked like a sixteen-year-old consumption patient.

"Eroticist, if you don't mind," said Jan.

"Escort, if you don't mind," replied Veronika.

Whatever was in Eloise's glass tasted like coffee grounds in elderberry juice. She tipped the dregs onto the cobbles below. "Sorry, Veronika, but that foul potion has no right to call itself wine. I'll open this red instead. The candle, please, Jan. Before I introduce Otto to my friends, I need to understand who he really is. I'm not getting burned again."

"I warned you," said Jan. "Beware the man whose weekends are never free."

"You did and you were right," Eloise admitted. "Otto is definitely not married. We have a lot of fun together and he treats me with respect. In my limited experience, that's a rare combination."

"Unheard of," agreed Veronika. "Are you sure he's human?"

"Time will tell. We've been friends for nearly six months and until now he's shown no inclination to ... how can I put it ... make advances?"

"Definitely not human," said Jan, holding the candle to illuminate Eloise's hands as she eased the cork from the bottle. "Or he might like boys. That's a thing these days. Apparently."

Veronika gave him a dry look. "Shut up, Jan, and give me a cigarette."

He shrugged and offered up his packet.

"Just for once, let's imagine the impossible." The flame of her lighter glittered in Veronika's eyes. "The pot of gold at the end of the rainbow, a whole meadow filled with four-leafed clovers each bearing a ladybird? Whisper it. Has Eloise de Fournier found the Holy Grail? By which I mean A Good Man?" She burst into wild laughter, triggering Jan's cough.

Veronika's flair for drama and outrageous fantasy entertained them for hours. When the church bells struck one, Eloise blew them both goodnight kisses and went inside. In bed, she curled up under the covers and returned to that clichéd phrase: *A Good Man*. Her mother's voice responded: *Let's wait and see.*

20

Spring 1928, Berlin

"Use the brake as you come to the corner, just until you take the curve. Yes, that's it. Now accelerate out the other side. A bit more so you don't lose power ... oh, dear. Well, never mind. Let's start the engine and try again."

"You're very patient but I'm honestly not sure I'll ever get better at motoring. There are so many things to think about all at once."

"Don't give up too easily. You're managing very well for a first-timer. Remember it's like riding a horse. Instead of using your heels to make the beast move on, you use that pedal there. When you want to turn his head left or right, move the steering wheel. To say, 'Whoa', you press on the brake. The only difference is we must not let our mechanical steed go to sleep. Keep the engine idling at all times until we're ready to return our trusty Treefrog to his stable."

Eloise concentrated on the starting sequence and brought the *Laubfrosch* back to life. The analogy of horse-riding was apt.

A sense of power tempered by fear rushed through her, exactly as it had when she first sat on a pony. Triumph or disaster lay ahead, dependent on her level of mastery. She followed Otto's instructions and drove around the entire factory, only causing the engine to stutter twice by being overcautious, but returned them both safely to the gate.

She switched the engine off. "I did it!" She threw her arms into the air.

"You did it!" Otto beamed, leaned in as if to embrace her then looked upwards to the factory windows. His gesture transformed into applause. "Congratulations! What do you say we switch seats and I will drive you to a discreet little bar for a glass of champagne? We must toast Eloise de Fournier, lady motorist!"

He ordered a bottle of Irroy, which Eloise knew was an extravagant purchase. She had read a recent feature on champagnes in *Elegante Welt* and filed the name in the useful knowledge part of her memory.

"Why is it called a Treefrog?" she asked as they sipped bubbles.

"To be honest, I don't know where the nickname originated. The headlamps? The fact it's green? Whatever the reason, it doesn't harm sales. The *Laubfrosch* is Opel's bestseller. The one you drove today was an original, but the Rüsselsheim plant is now producing a three- and four-seaters and not only in green. I apologise, I'm running off at the mouth again. Never ask me a question about cars or politics if you value your ears."

"As you once said to me, 'I asked a question, you answered'. So the factory we drove around today is not actually where they make the cars?"

"No, that site is not suitable for mass production. It's more like a giant tailor's shop for vehicles rather than clothes. Any adjustments the customer requires can be accommodated at my brother's facility. They also do repairs after accidents, and let me tell you, there are plenty of accidents. Taking control of a vehicle capable of a top speed of up to seventy kilometres per hour is not for amateurs. As you saw for yourself."

Eloise nodded her acquiescence. "I didn't know it was your brother's facility. We could have dropped in to say hello."

"Only if you are willing to be bored to death from both sides. He's worse than me on the subject of automobiles. Where would you like to dine this evening? There's a homely little place on Grenadierstrasse which does very good fish."

"Isn't that in the Scheunenviertel, the neighbourhood where Jewish people live? I hear it can be dangerous."

A brief frown crossed his face. "No more dangerous than the Wedding area where communists live. Neither place is unsafe in and of itself. The only thing that makes any of these areas problematic is outsiders who come to cause trouble for the inhabitants. No matter, we can eat elsewhere."

She realised her insensitivity. "Yes, that's a good idea. Let's avoid every *quartier* of Berlin, the Jewish, the communist, the Nazi, the political establishment, the ostentatious rich, the depraved middle class, the wretched poor, and pretend none of it exists. In fact, why don't we go back to your place? I assume as a single man of means you have learned to cook? I'm going to visit the ladies' room and give you a moment to think."

He made pork chops in a cream sauce with salted potatoes, carrots and chard. Not quite restaurant fare but wholesome, filling and with the personal touch. They drank red wine and sat at the table by the window, overlooking the square. His desk was untidy, with piles of books and pamphlets spilling onto the floor, but otherwise the apartment was clean and well organised. Conversation flowed less easily than usual and she understood why. She had changed gears in their relationship, just as clumsily as she had done in the Opel. Now she had the choice whether to accelerate or brake.

"That was delicious, thank you." She placed her knife and fork together.

"My pleasure. It's been a while since I cooked for someone else."

They watched trams rattle along the street. Eloise tried to formulate a sentence about her lack of cookery skills but got bored before she began. "Otto, may I ask a question? After I drove around the factory in your car this afternoon, you almost kissed me. But you didn't. Why not?"

He folded his napkin and met her gaze. "I wanted to. Then I remembered where we were."

She was about to make a pert comment about it being legal for two adults to show affection in public, but an instinct stopped her. Instead, she waited as he struggled to find the words.

"My brother was watching from his office. He's quite a bit older than me. In his opinion, that gives him the right to dictate how I live, from my politics to my friends. When I care about something, I keep it to myself, otherwise Gustav will find a way of ruining it. That's why I didn't kiss you today."

She brushed some crumbs from the tablecloth. "Older siblings can be absolute tyrants. My poor little brother suffered untold miseries by dint of being younger than me. Therefore I understand why the presence of your brother restrained you, today." That pause before the final word was infinitesimal, yet significant.

He swallowed and reached across the table to take her hand. "All the other times were due to my being a hopeless coward. I've never liked someone as much as I like you. The fear of scaring you away held me in check. But now that's out in the open ..." He released her hand, took her chin between his finger and thumb and pressed his lips to hers.

The rush of emotion affected her like a dozen glasses of champagne, bursting bubbles in her brain and sending molten gold through her veins. His thumb tilted her face upwards as his warm palm rested on her neck.

"Oh, Eloise." His forehead rested against hers.

She opened her eyes. "Yes?"

"All those moments I missed seem like such a waste, I could kick myself."

"I could kick you too. However, there is such thing as making up for lost time."

In previous sexual encounters, Eloise had always been the amateur, learning from her lover's experience. With Otto, the roles were reversed. She was his first. When she had recovered from that unexpected revelation, she regarded his innocence as a treasured gift. Like any artisan, she would teach her apprentice the skills of sensuality until he reached the level of mastery. The most important part of his education was regular practice.

The shift in their relationship barely altered their schedules. Eloise worked Monday to Friday at *Vogue*. Otto spent his week selling cars and every Saturday working for the SDP. From Saturday night to Monday morning, however, he was all hers. Love-making, food, driving lessons and culture occupied their weekends, filling the tank for the week ahead. When Eloise woke on a Sunday morning to see Otto's profile on the next pillow, her emotions overwhelmed her. She wanted to cry, to laugh, to thank her guardian angel for blessing her with such good fortune. Otto was more than her lover; he was her closest friend. At times, she wished she could confide in him, whispering intimate secrets about her wonderful new romance. Instead, she dropped unsubtle hints to Veronika and Jan, and asked Irmgard if she could invite a partner to their opening night. It was time to go public.

The launch of German *Vogue*: the most anticipated event in the entire 1928 Berlin social calendar. People tried influence, bribery, threats and trickery to gain an invitation but the guest list remained inaccessible. The great and good were in attendance, all dressed in designer gowns, fine jewellery, perfect tailoring and flamboyant accessories. Press photographers jostled for position and crowds gasped as each luminary entered the portico. Eloise only caught glimpses of the furore outside as she shook hands, greeted new arrivals and made introductions between people who already knew one another but pretended they didn't.

Anyone would have been nervous under the circumstances, yet her concern for Otto stretched her nerves to the point where she confused the names of two Viennese designers. One made the screwing-nose gesture, a signal he thought she was drunk. In a panic, she looked around for a window for fresh air. By the door, she saw Otto conversing with Dr Hirschfeld and that English author who found Berlin 'so very amusing'. Her intense stare attracted Otto's attention and he gave an admiring nod. He was relaxed, genial and in no need of her assistance. From that moment on, she unfurled her social butterfly wings and fluttered around the room, charming, laughing and sprinkling compliments like pollen.

As the band played an encore and the guests drifted into the night, Otto tapped her on the shoulder. "May I have the last dance?"

She leaned into his chest and he wrapped his arm around

her back, drawing her closer. "If my legs will still hold me, of course you may."

"How soon can we go home?" he whispered. "I know you need to winnow the wheat from the chaff of this evening with your colleagues, but maybe that's best left until tomorrow."

He bent to kiss her and a flashbulb startled them apart.

"Please don't do that!" he called, his tone firm but courteous.

"I said no more pictures!" Irmgard bellowed. "Hand over your press pass and get out of here! Did you hear me?"

There was no question of disobeying. Irmgard could project her voice across seven *quartiers* of Berlin and even Potsdam might hear an echo. The impertinent photographer held up an apologetic hand and made a hasty, inelegant exit.

Irmgard walked up behind them, draping her arms across their shoulders. "Darlings, what a night! You do realise this changes everything? Georges, did we keep the best bottles for last? Well then, what are you waiting for?"

It wasn't only Eloise's employer gaining column inches in the press. Opel was breaking new ground with its rocket-powered vehicles, which were quite the novelty. Added to that the company's determination to break land speed records, and interest sparked beyond the field of German car manufacturing. An upcoming event in Rüsselsheim excited Otto to the point where he could talk about little else. On April 28, the company planned a demonstration of the RAK 1, a converted racing car powered by rockets instead of an engine. The engineers hoped they would be the first to break the 100kph barrier.

"That's insanely fast!" exclaimed Eloise, as they ventured out to try another new restaurant on Saturday night. "I do hope you'll be well out of the way. Oh my goodness, you're not driving, are you?"

"Me? I should be so lucky. Fritz von Opel himself wanted to be behind the wheel, but his partners dissuaded him. No, we're using a racing driver called Volkhart, a fearless fellow well used to testing prototypes. If everything works as it should, we'll try the new improved version on Berlin's AVUS." He saw her blank look. "The automobile-only road used as a racetrack? Look, I know racing cars are not really your bag, but will you come along when we show it to the public next month? It's going to be a high-profile event with lots of well-known faces."

"I'd come along to support you even if it was only a gaggle of mechanics and a stray cat. After all, you suffered the *Vogue* party which must have bored you half to death. Count on me. What time are you leaving for Rüsselsheim tomorrow?"

He wrinkled his nose. "Early. Gustav will collect me at eight because the journey takes all day. I'm sorry our weekend together is so short. We are due to return on Friday, so I'll make it up to you, I promise."

Eloise squeezed his arm. "I'll look forward to that, my love. Don't feel too guilty though. Every now and then, it's a good thing to stay at Charlottenweg for the weekend. Since I hardly see them during the week, I'm rather looking forward to a chat with those reprobates."

"If you're including Hildegard in that description, I wish to register a protest on her behalf."

She laughed. "The very thought! Considering you've never encountered any of my housemates, you know them extremely well."

"Your stories paint vivid pictures. I was thinking, do you see an occasion when I might meet Jan and Veronika? I trust your judgement, naturally, and would never presume to intrude."

"Why not? Normal people would cook a meal and invite guests but those two are not normal. How do you fancy an evening sitting on a fire escape with a glass of wine?"

"So long as you are there, it sounds like fun. Let's fix a date. Oh, there's the Russian restaurant, across the street. Look at the queue! I suppose I should have expected this on opening night. Good job I made a reservation. Do you think there will be photographers?"

Eloise clasped his hand. He hated seeing his face in the newspaper society columns. "It's possible. Turn up your collar and pull down your hat. I'll use my fan. If they can't get a clear shot of our faces, they'll pick on someone else. Best foot forward, *mon brave*."

21

May 1928, Berlin

After she kissed Otto goodnight on Charlottenweg, Eloise trotted up the path to her front door, only stopping to check the new post box Jan had hammered onto the fence. She was the only one who ever did so. It was surprisingly full. Two notes for Veronika, a fat envelope for Jan, four letters for Hildegard and three for her. She laid those for Hildegard on her shelf and took the rest upstairs. She propped Veronika's against her door and delivered Jan's to the fire escape.

"*Danke sehr*," he grinned. "Wait a minute. Why are you here on a Saturday night? What have you done to Otto?"

"Nothing! He's off to some automobile thing early in the morning and I thought it would be nice to spend some time with my housemates."

"Housemate. Veronika's gone to some depraved house party in the country. We won't see her again before Sunday evening but she promised to bring home some kinky stories." He tore open his envelope and counted the notes. "Thank you very much, Dietmar. Cigarette?"

"Have one of mine. There was a restaurant opening tonight and I picked up some freebies. If you start with that boring don't-want-your-charity speech again, I'll push you off the steps."

"Let me see what you've got before I decide whether or not I want your charity."

She emptied her pockets onto the rug and spun the wheel on her lighter, to ignite her cigarette and illuminate her haul.

He prodded the items. "Vodka miniature, Black Russian smokes, steel shot glass, chocolates, butter pat, breadsticks, little pot of jam ..."

Eloise snorted smoke from her nostrils. "That's not jam, it's caviar. I don't much care for fish eggs, but everyone raves about the stuff. *Chacun à son goût.*" She flipped through her letters. One from Fribourg in a hand she did not recognise. One from *Vogue*, probably her new contract. The last was handwritten and it took a moment for Eloise to place the familiar sloping italics.

D*ear Eloise*
I had hoped to have this conversation in person but as you did not return on Friday, I assume I will not see you again until Monday evening. In strictly formal terms, that will be too late to deliver my notice. In four weeks' time, I shall take up a new position. A firm in Lichterfelde has offered me the role of office manager, meaning I can live with my family in relative safety and civility.

I will not pretend it is only the growing unpleasantness on the streets of Berlin which precipitates my move. Charlottenstrasse was once a respectable address but that has changed in recent months and my constant requests to you, as ersatz landlady, have fallen on deaf ears.

I shall pay rent for May but move out next weekend. Please understand that I bear you no ill will but cannot accept your lack of standards. I wish you all the best with your new job and new man.
Regards
Hildegard

"Oh dear. Hildegard is moving out. That's a real shame."

"Is it?" asked Jan, opening the little vodka bottle. "Can't say I'll miss her."

Eloise turned over the other two letters and decided not to open either until she was in her room. "You might not but I will. She was very nice to me when I first arrived. I know she can appear a little stuffy, but she has a proper way of doing things. She's disappointed in me."

"So am I. Fish jam and a tin cup? Thank God for Dietmar, that's all I can say."

Eloise nudged him with a knee, careful not to aim a swipe at his shoulder as she would have done with Bastian. On the one occasion she had pretended to smack Jan for impertinence, his cowering reaction had horrified her. "Shut up, you ingrate. I'm going to bed. Goodnight."

"Goodnight, Eloise. Say, that automobile event of Otto's? Didn't you want to go?"

Eloise had not been invited but that was a blessed relief. "Rocket-powered racing cars?" She cupped her hands over her ears. "I can't bear loud noises."

He nodded and looked up at the stars. "Nor me. Not anymore."

Eloise washed, brushed her teeth, changed into her nightclothes and closed the bedroom curtains. Only then did she curl up against her pillows and open her post. She wanted to savour the moment of opening that envelope. One full-year contract with *Vogue* Germany at an improved salary, backdated to the start of April. She pressed the letter to her chest and smiled at the ceiling. *Ladies and gentlemen, Eloise de Fournier,* Vogue *journalist and woman about town*!

The second letter was in dense German legalese and it took her a few minutes to comprehend what she was reading. The amount she was due to inherit after her father's death was twenty thousand Swiss francs. Her head spun and she closed her eyes. Then she laughed. First famine, now feast! Was it possible Fate bestowed two gifts at once? Why the hell had she given that vodka to Jan? In truth, she was dizzy enough without strong liquor. She rubbed her eyes and read the letter again. That time, she spotted the clause. Twenty thousand pounds would be available to Mrs Eloise de Fournier on the occasion she returned to live Fribourg with her children. Ah. Even from beyond the grave, Papa was still pulling strings. Well, she was now a career woman with her own income. If and when she returned to her home city, it would be on her own terms. Her last thought before she closed her eyes was of her dear departed husband. Sylvain's favourite saying was 'With a child, one must always lead by example'.

The RAK-1, or Opel rocket racing car had met expectations, reaching 100kph and killing no one. The papers were full of the news, yet Otto himself, when he returned, was strangely subdued. Eloise didn't press the point and chatted instead about her contract, Hildegard's absence and the oppressive nature of election campaigns.

"It's as if everyone is shouting in your ear, insistent on gaining one's vote. The problem is, I can barely remember a single candidate's name." They walked through the *Flohmarkt*, idly examining trinkets.

"What about the name Otto Graz?" he asked, his gaze intense.

She stopped. "You're going to run for election?"

"Only at a local level, because someone has to. If I don't take up the cause for people like me, what choice do those without a candidate have? Most people in Berlin have little sympathy with the far right and while tolerant of the communist agenda, have no desire to see a repeat of what happened in Russia."

Eloise gave an involuntary shiver and walked on past a stall selling mirrors. She looked old, watery, speckled, long or squat, depending on which glass reflected her face.

"You would stand as a Social Democrat?" she asked. "Maintaining the status quo?"

"There is no status quo. The Weimar Republic is an infant democracy taking its first steps and therefore trying to reach compromises with every faction which thinks it can do better. Leave alone external pressure from foreign powers. Our domestic situation is a powder keg. Extreme political poles could tear this country apart if the centre cannot hold. As a Social Democrat, I will represent common sense, the middle ground, supporting the government at a time when it needs it most. I want to stand for the German people. Hard-working, balanced, committed to rebuilding a great nation."

She considered his words as they examined a selection of pocket watches. "Your words are rousing and I can see the sense in adopting a solid central position. Such a candidate would get my vote. What concerns me is the febrile nature of politics these days. People coming to blows in a café, marauding youths using fists and weapons to silence the opposition, a refusal to listen to what you rightly describe as common sense. I suppose you will call me a coward, but the idea of entering the fray with tempers running high gives me cause for concern."

He took her hand and they strolled past some frankly terrifying works of art. She waved a hand at the garish images. "You see, this is exactly what I mean."

Otto studied the distorted depictions of ugliness. "The artist's perspective is no less valid than that of the politician. In some ways, it's more honest. This is one man's subjective interpretation of our unfair and corrupt society. One can agree with him, consider his point or simply walk past. Not so with politics. Revolutionary reds and Bavarian brownshirts impose their vision, demanding slavish devotion from their supporters and pointing fingers of blame at their opponents. Never trust an ideologue whose rhetoric is based on resentment and fear."

The stallholder asked which paintings they liked and Eloise answered. "Honestly? Each is striking in its own way but I wouldn't want to gaze on any of them over breakfast. Have a good Sunday." She steered Otto away from the market and across the road to the park. "I'm glad you're back. I missed you and your passions while you were in Rüsselsheim."

He lifted her hand to his lips. "I missed you more than I imagined. What I would have given for your good sense to counterbalance my brother's company. Five days was more than enough."

"What does Gustav think of your decision to go into politics?" she asked. In the ensuing silence, she drew her own conclusions. "I see."

"What do you see?"

"My supposition based on what you have told me of your relationship with your older sibling is that you have not told him of your plans. Your intention is to run for office, gain your seat on the council and present him with a *fait accompli*. That way he cannot derail your ambitions."

They sat on a bench in a patch of sunshine. "Very astute. If I gain my seat, that is. That is far from certain. I will have to work harder than ever to persuade people to vote for me. My campaign is not about crude imagery demonising a fictitious enemy. My appeal is to rational thought, which does not fit on a poster. I need to meet ordinary people and rather than bellow slogans into their ears, listen to their concerns. I don't have much time. The elections are on 20 May."

Eloise patted his knee. "In that case, we'd better get to work!" What could be achieved in fewer than three weeks, she had no idea.

"I have the results in my hand and now I can declare Herr Otto Wilhelm Graz of the Social Democratic Party the clear winner! Congratulations to you, sir!"

Otto shook hands with all the other candidates, expressed gratitude to his supporters, acknowledged the achievements of his predecessor and promised to deliver for the district. He left the stage to enthusiastic applause. His progress through the hall was impeded by well-wishers and back-slappers but finally he arrived at Eloise's side.

"I'm so proud of you," she said, resisting the temptation to throw her arms around his neck. Acceptable decorum under these circumstances was uncharted waters.

"Tonight, my love, I must join my colleagues for a celebration. I want nothing more than to return home with you but now is the time to put our plans into action."

"So you should! Go and enjoy your success. Irmgard and Georges will drive me home. I could not be happier for this evening's result."

Otto held her shoulders. "Yes, this changes everything. Tomorrow night, my place? Shall we say seven o'clock?"

"I'll be there."

He kissed her, ignoring camera flashbulbs and curious looks from the crowd. She squeezed his hand and walked away, searching for Irmgard. People moved aside, some smiling, some staring until one man stepped directly into her path.

"Excuse me," she said, trying to sidle past.

"We are yet to be introduced. My name is Gustav Graz. I understand you and my brother are close friends." He extended a hand. His height coupled with their proximity forced her to look up at a heavy brow, thick moustache and thin smile.

Eloise pressed her palm to his. "Eloise de Fournier. Glad to make your acquaintance. You must be delighted by Otto's achievement."

"Must I?" His expression was contemptuous to the point of caricature. "As a Swiss immigrant, naturally you approve of unqualified peasants influencing governmental decisions."

Her face flushed with anger. "Like your brother, I believe in democracy. The government is elected to serve its people. In my view, the Social Democratic Party offers a balanced ..."

"Since when did fashion journalists see fit to lecture anyone on anything other than this season's hats? Goodnight."

She stood there as he swept away like a pantomime villain, and tried to summon a laugh, but it died in her throat.

"Eloise!" Irmgard pushed her way through the throng. "Georges is waiting in the car. Who was that? *Nosferatu*?"

Her laughter finally escaped. "Something similar. Shall we go?"

For a Monday night, Otto had made an enormous effort. White tablecloth and napkins, wine glasses, polished cutlery and a posy of flowers in a bud vase elevated the kitchen table to restaurant status. He cooked Wiener Schnitzel with peas, carrots and fried potatoes, poured them a glass of Riesling and gazed at her in the lavender light of dusk. His good humour after such a triumph was to be expected but his intensity became unsettling. Surely the man should be spouting schemes, ideas, plans and policies, not studying her as if she were a work of art.

"That was quite delicious," she said, placing her cutlery together. "Dinner chez Otto from now on will be hotly anticipated."

He clasped his hands under his chin and studied her face. That unfocused look reminded her of Veronika's soft smile when she had taken morphine. Otto needed bringing back to earth and Eloise knew exactly how to do it.

"I met your brother, by the way."

His focus sharpened as if she had shone a torch in his eyes. "Where?"

"On election night. He introduced himself and told me fashion journalists had no business engaging in politics. Ironic, when you consider what a flair he has for drama."

Otto's laugh built like a volcano, erupting into a guffaw. "A flair for drama! That is Gustav in a nutshell!"

"It wasn't only me who noticed. Irmgard compared him to *Nosferatu*."

"Even better! How I wish I could tell him."

"Don't. I have a feeling he and I shall never be friends."

"Friends, perhaps not. But could you bear in-laws?" Otto stood to collect something from the untidy desk. Rather than sitting in his chair, he knelt beside her, holding out a small velvet box. "I have been planning to ask you something for quite some time. My promise to myself was this: if I get elected, I will delay no longer and seize happiness with both hands. Eloise, would you do me the greatest honour and consent to be my wife?"

22

Summer 1928, Berlin/Fribourg

Always a stickler for propriety, Otto wanted approval from Eloise's family before they could proceed with wedding plans. Personally, Eloise had never desired anything other than permission for any of her decisions, but her fiancé was cut from different cloth. The trip was fixed for August and of course, the only way to travel was by motor car. All the time not already taken up by Opel and the SDP, Otto spent planning the route and worrying about how to ingratiate himself with his future in-laws.

The reverse problem preoccupied Eloise. In June, Otto's parents threw a celebratory lunch to welcome her into the family. Neither her age nor her previous marriage seemed to bother them and they gave their blessings blithely. To Eloise, that showed a curious lack of judgement. Not that she wanted Frau Graz to clutch her son to her protective bosom or Herr Graz to accuse her of predatory behaviour, but a little concern for Otto would have been nice. The reason for their disinterest arrived in time for coffee.

Gustav Graz had all the ingredients of a handsome man, but somewhere in the baking of that cake, vinegar had entered the mix. His parents fussed over him like a returning hero, only introducing Eloise as an afterthought.

"Pleased to meet you, Madame de Fournier. I understand congratulations are in order. May I wish you great happiness in your future union." He said the words as if he were sucking on a lemon.

"Thank you, Gustav, although we have already met. On the evening of Otto's election, if you remember?" His look remained blank. "Never mind. Since we are to be family, I hope you will call me Eloise."

"As you wish." He turned to his brother. "I assume you are going to Hanover next week, Otto? This is the summer of land speed records and you would be a fool to miss it."

His elder brother's supercilious air left Otto unruffled. "Unfortunately, I have other plans that day, but high hopes the world will be convinced by the power of rocket science."

With a flip of his coattails, Gustav took his seat. "Other plans? What can possibly draw you away from our life's work? Oh, I see. You must be busy choosing wedding venues and selecting flower schemes." He pinched the handle of his coffee cup between finger and thumb. "The best china, Mutti? Really?"

Frau Graz glanced at her husband who refused to meet her eyes.

Otto gave an easy laugh. "Our wedding arrangements must wait until I have met Eloise's family. Without their blessing, we cannot proceed. The truth is that June 23 coincides with a major political conference, when we hope to find common ground with our opposition."

Gustav exhaled through his nostrils. "Anyone would think

he'd been elected to the Reichstag, not some tiny regional council. Are there no biscuits, no cake, no French fancies this afternoon? Next time, I shall bring my own."

Frau Graz flapped her hands at the maid. "Bring the tea platter, Agnes!"

"Now, *meine Dame*?"

"Yes, of course! You know how Gustav has a sweet tooth." Her frown smoothed into an indulgent smile as she directed her attention to her eldest son. "Would you say the Hanover event is likely to have a similar kind of attendance as the AVUS? According to the newspapers, all kinds of illustrious personalities were present: actresses, sportsmen, film directors and politicians."

"I wouldn't know. That kind of idle chit-chat belongs in women's magazines. The Hanover event is about pushing the boundaries of speed on land. June saw Fritz von Opel reach 238 kilometres per hour with a rocket-powered car. Now we apply the same techniques to the railway. Soon we shall travel from Berlin to Munich in two hours. Why not?"

The maid set a three-tiered, English-style tray on the table, laden with slices of cake, petit-fours and a variety of summer fruits.

Gustav ignored it entirely. "Those prepared to commit to Fritz von Opel and his vision will reap the finest rewards." He addressed his father. "As a matter of fact, I'm test-driving one of our newer models today. Why don't you and I go for a spin and leave the ladies to their gossip."

He strode down the driveway without a backward glance, his coat billowing behind him. Herr Graz stood up, gave a polite nod to Eloise and followed his oldest son towards the car.

"My favourite kind of visit from Gustav. Mercifully short," said Otto. His reaction to his brother's overt unpleasantness was calm and even mildly amused. "Agnes, would you take the tea things inside and save them for later? Thank you. Now what about a tour of the gardens, Mutti? I've told Eloise all about your green thumbs. Come, my mother's pride and joy is best viewed in the sunshine."

Your mother's pride and joy is best kept as far away as possible and if I never see him again, it will be too soon. "I'd love to stroll around the gardens! The perfect way to walk off our lunch. Tell me, Frau Graz, did you design all this yourself?"

They spent a pleasant hour amid the flowerbeds, admiring the variety of foliage and complimenting the lady of the house on her refined taste. At one point, she took her leave to accost the gardener, giving Otto and Eloise a moment alone together. He led her to a bench under a linden tree, where they sat in the shade.

"This is where I always dreamed of proposing to you."

Eloise took in their verdant surroundings, with scented blooms and the constant flutter of insects dancing from one bush to the next. "I can see why. If you want to do it again, I'll be happy to give you the same answer."

He took her hand. "I used to sit here as a boy, when I needed solitude. It soothes me in every season, but especially at this time of the year. Clear blue skies above, shades of green below, flowers like fireworks and jewel-coloured butterflies whispering promises of a brilliant future."

She kissed him. "The answer is still yes."

W ithout ever broaching the subject directly, Eloise and Otto avoided the subject of his objectionable brother. Visits to the Graz household were either carefully timed to coincide with another of Gustav's engagements or the spontaneous 'we were just passing and thought we'd say hello' kind. Eloise was grateful. She could take any amount of patronising belittlement on her own account, but when that puffed-up peacock sought to disparage her husband-to-be, she sharpened her claws, ready to ruffle his feathers.

His future Fribourg family held no such horrors, yet Otto fretted as if they were a firing squad. No matter how many reassurances Eloise gave, he believed himself nothing more than a sorry substitute for the late, great Sylvain de Fournier. He spent hours reading about Swiss medical advances to initiate conversations with Bastian, took more trouble than Eloise ever had to find the right kind of toys for her children, and asked endless questions about Charlotte's interests. Eloise couldn't help much. It was a topic she had never previously considered.

"She's an academic," she said, distracted by the latest copy of *Die Dame*. Once again, the cover was a painting by Tamara de Lempicka, almost shocking in its sensuality. A woman in a white hat, her shoulder and neck bare, cradled an armful of summer flowers; poppies, cornflowers and daisies. Her half-lidded gaze and parted red lips invited the viewer to enjoy this natural bounty. Who could resist?

"That much I gathered, my love. But what can you tell me about her field of study?"

"Serious things, I'd say."

Otto removed his glasses and rubbed his eyes, a sure sign he was tired.

Eloise put down the magazine. "Well, let me see. My sister wants to know what's going on in the world. She reads newspapers rather than magazines, or theoretical tomes on social development, eschewing fiction as a waste of her time. Charlotte introduced me to women's rights, for example. It was her choice to enrol my children in the Waldorf education system led by that Steiner chap. Now I come to think of, both my siblings have enquiring minds. I wonder where mine went?"

Otto replaced his glasses and came to sit beside her on the

divan. "Your enquiring mind is here," he tapped the magazine. "An understanding of what is happening on the streets is a different kind of enquiry, but shows no less enthusiasm for your fellow human beings. Each of us contributes to the advancement of knowledge in his or her own way."

"Promise me you'll say that to Charlotte. No, I'm not being flippant. Tell my sister that's what you believe and perhaps for once she will view me as something other than shallow and frivolous."

He kissed her. "How could anyone doubt your *joie de vivre*? I love you, Eloise, and consider everyone who doesn't quite mad. Are you absolutely sure you want to go back to Charlottenweg tonight? We have a very early start tomorrow."

"Absolutely sure. I am leaving the most irresponsible people of my acquaintance in charge of that house for two full weeks. That's why I am taking some little presents to bribe them into good behaviour. Rest assured, I will be ready and waiting for you at six o'clock in the morning, fresh as a ..." her eyes rested on the magazine cover "... as a daisy."

The journey took two days. The first leg was nothing special for Otto. It was the same route he drove every month to the Opel factory in Rüsselsheim. But the whole thing was a wonderful novelty for Eloise. Even the streets of Berlin looked different from the front seat of an automobile.

They stopped for lunch in Weimar, for no other reason than Eloise's curiosity. The city that gave its name to the new republic was the home of significant literary figures such as Goethe and Schiller, along with the Bauhaus movement led by Gropius, Kandinsky and Paul Klee. It also possessed several decent restaurants. Otto dismissed every one he had visited with his brother.

"He will only eat in places with white tablecloths. You and I will seek out somewhere rustic with a view and ideally, no tablecloths at all."

He got his wish. A rustic hostelry with a view over a town square had bare wooden tables, a dish of the day and earthenware jugs of local wine. They ate chard and barley soup with dark bread, alongside cold cuts of meats, pickles and cheese. Conversation turned to the little girls playing in the shadow of the church.

"Would you say those two are twins?" asked Otto. "At this distance, I can't tell them apart."

"I'd say so. So sweet with their ringlets bouncing in the sunlight. A pair of angels."

"Who needs a picturesque natural vista when you can gaze upon two children playing *Himmel und Hölle*?"

"*Himmel und Hölle*. Heaven and hell. You know, their golden blonde hair reminds me of Lili, my housemate who moved out."

"I thought that was Hildegard?"

"No, Hildegard left later. Lili was an innocent, fresh-faced Gretchen who adored fashion. The picture-perfect vision of a Teutonic female." Eloise's mood darkened. "Not anymore. She's a leading light in Elsbeth Zander's gang, the German Women's Order or whatever they call themselves. Now officially affiliated to the Nazis! Can you imagine a political organisation run by women actively campaigning to keep women out of politics?" She shook her head. "Poor Lili."

Otto's leg brushed hers. "This may not be the place, my darling."

Eloise noted the stillness and silence of their fellow diners. "Weimar is a charming place, don't you think? Can we stop here on the return journey? There is so much more to see."

When they returned to the car, she apologised for her outburst.

In this instance, Otto did not immediately absolve her of blame, simply reaching out a hand to pat her leg and raise his voice above the sound of the wind and the engine. "No harm done. Nowadays, we all need a little reminder to keep opinions to ourselves. Are you warm enough? There's a rug in the back should you need it."

After the first full day on the road, Eloise realised that motoring presented its own set of challenges for the modern woman. The effects of sun and wind might look free and romantic but they wrought havoc upon her skin and hair. She wound up the window after half an hour, thanking her stars Otto had opted for the close-bodied 'Limousine'. Only a few hours rattling along the roads and she began to think more fondly of trains. This trip was a pre-honeymoon, in a way, but on arrival at their lodgings at Gasthaus Adler in Rüsselsheim, Eloise made up her mind to forgo intimate relations in favour of a decent night's sleep. She slathered herself in cold cream and bid her future husband goodnight. Otto understood, kissed her shoulder and fell asleep before Eloise had finished saying her prayers.

Their arrival in Fribourg provoked great excitement. Everyone wanted to admire the car first and meet Otto second. Eloise herself attracted the least attention. Once Otto had promised to take Bastian, Julius and Laurent for a ride the very next morning, the party moved indoors.

"Charlotte, dear, would you show everyone to their sleeping quarters so they can freshen up before dinner? We've given you a guest room on the first floor, Mr Graz, with a view of the gardens. Eloise, your bedroom is the same as always."

They would be sleeping separately, Eloise realised. She gave Otto a rueful look.

"Certainly. This way, Mr Graz. The servants will bring your bags."

"Thank you. And please, there's no need to stand on ceremony. Call me Otto."

"Very well, Otto, and I hope you will address me as Charlotte. I've put you at the end of the corridor, right next to Eloise. I thought that might be more comfortable. Dinner is at seven-thirty this evening." She gave them a knowing smile and returned downstairs.

Eloise caught Otto's hand, pulled him inside the guest room and closed the door. "There! Not so alarming after all. And they've given you Bastian's old room, which has a connecting door to the old nursery, also known as my boudoir. My mother's and Charlotte's quarters are in the other wing, the children's rooms are on the second floor, which means you and I have a little privacy." She kissed him, the thrill at bringing her loved ones together overcoming her tiredness.

He held her close. "This house is very grand. I hope I won't embarrass you."

"Papa was fond of the finer things in life. It's strange coming home to the place without him here to welcome me. I wish you had met him. I know he would have approved." A knock came at the door. Eloise pressed her finger to her lips and ducked through the connecting door.

"See you at seven-thirty," she whispered.

Nine sat down at the dinner table that evening; Madame Favre at the head, Otto to her right and Eloise to her left. Seraphine took the chair next to Otto, and Bastian sat beside Eloise. At the other end of the table, Charlotte supervised Julius, Sylvia and Laurent. The two little girls, Etta and Antonia, remained at home with the nanny. Dinner was a lavish affair of five courses, quite out of the ordinary for the de Fournier household. They began with goose liver pâté on freshly baked bread rolls, followed by a rich chicken consommé. Main course was duck *à l'orange* with baby potatoes and garden vegetables, while dessert was one of Eloise's favourites: poached pears with French vanilla ice cream. Finally, a classic selection of Swiss cheeses with grapes rounded off an excellent meal.

"Quite a banquet!" Otto exclaimed. "Your kitchen staff are to be commended."

"Yes, indeed, without Cook and our head gardener, I do not know how we would manage. Most of tonight's food came from our own gardens, Mr Graz, and that includes the poultry. Since the war, we sought to be more self-sufficient, you see."

"Very wise. My mother, as Eloise will attest, takes great pride in her gardens. However she tends more to the decorative than the practical. Flowers are very colourful, but you can't eat them."

"What about cauliflowers?" asked Julius.

Everyone laughed at his astute observation.

"Quite right, young man. Both pretty and edible."

"Have you inherited your mother's green thumb, Otto?" asked Seraphine.

"I really couldn't say. My apartment in Berlin has no garden. Not as much as a window box. To be honest, I don't have much time for gardening. My weekends are spent on motor vehicles and political campaigns, and Eloise, of course."

"You have more than one motor car?" said Laurent, his eyes wide.

"No, no, but I work for Opel and spend a lot of time test-driving. Our aim is to break the land speed record, you see."

"Yes, we read about that!" said Julius.

"An exciting time to be in Berlin, without a doubt," said Bastian. "I also wanted to ask you about the political situation. We hear all kinds of dramatic stories, but I am sure you must be better informed about the reality." Her brother folded his napkin over his plate, a gesture Eloise recognised from when her father presided over the dinner table. Time for the ladies to withdraw and leave the gentlemen to talk. Part of her was incensed by being excluded, but her practical side saw the opportunity. Here was Otto's chance to gain Bastian's approval.

"Oh, politics!" said Madame Favre. "I'm afraid we shall have to leave you to it. I find the whole business most disagreeable. Ladies, children, let us retreat next door and speak of pleasanter things."

For a moment, Eloise thought Charlotte would argue, since she took a passionate interest in all things political and hated being treated as of lesser importance. But she caught her mother's glare and chivvied the children out of the room. "Half an hour's play then you must go to bed."

In the parlour, the boys immediately settled at a table on opposite sides of the chessboard. Eloise watched for a few minutes but soon lost interest. Sylvia had picked up a book and sat on a canapé beside Seraphine. The way her daughter nestled easily against her sister-in-law provoked a twinge of envy.

"What are you reading, my darling?"

"It's an English story, called *The Velveteen Rabbit*, or *Le lapin de velours* in French. I like it a lot although it has some sad parts."

"Reading in English now! You are growing up so fast."

"Sylvia has a talent for languages," said Charlotte, pouring tea. "The school encourages them to study whatever they enjoy most. That's a good thing, I'm sure you agree."

"I certainly agree," said Eloise. "I often read in English these days. It's important to keep up with trends in America, for example."

Charlotte gave her a dubious look but said nothing.

"Now about this beau of yours," said Madame Favre, accepting a cup from her eldest daughter. "I have to say, he seems quite charming, if a little young to be involved in politics. How long have you known him? Has he introduced you to his family?"

This was her mother's roundabout way of asking if their relationship was serious.

Eloise glanced at the children; the boys frowning over the black and white pieces, Sylvia's lips moving as she followed her story. She knew children listened to every word, even when apparently absorbed in another activity.

"Later, Maman," said Eloise with a shake of her head.

At that moment, the door opened and Bastian gestured for Otto to enter first. Both men were smiling. Bastian gave her shoulder a squeeze and stood by the table, watching developments in the chess game. She tried to catch Otto's eye, but he poured a cup of tea and sat on the armchair beside Charlotte.

"I understand you work at the university, Charlotte. What faculty would that be?"

"All of them." She sipped at her teacup. "You see, I'm a senior librarian, working across every department to maintain a huge repository of knowledge."

Eloise couldn't help herself. "Oh, is *that* what you do?"

It was a good thing the clock struck the hour and diverted Charlotte's attention. "Laurent, Sylvia, it's nine o'clock. Perhaps your mother would like to supervise bedtime this evening. Bastian, I think Seraphine and Julius are ready for home. Goodnight, children."

They said their goodbyes and Eloise followed her offspring up two floors, wondering what supervising bedtime meant these days. As it turned out, it involved her trying to comprehend Laurent's questions about motor cars with his mouth full of toothpaste and admiring Sylvia's neat rows of books as each child went through a well-practised routine. She tucked them in, kissed them goodnight and switched off the light. When she reached the ground floor, the maid was clearing away the tea things and everyone else had disappeared.

"My apologies, madam, did you want some more tea? Shall I bring a fresh pot?"

"No, thank you, Greta. Where is everyone?"

"Monsieur Favre and family went home, your mother has retired for the night and Miss Charlotte and Mr Graz are taking a turn around the grounds. It's still light, you see."

Pacing around the parlour made her look desperate, so Eloise thanked the maid and went to her room. She undressed, changed into her nightclothes, washed her face and cleaned her teeth. Still Otto had not returned. She opened the connecting door to await his return. Nothing moved in the shadows of the garden and she wondered what could possibly take him so long. Her feet grew cold, standing at the window, so she crawled under the bedcovers to warm herself. Until she knew her siblings' reactions to Otto's proposal, sleep was impossible.

23

Summer 1928, Fribourg

"Bonjour, madam. Did you rest well? It's a beautiful day outside."

Eloise scowled as morning light flooded the room. "What time is it?"

"Quarter to nine. The journey from Berlin must have been very tiring. Your mother suggested I bring you some coffee. Should I prepare your attire for the day or leave you in peace?"

Eloise pushed off the covers and sat bolt upright. "Quarter to nine? Is everyone else up and dressed?"

Greta poured a cup of coffee from the silver pot. The bittersweet aroma wafted across the room and up Eloise's nostrils, luring her out of bed.

"Yes, madam, everyone but you. Your friend Herr Graz took Laurent for a ride in his motor vehicle. I understand they intend to collect Monsieur Favre and Julius en route. Your mother is waiting downstairs with Sylvia so you can walk to the cathedral together."

"And Charlotte?" Eloise added cream to the thick black brew.

"Your sister left for university at the usual time."

"But it's Sunday!"

"She promised to attend Mass with the rest of the family. The service begins in just over an hour. Shall I help you dress?"

With Greta's assistance, Eloise was ready in half an hour. A cream tennis dress with black trim and dropped hem, a felt cloche and block-heeled court shoes conveyed style and respectability. The light shawl over her shoulders prepared her for the cathedral's chill, but nothing could withstand her mother's icy disapproval.

"Good morning, Sylvia," said Eloise, kissing her daughter. "I'm sorry to keep you waiting, Maman. I slept in."

Madame Favre glanced at the clock. "So I understand. Unless we leave now, we will be late and draw attention to ourselves." She took in Eloise's outfit. "We're going to a church service, not a garden party."

"Would you like me to change?"

"Good gracious, we'd be here all day. Come along, Sylvia, and don't forget your hat. The sun can be cruel to a lady's skin."

The walk to the cathedral took fewer than ten minutes, giving Madame Favre plenty of time to stand around making conversation with the neighbours before the main event. As the matriarch had predicted, Otto's arrival in a modern motor car, complete with her son and grandchildren, allowed her to step onto centre stage.

"Here you are! Oh, my nerves. You boys will be the death of me. I thought you'd never make it. Come, Otto, let me introduce you to our dear friends and neighbours."

Eloise's husband-to-be threw her a mock fearful glance before disappearing into the throng. Any hope of a quiet word with Bastian was quashed by the excitable chatter of Julius and

Laurent, bubbling over with glee at riding in a brand-new motor vehicle. She contented herself with an enquiring look. He returned a hearty smile. Did that mean yes?

Sunday lunch took place at the de Fournier property, once Eloise's marital home, now inhabited by Bastian and family. It looked as beautiful and well tended as the first time Eloise had set eyes on it. To the front, the garden was a cornucopia of colour, with every shrub adding a new shade to the floral palette. At the rear, the long lawn of her memory was a third of its previous length, the remainder turned over to a vegetable plot and chicken run. Aesthetically, it jarred her senses, but she could not deny her brother's pragmatism.

Again, the food they consumed was home grown, or locally caught in respect of the fresh river trout. Despite her impatience to hear the results of last night's conversations, Eloise relaxed into the simplicity of life in Fribourg. Here was a safe place. The children sat at the end of the table, including little Antonia, whose huge blue eyes regarded Eloise with curiosity.

When the main course of fish and fresh vegetables had been consumed and complimented, Bastian exchanged a look with Seraphine.

She nodded. "Children, you may leave the table now. A very special dessert is waiting in the nursery." The nanny took Antonia from her mother's arms and led the children out of the dining room.

Bastian waited until the staff finished clearing plates before he spoke. "Maman, I have something important to share with you. Last night, Otto asked for my blessing to marry Eloise."

"Oh!" Madame Favre pressed her napkin to her lips. Her misty gaze turned to Otto and Eloise. "This is wonderful news!"

"As I said, he asked for my blessing. My reply was that it is not mine to give. I am not my sister's keeper; she is her own woman. The only people whose opinions matter are Sylvia and Laurent. Personally, I believe Otto makes my sister very happy and I would welcome him to our family. Charlotte, do you concur?"

"I do, with the caveats I have already expressed. Like you, my chief concern is for the children." She looked into Eloise's eyes. "What are your plans? Will you stay in Berlin or move to Fribourg? Where are Sylvia and Laurent to reside? Do you plan your own family? How will you ensure the future of your older children?"

Otto rose to his feet, placing his hands on the table. "Thank you all for your kindnesses and even more so for your honesty. I never imagined a woman like Eloise, but when we met, I recognised my extraordinary good fortune. Meeting her family is another revelation. Your loyalty to one another is unmistakeable and I would love to become part of that. If you will accept me as your in-law, I fully intend to care for Sylvia and Laurent as if they were my own. Eloise and I are in love and plan the rest of our lives together. Whether that is in Berlin or Fribourg or somewhere in between is a practical question I'm sure we can resolve. But before we go any further, I must seek approval at the highest level. Please excuse me."

Eloise made to rise, but Bastian placed a hand on her arm.

"Let him do this. The children will respect him for asking. Seraphine, tell the maid she can serve dessert now, prepare the coffee and so on."

Under normal circumstances, wild horses could not have kept Eloise from chocolate mousse with summer berries. Failed imaginings of the scene upstairs stilled her spoon. Madame Favre made several conversational openings which Seraphine gamely attempted to return, but the prevailing sense in the room was one of bated breath.

Finally, the door opened and Sylvia looked in. "May I?" She asked permission of Bastian, not Eloise.

"Of course, *ma cherie*."

The girl scurried in to stand beside her mother, Laurent and Julius hot on her heels. "Herr Graz tells us he wishes to marry you. He says you make each other very happy. Our father, he knows, is irreplaceable but he would like to offer us what he can."

"And he has a car!" whispered Laurent.

"We asked him for a moment to decide and he went out into the garden. We watched him from the window, didn't we?" The boys nodded, eager for the story to progress. "Mitzy came across the lawn and he ..."

"... bent down to stroke her," finished Laurent. "She curled around his legs. Mitzy!"

Eloise glanced at Bastian for an explanation. "Mitzy is our cat. She hates humans and bites everyone. Then what happened?"

"Then we made a decision," said Sylvia.

"A unanimous decision," added Julius.

Bastian cleared his throat. "I believe Herr Graz addressed his question to Sylvia and Laurent, not you, young man."

"My cousins asked my opinion. Happily, everyone was in agreement. We think Herr Graz is a very good sort. And as Grandmère often says, we all want Tante Eloise to settle down."

Madame Favre feigned innocence of making any such comment, while Bastian and Seraphine could not hide their amusement

"Out of the mouths of babes," Charlotte laughed. "Well, it seems we have our answer. Thank you, children, for taking such an important question seriously. Laurent, go rescue the poor man from that awful feline and let us celebrate!"

Bastian fetched a bottle of champagne from the cellar and

Greta poured apple juice for the children. The family spilled from the dining room into the garden, where they toasted the future couple and welcomed Otto to the family. High spirits overtook the children and even Sylvia joined in an energetic game of tag.

The afternoon heat, intense emotion and a glass of bubbles left everyone limp and drowsy. Charlotte dozed off under the cherry tree, and Seraphine put Julius to bed for a nap, while Otto escorted Madame Favre and two of her grandchildren back to her house. Eloise saw an opportunity a walk along the river with her brother. They walked in relaxed silence beneath the beech trees until they found a bench in the shade.

"I hope you didn't mind my passing the responsibility to the children."

"It was a masterstroke, as you well know. They had the final word and now will accept the new circumstances with a positive frame of mind. It was also a risk, you realise?"

Bastian closed his eyes and crossed his ankles. "A calculated one. After the car trip this morning, Laurent was sold. If I'd told him Otto planned to chop you up and turn you into cat food, he would have said, 'Well, even cats have to eat'. Filial love is a fickle thing."

"Yet Sylvia is a different proposition. I'm surprised she didn't insist on a two-hour interview, quizzing Otto on his intentions."

"She didn't need to. Charlotte already took care of that last night. Poor Otto."

"Poor Otto," agreed Eloise. "It's a wonder she didn't put him off."

"He's made of stronger stuff and in any case, he loves you. That much is clear."

"I really think he does." They lapsed into a profound peace, watching leaves ripple in the breeze and silvery light dance on the river.

Bastian opened his eyes. "I know you've been bombarded with questions today. However, there is one thing I'd like to know because your plans will affect mine. What about the house?"

"Yes, the house, of course. I really don't know if we will stay in Berlin or if we can find work in Switzerland. It's a discussion we've not yet had. Since we plan to marry next summer, there's plenty of time to decide. As far as I'm concerned, you can stay permanently. There's plenty of room for all of us."

"That's true. Unless you plan to start your own family."

"Oh, Lord, Bastian, I don't want any more children! Let's be honest, no one could call me the perfect parent. Some people are naturally brilliant at motherhood, such as Seraphine. Others go through the motions and hope for the best. No, I'm grateful for Sylvia and Laurent but the thought of starting all that again fills me with horror."

Bastian shifted on the seat to look at her. "Does Otto feel the same way?"

"I'm thirty-three years old now and will be thirty-four by the time we tie the knot. Far too late to start thinking about babies."

"As a matter of fact, it's not, but that's a choice for each individual. All I'm saying is that you seem very sure about no future children. Is the same true of Otto?"

Eloise folded her arms. "It's not something we've ever talked about."

"I see. Shall we stroll up the hill?" He offered his hand and she took it.

They walked a while in a rather less comfortable silence than before.

"I'm not trying to bully you, Eloise. It's just that when two people decide to spend the rest of their lives together, both should be clear on how that life will look."

She sighed. "You are trying to bully me, and rightly so. I was so excited about the whole romantic side, I've been dragging my heels over the everyday aspects. And if you say, 'Twas ever thus', I shall push you into the river. While we're on holiday here in Fribourg, I will find a good time to raise the topic. Then let's pray he's not already hearing the patter of tiny feet."

Bastian squeezed her hand but said nothing.

During their ten days in Fribourg, a good time to raise the topic never presented itself. Eloise listened as Otto showed Laurent and Julius the principles behind a combustion engine, and marvelled at his patience with their questions. When she grew fatigued playing badminton, Otto asked permission to use her racquet so Sylvia could finish the game. One sunny afternoon, he drove her, Seraphine and the children to Murtensee for a picnic, apparently enjoying himself surrounded by women and children. Once she caught him playing peek-a-boo behind a cushion with Etta. She grew increasingly convinced he would make an excellent father. The thought depressed her profoundly.

Her spirits were already low as they departed for Berlin, with emotional farewells and promises of the next visit. The journey made things worse with sudden summer showers challenging the windscreen wipers and making visibility poor. Otto appeared animated and enthusiastic about the drive, making cheerful conversation over lunch and asking if all was well. She convinced herself she had made a colossal mistake by introducing him to her family, with her affectionate siblings, playful children and quiet, comfortable existence. He had seen an alternate vision of the future and was already planning two children and a vegetable plot. Bastian was right. If their dreams did not align, and vegetable plots had no place in her fantasy world, they would only bring each other unhappiness.

On the approach to Rüsselsheim, the car began to sputter occasionally, as if it were about to stop completely. Otto's brow creased and he tinkered with various instruments, but when it happened twice more, each occasion more alarming, he accepted there was a problem he could not manage. After dropping Eloise at Gasthaus Adler, he continued on to the Opel plant to see if an engineer could advise. She accepted without demur.

In the cosy wooden bedroom, Eloise gave the porter a coin for delivering their bags then sat on the bed and wept. How had it all gone wrong so quickly? Otto fitted in as if he'd known them forever, her family was pleased with her choice, the children were keen on a new father figure and she was about to destroy everyone's joy through her own selfishness. She cried bitter tears and even tried to imagine a scene of provincial domestic bliss, but shoved the thought away. Eventually, she washed her face, repaired her make-up and went downstairs to the dining room.

In Berlin, she never minded sitting alone at a dining table, but here in Gasthaus Adler it seemed more of a novelty. Other patrons whispered and when she told the waitress she was ready to order, the girl asked if she would prefer to wait for her husband.

"Eloise!" Otto stood in the doorway, looking as if he'd just climbed from under an engine, oil spots on his shirt and dirty smudges on his hair and forehead. "Give me two minutes to freshen up? Order me whatever you're having. With a huge beer!"

She could not help but laugh. He had the air of a boy just back from an escapade and she loved him for it. In an instant, the stares of the clientele shifted from judgemental to curious. She ordered them Schnitzel with *pommes frites* and two beers, one large, one small. The meal arrived the moment after Otto sat down.

"Great choice! I am so hungry I could eat this twice. About

the car, good news and bad news. Our poor little Laubfrosch needs an engine overhaul. Perhaps such a long journey was too much. Never mind. The chief engineer will take a detailed look next week. Meanwhile, he asked if I would like to put the new Opel 4/20 PS through its paces. Thus we have a brand new vehicle to take us home. *Prost!*"

They knocked their steins together and drank. The beer lightened Eloise's spirits, as did the hot, oily food, but the news they would not be stuck in Rüsselsheim for longer than one night made her giddy. "*Prost*! I'm very relieved."

"So am I! The last thing I need is vehicle problems. Your eyes look a little red, my love. Are you tired or already missing your family?"

She continued eating but acknowledged this was the perfect occasion to raise the topic. "Not exactly missing them quite yet. However, it is true my family changed my perspective. Up until now, I thought you loved me and I loved you and that sufficed. My blind faith convinced me everything would work out somehow. Spending time with my blunt sister and pragmatic brother, I realised I cannot just expect everything to fall into place. For example, one crucial question hangs over my head. Do you expect our marriage to bear fruit, by which I mean offspring?"

"Good God, no!" His response was immediate and emphatic. "Why do you ask? Do you yearn for more children?"

"Certainly not. Twice was enough."

"That's what I thought. So why did you get upset?"

Eloise sliced off another piece of Schnitzel and gave him a brilliant smile. "At this very moment, I have no idea."

He grinned and continued his meal, devoting all his attention to the food. Eloise was more preoccupied with her thoughts, eating only half what was on her plate. Finally, she placed her cutlery together.

"If you don't want that ...?"

"Help yourself. May I ask why?"

"Because I'm hungry. I ran halfway across the factory to find spare parts before the engineer told me I was wasting my time."

"I meant why don't you want to reproduce?"

"Oh!" He took another swig of beer. Then he met her eyes and dropped his voice to a serious murmur. "Because bringing a child into the world as it stands at the moment is an act of sheer irresponsibility."

24

Winter 1928 – Spring 1929, Berlin

Eloise had the notion she was walking through a hall of mirrors. This one grotesque, that one sublime, so many others merely mundane, yet each reflected an aspect of her life.

In Charlottenweg, the house was now devoted to sex work: Veronika serviced clients on the ground floor and upstairs Jan wrote pornography. No more wealthy benefactors whisked Veronika away for a weekend or sent her home with a hamper of luxury goods. Demand for her erotic evening performances where she writhed and twirled in wisps of chiffon had shrivelled to nothing, much like her body. Dietmar, on the other hand, had a waiting list for everything Morgengrauen could produce.

Eloise rolled up her sleeves and applied basic hygiene measures to the kitchen and bathrooms the first few times she visited, but soon accepted she was fighting a losing battle. One day, she noticed the connecting door to Ruth's half of the building hung open. She confronted Jan, as Veronika was otherwise engaged. He confessed that he had broken in, stolen whatever trinkets he could sell and bartered dusty ornaments to buy cocaine.

"For you?"

His fierce blue eye stared back. "For her. It's always for her."

Eloise believed him and it hurt her heart.

Bit by bit, she moved her belongings to Otto's apartment until Charlottenweg was nothing more than somewhere she used to live. Or at least that's what she told herself. She wrote to Ruth at her new address, absolving herself of all responsibility for the property. There was no reply. At least once a week, Eloise happened to be passing with a package of food, cigarettes and toiletries to help her friends survive. Each time, things had become just a little bit worse.

Meanwhile, in her working life, she attended fashion weeks, art exhibitions, motor shows and theatre performances. Wearing a Jeanne Lanvin dress and sipping a cocktail, she discussed with her friends the irony of Brecht's *The Threepenny Opera*. A scathing critique on social injustice, it was the hottest ticket in town for everyone from bankers to government ministers. How they laughed!

Otto was deeply absorbed in his work. The American automobile firm General Motors had shown an interest in Opel's Rüsselsheim production line system and paid over $33 million for an 80% stake in the company. It was a huge boost to the car manufacturing sector and Opel was the jewel in its crown. At first dubious about the takeover, Otto soon found that his unexpected bonus eased his fears and they dined at The Wintergarten in celebration.

Eloise spent hours poring over trends for summer dress

patterns while snow piled up on the windowsill. Each night her umbrella dried in the hallway while she sliced celeriac, leek and turnip for a winter soup and thought about a new angle on bikinis. On the evenings Otto led one of his political meetings, her courage failed her. Rather than venture out into the bitter sleet and walk to a steamy town hall where people puffed up with emotion or aggression shouted and shook their fists, she stayed home and planned her wedding. It still seemed an impossible fantasy, but the fact of the matter was that she and Otto had fixed a date – Saturday June 1st – to become husband and wife. Now she had to find the dress, the venue, and decide on a constantly changing guest list, musical accompaniments and why not, flowers.

For reasons of practicality, they planned two events: the official ceremony at Fribourg Cathedral and wedding breakfast with her family; and a party two weeks later in Berlin, with less focus on religious vows and more on the celebration. In each location, she had an ally. When Eloise had proposed the role of maid of honour last Christmas, Seraphine voiced only the slightest quibble: surely that was Charlotte's privilege? All Eloise needed to do was raise her eyebrows and the idea of Charlotte embracing pomp made them both giggle. Seraphine accepted the responsibility with unforced joy. Three little bridesmaids and her lovely sister-in-law would make the photographs perfect.

One might have expected Otto's family to step forward and organise the Berlin festivities, but they showed only passive acceptance of their son's upcoming nuptials. Gustav said he would check his diary, but parties were not really his scene. Instead of her future in-laws, the force of nature that was Irmgard took control.

"A costume ball! I can picture it already! The great and the glamorous all in the most beautiful gowns, photographers and society columnists clamouring for an invitation, everyone desperate to see the most modern couple tie the knot: him a motoring legend, her the *Vogue* columnist on everyone's lips. It's the wedding of the year and all of Germany will be watching."

"You do exaggerate wildly. That sounds thrilling, but we don't have the funds for an extravagant party. The marriage itself will cost us enough. We wanted something muted and personal, just for our friends."

"*Quatsch*! You won't pay a Pfennig. I will secure sponsorship, from the venue to the catering and even the music. If I put my mind to it, I can probably even get someone to design your dress. Since it's a summer wedding, what about calling it a Butterfly Ball? Colourful, fabulous, and exactly what people need after a long grey winter. Please say yes, Eloise darling, I need something to look forward to because I hate Berlin winters with a passion."

Helpless and hopeful, Eloise said yes, sure she could convince Otto of the need for publicity once the wheels were in motion. After all, who doesn't love a party?

Berlin's Chief of Police, for one. In December, Karl Zörgiebel had banned all outdoor political gatherings in the entire Berlin metropolis, citing factional violence as a good reason to keep zealots off the streets. To Eloise, that sounded reasonable. Violent battles between paramilitary groups whether allied to communists or the far right, encroached upon normal life, stretching law enforcers and distressing ordinary citizens. Fewer placards and less aggression would brighten her day.

Otto saw it differently. "It's a regressive move. We are a republic. An immature, squabbling republic still in short trousers, perhaps, but one obliged to represent every last one of its citizens. Our government has a duty to hear all views, dissenting or otherwise. For Berlin, the most open-minded and progressive city in Prussia, Zörgiebel banning political protest is a dictatorial act. It's tantamount to banning free speech. This will end badly."

"He sounds frightful." Eloise was at the ironing board, removing creases from one of Otto's work shirts. "Can't you replace him with one of yours from the SDP?"

Otto exhaled a sharp laugh. "He is one of ours from the SDP."

"Oh. I see." She didn't.

"You need to understand the situation, Eloise. The Social Democratic Party might look like it's in charge, but the reality is we're in the middle, trying to appease the extreme left and the far right. Communists wield a great deal of power with so many seats in the Reichstag, claiming to represent the true working classes. They are unwilling to compromise and use small groups of Red Front Fighters to disrupt what they describe as the bourgeoisie. The Nazis take a similar stance, unleashing violence against the status quo via their Storm Troopers, saying they stand for the honest German family. The face of the status quo, AKA the bourgeoisie, is the SDP. That makes us everyone's *de facto* enemy."

Eloise noted the droop at the corner of his eyes. "What's the difference between the true working classes and the honest German family?"

"That, my love, is a very good question. If either party stopped shouting and listened, they might find some common ground. I place my faith in dialogue over dogma. The danger is in polarisation. Nature may abhor a vacuum, but the Nazi Party loves nothing more."

It seemed to Eloise, as she starched Otto's collars, that the whole of Germany was a schoolyard, with one gang of kids trying to gain precedence over another. A cloud of steam rose from the wet tea towel as she pressed the iron across yoke and cuffs. "If the left have fighters and the right have troopers, in what kind of force does the centre place its faith?"

Otto ran a hand from his forehead to his crown. "That would be the police."

With two months to go before the wedding, Eloise had her last fitting for a Schiaparelli dress. The silvery fabric caressed her form, accentuating her curves and minimising her waist. It was unconventional but individualistic, suited to both formal ceremony and flamboyant party. When she walked around the designer's atelier, she had tears in her eyes. On the occasion of her second marriage, she would look even more beautiful than she had on her first.

Everything else on her list was either already organised or in the hands of Seraphine and Irmgard. All that remained was to pin down Otto's role in the proceedings. She kept it simple, knowing how preoccupied he was with party politics, and waited till they were ready for bed.

"I'm sure you'll be pleased to hear that arrangements for our marriage are now final. Nothing left for us to worry about." She swept cold cream in long strokes from her collarbone to her cheek.

"I'm very grateful to you for doing all that work. Please understand, I don't consider it 'a job for a woman', but you enjoy paying attention to finer details and I trust your judgement. Do you need anything from me?"

"Very little, in fact. A suit and a best man, that is all."

He buttoned up his pyjamas. "Of course. I will call on my tailor before the end of the week and order a formal suit."

"Choose something you can use again. This is no time for frivolous spending on something you will only wear once." She bit her lip, recalling how much *Vogue* had spent on the shantung silk for her gown. "What time do you have to leave in the morning?"

"Five. We'll be at AVUS all day and in the evening, I must give an interview to *Vorwärts*, our newspaper. I may not be home until late. I'm sorry, Eloise. This weekend, I promise to spend all my time with you." He placed a hand on her shoulder.

"No need for apologies. You're working hard for your ideals and I admire your energy."

"Thank you." He kicked off his slippers and got under the blankets. "It's so cold! Are you coming to bed?"

"Yes." She tucked herself, switched off the lamp and curled into his warmth. "Thank you for ordering a suit for the wedding. As for the best man, I assume you'll ask your brother."

His body stiffened. "Under no circumstances would I consider Gustav for my best man."

"As I said, my darling, your choice. Sleep well, Otto." She kissed him lightly.

"Exactly. You have a good night's rest too. I love you, Eloise."

She lay awake for a few moments, waiting for him to fall asleep, worried she had upset him with the mention of his brother. Soon his breathing deepened and his embrace loosened. Only then could she relax and close her eyes. Everything would be fine and even if it wasn't, worrying ahead of the event was unlikely to help.

Trouble was brewing long before the end of April and no one was surprised. International Workers' Day bore its own significance depending on one's political affiliation, but tradition stated that 1st of May was a day to honour labourers of every ilk. The difficulty was that political gatherings of all kinds were still banned across Prussia. The Communist Party's newspapers and leaflets insisted the workers' right to march superseded any governmental prohibitions. The government upheld its decision, citing previous violence and reiterating its intransigence. A spiral began: the government warned against any public events; the communists pointed at oppression; the police prepared for street battles and the Nazis rubbed their hands together in glee.

Reports of sporadic incidents of violence made their way onto trams and into cafés, sending people scurrying home. One of those was Eloise. With a nod to *Walpurgisnacht*, she prepared *Hexensuppe*, or witches' soup, with beans and spiced sausage. She left it simmering on the stove and sat at the dining table to browse the newspapers. Dramatic warnings of 200 potential deaths from the SDP (voice of reason/reactionary establishment, according to perception), were countered by calls to action from the KDP (revolutionary troublemakers/working-class heroes, varying by publication) accusing the Reichstag of brutally suppressing the voice of the people.

Eloise reflected on her own florid prose. In an article she had recently written on motoring accessories for the lady driver, she had committed the cardinal sin of excess alliteration, describing scarves as soft, sensual and silken. Compared to political soapboxers, she decided, she was rather restrained. On her way to the kitchen to stir the soup, she heard a key in the door.

"Otto?"

He came around the corner with an older man, who took off his cap. "Hallo, Eloise, this is Konrad. Sorry but we can't stay. Some of us are going down to Neukölln and Wedding, hoping to calm the temperature. Oh, what's that smell?"

"*Hexensuppe*. Good evening, Konrad, pleased to meet you. If you have to hurry off immediately, I completely understand. But it only takes a few minutes to eat a hearty soup. Consider it fortification for the evening."

"Good evening, Frau Graz, and thank you. A bowl of soup would be very welcome." His eyebrows were like furry caterpillars and his forehead as grooved as a breadboard.

Both men shrugged off their coats and sat at the table.

She didn't correct his term of address, merely sharing a smile with Otto as she scooped two large portions into each bowl. Frau Graz would be her title in almost one calendar month, so why quibble?

"Please start and I will bring some bread. What takes you to those quarters of the city?"

They ate, scooping chunks of vegetable and sausage in a regular rhythm.

"That's where the problems start." Otto blew on a spoonful of beans.

"It's a poor neighbourhood, you see," said Konrad. "Exactly the kind of place communists find willing ears. A rational voice is required to counter that propaganda. I must say, this soup is very fine."

Eloise acknowledged his compliment with a nod, placing the bread on the table.

"Someone has to argue our side," Otto continued. "The government is not the enemy, but it's easy to perceive us that way if we sit in the Reichstag issuing limitations on everyday behaviour. That's why we need SDP representatives on the ground, talking sense to people. Konrad is an excellent communicator and I am learning the art of persuasion."

"Oh, dear. You would think people had had enough of fighting."

Konrad had finished his soup and was already putting on his jacket. "The fact is, dear lady, Germany is still at war. If not with its enemies, then with itself."

"Please take good care, both of you. I wish you luck."

"Soup was exactly what we needed. Thank you, Eloise. You're a staunch supporter."

Otto kissed her, an outdoor chill still lingering on his coat, and led Albert out. They had stayed no longer than ten minutes. Eloise put a slice of bread in her bowl and poured the remaining soup on top. As she ate, she watched the black skies of *Walpurgisnacht* cover Berlin. Tonight there would be none of the traditional bonfires to chase away witches. The best way of avoiding evil spirits would be to stay home.

That night she slept badly, alert for the sound of her fiancé's return. Finally, as dawn broke, she got up to use the bathroom. When she came out, she saw Otto's boots by the front door. She tiptoed down the corridor and found him asleep on the divan, covered by a crocheted blanket. She gazed at him for a moment, relieved he was safe, grateful for his thoughtfulness and filled with a protective urge to lock the door and keep him safely by her side. Then she returned to bed and slipped under the blankets for another hour, planning to get up and make breakfast at seven.

When she awoke, it was quarter to nine. In the living room, the divan was empty, the blanket neatly folded and the only sign of Otto's recent presence was a pot of coffee on the stove. A note was on the kitchen table.

Darling Eloise

Apology No. 1: I'm sorry for not saying goodbye, but you were sleeping so peacefully, I did not have the heart to wake you. You looked like a little dormouse curled into a ball.

Apology No. 2: The streets are going to be wildly unpredictable today and I strongly suggest staying home. Vogue *can manage without you this once. Use the telephone!*

Apology No. 3: That said, I'm afraid I used the last of the bread for my breakfast, so an early trip to the bakery is permissible.

I love you, my little dormouse, and if all goes well, I plan to be home for dinner.

Your Otto

She kissed her finger to her lips and pressed it onto his signature.

25

Spring – Summer 1929

She did as she was told and used the telephone. Otto often picked up the handset without a second thought, but Eloise always weighed cheaper alternatives. It was a long-running joke between the two of them that she'd rather run the length of the city with a message than incur the costs of telecommunication. Considering her general profligacy with expenses, it was a strange behavioural quirk she attributed to her father's influence.

Irmgard agreed with her decision not to venture outside. "Naturally! Everyone's staying home, my darling. It's like a war zone out there, what with the commies and the unions and the police and the Nazis. Ideologues, the whole rotten lot, who use impressionable youths to do their dirty work. Yesterday, I saw children throwing stones at traffic wardens! Can you believe it? This will all end in tears, mark my words. Georges thinks I should go to Paris and escape the whole mucky business. I'd go in a heartbeat, if I wasn't having far too much fun planning a certain wedding party."

"Yes, that's where I should be directing my attention, rather than worrying about Otto. He came home so late last night, he slept on the divan rather than wake me. But he's back out in the thick of things again today."

"Your fiancé is a man of principle and I admire him for his ethics. I just wish he'd write books on the subject. So much safer than making speeches at assemblies. But Otto is fond of dangerous sports. Talking of which, what do you say to a different slant on winter activities this year? No more 'what's suitable for the slopes' because that's what *der Daumen* will be doing."

Irmgard's bitterness towards Eloise's former employer and their rival publication led her to create all kinds of alternative names for the magazine – currently she favoured *der Daumen (The Thumb)* as a snide reference to Ernst Dryden's masculine influence as creative director of *Die Dame*.

"By a different slant you mean another sport?"

"No, no, we're never going to ignore skiing. Our readers love the idea of looking elegant in the mountain resorts. But after a day rushing down snowy runs, one can enjoy the après-ski! Classy attire to wear by the fire. We'll have a skincare feature to run alongside and showcase lots of beautiful leisure clothes. I'll get a few designers to send you samples for tomorrow."

"Tomorrow?"

"Oh, all this nonsense will be over by the morning. Don't worry, Eloise. I can hear in your voice that you're fretting. All will be well. You set yourself to thinking about après-ski once you're done with that change-of-season lipstick piece. I must go, darling. Stay inside and take good care."

In some ways, Irmgard's blithe belief in the future was a counterweight to Otto's harsh realism. Between the two, Eloise found something approaching harmony: natural optimism with a healthy pinch of caution. She buttoned up her coat against the wind and scuttled along the street to see if the bakery was even open on a workers' holiday. Thankfully, it was operating as usual and she purchased a loaf of bread, two beigels and one of yesterday's filled rolls for her lunch. That should keep them going until life returned to normality.

She spent the morning editing her article on lipsticks for every colouring and found herself distracted by a photograph of Josephine Baker. There was a woman who knew what suited her face. Eloise had seen her perform twice at the Nelson Theatre, mesmerised by her extraordinary fluidity of movement and dazzling smile. She was just thinking how glad she was Otto had not witnessed the woman dance when the telephone rang.

"Hello?"

"Frau Graz, here is Konrad speaking. Is Otto with you?"

"No, I haven't seen him since this morning. Is everything all right?"

"I don't know. The police charged us when we came out of a meeting and we got separated. Several people were hurt and I lost Otto in the confusion."

"Do you think I should come and help you find him? Konrad, are you still there?"

"No, don't come anywhere near Wedding. It's worse still in Neukölln where the police have lost their minds. Stay home. Otto will return when he can, and when he does, tell him to call HQ." He rang off without another word.

All interest in cosmetics disappeared and Eloise hurried to the window. Life appeared to progress, if a little quieter than normal. Alexanderplatz was a good forty minutes from Wedding and she wasn't exactly sure where Neukölln might be. She opened the window in order to catch any gossip and sat on the window seat to wait. The bells rang for midday, but Eloise had no appetite for a day-old roll wrapped in brown paper. Time slowed to the point she became convinced it was going backwards. Trams rattled under the window, motor cars negotiated junctions, horses dragged carts and people dodged between the three to reach the relative safety of the pavement, only to be accosted by beggars.

Come home, Otto. Your fight will still be there tomorrow. Please come home.

Twice she picked up the phone but couldn't think who to call. Then she gave herself a stern talking-to. Otto was a respected politician who could reason with anyone, no matter how extreme their position. Local people had elected him to do a job which he was trying to perform under challenging circumstances. If he came home to find his wife frozen by phantoms of her own imagination, she would be more of a hindrance than a help. Cooking, she decided, was the best way to use her time. Her fiancé must be ravenous after a day on the streets, so *Rösti* with bacon and a fried egg was the obvious choice.

The process of grating potato calmed her nerves and she took comfort in the usual cacophony of bells, horns, shouts and whistles through the window. *Life flows on*, she thought, *and we are swept along in its wake, whether we like it or not*. When the telephone rang – twice in one day! – she wiped her hands on her apron and answered with an optimistic tone.

"Otto?"

"Sorry, no. My name is Rapp and I am a doctor at the *Kinderklinik* in Wedding. Your name is Eloise de Fournier, yes?"

Kinderklinik? Why was a children's hospital calling her at home? Sylvia and Laurent were in Fribourg, surely?

"Yes, I am Eloise de Fournier."

"I apologise for bearing bad news, Frau de Fournier, but we have Herr Otto Graz in our care. His wallet contained this number and your name."

"Herr Graz is my fiancé. Why is he in a children's hospital?"

"Your fiancé had an accident and we are the closest medical centre. Unfortunately, he got caught up in the disturbances and fell against a kerbstone. Since it is a head injury, we took a Röntgen picture. You are familiar with the concept of X-rays? It shows a swelling which puts pressure on his brain. We intend to operate immediately and in my opinion, you should be at his side. The success rate of such procedures is unpredictable. Please hurry. Here is the address."

Ten minutes before the surgeons could begin the operation, forty minutes before Eloise's taxi navigated a route through the raging protestors, six hours after a water hose pushed a political moderate off his feet, cracking his skull against the pavement, Otto Graz drew his last breath.

Eloise knelt by his body. She was not permitted to see his face, due to the damage. Instead, she kissed his cold, stiff hands, committing every crease, vein, freckle, fingernail, graze and mole to memory. The hospital gave her time, despite the number of emergencies they were handling. Finally, she let him go, walked almost half the way home until she found a functioning tram stop and returned to their apartment. The weight of obligations crushed her. Once inside the door, she took off her boots and coat, lay on the divan and covered herself with the crocheted blanket. Four times the telephone shrilled its intrusive cry for attention and twice somebody rang the doorbell. Eloise lacked the energy to attend to anything. Night crept into the room and brought the chill along, causing her to stiffen and shiver. Finally, she forced herself to get up. For want of a better idea, she put on her coat. By the light of the kitchen lamp, she saw a pile of browning potato shreds. Whether it was the waste of food or the pleasure she had imagined while planning the meal, the act of scraping the starchy mess into the bin released her from frozen shock into grief. She wept at the sink, splashing cold water on her face between wrenching sobs. Unable to bear the truth, she sought reassurance, scattering the papers on the table in search of his note.

I love you, my little dormouse, and if all goes well, I plan to be home for dinner.

Your Otto

Her Otto would not be home for dinner.

When her vision cleared, she read the note again and saw his instruction. *Use the telephone!*

Her first thought was Bastian, her haven in times of trouble. Had he not shielded her from the dreadful business of funerals when she lost her first husband? Even before she finished the thought, she dismissed it. Otto was not yet her husband and she was an independent woman with capable friends. She picked up the telephone and dialled the only number she knew by heart: Irmgard.

All the papers reported on *Blutmai* (Blood May), each with a different opinion on who was to blame. The number of dead and injured varied between 30 and 200. Fingers pointed at the police, accusing them of excessive violence and blaming military tactics on the SDP. The government retaliated by banning communist newspapers and imposing martial law in two districts. Eloise understood all the words yet the meaning escaped her. Perhaps she could have made more sense of it if she had stayed in Otto's apartment, watching from the windows as angry crowds gathered on Alexanderplatz. However, when Irmgard took control, resistance was futile.

Eloise spent a week in the guest room of Irmgard's beautiful villa, tackling one task at a time. Gathering strength to tell family and friends of her loss took enormous effort, leaving her drained and limp. The worst call was to Otto's parents, where they simply refused to believe her. Herr Graz Senior insisted she speak to Gustav, as if he was some kind of translator. Eloise's throat swelled to the point she could no longer trust her voice and whispered a farewell. She could not, would not speak to Otto's hateful brother.

Irmgard, always hovering in case she was needed, took charge. "Fear not, I will handle Gustav Graz. Leave this to me, dear girl, I've met his type before."

Old Eloise would have listened outside the door, intrigued by a mongoose tackling a snake. Bereaved Eloise had no stomach for the battle and retreated to her room, sitting as usual on the sunny balcony. Death should not happen in summertime. It was inappropriate. The correct time for an untimely demise was November, or October if one was in a hurry. Not spring with fruit trees in full blossom, clear skies and what else was it he said?

Clear blue skies above, shades of green below, flowers like fireworks and jewel-coloured butterflies whispering promises of a brilliant future.

Whatever the season, this was a time for gratitude and treasured memories. She inhaled, stretching her lungs to their capacity, and on her exhale, picked up a pen and paper.

Dearest Otto

Please know you were the love of my life. Never before had I known the level of trust in another person as I did in you. Our fields of interest differed, yet I cheered for you, rejoicing in your successes. My admiration for your passion and determination only ever grew. With your encouragement, I became myself, confident of your support. Our life together, I am sure, would have been a journey of discovery. I mourn the loss of my husband-to-be but treasure the precious time we spent as a couple. One day, we shall be reunited forever.

With more love than words can contain,
Your Eloise

She folded the note, kissed it and picked up a box of matches from the mantelpiece. He would have laughed at such symbolism but he wasn't there. Leaning from the window, she lit the paper and watched her words burst into flame. When the paper burned close to her fingertips, she released it, a tiny glow floating to earth, soon nothing more than ash.

26

Two weeks before her wedding day, Eloise buried her future husband. Thanks to Irmgard's offer of medication, her memories of the occasion seemed fractured and surreal, as if she'd only watched a film of the event. The coffin, Irmgard's firm grip on her elbow, SDP officials and uniformed police, the Graz family, newspaper reporters and a priest intoning a meaningless recital. As nothing more than his fiancée, she was in no man's land, without a place in the hierarchy. She sat in the second row of pews, behind the family, who thanked her for coming as if she were any other guest. She wept as silently as she could behind her veil. The only moment of reality breaking through her distanced fog happened when she got up to follow the mourners into the graveyard. Veronika and Jan stood by the church gates. Hollow-eyed and skeletal, they looked like a pair of resident ghosts whose job was to haunt the living. Eloise raised a black-gloved hand in greeting and they bowed respectful heads.

Once the ceremony was over, her friends had gone. She wished they had waited so that she could join them in some form of oblivion, rather than leaving her to face all those sympathetic eyes. She accepted all the condolences, bid Otto's family goodbye and asked Georges and Irmgard to drive her home to her apartment. They did their best to dissuade her, saying she should not be alone on such a day. Eloise insisted, careful to express her gratitude but equally determined to make her own decisions about the rest of her life.

Regardless of what she expected, returning to the apartment came as a shock. The post box overflowed, cards of condolence jammed amongst all the usual bills and political fliers. Inside, the air was sour, with a fetid, rotting thickness. This was Otto's place and she had the impression of being an intruder. She changed into a day dress and set to work, first pouring all the spoiled food into the waste bin and opening all the windows to admit a fresh breeze. Next, she watered all the wilted, browning plants with a whispered apology. Then she began packing all Otto's clothes and shoes into a suitcase. Her plan was to take the tram across town and deliver them to Jan. They wouldn't fit him, since Otto was tall and muscular while a gust of wind could topple Jan. But clothes were clothes and Eloise had to be practical. Her skin seemed to grow thinner so that random objects left a bruise. His shaving brush, the inkwell and fountain pen she had given him for Christmas, even his shoehorn provoked memories and consequent tears. The effects of Irmgard's remedy were evidently wearing off. In her purse was another pill, 'in case of emergencies'. Reality was not an emergency. The sooner she got to grips with her new situation, the better.

She worked until five, boiled some rice and ate it at the kitchen table while tackling their correspondence. Halfway through a loose tally of the bills due and wedding RSVPs, there was a ring at the doorbell. She took off her apron and went to greet her visitor. On the threshold stood Gustav Graz, his top hat in his hand.

"Good evening, Gustav."

"Eloise." He dipped his head. "May I come in?"

He smelt somehow oily, perhaps from a vehicle or his hair. Whatever its source, the scent repelled her. Yet she could not refuse him entrance. "Please do. I found today's ceremony quite touching. Were your parents satisfied with the arrangements?"

He stalked into the living room and surveyed the dusty room, browned plants and smudged windows lit by late afternoon sun. "I made all the arrangements. Naturally they were satisfied." He tweaked up his trouser legs and sat on the divan, tossing the crocheted blanket to the other end, as if it were dirty.

"I'm afraid I have just returned home this afternoon and did not expect visitors. But I could offer you a cup of tea or a glass of water?"

"No. I am here on official matters. It will not take long."

Eloise stood beside the armchair, fists clenched, her gaze on the carpet, and thought about the pill in her purse. "I'm pleased to hear that because I'm currently occupied in sorting out my affairs. What is it that you want?"

"It's more a question of what you want. According to that overblown oration from his political party, my brother was 'an idealist, driven to make the world a better place'. That seems to be true. Idealists rarely deal in facts. The reality is that my brother never made a will. He died a bachelor and everything he owned now goes to his legal next of kin: by which I mean his family. His money, his possessions, his apartment and anything else of value belongs to us."

She looked up and saw the deadness in his eyes had been replaced by a glint of light.

With a deep exhale to steady her breath, she replied. "I understand. You'd like me to leave the home Otto and I shared, taking nothing but my possessions, and leaving you the key. Am I correct?"

He placed his palms together, resting his chin on his fingertips. "That is one course of action. The sad fact is that you have nowhere to go, unless you return to that pit of immorality on Charlottenweg. I assume those degenerates lurking in the graveyard are the kind of people you call friends."

"Yes, they are my friends and both good people. Jan lost his eye in the war, fighting for Germany. Veronika is a modern woman who ..."

"... charges by the hour. Please listen to what I have to say. I am not devoid of compassion and it is clear you need support. For my brother's sake, I am prepared to offer you an alternative."

She knew Gustav well enough to suspect his alternative involved taking away her professional status. A live-in job as his mother's gardener? A secretarial role with the Opel firm?

"And what would that be?"

"Tradition dictates that when a groom leaves his bride before the marriage ceremony, the best man has a duty to honour that obligation."

The idea was so absurd Eloise wanted to laugh. She stared at his supercilious expression a second, unable to hide her incredulity. Her legs threatened to buckle, so she eased herself into the armchair and covered her face with her hands.

Otto did not leave me. Otto would never have left me because he had more decency in his little finger than you will achieve in your lifetime. You were never intended as his best man. He detested you and so do I. To marry you would be dancing on his grave.

It took a moment until she regained control of herself. "I'm afraid I cannot entertain such a proposal on the day I buried the love of my life. Marrying another man, regardless of who he might be, is absolutely unthinkable."

"Think a little harder. This arrangement is mutually beneficial. You wed into a wealthy family, just as you planned. I am spared the inconvenience of finding a suitable wife to provide me with an heir. The question of your employment can be discussed in due course."

His words turned her blood to ice. "I will consider your suggestion. Today has taken its toll, as it must have done on your whole family. If you don't mind, I'd like some private time this evening. Thank you for paying a visit." She stood and gestured to the door.

He unfolded like one of those measuring rulers and stepped closer to her, not to the door. His shadow blocked the setting sun. "Entirely your decision, of course. I will enquire in another week and if your answer remains the same, you shall vacate these premises by the end of July. One word of advice; try to be the pragmatist my brother never was. Good evening to you."

The following Monday, Eloise returned to work, blocking every thought of Gustav Graz and his patronising 'arrangement' from her mind. For the first few days in the office, she thought the sober atmosphere was a sign of respect for her grief. Only when she caught a snatch of conversation between Eloise and Georges did she realise her personal tragedy belonged in the last issue, i.e. yesterday's news. What ailed German *Vogue* was kept from Eloise's ears until she opened them.

Lack of advertising revenue. Unpopular editorial focus. The wrong kind of writers. Un-German ethics. Niche market catering to the bourgeoisie. Powerful competition.

"What's going to happen, Irmgard?"

The two women sat at a sunlit table outside Victoria Café, their smiles at odds with the sober tone of their conversation. But this was Friedrichstrasse, where people came to look happy. Sad faces were met with frowns.

"Unless we get a financial injection from some generous beneficiary, our last edition will be in August. It breaks my heart, Eloise, but we simply cannot function in Berlin. How can one discuss fashion and style while deadly fights break out on our streets? I'm so sorry, my dear, this is the last thing you need to hear after your bereavement. Yet there is still hope. Georges has connections in Paris and an enormous apartment in the 2nd arrondissement. He knows everyone: Picasso, de Lempicka, Dalì, Chanel, everyone! We intend to depart for France in a matter of weeks and you are welcome to join us. After all, Germany is becoming intolerable. Will you come, my darling? You speak French, you have classic style and everyone will love you. Please say yes."

Eloise smiled, because she had no choice. People were watching. "You are my best friend. Where I succeed, you applaud. When I stumble, you catch my hand. You were the first person I called when Otto died. But I can't come to Paris with you and Georges, no matter how tempting the offer."

Irmgard beckoned the waiter with a perfect red-polished fingernail. "Because I'm your best friend, you refuse my invitation? Two glasses of the house champagne, *mon brave*."

"I can never repay you for all you have done and will never forget your kindness. Never. But I moved to Berlin to learn independence. A modern woman is in charge of her own life. She sometimes falls flat on her face but takes responsibility for her mistakes. If I went with you to Paris, I'd be running away."

"You're writing a column, I can hear it in your voice. Some would say running away is the best thing to do in the face of a hurricane."

"True, but once again, I would be dependent on others. There has to come a time when I stand firm, draw on my resilience and refuse to shelter behind someone else. It might make no sense to you, but I have to plumb my own well. Otherwise, I must marry Gustav and be a brood mare."

"Gustav?" Irmgard's eyes widened. She flashed a dazzling smile at the waiter as he placed two coupes on the tablecloth.

"He proposed? I cannot imagine that vile man expressing romantic feelings. *Santé!*"

Eloise stuck to the German toast rather than echo the French, as a way of marking her identity. "*Prost!* He didn't. His offer was transactional. He rescues me from financial ruin and I bear him a child." She shook her head, banishing the thought, and sipped her champagne.

Irmgard covered her eyes. "One more reason why you should come to Paris." She looked up under the hood of her hands and dropped her voice. "Germany, I am sorry to say, is going bust. Even here in Berlin, things will soon get worse for 'the modern woman'. The Nazis want us back in the kitchen, or maybe the bedroom. We have made so much progress we think ourselves invincible but it could all be snatched away in a heartbeat. Winds of change are upon us, believe me."

"Is that the angle of your next editorial? Because I think you might frighten our readership."

"The way things are going, our readership will soon cease to exist. The stock market is sliding, our economy has more sticking plasters than strategies, plus the Americans will soon stop lending us money. Disposable income tends to disappear in a depression. That means no music, no theatre, no cinema, no art and certainly no fashion."

Her perennially optimistic friend sounded so unlike herself, Eloise scarcely recognised her. "A depression? That's a rather bleak outlook."

"Sadly not. We live in a bubble, you and I. Berlin's hedonistic lifestyle of designer clothes, glamorous parties, wealthy people and champagne at lunchtime insulates us from reality. The bloom has faded, exposing the rot beneath. Read the newspapers." With some effort, she threw off her careworn air and adopted her professional smile. "That is why you must come with us to Paris, where joy is still in abundance, where art and beauty reign supreme."

"I promise to think about it."

"In the same way you'll consider Gustav's proposal? You are an articulate woman with a voice which deserves to be heard. That won't happen here. When *Vogue* closes, what will you do?"

"I honestly don't know."

Irmgard tossed the remainder of her champagne into her mouth. "Stubbornness is your least appealing feature. Think very hard and make realistic plans. Our lives can change overnight, so we must be prepared. Will you not consider returning to Switzerland and your family if you refuse to join us in the style capital of the world?"

"What I am going to do is weather the storm, stand firm and refuse to be intimidated by arrogant men, whether that is a brownshirt or a brother-in-law. Otto loved me as a risk-taker, a pioneering modern woman. I cannot betray that regard."

"Otto loved you for many reasons, my dear. One of many was your good sense. Do not permit bullishness to overcome your instincts. Shall we get the bill?"

27

Summer – Autumn 1929

By the time Gustav returned to request an answer, Eloise decided, he would find the apartment already vacant. Her absence was an unmistakeable way to communicate her decision. She packed her belongings into two suitcases and a cardboard box, scrupulously separating Otto's possessions from her own. When she had finished scrubbing, brushing, dusting and wiping, the apartment looked sad. Clean, but sad. The one item she took which did not belong to her was the crocheted blanket. That, and the spare set of keys. Just in case.

The taxi conveying her to Charlottenstrasse would be the last time she afforded herself such luxury. With two months' more income from *Vogue*, she could live cheaply until she found work. For some reason on the taxi ride across the city, signs of Switzerland appeared everywhere. She heard two men speaking Berner-Dütsch as she helped the driver load her bags. An advertisement by the road trumpeted Swiss cheese. Bells ringing from a little church reminded her of the *Viehschau*, or cattle parade when farmers brought their herds down from the mountain in autumn. Omens she should return? She shook her head. *Not yet. Give me one last chance.*

At her old address, the building was in darkness. Even the driver was reluctant to leave her at such an evidently abandoned place. Eloise reassured him, paid the fare and made three journeys up the path. Her key still worked. Inside, she reeled from the scent of mould and decay. If anyone still inhabited these rooms, they had no sense of smell.

"Veronika? Jan?"

A small creak came from the first room, so Eloise took out a handkerchief and turned the door handle. The room was dark, curtains closed against the street lamps, and when she pressed the light switch, nothing happened. "Veronika? Are you there?"

Some rustling came from the centre of the room, making the hairs on Eloise's neck rise. This place could be inhabited by a gang of beggars, waiting to kill and rob an unwary stranger. Someone struck a match.

The room immediately took shape: the same bed Eloise used to sleep in with its pile of cushions against the headboard like a rockery. In the centre, soft and white as an Edelweiss, lay Veronika holding a match.

"Light a candle, will you?" Her voice was a croaky whisper.

Eloise lit a votive candle on the dresser which had the added benefit of reflecting in the mirror. She used it to light another next two beside the bed, each heavy and white, probably stolen from a place of worship. Three small flames filled the space with a warm glow. Veronika's phlegmy cough didn't reach far enough to blow them out.

Entering a person's bedroom without permission demanded a certain etiquette, so Eloise did not allow herself to dwell the empty bottles of wine, the bloodstained bandages or tray of phials and syringes, but registered them in a second.

She trod carefully, three candles barely enough to throw illumination on the floor, and sat on the bed, at the level of her friend's knee. She forced herself not to flinch at the grey, sunken face of a former beauty and instead looked into her clouded blue eyes.

"I'm so sorry about Otto," Veronika wheezed.

"Thank you for coming to the funeral."

"We cared. For both of you." Every word sounded a huge effort. "What now?"

"I'd like to move in here. My journalism work will soon run out. With your permission and Jan's help, I can turn this place into a boarding house. I want to rent rooms to those who can afford them while keeping the three of us afloat. After all, Ruth left me in charge."

Veronika closed her eyes and tears leaked down her cheeks. She said nothing, simply nodding her head.

In Ruth's part of the building, they began work the very next day. Eloise and Jan took down all the battens from the front windows and let fresh air blow in. Bit by bit, they dusted every surface, swept the floors, threw out rotten rugs and washed the curtains. Eloise paid the electricity bill and had the gas reconnected. She arranged the remaining furniture and Jan painted a third coat over the front door. In what used to be Ruth's office, they sat down and planned how best to use the property. A salon and kitchen downstairs for guests, two rooms on the first floor and another on the second. The mirror image of their own lodgings could accommodate six. If guests paid a deposit and regular rent, Jan, Veronika and Eloise could pay all the bills and fund their own lifestyles in the shadows.

Because the only guaranteed income for the next two months was Eloise's salary and the pittance Jan received for his smutty stories, Eloise hoarded her cash like a dragon did gold. As the German *Vogue* representative, she squirreled away free gifts, persuaded designers to part with fabric samples or fine china, scoured sales for quality linen and pressured every person she knew for recommendations. Jan reported for duty every single morning, once he had finished his coffee, and threw himself into his work with relish. Veronika could barely get out of bed.

Ruth's house went from an empty shell into a welcoming residence for visitors over three exhausting weeks. On the first night after it was more or less complete, Eloise helped Veronika along the corridor and settled her into the divan. She uncorked a bottle of cheap spumante and Jan assembled a platter of meats, cheeses and pickles. The trio sat in a line along the divan, admiring the basic but functional interior.

"It's weird," said Veronika. "This place used to be so lively. Now no one's here."

"We're here!" Jan clashed his beer bottle against Eloise's glass. "We made this."

"You made something ..." she started to say, but a sudden explosion of coughing overcame her.

"... fit to rent," finished Eloise, patting her back. "Our first guests are due on Monday. Herr and Frau Schwarzkopf come from Lübeck and both work in the insurance industry. They will pay a month's rent in advance and have already committed to a one-year contract. That is our life raft for now. The following weekend, we have four viewings but unfortunately most of them seem to be single. We need couples so we can charge for a double room."

"If a man wants a room to himself, he can pay full price," said Jan.

"Good point. The room has a flat rate, regardless of how many occupants."

Veronika had recovered, only occasionally spluttering into a man's handkerchief. "But are they respectable?" She raised what remained of her eyebrows. "I have standards, you know."

"She's right," added Jan, with a straight face. "We don't want the place infested with low-life pornographers, drug addicts and prostitutes, do we?"

"On Charlottenstrasse?" Eloise pulled an expression of outrage. "Never!"

They laughed the laughter of last chances, blindly clinging to optimism while knowing all their efforts might be wasted. Ruth might return to reclaim her property and throw them out for sheer effrontery. The brownshirts might recall the owner was Jewish and burn the place to the ground. Neighbours might object to a boarding-house run by three unemployed people of low reputation. They were flying in the wind, likely to hit the ground at any moment, which was why they aimed for the sun.

The Schwarzkopf couple were very serious, checking the bed-linen, carpets, kitchen cupboards and bathroom facilities like hygiene inspectors. Eloise was ahead of them, having tested everything herself. Frau Schwarzkopf, whose face seemed accustomed to disapproval, questioned the mismatched crockery. Each item collected by Eloise was of the highest quality with a designer stamp. All different, because companies did not offer 24-piece dining sets to a journalist at a failing magazine, but every last plate or cup was a thing of beauty.

Eloise was ready for her. "When accommodating international guests with a variety of tastes, one can opt for universal and bland as a way of keeping everyone happy. Or fill the space with beautiful elements to delight the eye. No, that brilliant blue divan does not blend into the background. It stands out, demanding admiration. The delightful coffee cups and colourful glasses are equally individualistic, speaking of a home furnished with good taste rather than uniformity. Our parents' generation preferred to keep their heads down. Not anymore. In 1920s' Berlin, we are all about flamboyance and visibility. This is what you have here – a property designed for luxurious relaxation or a space for vibrant entertainment. Can you not see this salon filled with gaiety, music and cocktails made behind your own little bar? That Art Deco design is quite unique."

Because it was made from broken bits of coloured glass assembled into a random mosaic by a one-eyed ex-soldier. She and Veronika each owned a miniature personalised version; Veronika's red, Eloise's blue. Hung in front of her bedroom window, the coloured glass refracted morning sunlight like rainbows.

"That is pretty," agreed Frau Schwarzkopf. "Not that my husband and I plan to entertain. We are new to the capital and yet to venture into society."

"I too am a newcomer originally from Switzerland, but Berlin is a very easy place to find friends. You need nothing more than time. Talking of which, my husband will be waiting for his dinner. The last formality is the deposit?"

Herr Schwarzkopf handed over an envelope.

"Thank you. I shall leave you to settle in. Should you find anything missing, simply knock on the adjoining door between the evening hours of six till ten pm because otherwise I am at work. Sleep well and welcome to Berlin!"

Their next guest was far less interested in the detail. Herr Fromm was a travelling salesman who wanted somewhere to stay whenever he was in town and had no difficulty paying his rent when he wasn't. Eloise never found out what he sold. As long as he had ready cash, she didn't care.

Charlottenstrasse was earning enough to fill the shortfall

between Eloise's salary and the property's running costs. But when her money ran out, they would be on the bread line. She advertised by word of mouth, hustled for any kind of extra work, lined her stomach with free food at fashion events and resisted Irmgard's entreaties to flee to France. One more tenant and she could take care of Veronika, Jan and herself, while trying to restart her career.

The final guests appeared out of nowhere. On one July evening, someone rang the bell of Charlottenstrasse, interrupting dinner. Eloise went to answer, closing the connecting door on Jan and Veronika. A lean, well-dressed man announced himself as Herr Zarin. He was an academic, specialising in philosophy and psychology, who spent his days educating students in the science of thought. His wife had a job at the maternity hospital. They had been forced to leave their previous accommodation due to 'a particular unpleasantness' with their landlord.

"We should tell you from the outset that we are Jewish. Is that a problem?"

"Not in the slightest. As long as you can pay the rent, everyone is welcome. Shall I give the tour and let you decide if it meets your requirements?"

"If it's not too much of an imposition."

Eloise abandoned her meal and escorted them around the building. She showed them the attic room and did the deal right there in the office. Three rooms rented, meaning a year of no worrying over money.

Her new outlook showed in that she did not rush out to buy champagne, but bought a padlock for her bedroom. She loved Veronika and Jan dearly but when sharing a house with an addict, one should never give them a chance to disappoint you. It would always end in tears.

. . .

Vogue closed in September, releasing its ultimate issue in October 1929. By the time the magazine hit the stands, Irmgard and Georges had long since departed for Paris. The magazine's former offices were now occupied by an advertising agency. Eloise kept her copy in her bottom drawer, hoping one day it might be worth some money as a collector's piece. She didn't even open it, knowing the very act of flicking through the pages would make her sad, plus with her cynical hat on, depreciate its value.

Her final salary arrived at the end of the month, which coincided with her getting semi-regular work as a writer for the *Berliner Tageblatt*. That was Irmgard's parting gift: an introduction to Theodor Wolff. The editor-in-chief was well known for his erudite journalism, along with novels, plays and liberal politics. He commissioned her to write three or four pieces per month for the *feuilleton* section of the paper; entitled *La Flaneuse: What the Modern Woman needs to know*. Such a broad remit meant Eloise could exercise her mind penning something more complex than seasonal colour schemes. She reviewed films, critiqued cabarets, reported on women's rights in Germany and noted significant shifts in other European countries. Once again, she spent large swathes of her day in the library, reading every contemporary publication she could find. The *Tageblatt* (daily sheet) was a different beast to a magazine. Newspaper journalism was fast, reactive and exciting. She would write a piece on contemporary events one day and the next it was in the paper.

Even if she was no longer working in fashion, she had to maintain a certain level of elegance. The only additions to her wardrobe these days she could afford were thrifty purchases to update existing items. She thanked her mother's sensible policy of buying one expensive coat and two pairs of quality footwear, then keeping them regularly maintained. With a bright scarf or new buttons, she could make such items look fashionable for years.

The tenants paid their rent on time, and once a few early problems such as a wobbly banister or troublesome cistern were fixed, she rarely saw the guests. Jan's enthusiasm for home improvements transferred to their own accommodation, to the extent of making Charlottenweg's own post box and fixing many of the broken fittings. Most evenings a week, Eloise cooked a meal for three people in a pleasantly clean kitchen. Whether it was regular food, the positive ambience or the warmth of her room, who could tell, but Veronika rallied, shaking off her cough and getting out of bed to help with the housework. One October evening she asked Eloise if she still had a sewing machine.

"There's one upstairs, but it's not actually mine. Hildegard left it behind. What do you want it for?" She was busy picking the bones out of some soaked dried cod.

"I'm pretty useful with a needle and thread. When I was a dancer, I made my own costumes. Maybe I could offer a repair service, just until I'm back on my feet. Earn a few Pfennigs to chip in to the kitty, you know?"

Eloise shrugged. "If you like."

"Great! I'll use the spare room to keep out of the way and save making a mess in the kitchen. I can sew things for you, too, as my contribution. You've been very good to me."

Her head bent to hide a sudden rush of emotion, Eloise swallowed and nodded her agreement.

"I'll go up there now and rearrange things." She squeezed Eloise's shoulder. "Thank you."

That night they ate cod in mustard sauce with spinach and potatoes, drank some cheap white wine and talked about their plans for the following week. Eloise noticed the way Jan gazed at Veronika. She recognised that look of absolute adoration in his eye. Rather than feeling sad she had lost the love of her life,

Eloise felt lucky to have spent a short glorious time with Otto. Love was nothing more than a sequence of odd moments where you realised what it meant to share yourself. At that particular moment, sitting with her damaged housemates, a surge of real affection filled her heart.

28

October – November 1929, Berlin

Thursday October 24 was one of her office days at *Berliner Tageblatt*, otherwise 'Black Thursday' or the Wall Street Crash would have signified little more than some other country's problems. Her colleagues' grim expressions told a different story. The atmosphere was one of barely disguised panic: urgent telephone calls and hastily called meetings in a scramble to make sense of the crisis. Only then could the editorial team explain its significance and what the implications might be for the citizens of Berlin.

Her direct boss, Fred Hildenbrandt, passed her desk a little after four and looked surprised to see her bent over her typewriter. "What are you still doing here?"

"Finalising that article describing which investment pieces women should buy this season, handbags, fur, jewellery, ... or do you think that a bad idea under the circumstances?"

He took off his glasses and rubbed the bridge of his nose.

"Under the circumstances, you'd be better off advising them to sell anything of value. Because very soon, everyone will be looking for a buyer. Look, just file what you've got and go home. See you next week, if we're still in business."

The idea of selling her possessions occupied Eloise's mind all the tram ride home. She must always have enough money for her train fare to Switzerland, just in case. In a safety deposit box at the bank, she had half a dozen pieces of jewellery, all gifts from Sylvain. Together they would be worth several hundred Swiss francs. In Reichsmarks, it was anyone's guess. But enough to buy three tickets if necessary, with plenty left over. When she had originally placed those items in a secure vault, she cared more for their sentimental significance than what they would fetch on the open market. Now, she feared their value would drop dramatically if everyone started selling their treasures at once. She made up her mind to visit the jeweller's shop tomorrow and ask for a quotation.

At Charlottenweg, all was activity. At the doorstep, a woman was taking her leave of Veronika and through the kitchen window, Jan was cooking at the hob. The smell of frying onions wafted from the window. Eloise bid the woman good evening as she passed. Veronika, with all the strength of a cobweb, was trying to lift a heavy laundry bag across the threshold. She saw Eloise and gave her a huge grin.

"That was another customer! I put an ad in the newsagent's this morning. A neighbour came round and asked me to repair her children's school uniforms. It took me all afternoon but I earned one Mark fifty. She was very pleased and told her friends. That lady just brought four pairs of trousers for me to fix. I sent Jan to buy each of us a *Wiener* for dinner so you don't have to cook tonight."

"Congratulations!" Eloise recalled that a copy of *Die Dame* cost 1.50. "Thanks for spending your first payment on food for us all."

"It's only a *Wiener*." Veronika blushed. "But it's something."

It was more than something. Her housemates taking the initiative became a precious moment, all the more so because of its rarity. Eloise carried the laundry bag upstairs for Veronika, complimented Jan on his cooking, cut slices of bread and poured glasses of water, soaking up the sense of companionship. They talked about their days, in which each had worked and earned some money, laughing at the absurdity of it all. She didn't mention the financial disaster in America. Hopefully its impact would cause no shockwaves. The smallest ripple might be enough to destabilise their fragile little household.

The jeweller agreed with Eloise. The necklaces, that brooch, those earrings were all high-quality examples of Swiss craftsmanship. Each piece was indeed in pristine condition and worth a lot of money in a buyer's market. Under normal circumstances, he would have offered her 1,000 Marks, convinced he could raise that and more at auction. Then he shook his head, an expression of infinite sadness crossing his face as he folded each item back into its velvet pocket.

"I'm sorry, dear lady, but I cannot pay you what these are worth. Do you know how many women have come here in the last year, trying to get the best prices for their family heirlooms? Now the Americans are calling in their loans, there is no money. Nobody wants to buy jewellery. My advice to you is to keep them, if you can." He looked up at her with deep brown eyes. "Your collection is not only lovely, but I sense every jewel means something to you. Keep them. Take them home to Switzerland, where people are still spending. Good luck."

She tried three more places with similar responses or insulting offers. Finally she managed to get 200 Marks for the diamond brooch, around a third of its true value. Nonetheless, it represented an escape route to somewhere safe for her, Veronika and Jan. Next week, her tenants' rent was due and she intended to take a tiny percentage from each to add to her hoard. The rest she would spend on bills and other essential expenses. If she still had a job next month, none of her wages could go on buttons, scarves, lipstick or magazines. Every last Pfennig was destined for her emergency fund.

By Tuesday, no one could ignore the alarm bells from across the Atlantic. Cheap rags published hysterical headlines and even sober newspapers warned of approaching disaster. Conversations in coffee shops ranged between doom and fatalism. While people disagreed as to the reasons why, everyone agreed Germany was deeply in debt and now America was calling in its loans. Eloise's hope for ripples rather than waves was soon dashed against the rocks.

Berliner Tageblatt reduced their staff to a skeleton crew, dropping all casual contributors. Every enquiry she made to other publications met with the same response: whether a regretful shake of the head or a bitter laugh, it was always no. When she went to collect the rent from her guests on the first of November, the Schwarzkopfs paid for next month, optimistic the insurance trade would keep operating as usual, and wished her a pleasant evening. However Herr Zarin handed her one month's rent and their notice.

"With sincere apologies, Frau de Fournier, but if the university cannot afford to pay me, we cannot afford to live here."

She commiserated with their plight, struggling to hide her disappointment. When she knocked at the door of Herr Fromm's room, the keys were dangling from the handle. Inside, the room was empty. No note, no apology, no rent, just an empty space.

She gritted her teeth and considered the chances of finding someone who could afford a room on Charlottenstrasse. Slight, yet she had to try. She followed Veronika's example and put a card in the newsagent's. Then she went home to make *Rösti* with whatever else was left on the shelf. Before Christmas, she had to get out of Berlin.

Dearest Bastian

As you may have seen in the broadsheets, circumstances look dire for Germany. Businesses are closing, unemployment is reaching crisis proportions (my piecemeal employment has recently ceased) and the political situation is a constant concern. In uncertain times, more than one violent faction will try to grab power.

All things considered, I think it best to return to Fribourg. The difficulty I have is in leaving my beloved friends: Veronika and Jan. If they agree to travel with me, which is far from certain, do you think we might be able to offer them shelter? I cannot bear to forsake them in this increasingly uncertain climate. My savings will cover our travelling expenses. It is simply a matter of receiving a welcome in Switzerland.

Please give my love to Sylvia and Laurent, greetings to our entire wonderful family and I hope to hear from you soonest. My intention is to return before Christmas.

Your loving sister
Eloise

On her way home from another fruitless day searching for work in late November, she saw a man on the front lawn of the Charlottenstrasse house, banging a For Sale sign into the earth.

"Excuse me? Who gave you permission to do that?"

He gave her a dead-eyed stare and pointed to the name of the estate agency on the sign.

"But we live here. You can't just sell this house without giving us notice."

Again, he pointed at the sign. "This is your notice." He lit a cigarette, walked to his van and drove away without giving her a second glance.

Eloise's hands shook as she walked around the building to Charlottenweg, only to hear yet more banging. This time it was a woman hammering on the back door.

"I know you're in there. Open this door!" She rattled the handle. "Veronika, open up!"

In a second, Eloise decided against going up the path to home and instead continued walking along the street. Once she had gone past three houses, she crossed the road and hid behind a horse and cart. The animal was covered with a blanket, making it the ideal shield. The woman was now rapping on the window of Veronika's bedroom.

"I want my sheets and my money back. Do I have to call the police?" She waited a few more seconds, then stomped down the path with a furious snort. She turned in the direction of the main road, muttering to herself.

Eloise waited a full five minutes to be sure she had gone and noticed a movement at the kitchen window. Jan was peering down the path. He spotted Eloise and her eyes met his for a second. His expression was unreadable and then he pulled the curtain across the window.

The house was silent when she entered and the kitchen was empty, with a couple of letters lying on the table. She went into the hall and was about to knock on Veronika's door when a voice said, "Don't."

Jan was standing in the bathroom doorway. "She's sleeping it off."

"Sleeping what off?"

"Whatever she took. That woman was the housekeeper from the hotel down the road. She came round this morning with a big pile of bedclothes for Veronika to mend. She paid her 20 Marks in advance because it was a rush job. I took the sheets upstairs, because they were heavy, and returned to my room. But instead of starting on the needlework, she went out. She was gone for hours and when she came home ..." He tailed off, just waving a hand in front of his face.

"You think she'd taken drugs?"

Jan nodded, his expression grim. "I don't know what she could get for 20 Marks, but whatever it was, it worked."

"And now that housekeeping lady wants her money back. Hellfire and damnation! What if she brings the police here?"

"I would have sewn the sheets myself, but I don't know how to use the sewing machine."

"We'll have to do it between us. I'll show you how. We can't afford to give that hotel woman 20 Marks and we definitely don't need the police. Come on."

Eloise taught Jan how to use the machine and left him to repair the first batch while she opened the post and waited for the woman's return. The first letter was from the same agency as printed on the sign at the front of the house, informing all tenants that the house was now on their books. The property was up for sale and they had until the end of the year to vacate the premises or they would be forcibly evicted in the first week of January. Eloise sat down with her head in her hands but was immediately interrupted by more banging. This time the knocking came from inside the house, the connecting door to the front of the building.

She opened it to see the Schwarzkopfs, arm in arm and clearly furious.

"Good evening to you."

"What is the meaning of this? We signed a one-year lease with you and now the property is for sale? This is an outrageous way to behave."

"I'm as shocked as you are, Herr Schwarzkopf. I had no idea the owner intended to sell."

"You are not the owner?" Frau Schwarzkopf's voice was shrill.

"No, I am the owner's deputy. She handed over the management role to me when she left Berlin. Since the economic situation has worsened, I assume she now seeks a buyer for the place."

"And what are we supposed to do?"

"The same as I will have to do, I'm afraid. Find somewhere else to live." Someone began banging on the back door. "I'm truly sorry, but I have to go. I wish you a pleasant evening." As she closed the door, she had the distinct impression they were so puffed up they might explode.

On the back step stood the hotel housekeeper, her arms folded, brow furrowed and with a large man by her side.

"Good evening to you," repeated Eloise. "Unfortunately my housemate was taken ill this afternoon. We are most concerned for her health and a doctor is on his way. I understand you deposited some bed linen to be repaired this morning. Please be assured we will complete the work as promised and as a gesture of goodwill, deliver it personally to your establishment first thing tomorrow morning."

"I want my money back," said the housekeeper but her demand was cut off by the large man's question.

"What's wrong with the young lady?" His bass voice contained nothing more than neighbourly concern.

"My housemate has been unwell for some time with a persistent cough. As you probably saw for yourself, madam, she is very thin and frail, her complexion whiter than paper."

"Tuberculosis, by the sounds of it," said the man, tipping his head to one side in a sympathetic gesture. "I've seen it before when I worked at the hospital. Patients always think they can do more than they are able. Be aware, *meine Dame*, that it can be infectious. You should take precautions. Did she touch the sheets?"

"She had no opportunity to do so. My colleague took them to our sewing room and when he came downstairs, he found she had collapsed on the kitchen floor." The more Eloise lied, the easier it became. "Your sheets are uncontaminated, I can promise you that with my hand on my heart."

A car turned into the street and stopped outside the house. Eloise recognised the model immediately, an Opel *Doktorwagen*, but couldn't see who was behind the wheel.

"Oh, that must be the doctor! Thank you so much for your understanding and I will deliver your sheets in the morning. Good night to you."

The housekeeper was prepared to argue but her companion offered positive wishes for Veronika's recovery and led the way down the path. They shot curious looks at the man getting out of the car, who ignored them completely.

Gustav Graz wore a top hat, long coat and leather gloves. Eloise stared, stony-faced, as he walked up the path. It took all her self-control not to burst into wild giggles. Had he never been to the cinema or did he actually style himself on a dastardly schemer? All he needed was a moustache he could twirl.

She began as politely as she had done with the last two confrontations. "Good evening to you, Gustav. I hope you are well."

"A courteous greeting from a discourteous woman. It was rude and ungrateful of you to depart from that apartment without the decency to respond to my generous offer. Not that I expected anything better. Whether at work or in a romantic attachment, you bring bad luck. In many ways, an alliance with you would have been an albatross around my neck. A lucky escape for me."

"How pleasant to see you again. I would invite you in for a chat about old times, but my dinner guests are due imminently. I really should keep an eye on that boeuf bourguignon. Was the purpose of your visit to upbraid me for departing without a formal farewell? If so, you could have done that months ago."

He cast a contemptuous eye over the property, "As they always say, a person always finds their own level." He glanced behind her, and Eloise sensed the presence of Jan at her back.

"Everything is in order, Jan. This gentleman is Otto's brother and he was just leaving."

"Ah, I see the rumours are true. You do indeed live among beggars, thieves and prostitutes. Or perhaps you have joined them?"

Instinctively, Eloise thrust out an arm to prevent Jan rushing outside.

"Go indoors, Jan, we have a lot of work to do before tomorrow. Thank you for your support, but I am perfectly capable of dealing with this alone. What is that brings you here, Gustav? Say what you must and let's proceed with our evenings. Mine has been quite long enough already."

He cleared his throat. "My brother drove you to Switzerland last year, correct?"

"Yes, to seek my family's blessing for our marriage." Her voice faltered and the weight of exhaustion dragged her shoulders downwards.

"The car broke down and he left it in Rüsselsheim for repairs."

"Yes, but that was over a year ago. What relevance does it have now?"

"Otto registered that motor vehicle with you as the legal

owner. I assume he planned to give it to you as a wedding present. But the thing broke down and it was low on the list of the factory's priorities, especially after General Motors took charge. To be honest, I'm astonished they ever fixed the infernal machine. But they did. It is now fully restored and legally in your ownership."

"Otto gave me a car?"

"As I said, my brother lacked any sense of practicality. Dear Lord, you cannot even drive! Neither can you afford road tax, fuel or insurance, especially not in these straitened times. He gave you a white elephant. Something useless, unaffordable, expensive to maintain and hard to sell. This is where I am prepared to extend my last offer of generosity. I am willing to purchase the vehicle for 1,500 Marks. Simply sign the transfer of ownership and I shall collect it on my next trip to Rüsselsheim. You would be foolish to refuse."

Eloise stared at the papers in his hand, her mind flooded with memories of that long journey. She could picture Otto, his face smudged with oil, grinning as he said, 'Give me two minutes to freshen up? Order me whatever you're having. With a huge beer!' The hollow pit of grief opened its maw beneath her once again and a cold wind crept around her ankles. She should be indoors, not standing on the chilly doorstep with Gustav.

One and a half thousand Marks would change her life. But the car was a wedding gift from the man she had planned to marry.

"It's very kind of you to bring me the papers. I appreciate your offer to take it off my hands, but that is not what I want. I will keep the car, thank you."

Gustav made a sound of exasperation. "Be practical, Eloise! What are you going to do with a motor vehicle? No one wants to buy a car these days, believe me. I am the best chance you'll get."

"I said no, thank you. Could you kindly hand over the documents and the keys, because I have a lot to do tonight."

He thrust a sheaf of papers at her and held out the keys. "Here, you stupid woman. You realise you are throwing money down the drain."

"Goodbye, Gustav. I wish you a pleasant evening." She went inside and closed the door.

29

November 1929

The receptionist at Hotel Metropole lifted his brows as Jan and Eloise used the last of their strength to drag two laundry bags up the steps. He intercepted them at the door.

"Tradesmen's entrance is around the rear."

Eloise gave him a murderous glare. "I'm not a tradesman." She dumped her bag at his feet and indicated to Jan he should follow suit. "Tell your boss we are grateful for her patience. Come, Jan, let's go. I am going to sleep for a week."

In the event, she managed four hours before Jan climbed the stairs to knock on her door, worried about Veronika. With a weary groan, Eloise got dressed and joined him in the kitchen.

The moaning was even less bearable than the coughing. Veronika seemed in terrible pain, but Eloise knew it must be withdrawal symptoms. Once all the drugs were out of her system, she would recover. They only had to wait. Jan paced outside her room like an expectant father and they had the same conversation at least every couple of hours.

"We have to do something, Eloise. She's suffering."

"What do you expect me to do?"

"She needs medication for the pain."

"That will only delay the torment. Jan, face it. She's an addict. Giving her more drugs is the worst thing we can do. Even if it were a good idea, where would we get the money?"

That shut him up for the first few times. As the moaning turned to howls, he finally said what was on his mind.

"There's the rental money. We could use that cash to help her through this."

She gaped at him, open-mouthed. "That money pays for our electricity, our heating, our food. Are you seriously suggesting we live like rats to feed her habit?"

"What about the car, then? That man said he'd pay 1,500 Marks for it."

Her temper was threatening to boil over, so she dropped the potato peeler and clutched the sink. From the room across the hall, Veronika let out a banshee wail.

"Close the damned door, will you!" Her curse shocked Jan, who did as he was told.

"Listen to me and know that I mean every word. We both care about Veronika. Where we do not agree is on how to help her. I want her to get better in the long term. You want her to feel better in the short term. If you think I am going to sell the only present my fiancé left me so she can inject poison into her body, you are an idiot. The only way through is to let her sweat it out."

Jan collapsed into a chair, clutching his forehead. "Have a heart, Eloise. She's in a terrible state. Let's take her to hospital."

"And how do we pay for that?"

"We have to do something. I can't stand much more of this."

It seemed the Zarins had the same thought. They knocked on the connecting door to complain about the noise. The incessant sewing machine last night was bad enough, but screams of agony were too much to bear.

Eloise asked the same question she had posed to Jan. "What do you want me to do? I can't take her to hospital because she has no health insurance. Even if I could find a doctor willing to come to the house, we have no way of paying him."

Frau Zarin raised a tentative hand. "I am a midwife, or used to be until the hospital decided they no longer need Jewish nurses. If I bring my medical kit can I take a look at your friend?"

"I don't think she's having a baby," blurted Jan.

Frau Zarin didn't even blink. "Probably not, but best to be certain, no?" She turned to her husband. "Wait here, *mein Schatz*, I won't be long."

Eloise led the two men into the kitchen and instructed Jan to make tea. When Frau Zarin returned with a brown leather bag, Eloise showed her into Veronika's room, recoiling at the stench. Frau Zarin strode directly to the bed and examined the pitiful figure writhing like a maggot on top of the covers.

"Open the windows, Frau de Fournier, if you would be so kind. The air in here is foul. One question, then I would ask you to leave us for a moment."

"Of course." Eloise opened the windows and gulped in fresh night air.

"Do you have any idea what she took?"

"None. I know she sometimes uses cocaine, opium, morphine and other substances. All I can say for certain is that she spent 20 Marks to get out of her mind and this is the result. I will be right across the hall if you need me."

In the kitchen, Herr Zarin was chopping onions and Jan was peeling potatoes, conversing as if this was an everyday occurrence. A slab of something wrapped in greaseproof paper, which certainly wasn't there earlier, lay on the counter along with a fresh leek, a loaf of bread, some butter and half a dozen eggs.

"Frau de Fournier, I apologise for the intrusion. I suggested we pool our resources and cook dinner together whilst you were otherwise engaged. This fine young fellow tolerated my intrusion with good grace. As for what we shall eat, well, I don't have a name for this dish but it's somewhere between a Spanish tortilla and Swiss *Rösti*. In the two years I spent working at the University of Murcia, I learned a great deal about food. Eggs are easily digestible if the patient feels strong enough, and this dish will provide a hearty meal for the five of us. I brought a bottle of wine, which I admit is not a fine vintage, but it will suffice around the campfire. Dear lady, you look on the verge of collapse! Sit down and drink some water. You are captain of this ship therefore you must maintain your strength."

Eloise sat, so weary she wanted to cry or laugh hysterically. Herr Zarin tore off a corner of bread, slathered one end in butter and handed it to her. "Let's call this an *amuse bouche*. Jan, pour the lady a glass of wine and fill the rest with water. For my part, I shall sweat the onions."

She took a bite of bread, and as if her stomach suddenly remembered what food meant, she found herself ravenously hungry.

The unlikely pair chatted, Herr Zarin shouldering at least 80% of the conversational burden, and the kitchen filled with mouth-watering aromas. She positioned her chair so she could see Veronika's door, and half-listened to what the cooks were discussing.

"Splay the leaves like a fan, that's the best way of washing a leek. You sustained that injury during active duty, I assume. Where were you fighting?"

"Amiens."

"Good God, man. May I shake your hand? Wait, let me dry

mine first. There. Thank you for your service to our country. Do you possess such a thing as black pepper?"

"We only have white."

"Which will serve the purpose equally well. I saw no action during my time in the military, since I was stationed in a communications centre. The reason for that was my facility with languages. French, English and Italian speakers were readily available at my barracks, but someone with a working knowledge of Russian was rare. Is there a lid for this pan? Thank you. I had learned it in order to read the great philosophers in their original tongue, you see, with no idea it might be put to use in a conflict situation."

"Can you still speak it?"

"Of course! I spend Sunday mornings in the cafés of Charlottenburg, reading the papers and talking to whoever will tolerate me. Russians everywhere, mostly of the intellectual sort who love to debate. Fascinating minds, albeit with a tendency towards pessimism. You must have been a mere boy during the war."

"I joined the army at seventeen. Lost my eye at twenty-one."

"Poor devil. Was it a grenade? I heard the French used to make theirs from empty *foie gras* cans jammed with stones and explosives."

"Not a grenade. That would have taken my hearing as well. Shrapnel from an artillery shell did this." With his back to Eloise, he faced Herr Zarin and lifted his eye patch. Zarin did not flinch but reached out a hand and squeezed his shoulder.

"Your generation sacrificed so much."

"Yes, we did. But what for?"

Frau Zarin appeared in the doorway, beckoning Eloise. She led the way into the other half of the house, careful to close the door behind her. They sat on the blue divan, side by side.

Before she spoke, Frau Zarin checked the Schwarzkopfs

were not in the vicinity. "I am not a doctor, you must understand, and I would recommend you get a real medical opinion. My diagnosis is your friend is dying of tuberculosis. She is also addicted to opium, morphine and cocaine. Her lungs are barely functional. At the time we spoke, she was conscious, but far from lucid. If I understood her correctly, she bought a phial of morphine yesterday and is now begging for more. I have given her a mild sedative to calm her temporarily. You can give her another later if necessary. I'd rather give it to you than leave it in her room. Frau de Fournier, Veronika requires urgent medical intervention. Similar cases have been treated successfully in Swiss sanatoriums but transport is the issue. I doubt she would survive the journey."

Eloise wanted nothing more than to lie down and sleep for the rest of the week. Instead she looked into the kindly gaze of Frau Zarin and said, "What do you think I should do?"

"Fight to keep her alive, with no guarantee of success. Or ease her path, comfortable and without pain. The first option will be extremely expensive. The latter?" She shrugged. "A hundred Marks should do the trick, if you can find someone to sell you that much. Sometimes, it's kinder to let a person leave when they're ready. I believe Veronika is ready."

"I understand." Eloise rubbed her eyes. "I need to eat and sleep on it before considering this decision with a clear head. Your advice is most welcome. Dinner should be ready soon. Shall we?"

Even in her exhausted frame of mind, she noticed the connecting door was ajar. But the smells emanating from the kitchen distracted her from everything but her appetite.

. . .

Eloise awoke from a profound sleep with complete clarity of mind. Veronika must be hospitalised, regardless of the cost. If they could treat her to the point where she was able to travel, Eloise would take her to Fribourg. There she would either find a sanatorium or plead with Bastian to nurse her friend back to health. Determined to make the most of her Saturday morning, she rolled over to check the clock. Ten to twelve!

She had slept half the day. In a hurry, she washed, dressed, fastened the padlock and went downstairs. From Veronika's room there was no sound, and Eloise held her breath as she opened the door. The bed was empty. Then a ragged bout of coughing came from the downstairs bathroom, followed by a groan of pain. When the wretched waif opened the door and saw Eloise, her wild look of desperation made Eloise retreat several paces.

"Good morning, Veronika. How did you sleep?"

"You have to help me, Eloise, please. I'm in terrible agony."

"I intend to help you. Today, I'm taking you to the hospital to receive professional treatment for your condition."

"*No!*" Her shriek triggered another bout of coughing and Eloise moved out of range, into the kitchen. A few seconds later, Veronika followed, her nightgown speckled with blood.

"Eloise, listen to me. I can't go to hospital. I can't pay."

"I can and I will. You realise you could infect Jan and me with TB? Every time you cough, you spread your infection in the air. It's clear you don't value your own life, but to risk the health of your housemates is worse than selfish. I am going find the money to pay for your recovery in hospital."

"You don't have to do that. I just need something to get me through the next few days. It's a lot cheaper than hospital. I can tell you where to buy what I need. Please, I've never felt so bad in my life."

"I will never buy you drugs. Never. I want to save your life, not hasten its end. Excuse me, I have errands to run." She dodged Veronika's feeble grip and snatched up her coat.

"Eloise! You're my only friend," she sobbed.

"I'm not your only friend. But I might be the only one prepared to do the right thing." She slipped out the front door and locked it behind her. Then she walked outside towards the tram stop.

The journey to Otto's apartment was familiar and yet not. This time, she was an unwelcome visitor. The apartment itself would be similarly changed since Gustav had moved in. She made up her mind not go inside. His eradication of Otto's presence would be insufferable. He opened the door on the second ring with his customary scowl. It lifted only marginally when he saw her.

"Eloise? What do you want?"

"My apologies for interrupting you at home on a Saturday afternoon, but I have changed my mind. When you arrived yesterday, I was fighting several crises at once and my reaction was ill-considered and foolhardy. You are absolutely right about the need to be practical when everyone is under pressure. If your proposal still stands, I would like to accept it."

His gaze flickered back and forth between her eyes, as if he was trying to catch her in a lie. She stood still and unsmiling, the papers and the key in her hand.

"To which proposal are you referring? Your hand in marriage or my offer to purchase your motor vehicle? Or have you seen sense and are willing to accept both?"

A flush of embarrassment overcame her, robbing her of speech for a moment. While she had not forgotten his suggestion that he take his brother's place, her focus on selling the car had entirely blocked it from her mind. She realised her opening speech had been misleading and winced.

"My mistake. I was not clear. For that, I am genuinely sorry. You offered 1,500 Marks for the repaired Laubfrosch. I confess sentimentality clouded my judgement because it was a present from Otto. Now I see it would be far more intelligent to accept the money in return for the car."

His brow lowered, hooding his eyes. "What on earth are you doing, Eloise? It's as if you want to spite yourself, living in that ghetto."

Heat rose in her face again, this time from anger. "I came here to discuss your offer to purchase my car, not to debate my lifestyle."

"I am willing to take that machine off your hands for 750 Marks. Yes, the price has changed. Economic hardship, financial depression, etcetera."

"It's worth twice that. You offered me double the amount yesterday."

"If you'd prefer to try your chances on the open market, *viel Glück*." He made as if to close the door.

"If you can pay me in cash right now, I'll take it."

"Very well. Would you like to come in out of the cold while I gather the money?"

"I'm fine here, thank you."

He closed the door and left her waiting for ten minutes. When the cold started to make her teeth chatter, she walked briskly up and down the street, patting her upper arms with vigour. When he finally emerged with an envelope, she counted every note before handing over the key and documents.

"Thank you. Goodbye, Gustav, and I wish you luck with *your* chances on the open market." She strode around the corner, her heels tapping a staccato rhythm on the pavement that sounded like applause.

30

November 1929

Stormtroopers were marching along Potsdamerstrasse, shouting anti-communist slogans and carrying shawms, led by that troublemaking agitator Horst Wessel. Marches usually ended in violence, which for Eloise necessitated a change of route. A streetcar breakdown delayed her further and she walked the rest of the way. Her last detour was via the market to buy some overpriced chicken and stunted vegetables, which would be easily digestible and nourishing if Veronika was able to eat. Then after dinner, Eloise would clean her friend as best she could and find a taxi to take them to hospital. Light was already leaching from the sky when the fog rolled in over Charlottenstrasse. Eloise closed the door on the city and sent a little prayer that things would not get worse.

The house was silent and in darkness. She put the food in the kitchen and knocked on Veronika's room, to no response. She eased open the door and switched on the light. On the bed lay a body covered by a grey sheet.

Her hand flew to her mouth. "No! Oh, please no, not yet."

"Veronika?" She took a few faltering steps closer. Her hand shook as if she had the palsy but she forced herself to lift the sheet. Veronika's eyes were closed, her skin waxy, and a strange smile remained on her violet lips. A cliché leapt into Eloise's mind. *She looks at peace.* She folded the sheet across her friend's bony shoulders, knelt by the bed and prayed for her dear departed soul. Tears leaked down Eloise's cheeks and spilled onto her coat. Eventually, she stood up to bestow one last kiss on that pale forehead. She drew back with a gasp.

Veronika's skin was warm. Eloise pressed two fingers to her neck but could detect no pulse. She snatched up a mirror from the dresser and held it close to Veronika's nose. For a second, nothing happened and then a small puff of condensation clouded the glass.

"She's alive," sobbed Eloise. "She's still here." In an instant, she removed the sheet and rolled up the sleeves of her nightdress. As expected, several fresh puncture wounds bled from her right arm, suggesting she'd had problems finding a vein. On the night table were two phials of morphine and a used syringe. A thought occurred. She rolled up the left sleeve of the nightgown, where the usual scars and marks of an addict told their story. She racked her brains to picture Veronika using a pen, a key or a corkscrew. She was right-handed. Whatever she injected went into her left arm.

Finally she understood.

She left Veronika's room and took the stairs two at a time. On the landing, all was dark. She banged on Jan's door, tried the handle and yelled his name, to no avail. Then she ran up to her own room to see the padlock still in place but the door hanging limply from the staved-in jamb. She stepped over the broken wood and looked straight at the jewellery box on the top of her wardrobe. It was not there. Instead, it was on her bed, the bottom drawer yanked open. That was where she kept the rent from the lodgers, her savings and the money from selling her brooch, around 600 Marks in total. She placed her hands over her eyes, taking deep shaky breaths in the freezing cold.

When she looked again, she saw something remained in the drawer, showing green against the white velvet interior. It was a 10 Reichsmark note, wrapped around a bundle of others. She counted with great care, and found she still had 450 Marks remaining. Jan had broken down the door to steal 150 Marks and left her the rest. Frau Zarin's words from the previous evening echoed in her ears: *A hundred Marks should do the trick, if you can find someone to sell you that much. Sometimes, it's kinder to let a person leave when they're ready. I believe Veronika is ready.*

She put the money in her coat pocket and sat on her bed to try to make sense of this series of nightmares. Jan had broken into her room, with no attempt at hiding his actions, to steal 150 Marks. Veronika lay in a drug-induced stupor with two phials of morphine by her bed. It did not take a genius to connect the two events and the reasoning behind them. Jan loved Veronika with his whole heart, Eloise knew that. Had he meant to assist her in leaving this life? If so, he had failed. A flash of empathy struck her, imagining the pain it must have caused to administer a lethal dose. Helping the person you loved most in the world to leave it was an exceptional act of altruism.

For some reason, she thought of Shakespeare's star-crossed lovers. Juliet takes the potion and falls into a profound sleep. Romeo arrives at the tomb and believes her dead. Unable to live without his beloved, he takes poison and dies. Juliet awakes, sees Romeo's body and kills herself with his dagger. A tragedy.

She shivered, partly from the cold and partly a chilling thought, and sat bolt upright. Was that what the extra 50 Marks was for? A third phial to end his own life? Eloise ran down the stairs and banged on his door.

"Jan, open up. Everything is all right. I know what happened and I understand. Jan? Listen to me, Veronika is alive. She's breathing. Come with me and see for yourself!" Her voice grew higher in pitch and she began to panic. She crouched to look through the keyhole but either the key was in situ or the room was in darkness. Twice she ran at his door, barging her shoulder at the wood. The second time she acknowledged she was more likely to break her collarbone than make the wood concede.

There was another way of accessing that room – the fire escape.

She ran down the stairs, another foolish way to trip and break bones, and rushed outside. She stopped on the step. The fog had thickened to a blanket, muffling sounds and smothering warm glows from the building opposite. Street lights pierced the gloom as effectively as fireflies.

Something drew Eloise's gaze upwards. Swinging from the fire escape was a man's body, spinning slowly like a leaf caught in a spider's web. When a car came down the street, its headlamps threw the macabre spectacle into horrific relief. The eye patch, the protruding tongue, the limp corpse seemed at once shocking and familiar. Eloise clamped her hands over her mouth and rushed to the bathroom, where she vomited twice. She washed her face and drank a glass of water. Then she ran upstairs to turn off the lights. No one must see Jan's body until she had calmed down and made a plan.

She had to act quickly. But how? Her mind flapped and swooped, a panicked bat in an attic, trying to find a way out of her confusion. Police, drugs, hospital, morphine, money, attempted murder, pornography, illegal sub-letting, suicide pact ... that thought pulled her up short. She entered Veronika's room to find her in exactly the same position. Still unconscious, still smiling but barely alive. The nightstand held an Art Deco tray littered with detritus Eloise didn't care to touch. So she plucked a pair of velvet gloves from the dresser and examined each piece with care. Cigarettes, empty phials, syringes, a silver powder box, a bloodied handkerchief, a hip flask, a perfume atomiser and a black cigarette tin Eloise recognised. She lifted the lid and saw it contained no cigarettes but a third phial of morphine. There was also a scrappy piece of paper in Jan's spidery handwriting.

Just in case. Yours eternally, J.

Eloise took it all into the kitchen. She placed the tray on the table, along with the money from her coat pocket. Her mind calmed to a cool decisiveness. Each step was clear and she ran through each connecting scene like an actor preparing for the stage.

When she was ready, she reapplied her make-up in the mirror of her compact, smoothed her hair and sprayed a little perfume behind each ear. Then she filled the syringe with morphine, flicked out the air bubbles, placed it on the tray and returned to the patient. With one hand she clamped the skin of Veronika's left arm until she could see a prominent blood vessel. With the other, she pierced the vein and injected her with the entire contents of the syringe. Then she waited, holding her friend's hand and whispering her goodbyes.

It took seventeen minutes before Veronika's heart stopped beating. Eloise blew her a kiss and said a prayer. Then she put her plan into action.

Gloves onto a pile of dirty laundry, lights off and door closed. She picked up the chicken, carrots and kohlrabi she had purchased and left the house to walk two blocks. She waited, cold, tired and tense, then boarded a tram in the direction of Charlottenstrasse. The moment it moved away, she rang the bell, walked to the front and handed her scarf to the driver.

"I think someone dropped this. Should I give it to you or take it to the depot tomorrow?"

"You can give it to me. Very decent thing to do, not many honest people around these days."

"It's our civic duty to help each other. I wish you a nice evening."

"Likewise, lady."

She smiled and got off at the next stop. At the front door of Charlottenstrasse 125, she practised her weary face before knocking and hoped the Schwarzkopfs would not answer. This time her prayers were answered.

"Herr Zarin, I apologise for yet another disturbance, but I'm just on my way home. This is a small gesture of gratitude for your assistance last night. We were all most appreciative of your support. Please enjoy it with my heartfelt thanks."

"There is no need to thank us, Frau de Fournier! What are neighbours for? A chicken? That is most generous. A roasted bird is a rare treat. Unless you have plans tomorrow lunchtime, please come and enjoy it with us. You, Jan and Veronika, if she is able."

For a second, Eloise lost her composure, but gathered herself. "Sorry, today has been difficult. Veronika will be in hospital, I hope, since I sold my car to pay for her healthcare. We do what we can. Yes, I'd love to join you if I can and I know Jan will enjoy your company. He certainly did last night."

"Well done. You are a loyal friend to that poor girl. Thank you for the chicken and we look forward to welcoming you tomorrow. Good evening, Frau de Fournier."

She walked around the corner and prepared herself for what must happen next. First things first, a terrified scream. As it turned out, someone else got there first.

"Oh my God, a man has hanged himself! Call the police! Keep the kids inside, this is a nightmare. Look, up there! He jumped off the fire escape, poor soul. Who lives in that house? *Polizei! Polizei!*"

Eloise broke into a run and reached the shrieking woman. "What's the matter? Is there a fire? Why are you calling for the police?"

The woman, her grey hair frizzing from her head like a halo, pointed upwards. Eloise followed her finger and collapsed to her knees. "No, please no. Why would he do such a thing?"

The circus began. Neighbours came running, someone put a shawl around Eloise's shoulders, another gave her tea. The police arrived amid much fanfare. A senior officer requested her key and half a dozen uniformed men entered the property. By this time, the Schwarzkopfs and Zarins had come around the corner to see what the fuss was about. Frau Zarin crouched beside Eloise, holding her hand. Finally the police ushered her into a van and drove her to the station.

It took hours of repeating herself, until corroboration from the Zarins, the street neighbours and even the tram driver proved she was telling the truth. It was, as she said, a tragedy. Arriving home from a long day selling her car and seeking work, she finds a Shakespearean scene. One love-struck housemate kills a dying woman in an act of mercy, and takes his own life. Eloise's best friends, both gone in an instant.

Eventually they let the Zarins take her home to Charlottenstrasse, where they prepared what used to be Herr Fromm's room for their unexpected guest. Access to the rear of the building was prohibited until the police had finished their examinations. Eloise ate a bowl of soup, drank a brandy and thanked them for their kindnesses. Then she slept, her body and mind too exhausted to entertain emotions.

31

November, December 1929, Berlin, Rüsselsheim

Herr Zarin was a man of his word. For Sunday lunch, he cooked roast chicken, with roast potatoes, kohlrabi, carrot and spinach. Conversation was nothing more than a series of platitudes. Just as they finished eating, the police interrupted with news the house had been 'cleared'. Should Eloise wish to retrieve her belongings, she was welcome to do so.

She could not penetrate the shell-shocked distance between herself and the rest of the world, but summoned enough strength to thank them. "When can I return to my own room?" she asked.

The officer rubbed his forefingers down his moustache. "You are at liberty to do so whenever you wish. I assumed you might prefer to live somewhere else seeing as the young man jumped from outside your window."

Eloise closed her eyes. She had been sitting in that room, counting her remaining cash, shivering in the draught while Jan dangled from the metal steps outside. Tears spilled down her cheeks and she reached for a faded napkin.

"My apologies, Frau de Fournier. I leave you now to enjoy your Sunday."

Frau Zarin placed a comforting hand on her shoulder while her husband saw the officer to the door.

"If you need any assistance removing your things to this part of the house, Eloise, I would be happy to lend a hand."

"You're very kind, but this is something I need to do alone. May I borrow some newspapers to wrap my breakables?"

It was also part of her plan.

All afternoon she walked up and down the stairs, taking her clothes, shoes, books, sewing machine and typewriter to fill two trunks. At the bottom of one drawer, she found a mini bottle of champagne from when life was all glamour and parties. Then she wrote her address on the labels and left them in the hall. The act of writing an address reminded her of the post box. She collected the contents and sat at the kitchen table to read three letters, only one of which was addressed to her.

Dear Eloise

Your letter filled us with joy. Everyone rejoices that you will return. To have my sister home and safe from the turmoil in Berlin came as a tremendous relief to me in particular. Naturally you can bring your friends. We have spare rooms and would welcome extra hands to work the land. As you know, financial pressures weigh upon us all, so we make good use of the garden. Your own property as well as that of our parents is now entirely given over to growing food and raising animals. Herr Bastian Favre, doctor and farmer, at your service.

Please let me know your arrival time and I guarantee I shall be there at the station to welcome you, Veronika and Jan.

Sylvia and Laurent are beside themselves with happiness.

With love from all of us, Bastian

The second envelope, addressed to Jan, contained 5 Marks and a suggestion for a different angle for the next story. Eloise read the first sentence, curled the letter into a ball and threw it into the waste basket. She pocketed the money, though. Times were hard. The final letter was from the estate agent.

To all residents of this address
REMINDER – DATED 1 DECEMBER 1929
This legal document is to inform you that the entire property of Charlottenstrasse 125 is now sold and you are required to depart in one calendar month or be forcibly evicted in January. Thank you for your attention.

Colours bounced around the kitchen as if fairies were dancing. For a second, she caught her breath. Yet the phenomenon was an indication of neither departed spirits nor reflected flames. Instead, afternoon sun shone through Veronika's glass mosaic which she had hooked at the kitchen window. Eloise stared at the shape, an oblong lump made up of red, pink, yellow and white and realised it was a heart. Not the clichéd mulberry leaf beloved of the media, but a physical representation of the human organ. Jan had given Veronika his heart.

Eloise unhooked it and returned to the second floor. There she studied her own prism and finally understood that the almond shape in shades of blue, violet and turquoise was not a lake or pool but a single blue eye. With great care, she wrapped both ornaments in newspaper, one red, one blue, and placed them in her holdall. She added the contents of her jewellery box and sufficient essentials for a few days' travelling. Then she sat down her desk to pen two letters: one to Veronika and one to Jan.

Once she had finished, she took both papers out into the garden and burnt them, watching tiny sparks rise up the fire escape until nothing remained but ashes. The little champagne bottle served to toast her friends' lives and mourn their losses: *To Jan and Veronika*. Then she dried her tears and went next door to spend her last night in Berlin.

You are a modern woman. You can do anything. She repeated it like a mantra from the minute she awoke. The sun had not yet risen when she slipped out of Charlottenstrasse, leaving nothing more than a thank-you note for the Zarins and her door keys on the dining table. Dressed in the mannish suit, white shirt and fedora she had worn to Irmgard's birthday party, she took the tram to Alexanderplatz. There she sat in a café opposite what used to be her home, watching the gate and trying not to think about the number of things that could go wrong. As for those that already had, she kept that door closed. *You are a modern woman. You can do anything.* Gustav's *Doktorwagen* drove out of the courtyard at ten to seven. When he got out of the vehicle to lock the gates, he was wearing his top hat. Resisting a snort, Eloise drew down the brim of her fedora. She sipped at her coffee, waiting until he had driven out of sight. Only then did she pay her bill, stride across the street and, using her spare set of keys, enter the building.

On the first floor, she held her breath as she inserted her key into the apartment door. It would be typical of Gustav to have changed the locks. But the tumblers fell into place and the door opened smoothly. She exhaled and slipped inside, silent as a cat. The apartment was warm in temperature but cold in decor. Everything seemed dour and forbidding, particularly as all the doors leading from the hall were closed.

Gustav was an orderly person, so Eloise followed his logic. Where would he keep important documents? She entered the living room and gazed at the writing desk where Otto used to labour late into the night. No longer was it longer strewn with books and papers. In fact, nothing cluttered the surface but a leather-bound blotter and a fountain pen. She searched each drawer, shelf and pigeon-hole systematically, praying he had not already taken them into the office. In the last drawer on the right-hand side she found what she sought: the paperwork for her *Laubfrosch* along with a Transfer of Ownership document. Relief rushed through her like a fresh breeze. She took the transfer paper she had signed and considered setting fire to the thing, but wanted to leave no trace of her presence. Not even ash. Instead she stuffed it in her pocket, ready to dispose of it en route to her destination. The vehicle documents she tucked safely in her holdall. From her jacket, she withdrew an envelope bearing the name Gustav Graz, which contained 750 Reichsmarks. As an afterthought, she borrowed his fountain pen and added a note on the back.

Sorry, I changed my mind. Again.

She left it in the same drawer she had found the documents and replaced the pen at the precise angle he had left it. With any luck, he might not discover her double-cross until she had left the country.

When the bells rang for seven o'clock, she left the building to navigate the streets of Berlin on a busy Monday morning. If anyone had seen the slight young man enter the property and leave five minutes later, they would be hard pressed to pick him out in a crowd.

You are a modern woman with a list of errands, that is all. She visited the main Post Office to arrange collection and transportation of her trunks. While there, she sent a telegram to a boarding house in Rüsselsheim. At the railway station, she purchased a first-class ticket, some bread, cheese and fruit to sustain her over the next seven hours, and a copy of *Motor und*

Sport to prepare for the second part of her journey. When the train heaved its way out of Berlin, Eloise was grateful the carriage was sparsely occupied, since she could not stem her tears. She pressed her handkerchief to her face and wept in silence. For Otto, for Veronika, for Jan and for so much lost potential. She wept for the city itself, riven by rivalries and unable to accept its circumstances. She wept for the woman she had been three years ago and pitied that blue-eyed ingénue.

Images loomed large in her mind: Jan's body revolving in the fog like a giant chrysalis from which no butterfly would emerge. Velvet gloves squeezing a thin bicep and a needle slipping into a vein. An act of mercy. Or was it an act of selfish convenience? Otto asleep on the divan, covered by a crocheted coverlet. Her break-in to that same apartment and subsequent theft. She could scarce believe herself the things she had done.

Otto, if you could see me now, what would you think?

In Leipzig, the train stopped for half an hour to take on more coal. Eloise disembarked to stretch her legs and use the facilities at the station hotel. She remembered her overnight stay all those months ago and looked out for a waitress in a modern hat. There was no one of that description. In the ladies' room, she cleaned her puffy face, changed into a warmer dress and added a cardigan beneath her coat. Then she returned to her first-class seat and tried to recall everything Otto had taught her about motoring.

Her holdall and block heels came in useful. A delayed arrival in Frankfurt meant she had to run between platforms, just making her connection as the stationmaster's whistle blew. Her pulse took some time to return to normal and she regretted not being able to use a latrine. Her spirits sank further when she alighted in Rüsselsheim to darkness and pelting rain.

The sensible thing to do would be to register at the boarding house, use the bathroom and collect the car in the morning. But the threat of Gustav making a telephone call to warn Opel employees pushed her onward. She hired a taxi to the factory and paid the driver for a single fare, assuring him she would be fine from then on. The factory closed in twenty minutes, so she was making quite an assumption.

The reception area stood empty, although the lights were illuminated. Eloise was about venture into the main building when the telephone rang. The noise startled her and in an instant, she was convinced it was Gustav. She picked up the handset and replaced it, appalled by her own effrontery.

A door opened and an elderly gentleman emerged, looking surprised to see her. "Good evening! My name is Schiffler. I apologise for keeping a lady waiting while occupied with some paperwork. Was that the telephone?"

"Good evening to you, Herr Schiffler, and I assure you I have been waiting no more than a minute. The telephone did ring but only once. I am here to collect a vehicle." She presented her documents with a smile.

The old fellow peered over his eyeglasses and read the detail, making little sounds of *hmm-hmm*, *ah-ha* and eventually wrinkled his brow in sympathy. "I am very sorry for your loss, Frau de Fournier. Otto Graz was an excellent young man who only ever wanted to make things better."

"Thank you." Eloise bent her head and swallowed. When she was in battle mode, she could handle aggression, rudeness and obstruction. Only kindness penetrated her armour.

"Your car is fully repaired and ready for the road. Do you have a driver?"

"That is good to hear. No, I plan to drive the vehicle myself."

He scratched his head. "How far are you planning to go?"

"Tonight, only into town. I reserved a room for the night at Hotel Mainz."

"In that case, I can drive you. I would be glad to take you to your lodgings. My home is no more than two minutes down the road."

"What a generous offer! Thank you, Herr Schiffler, I am most grateful."

"Take a seat for a few moments, *meine Dame*, and I shall bring your Laubfrosch around to the front. There is a bathroom to your right should you wish to powder your nose." He left through the door he had come.

Eloise almost moaned with relief.

On the short drive to the hotel, she remembered a great deal about the Laubfrosch and learned still more from Herr Schiffler.

"It is imperative to fill the tank every 200 kilometres, which means four times if you are returning to Berlin. I assume that is your destination?"

She avoided answering directly. "Do you think that might be too much for such a car?"

"Certainly not! This workhorse is capable of much longer journeys. Just ensure the tank never drops below one quarter and maintain a regular speed."

"Good advice." She looked out at the rain. "I hope the weather improves tomorrow."

Herr Schiffler parked in the well-lit backyard of Hotel Mainz. "A little rain is not a problem. But snow is a different matter. In any kind of inclement weather, I advise you to find shelter and wait until it stops. Good luck, Frau de Fournier, and I hope your Treefrog brings you joy."

They shook hands and wished each other a pleasant

evening, both in a hurry to get out of the rain. She waited inside the doorway until he had crossed the street, then got behind the wheel and with only minor hiccups, drove her own car from the expensive Hotel Mainz to the homely and affordable Gasthaus Adler. If she had learned anything in the last three years, it was how to maintain appearances.

32

December 1929, Basel

Her first thought upon waking in the little wooden room was to reach Switzerland by nightfall. Five hundred kilometres, crossing a border, filling the fuel tank, finding her way on unfamiliar routes and the wild card of weather were all challenges. *You are a modern woman. You can do anything.* In Gasthaus Adler's parlour, a maid was lighting a fire. Eloise wished her a good day and was on the road by six o'clock. The fuel gauge showed a full tank and the rain had given way to a clear dawn. She drove south as the sun rose, bumping along in the driver's seat, her whole body aching, cold and complaining of hunger. The Laubfrosch was not much happier, sputtering and threatening to stall every time she changed gear. Eventually, they came to an arrangement as she attuned to the sound of the engine and they motored in relative peace into a bright morning.

The sun made intermittent appearances and the little car reached dizzying speeds of 50kph on the open road. Of all the dangers Eloise had considered when deciding to drive from

Germany to Switzerland – causing an accident, falling foul of thugs, sleeping at the wheel, losing her way, being apprehended by the authorities or running out of fuel – the one factor she had not considered was having time to think. Her mind must have spent the last few days in shock, but had now recovered and was asking insistent questions. She shut out every *how could you?* and *what were you thinking?* and the most plangent of all, *who are you?* to concentrate on her woefully inadequate motoring skills.

In her naïveté, she assumed she could refuel at a garage in Karlsruhe like any other driver. Undisguised curiosity from the attendant and amused stares from fellow motorists shook her confidence. She paid the attendant with a small tip and asked permission to park her car on the forecourt while she sought sustenance in a nearby café. He took her coins and agreed, still smirking.

The scent of fresh coffee lured her across the road and through the door before she had even registered the clientele. Ladies whispered behind gloved hands and one waitress actually stifled a laugh at her practical motoring clothes. Her temper flared. They ought to recognise and admire a trail-blazing modern woman, instead of measuring her against their own provincial yardstick. But this place was a long way from Berlin. Rather than wilt under their judgemental gaze, she ordered a Bratwurst with mustard and onions to raise eyebrows still further. Once finished, she paid the bill, wished everyone a good day and returned to her car. By midday, she would be in Switzerland. Home at last.

Three hours driving under the grey monotony of low skies and the landscape became a blur. Her concentration strayed. Twice she had to right herself after drifting to the centre of the road. All she had to do was keep going, watch the fuel gauge and stay awake. One mistake would prove fatal. *You are a modern woman. You can do anything. Keep going.*

. . .

At the Swiss border, she hardly imagined a welcoming fanfare. However, the smooth re-entry to her homeland she expected was anything but. This time, it was not her innocence that betrayed her, but her confidence. The *Grenzen* guards regarded the Laubfrosch with its Berlin plates as suspicious and treated her with aggression and hostility. First they studied her papers and asked her to come inside while they examined the vehicle. She spoke Swiss German and answered politely. Then she answered the same questions again and invoked her family name.

The younger man raised his shoulders to his ears. "What were you doing in Germany?"

"As I said, I was a journalist for *Vogue*. It's a women's fashion magazine."

"You must have been very well paid to afford one of those." He nodded through the window towards the Laubfrosch, where two German Shepherds were sniffing the chassis.

The older man sporting a dense moustache chuckled, an unfriendly sound.

"Once again, Frau de Fournier, your address in Berlin?"

Her brain froze and she looked down at her hands, still clad in leather. She pulled at each finger, easing off her gloves and giving herself time to think.

"The last place I lived in Berlin was Charlottenstrasse 125. A boarding house which is currently up for sale."

The two men had a muttered conversation and the older one left the room. The younger soldier folded his arms and watched as his colleagues removed her holdall from the car.

She shifted in her seat. "What do the guards want with my luggage?"

He ignored her.

"Sir? I would like to know when I can continue my journey. I am a Swiss citizen, returning home to my family."

"You can continue just as soon as you tell us who's paying you."

"I'm sorry?"

The door opened and the older man returned with a senior officer who did not introduce himself. With a jerk of his chin, he dismissed the younger soldier and took the seat opposite Eloise.

"Who are you and who are you working for?"

"As I said, my name is Eloise de Fournier from Fribourg. I'm a mother of two children and until recently, I was a journalist for *Vogue* magazine in Berlin."

He shook his head with a patronising sneer. "I'm sure you thought it would be easy to slip past some country soldiers with no experience of foreign agents. Wrong. We are professional Swiss border guards, trained to identify and apprehend malignant forces which threaten our nation."

Eloise was so blindsided that she actually laughed. "Don't be ridiculous!"

The atmosphere cooled.

"Let's try that again, shall we?" The officer curled one hand into a fist and covered it with the other. "I am a military man, well disciplined, fair minded and not prone to fits of temper. The interrogation squad are rather less predictable. That said, no one can deny they certainly get results. Your choice is simple, madam. You can talk to me or I hand you over to them."

Eloise stared at him, unable to think of a thing to say.

"I have a few questions about some anomalies in your story. If you answer them to my satisfaction, you may go on your way. If not, the interrogation squad will get the information we need using their own methods. Do you understand me?"

"I ... yes, of course. I have nothing to hide. I am a Swiss citizen, returning home to her family. There is no need to treat me like a criminal."

"Good. In that case, please allow the sergeant to inspect your handbag."

Instinctively, Eloise clutched it tighter. The moustached man held out a hand and she relinquished it with as much dignity as she could manage. Her throat swelled at the injustice, but she would not allow herself to cry. Tears should be reserved for people who mattered.

"To business: I want to know why you are driving an expensive vehicle whilst unemployed. Please tell me why you are travelling home with nothing but a holdall, which contains a large amount of jewellery. For what reason would you be carrying a valuable artwork wrapped in Russian newspapers? Who are you working for and what information do you seek?"

"And why are you carrying a large amount of Reichsmarks?" added the sergeant, showing the contents of her purse.

Eloise closed her eyes and placed a hand over her mouth. She had a sudden recollection of a visit to Bastian when he was studying in Zürich. An elderly couple on the train had regarded her with some censure and she chose to make sport of their obvious disapproval.

Oh, Bastian! With all manner of allusions and hints as to my top-secret mission, I more or less convinced them I was Mata Hari. Ha, ha! They'll be talking about me the entire weekend.

She inhaled deeply and wished she hadn't. The air was stale, the soldiers smelt of sweat and mouldy uniforms and she herself was none too fragrant after driving all morning.

"Are you seriously accusing me of being a spy?"

"Unless you can prove otherwise, madam, a charge of espionage looks likely. Treason carries a heavy penalty."

Unbidden, her brother's response floated into her mind. *As a matter of fact, Mata Hari was executed by firing squad during the war.*

At quarter to four, after several telephone calls to Fribourg, Berlin and Paris, they released her without apology. She signed for her belongings and stumbled outside to her little green car, hungry, thirsty and exhausted. Dirty yellow clouds threatened snow.

She pushed the little car harder as the first white flakes whirled like ash around the windscreen. Snow fell, gentle yet relentless, for another hour and a half, initially light and melting on impact with the ground. Then it began to stick, creating a slushy carpet beneath her wheels. Her motoring lessons had always taken place in the sunshine, on a private track. No one said anything about driving in snow.

Apart from the mechanic, whatever his name was. *A little rain is not a problem. But snow is a different matter. In any kind of inclement weather, I advise you to find shelter and wait until it stops.*

Eloise's sensible side advised caution and pointed out the encroaching dusk. There was a signpost for Bern, where she could rest and shelter from the storm. Her impetuous self encouraged persistence. If she stopped, she might not be able to continue her journey the following day. Best to keep going and she'd be in the arms of her family by dinnertime. And wasn't the snowfall lightening already?

The final hour from Bern to Fribourg was the most frightening of her life. She gripped the steering wheel, peering out at the night sky between sweeps of her windscreen wipers, aiming for the tracks previous vehicles had cut through the snow. There were precious few. Her tyres slid and skidded on more occasions than she could count and she slowed to second gear every time she took a bend. Fears jostled for dominance: an accident where she would not be found until morning, her body frozen in a ditch, leaving her children orphans. The fuel tank running out before she reached the city, so she would have to sleep in the car, at the mercy of robbers. The snow changing from the occasional light flurry to a blizzard, forcing her to drive at 15 kilometres per hour until she was covered by a giant snowdrift only to be discovered next spring.

The last dramatic scenario actually made her snort with tearful laughter. She wiped her eyes and called on all her willpower, resilience and concentration. It was nearly Christmas and she would spend it with her family. She began to sing. "*O Tannenbaum, o Tannenbaum, wie treu sind deine Blätter ...*" Her spirits rose with every verse.

The sign for Fribourg made her gasp in disbelief. She navigated her way through the streets, scarcely able to believe she was so close, and steered through the gates of the de Fournier property. She turned off the engine and sat shaking in the driver's seat until the front door of the house opened, spilling light down the white-dusted steps.

Footsteps crunched across the snow and a figure crouched to look inside. "Eloise?"

"Bastian!" She fell out of the door and into his arms. "I'm home."

33

December 1929, Fribourg

For the first time in far too long, Eloise awoke in her own bed, warm, rested and with no urgent need to get up and fight whatever disasters loomed on her horizon. Because two of her worst nightmares she had been unable to prevent. No, that was dishonest. One death was beyond her control, the other she had actively expedited. She sat up in bed, her breath short and ragged, wondering if she should pray for forgiveness. A knock came at the door.

"Come in, Greta."

A blonde head popped around the door. "Eloise, I hope you can forgive me. I asked Greta if I could bring your breakfast myself."

"Seraphine! Of all the people I wanted to see, you are the most welcome. I really should get up and join everyone in the breakfast room."

"What you should do is rest and recover your energy." Seraphine set the tray on the table and poured two cups of coffee. "We have muesli, fried eggs, fresh bread, ham, cheese and apple juice. Are you feeling strong enough for this?"

Eloise got out of bed and tucked her feet into slippers. "For breakfast, yes. For the family questions, we'll see."

"Don't worry. Everyone is astounded by your courageous journey. Your children cannot stop relating the tale. I should say that others are more shocked than impressed."

Neither needed to state names. "My mother will have to bear it. But what of Bastian?"

Seraphine placed a *Spiegelei* on a slice of bread. "Eat. Drink. Your brother, as always, is horrified, impressed, worried and proud, but most of all surprised by his sister."

"Thanks. You forgot disappointed."

"Never disappointed. Bastian has spent his life being sensible. Truthfully, Eloise, I think he envies you. It's not part of his personality to take risks and to dive headlong into adventure, because he is rooted in responsibility. But in a little corner of his mind, he admires your high-wire act."

Eloise took a sip of the tart juice, recalling some acrobats she had once watched. "My high-wire act always had a safety net. Its name was Bastian Favre."

Samichlaus Abend or Saint Nicholas Parade on 6 December marked the official opening of the festive season. The children were already excitable, eager to see which gifts the jolly old gent would bring them. Such occasions required every family member's presence. After a day's rest, Eloise was ready to play her part. She dressed in a midnight-blue gown which hung off her frame, arranged her hair and painted her face. The procedure seemed unfamiliar, as if it belonged to another time. The face in the mirror was gaunt and shadowed, with evasive eyes.

The family walked to the cathedral to watch St Nicholas

arrive by donkey, accompanied by torch-bearers, bell-ringers and musicians. They gathered with all the other citizens, many returning home especially for this event, in the cathedral square to hear his speech from the tower. Neighbours and acquaintances made their way through the crowds to welcome her home. She smiled, shook hands and exchanged a few words of appreciation for the city of her birth.

When the ceremony was over, the family walked home along twinkling streets, preparing to receive half a dozen guests for dinner. Laurent was scooping up handfuls of snow to hurl at Julius, but Sylvia slipped a hand into hers. She smiled up at her mother, her face framed by a knitted bonnet, her serious eyes filled with questions.

"Maman? Are you staying in Fribourg or going back to Berlin?"

"Darling, this is my home now. I have left Berlin for good."

"I'm happy about that. Laurent and Julius say you drove a motor car from Germany all on your own? Weren't you scared?"

"At times I was absolutely terrified. Driving in the snow was foolhardy and dangerous. I shouldn't be surprised if Uncle Bastian soon gives me a lecture on responsibility."

"Uncle Bastian will do no such thing." His voice from behind them made mother and daughter jump. "Sylvia, my sweet, I need you to run ahead to your *grandmère*. Tell her I said to seat Monsieur Pièce next to Eloise. Good girl."

Sylvia scurried off, eager to be helpful.

"I hope you're not matchmaking, Bastian Favre."

"Not in the romantic sense. He's a pioneer in the field of radio and on the lookout for talented journalists. The way he tells it, Switzerland could be a trailblazer in radio transmission. All you have to do is listen."

She laughed and tucked her hand in the crook of his elbow. "Very droll. Oh, I cannot tell you how good it is to be home."

"We are all relieved and overjoyed. Be warned, a lecture on responsibility is due, but not from me. The matriarch is biding her time until you are fully recovered. On the subject of your friends ..."

"Please don't ask me to talk about that yet. I badly want to discuss what happened, because I need your advice, but it's too soon. I'm not brave enough."

"You are the bravest person I know, Eloise. When you are ready to talk, I am willing to listen. Argh!"

Laurent ducked past and a snowball caught Bastian between the shoulder blades.

"Sorry, Papa, that was a mistake. It was meant for Laurent!" called Julius.

Bastian scooped some snow from a hedge and packed it into a ball. "This is no mistake and it's meant for you!" He hurled the missile with impressive accuracy and caught his giggling, fleeing son on the back of his neck.

Laurent burst into raucous laughter, pointing at his cousin. "He got you! Your own father!"

In one move, Eloise grabbed a handful of snow and stuffed it down Laurent's collar.

"And I got you! Your own mother!"

The snowball fight continued, adults versus children, until the driveway of the Favre house. Both parties claimed victory.

Sunrise woke her and she lay in bed awhile, phrases from the previous night's conversation floating through her mind. Roland Pièce was passionate about his medium.

Refined prose and stylish images always attract the eye. Precise words in a persuasive tone capture the ear. Both cast a spell on the audience and bid them act. That action might be a purchase or an opinion, but no one can deny its influence.

She watched the morning light refract through Jan's blue-eyed mosaic, throwing a waterfall of colours over her bedroom. In the afternoon, the sun would come through the west-facing window, creating a blaze of brilliance and warmth through Veronika's heart.

Can you imagine the voice of reason transmitted into every parlour in the land? It could change the way we perceive the world. That is why female voices on Swiss airwaves are vital.

Someone knocked on the door.

"Come in, Greta, I'm awake. Good morning."

"Good morning, Frau de Fournier. Would like breakfast in your room today or ... oh dear, did Caroline forget to close the curtains?"

"No, I left them open, so the sun shines through my mosaic. Don't you find it pretty?"

Greta gazed at the dancing palette of blues and violets. "Beautiful. Like butterflies."

Otto's voice echoed in her ears. *Jewel-coloured butterflies whispering promises of a brilliant future.*

"Yes, you're right. Exactly like butterflies."

For Toni and Cécile Späni

ACKNOWLEDGMENTS

I found the following works invaluable for my research: *The Coming of the Third Reich* by Richard J. Evans, *Women in Weimar Fashion* by Mila Geneva, *To Hell and Back: Europe 1914-1949* by Ian Kershaw, and *Tamara de Lempicka: A Life of Deco and Decadence* by Laura Claridge. Any errors or omissions are entirely my own.

I am grateful for editorial support from Florian Bielmann and Gillian Hamer, a classic cover from JD Smith Design and the proof-reading skills of Julia Gibbs.

ALSO BY JJ MARSH

The Beatrice Stubbs European crime series

(Tap title to buy)

BEHIND CLOSED DOORS

RAW MATERIAL

TREAD SOFTLY

COLD PRESSED

HUMAN RITES

BAD APPLES

SNOW ANGEL

HONEY TRAP

BLACK WIDOW

WHITE NIGHT

THE WOMAN IN THE FRAME

ALL SOULS' DAY

TRUE COLOURS

SIREN SONG

The Run and Hide series (International thrillers)

WHITE HERON

BLACK RIVER

GOLD DRAGON

PEARL MOON

Historical Fiction

AN EMPTY VESSEL

SALT OF THE EARTH

My standalone novels

ODD NUMBERS

WOLF TONES

And a short-story collection
APPEARANCES GREETING A POINT OF VIEW

For occasional updates, news, deals and a FREE exclusive novella, tap the link to subscribe to my free newsletter www.jjmarshauthor.com

Printed in Dunstable, United Kingdom